Sharon Kendrick once won a national writing competition by describing her ideal date: being flown to an exotic island by a gorgeous and powerful man. Little did she realise that she'd just wandered into her dream job! Today she writes for Mills & Boon, and her books feature often stubborn but always *to-die-for* heroes and the women who bring them to their knees. She believes that the best books are those you never want to end. Just like life…

USA TODAY bestselling and RITA® Award-nominated author **Caitlin Crews** loves writing romance. She teaches her favorite romance novels in creative writing classes at places like UCLA Extension's prestigious Writers' Program, where she finally gets to utilise the MA and PhD in English Literature she received from the University of York in England. She currently lives in the Pacific Northwest, with her very own hero and too many pets. Visit her at caitlincrews.com.

Also by Sharon Kendrick

Di Sione's Virgin Mistress
Bound to the Sicilian's Bed
Crowned for the Sheikh's Baby
The Greek's Bought Bride
The Italian's Christmas Housekeeper
The Sheikh's Secret Baby

Also by Caitlin Crews

My Bought Virgin Wife

Bound to the Desert King collection

Sheikh's Secret Love-Child

Stolen Brides collection

The Bride's Baby of Shame

The Combe Family Scandals miniseries

The Italian's Twin Consequences
Untamed Billionaire's Innocent Bride

BOUGHT BRIDE FOR THE ARGENTINIAN

SHARON KENDRICK

HIS TWO ROYAL SECRETS

CAITLIN CREWS

MILLS & BOON

First Published in Great Britain 2019
by Mills & Boon, an imprint of HarperCollins*Publishers*
1 London Bridge Street, London, SE1 9GF

ISBN: 978-0-263-27347-2

FSC
www.fsc.org
MIX
Paper from
responsible sources
FSC™ C007454

This book is produced from independently certified FSC™ paper
to ensure responsible forest management.
For more information visit www.harpercollins.co.uk/green.

Printed and bound in Spain
by CPI, Barcelona

BOUGHT BRIDE FOR THE ARGENTINIAN

SHARON KENDRICK

With special thanks to Melbourne-based Pat Conway for his invaluable insights into the high-octane world of Formula One—and a big shout-out to his dynamic wife Chris.

Thanks also to the equestrian genius Alison Clark, who inspired me with helpful details about polo and Argentina. Woof to Pop!

CHAPTER ONE

It was worse than she'd thought. Much worse. Past and present merged into one heartbreaking reality as Emily buried her face into the rough texture of the horse's mane and wept. 'Oh, Joya,' she whispered. 'Whatever has become of you?'

The horse gave a weak whinny and Emily couldn't stem the tears even though she hadn't cried in a long time. Because tears got you nowhere. Crying didn't actually *change* anything, did it? It wasn't as if someone was going to suddenly turn up and wave a magic wand and make it all better. For a few moments she just stood there before forcing herself to pull away, not wanting the animal to sense any more of the distress which had been swamping her ever since she'd arrived in this place.

Distractedly, she glanced around. A place which had been such a big part of her upbringing and was tied up with a swarm of memories. Bittersweet memories. Of a man with a hard body and warm, green eyes. A man who had brought her alive with his lips and his fingers and a whole lot else besides. Who had made her feel stuff she'd thought herself incapable of feeling. When she'd walked away from Alejandro Sabato it had felt as if someone were ripping her heart from her chest and then crushing it. In those few moments and all the months which had followed, she had truly known the definition of heartbreak. But she'd done it because there had been no other choice. Or at least it had seemed so at the time. Now she wondered if she had been a fool.

With an impatient hand she fisted away a tear, angry at herself for indulging in pointless reflection as she watched it tumble and soak into the rich Argentinian soil. Because she wasn't here to feel sad, or look back. And she certainly wasn't here to start thinking if only things had been different. Because there were no *if onlys* in life. The only certainty was that you took your choices and then had to live with the consequences, no matter how bleak they sometimes seemed.

She heard the sound of footsteps and turned to see Tomas walking slowly towards her, thinking how much the elderly retired groom had aged in the eight years since last she'd seen him. She had met him in the lawyer's office, and he and his wife had agreed to accompany her here today, insisting on bringing a bag of provisions to the now-empty house. She'd been pleased to have their company, yes—but, more importantly, pleased to have someone to share her shock at what had awaited them here.

Because the last time she'd stood on this spot, the estate had been thriving and the enormous ranch pristine and elegant. But not any more. Now it looked like a ragged ghost of a building, with none of its former glory remaining. Everywhere she looked she could see decay and neglect—from the overgrown veranda, where once socialites had laughingly sipped mint juleps, to the main house itself. Or what remained of it. There was no trace of the gleaming paintwork, near which had nestled fragrant white flowers amid glossy green leaves. A couple of upstairs windows were broken and one of the doors was falling off its hinges. Evidence of mice was everywhere in the empty and echoing rooms. And as for the stables… Well, they were something else.

Emily swallowed. There was nothing left of the stables other than the once-proud horse she had loved with all her heart, who now bore little resemblance to the powerful creature on which she had learnt to ride. Her body trembled with pain as she stroked his dusty coat.

'Oh, Tomas,' she said as the old groom reached her side. 'This is so *awful*.'

'Sí, señorita,' he agreed, his voice full of sadness.

'How on earth did it *happen*?'

Tomas gave a weary shrug. 'There was a little money left for his upkeep and I did what I could, but that money is now gone and the house is about to be sold to new owners who do not want him—or me. I would keep him if I could, but there is no room at my house for any animal—not even Joya.'

Emily dared to voice the fear which had been growing inside her ever since she'd walked in through the rusting gates of the property. 'Why on earth did my stepfather leave me the horse?' she demanded, but inside she suspected she knew why. It was to punish her. To lash out from beyond the grave and to cause her pain for daring to be the unwanted witness to his fiery marriage to her mother. The daughter he had never wanted, who had dared to fall in love with the son of the hired help.

Tomas was quiet for a moment and then spoke with the authority of someone who had observed a great deal during the years he had worked at the huge estate.

'He bequeathed him to you because you loved him,' he said slowly.

Emily nodded. Yes. She had loved Joya. With all her heart she had adored that horse, who had been such an important part of her teenage years. She'd been taught to ride on that horse, by the man with the green eyes and the hard body. She'd sought refuge from her mother's hysteria by galloping out over the lush green of the Argentinian landscape for hours on end. And it was hard to see the welfare of a creature you loved threatened like this.

Yet she'd hardly followed his progress avidly in the years since the divorce and her mother's subsequent death, had she? She had cut her ties with Argentina ruthlessly for all kinds of reasons, but now fate had brought her back to this vast land and she was shocked by what she had found. 'I can't bear the thought that Joya might have to be...*put down*, Tomas,' she whispered. 'I've racked my brain and tried to come up with some kind of solution but I can't think of anything.'

She had expected gloomy agreement but, surprisingly, the grooves on Tomas's weathered skin began to deepen as, unexpectedly, he smiled. 'But there is a solution, *señorita*,' he said. 'And it has arrived sooner than even I imagined.'

He was looking at the sky as he spoke. The clear, blue Argentinian sky. It took a moment for Emily to realise that its unspoiled surface had been marred by the tiniest black spot in the distance, which was growing bigger all the time, and that a peace-shattering buzzing sound was gradually getting louder.

Shielding her gaze against the brightness of the sun with the flat of her hand, she frowned. 'What's that?'

she questioned, even though it was perfectly obvious what it was. A flashy-looking helicopter, and it was heading this way. A sudden inner misgiving made her skin grow cold, despite the heat of the day.

'My prayers have been answered,' said Tomas emotionally. 'For he flies to us like a bird of prey! *El cóndor!*'

It was then that goosebumps began to ripple over Emily's body as if an icy wind had suddenly started whipping through the warm day, and she wrapped her bare arms tightly over her chest as if to protect herself. Her heart started to pound as the helicopter grew closer and she watched it hover overhead before beginning its swaying descent. She wanted to run as far as her feet would take her. To seek refuge from the dark figure she could see seated at the controls, displaying the kind of powerful mastery which had always been so much a part of his appeal. But not all of it, no, she reminded herself painfully. He had been tender, too—and it had been that tenderness which had been her undoing. He had demonstrated an affection which had been like a revelation to her, for she had never experienced anything like it before. And hadn't it been that more than anything else which had made her fall head over heels in love with him? Hadn't it been that which had made the pain of leaving him so bitterly hard to bear?

During the intervening years since their last tumultuous meeting, Alejandro Sabato had become an icon and international heart-throb. He had dramatically ended his career as a world-class polo player—though nobody knew why—but hadn't taken any of the usual paths after leaving the sport behind. No riding schools or polo club for him. Instead he had become a hugely successful businessman who operated on a global scale, though he'd never been able to shake off the stormy reputation which had grown up after a bitter book written by his ex-mistress.

But Emily didn't associate him with riches beyond most people's wildest dreams. She remembered him as the man who used to slowly trace the line of her lips with his fingertip before bending his head to kiss her. The man who had taught her the true meaning of love.

And she had thrown it all back in his face.

The wind created by the clattering craft was flattening the grasses and playing havoc with her hair, even though she'd tied it back into a plait when she'd stumbled out of bed that morning, still jet-lagged after her long flight. Her jeans were clean but that was pretty much all you could say about them, and her T-shirt was plain and unremarkable. Briefly, she wondered why she was worrying about her appearance at a time like this. But deep down she knew why.

Because he had been her lover.

Her only lover.

The man to whom she'd given her innocence, and in doing so had sealed her empty fate for ever.

She smoothed a flapping strand of hair away from her cheek, wishing she could quell the painful thundering of her heart. She hadn't realised he could pilot a helicopter, but that shouldn't have come as any surprise. Hadn't he gone from being a dirt-poor boy who possessed an extraordinary gift with horses to becoming one of the world's richest men? Financial success stuck to his skin like stardust—but not personal success, she reminded herself. The newspapers always described him as a playboy and commitment-phobe—as a man who had left countless broken hearts in his arrogant wake.

The rotor blades slowed to a halt and as the door of the craft opened, Alejandro Sabato leapt to the ground. He landed with a light thud, giving a brief masterclass in agility and strength and reminding her of his nickname earned during his polo-playing days—*el cóndor*—the one which Tomas the groom had just breathed in wonder. Emily swallowed. They used to call him that because he was dark and menacing and because he used to swoop down like a graceful predator, always getting the ball he was chasing. He'd been on the winning side of three World Polo Championships—and it had always been Alejandro who was pictured holding the trophy aloft, his dark head thrown back, his face grinning with victory and vitality.

Yet he had started out from the most humble of places—the illegitimate son of her stepfather's housekeeper who, from the age of three, had grown up on his ranch and learned to ride almost as soon as he could walk. His talent had been spotted early and he'd moved to a polo stable on the other side of the country, where he had been intensively schooled in the sport. Six years older than Emily, he returned to the ranch only infrequently and she'd met him first at the age of twelve, soon after her mother had married Paul Vickery.

Had he recognised how lonely and out of place the English city girl had felt in that sweeping great country, in the home of a man who didn't really want a stepdaughter? Was that why he'd been so kind to her? He'd taught her to ride—and to recognise the stars. He'd given her *yerba maté* to drink and taught her how to light a fire and then how to put it out again safely. A friendship had grown between them, although inevitably she had grown to idolise him. And then, when she was seventeen, something had shifted and changed. Desire had entered into their easy camaraderie and nothing was ever the same again.

But that was a long time ago. They'd both lived a lot of life and were adults now. Yet Emily found herself standing watching as Alejandro raked his windswept waves back from his forehead and the clench of her heart reminded her just how much he had meant to her. Suddenly a wave of nerves was rushing through her and she felt as if she were back in the shoes of that gauche young girl who had so adored him.

He must have seen her but he completely ignored her, going instead to Tomas and gripping him in a bear hug, before slipping into a stream of velvety Spanish, which caused the aging groom to beam with delight. Emily's command of the language was rusty these days but she understood enough to realise that Alej was making a request for refreshment and Tomas nodded and began to walk slowly towards the house, presumably to relay the message to his wife, Rosa.

And once the groom had disappeared, the two of them were alone and just at that moment the sun disappeared behind a cloud, so that all the light and warmth seemed to leave the day. Slowly, the Argentinian turned around to survey her with a look which was cold. So cold. She was shocked at how the vibrancy seemed to have left the gaze she remembered so well. How his once-warm green eyes were now like leaves which had been coated in ice and the curl of his lips bordered on contemptuous. Yet that didn't stop her breasts from tightening beneath her cotton shirt, or a long-forgotten hint of awareness from rippling sweetly over her thighs.

'Alej!' she said, the word much shakier than she would have liked—but there was no answering smile in response.

'Only my close friends and intimates call me that these days,' he corrected coolly, the curve of his mouth flattening into a cruel, hard line. 'Let's stick to Alejandro, shall we?'

It hurt, as it was probably intended to do, but Emily nodded as if it didn't. As if all those years of friendship and companionship and then love had never happened. As if the man who'd used to suck on her breasts as if they were freshly peeled grapes had just made the most reasonable of requests. She'd learnt many things over the years but one of the most important was to keep pain hidden away, where nobody could see it.

'Of course,' she responded, before adding a somewhat flippant amendment of her own. 'It's probably the shock of seeing you again, *Alejandro*.'

'Would you really describe it as a shock, Emily?' he questioned, his richly accented voice thoughtful. 'Or a deep and abiding pleasure? From the darkening of your eyes and the tension in your body I recognise so well, I would guess it's the latter.'

Emily worked in PR, so she knew everything there was to know about putting a positive spin on things, but never had an upbeat mindset seemed so distant as it did right then. He was talking to her with sensuality dripping from every word, yet he was staring at her with a flicker of contempt in his green eyes, as if she meant nothing. And yet that didn't seem to have any effect on her reaction to *him*. All the feelings she'd thought were dead and buried started bubbling up inside her and she couldn't seem to stem them, no matter how hard she tried. She wanted to feast her eyes on the liquorice-black waves of his just-too-long hair and the burnished bronze of his glowing skin. Just as she wanted to ogle his body in the way that someone who'd been wandering around in the desert for days might stare greedily at a cool flask of water. And most of all she wanted to hurl herself into his arms and kiss him.

Concentrating very hard, she fixed him with an expression of polite curiosity, trying to behave as if he was someone she'd just met. But her outward calm didn't mirror what was happening inside, because suddenly it felt as if her hormones had remembered what they'd been designed for. As if his presence had the power to make her body prickle with desire and heat and expectation. Her nipples were thrusting uncomfortably against her bra and she felt a long-forgotten twist of lust low in her groin as she looked at him.

In the past he'd always worn jodhpurs or faded jeans, which hugged his hips and thighs in a way which had seemed indecently provocative. But not today. Today, clad in an immaculate lightweight suit, he was looking like the billionaire he'd become—not the rookie polo player she'd fallen in love with, who'd barely had two pesos to rub together. And love was the last thing she needed to think about if she was going to get through this, she reminded herself fiercely. She needed to find out what had prompted his unexpected appearance and then for him to leave as quickly as possible. She certainly didn't need to respond to his provocative observations about her body. Even if they happened to be true.

'Why are you here, Alejandro?' she questioned, instantly becoming aware of the slight edge to her voice and trying her best to iron it out. 'Why have you turned up out of the blue?' Briefly, she cast her gaze towards the sky. 'Quite literally in this case?'

'Don't play games, Emily,' he said softly. 'It's a waste of both our time. I came because you need me.'

Emily blinked very fast. 'I *need* you?'

'Are you going to repeat everything I say?' His voice was silky. 'Haven't you grown out of that kind of docile behaviour by now?'

Don't react to that either, she told herself. You don't need to get into a fight with him. You're no longer that giddy teenager who used to follow him around like a tame dog and lap up everything he said to you. And you're not the young woman who cried every night for months after she'd walked away. You left that person behind a long time ago. You became somebody else. Somebody grown-up and together.

So Emily tilted her chin in the way she'd learned from watching other women. The way which sent out a message to the world that you were super-confident, even if inside you wondered why you couldn't ever seem to lose that little stone of sadness which was buried deep inside you.

'I'm not here to trade insults, Alejandro,' she said calmly. 'I asked you a perfectly reasonable question about why you were here.'

For a moment his green eyes narrowed. 'Tomas emailed me. I assumed with your blessing.'

She screwed up her brow in a frown. 'What did the email say?'

He shrugged and she wished he hadn't because it made her uncomfortably aware of the iron-hard muscle which lay beneath the fine silk of his shirt. Just as it made her aware of the rocky power of the arms which used to hold her so tightly, so that all the troubles of the world seemed to ebb away.

'That your stepfather had died—which I already knew, obviously, since news travels fast—and that he had bequeathed you your old horse. And since you didn't have the means to look after him, you were desperate for someone to step in and help you out.' He stared at her. 'Is that true?'

Desperate? Was she? Emily met the question in his piercing green gaze. She was certainly still reeling from the recent events which had recently turned her life upside down. Her loathsome stepfather had finally paid the price for his long-standing love affair with the bottle and had died a lonely death, which she couldn't really be sad about. She hadn't seen him since the bitter events following his acrimonious divorce from her mother and had been shocked to find herself listed as a beneficiary of his will. She still wondered what had possessed her to beg her business partner for some unplanned leave and then to turn up in a dusty lawyer's office in Buenos Aires to discover what he had left her. Was it simply curiosity or just a sudden desire to lay to rest the ghosts of her past?

Either way, she had been disappointed. It seemed there had been no deathbed conversion which had made Paul Vickery want to make amends for the harsh treatment he'd meted out to her and her mother. It had been just another twist of the knife really.

'Some of it is true,' she said huskily. 'My stepfather *did* leave me Joya. But no way did I ask Tomas to get in touch with you. You're the last person I'd ever choose to contact.'

Alejandro's mouth flattened as her soft English voice washed over him. Of course he was. He was disposable, wasn't he? A poor boy with a hard body who could be dispensed with once he'd done his job as stud. He had been deemed suitable enough to introduce her to the art of pleasure and then afterwards tossed aside like a piece of trash. And Emily Green had played him for a fool, hadn't she? Stared at him with those big sapphire eyes. Tossed her fair hair like a feisty pony, so that it rippled down her back like a field of golden wheat. He'd been transfixed by her Englishness. By her pale beauty and the pert vigour of her young body. Long legs and slender arms and a pale bottom, which curved like the moon.

She'd driven him mad with frustration and desire those hot summer nights when he'd lain alone on his narrow bunk next to the stables, sweat pouring from his brow and his groin close to bursting as he imagined losing himself in all her sweet, secret places. And then, when his dream had finally come true and he had bedded her at last—she had turned around and crushed his honour and his hopes beneath one of her costly leather shoes, before walking away from him without a backward glance.

At the time he had been astonished by her behaviour—but not for long. Because soon after that he was to discover that all women were liars and cheats. But it had been Emily who had hurt him the most, who had wielded the sharpest blade, which felt like it was digging deep into his heart. And didn't they say that the first cut was the deepest?

'So what are you planning to do?' he said, slanting

a compassionate look towards the horse who was still trying to summon up the strength to nuzzle Emily's hand. 'Put a bullet to his head?'

She recoiled, staring at him as if he had just ascended from the depths of hell.

'Are you advocating I kill my horse?' she accused shakily. 'You, who always loved animals?'

'Yes, I loved them and still do,' he grated. 'More than I ever loved any human, that's for sure—and way too much to want to condemn them to a life of neglect. Is that what you want for Joya, Emily? For his eyes to grow so dull that he can barely see and he doesn't even have the strength to put food in his mouth?'

'Of course that's not what I want,' she declared, the quick shake of her head drawing his eyes reluctantly to the thick shimmer of her blonde hair. 'But I don't have…'

'Don't have what?' he prompted silkily.

Emily stared at him, not wanting to divulge the truth—not to him of all people. But what good was pride in a situation like this? Shouldn't she be thinking about Joya, rather than how humble her life must appear to this new and very different Alejandro, who breathed wealth and power from every pore of his spectacular body?

'I don't have the means to look after him,' she admitted. 'I live in a small apartment in the middle of London and I couldn't possibly move him there—'

'I doubt he would survive the journey anyway.'

She nodded, wishing he hadn't made the curt intervention because she didn't need reminding of how frail Joya was. 'I also have a very modest lifestyle,' she continued, a rush of blood heating her cheeks as he continued to look at her with a trace of scorn. 'Which certainly wouldn't allow me to fund Joya's care here in Argentina.'

He appeared to be mulling over her words when Rosa appeared on the veranda carrying a couple of the wooden drinking cups known as gourds, and Emily felt a quick pang of nostalgia as she recognised the traditional Argentinian drink of *yerba maté*. Because it had been Alejandro who'd first introduced her to it—showing her how to suck it up out of the straw-like strainer, which prevented the leaves from clogging up your mouth. Who had told her laughingly that if she wasn't careful, the caffeine would keep her awake all night—but that was okay by him. She remembered how cosmopolitan he'd made her feel and how the whisper of his fingertips over her skin had made her stomach turn to jelly.

'Why don't we go over to the veranda and have this discussion in the shade, while Tomas takes Joya back to the stables?' Alejandro suggested smoothly.

To Emily's surprise she found herself agreeing, even though instinct was telling her it might not be such a great idea. Maybe it was the shock of seeing him again which made her follow him up the old wooden steps. Or maybe it was just that old habits died hard, because she'd always been a sucker for his suggestions. Either way, she was glad to take a seat on the veranda, taking a thirsty pull of the bitter drink Rosa had left for them.

Once her thirst had been quenched, she became aware of the Argentinian's cool gaze fixed on her and she fidgeted a little. He had undone a third button on his white shirt and was stretching his long legs in front of him, drawing her attention to the taut fabric of his trousers, which stretched across the muscular definition of his hard thighs. She could feel beads of sweat breaking out on her forehead as she found herself remembering those thighs hair-roughened and naked as they thrust against the smoothness of her own skin. Yet their physical relationship had been cut abruptly short, she reminded herself, wondering how something so brief could have had such an enduring impact. And then she remembered something else.

'Tomas told me that your mother had died last year,' she said quietly. 'I'm very sorry for your loss.'

It was then that his face changed. She watched it darken with anger and she shrank back a little against the battered wicker chair.

'You are hypocritical enough to express your condolences?' he demanded. 'When it was your spite which meant my mother lost her job?'

CHAPTER TWO

THE LOUD SWELL of the cicadas was the only sound which could be heard above the loud beat of her pounding heart as Emily stared at Alejandro across the faded veranda. 'I don't know what you're talking about,' she breathed. 'How could I have possibly been responsible for your mother losing her job?'

He sliced his hand through the air with a gesture of disdainful impatience. 'Don't give me that false wide-eyed look of innocence, Emily.'

'It's not false. It's genuine. I don't know what you're talking about.'

His brow darkened, his green gaze narrowing. 'After we were discovered together and you flew back to England as if the hounds of hell were at your heels, my mother was called into your father's study and told to leave the property immediately, never to return.' His face contorted with contempt. 'Twenty-one years of devotion thrown back in her face.'

Emily's lips fell open and she shook her head in vehement denial. 'I swear I didn't know that. I thought she'd left of her own accord.'

'Oh, come on. Women of such subservience don't just *leave of their own accord*,' he mimicked cruelly.

'Did you know your stepfather refused to provide any references for her, so she couldn't get any more work? And although I was able to provide some means of support, she complained that her life felt empty without work.'

Alejandro felt his mouth harden with anger and frustration. He had wanted to help his mother in more practical ways than simply buying her a small house. Having given birth to him at just seventeen, she'd been young enough to retrain in something different. Young enough to start again. But she hadn't wanted a new life. She had just smoked cigarette after cigarette while continuing to spin him the same old lies, which for a time while he'd been growing up had made him feel special and different. And wasn't it crazy that he'd hung onto the myth he'd been spun for so long—so that when he had finally learned the truth, it had nearly broken him?

He stared at Emily. Maybe it was true what she said and she hadn't been directly responsible for his mother's sacking, but that didn't change the anger he felt towards her, did it? Because he had loved her in a way he had never loved anyone else and he'd thought she loved him, too. But she hadn't. She had been the only woman who had ever rejected him and she had done it in a cruel and dismissive manner which had emphasised his subservient status. He would never forget the way she had looked through him, as if he had been invisible. *As if he were nothing.* Was it that which had planted the bitter seed of anger, deep in the empty place he called his heart?

He watched as, with an unsteady hand, she put down her half-empty gourd and fixed him with those incredible sapphire eyes of hers.

'You still haven't explained what brought you here today, Alej.'

He leaned his head back against the chair and surveyed her from between slitted eyes. 'Because I think I can help you. Or rather, I think we can help each other.'

She shook her head. 'After the things you've just accused me of, I'm amazed you're offering, but I'll decline if it's all the same to you.' She gritted him a polite smile. 'I don't need your help.'

'Oh, I think you do,' he contradicted softly. 'That is, if you want to save Joya. If you'd like him to live out his days happily in a flower-filled meadow, with a loving groom to tend to his every need rather than ending up on the scrapheap, which is where he's heading right now.'

'Are you trying to use an old, sick horse in order to blackmail me?'

'Not at all. I'm simply stating facts,' he said. 'And suggesting we do a trade-off.'

Still reeling from the fact that he held her responsible for his mother's sacking, Emily wondered what on earth he was talking about. Because what could someone like her do for someone like him, when he was an iconic billionaire and she was…? She stared down at her jeans and canvas sneakers. At the unmanicured hands which were resting on the sides of the chair. She was just an ordinary woman trying to find some balance after a tumultuous upbringing, which had bounced her round like a rubber ball. A woman who had been chasing independence since she'd graduated from college. Normality was what she craved more than anything and contact with Alejandro Sabato certainly wouldn't go anywhere towards helping her achieve that aim. Because he made her want something it was dangerous to want and that something was him. He made her think of slow touching and long kissing—both of which she'd like to do right now, even though he was looking at her with an expression of barely veiled contempt. And hadn't that been the root cause of her mother's tragic story—that she had been hooked on a man who had secretly despised her? Did she really want the same thing for herself?

Her instinct was to finish her drink, to smile politely and tell him she would manage somehow. She would find a way to save Joya, though she wasn't quite sure how she was going to go about it in a country which now felt distinctly foreign to her, despite having spent so much time here.

But Argentina was Alej's homeland, wasn't it? If anyone knew how best to deal with rehoming an ancient horse and rescuing him from certain death, it was him. And because he looked so powerful and dependable as he sat opposite her on the shaded veranda, she found the words leaving her mouth before she'd had time to consider the wisdom of saying them. 'What kind of trade-off?' she questioned cautiously.

Reflectively, he stirred his drink with the *bombilla* before lifting his gaze to hers, rugged features darkened by the shade cast by the overgrown shrubs which tumbled down the side of the veranda. 'How much do you know about me, Emily?'

It was an unexpected question and Emily wished he hadn't asked it. Because she knew him intimately, as only a lover could. His hard body. That low, exultant moan he'd given as he had bucked to fulfilment—over and over during that night. The only night. Flustered, she shrugged, trying to dredge up some of the facts she'd buried deep in her mind, where she rarely allowed herself to venture. 'I know you came from a poor family and that your mother—'

'No, not back then,' he interrupted, and suddenly there was a bitterness about him which she'd never seen before. Or maybe she just hadn't hung around long enough to see it.

'Spare me the rags-to-riches story which has been told a million times,' he ordered roughly. 'I'm talking about modern day. Real time. Now.'

Emily screwed up her eyes. If she admitted to knowing stuff about his current lifestyle, mightn't that seem as if she was somehow *trolling* him, like some sad ex-lover who couldn't bear to let go? But Alejandro Sabato wasn't just anyone, she reminded herself. Everything he touched made headlines—both work *and* play. Who *hadn't* heard of him?

'I know you suddenly retired from polo,' she said. 'And that your decision took everyone by surprise.'

He nodded but provided no explanation. His verdant gaze just continued to cut through her, like a knife slicing through a ripe melon. 'What else?'

She hesitated. After all the drama and fallout she'd experienced while growing up, she tried not to place too much importance on wealth—but in this case that would be like trying to ignore a whole herd of elephants who were trying to trample their way into a small cupboard. Especially with that top-of-the-range black helicopter, which was shining like a giant beetle in the field not far from where they were sitting, and the fact that Alejandro had recently come in at number thirty-four on a list of the world's richest men.

'That you invested in an energy drink which is pretty much drunk everywhere and used some of the money you made to help a friend set up a social media app. And then you bought into a motor-racing team, which has reaped its own rewards,' she offered. 'So you've exchanged one kind of high-intensity sport for another.'

'Very neatly summarised,' he said, raising his dark eyebrows. 'Perhaps I should be flattered that you've taken such an interest in my progress, Emily.'

'Please don't be,' she said sharply. 'I work in PR and it's my job to read the papers. And since you take up a lot of column space in the international press, it's hardly surprising that I should have picked up some facts about you over the years.'

From the thick lashes which framed the startling green eyes, he continued to survey her. 'Then you will know about Colette?'

There was the briefest of pauses before Emily nodded, surprised by how much it hurt to hear him say another woman's name. 'Doesn't everyone? Supermodels of her stature are few and far between. I gather you broke up,' she added blandly. 'And she wrote an unauthorised biography about you.'

'Did you read it?'

Emily shook her head. Was he mad? Of course she hadn't read it! She'd seen the title and hadn't even been able to face giving it a quick skim-through. Because what woman would want to absorb details of her ex-lover's wild sex life with one of the world's hottest supermodels? 'No,' she said, and then—because he seemed to be waiting for more—she forced herself to continue. 'But I gather it wasn't favourable towards you.'

Alej almost smiled. He'd forgotten the English penchant for understatement, just as he'd forgotten how Emily's cool beauty had the ability to ignite something deep inside him. It always had. He hadn't seen her in eight years, yet the lust which was pulsing through his body was as powerful as it had been when he'd met her way back when. Back then, she had been forbidden fruit for all kinds of reasons. Too young, for a start—even before you factored in that she was the stepdaughter of his mother's employer and that nobody in their right mind would dare mess around with the boss's family.

But desire was a powerful driver. It had eaten him up from the inside out. Plagued and tormented him like a fever, so that he'd had to work extra hard to concentrate on the polo which had always consumed him and had promised a route out of the poverty into which he'd been born. And wasn't the truth that Emily hadn't been like the other girls who hung around the polo field with their breasts practically falling out of their shirts? An out-and-out tomboy, she'd somehow made him *feel* stuff. Stuff he wasn't used to feeling, which had made him want to buy her flowers and brush her hair in the moonlight and tell her that her skin was paler than the stars. He'd thought it had been the same for her—that she had reciprocated his see-sawing emotions during those long months of stolen kisses and furtive embraces before he had finally made love to her.

His groin hardened. Because of her innocence and relative youth he had employed an uncharacteristic restraint around Emily Green. It had almost killed him to hold off until her eighteenth birthday, though in the end they had missed it by a day because they just couldn't wait any longer. Never had a sexual build-up been so exquisitely slow or sweetly torturous, so that when he had finally slipped inside her, he'd come almost as quickly as she had done. He'd been having safe sex with willing partners since the age of sixteen—but nothing could have prepared Alej for his first time with Emily, when he plunged deep into her tight and molten heat. The only time, he reminded himself bitterly, before forcing his attention back to the present and the sapphire-blue eyes which were regarding him with a curiosity which was somehow adding to his frustration and long-suppressed anger.

'It was, as you say—an unfavourable piece,' he conceded, his temperate tone at odds with his turbulent thoughts. 'But, unfortunately, mud sticks and she told a lot of lies about me.'

She tilted her head to one side, so that her thick blonde plait fell forward and lay enticingly against the firm thrust of her breasts. 'What kind of lies?'

'What man would wish to list their supposed transgressions to another woman? Why don't you just read the book for yourself?' There was a pause. 'And in the meantime, I could make sure that Joya is taken care of.'

Her attention was momentarily distracted as she watched a lizard slithering its way across the decking before looking up at him.

'That's a very generous offer,' she said uncertainly.

'Which obviously isn't motivated simply by my love of horses.'

'No?'

He shook his head and gave a glimmer of a smile. 'Of course not. I expect to extract a reward for my benevolence.'

Behind the smile an undeniable threat was underpinning his words and as Emily stared into his eyes she felt a sudden chill whisper its way over her skin. If she hadn't been so worried and in such a helpless position about helping Joya, she wouldn't have needed to ask the question, but the reality was that she did. 'What kind of "reward" did you have in mind?'

The slow smile he flicked her was tinged with sensual promise, but the words which followed were the last thing Emily was expecting to hear.

'You work in public relations, don't you?'

She blinked. 'How did you know that?'

'It wasn't difficult. I did a little research, before you arrived. Your reputation is modest, but it's growing. I read nothing but good things about you.' There was a brief pause. 'So how about you come and work for me, as my PR representative?'

'You don't have one at the moment?'

'Never saw the need.' He shrugged. 'But if you can polish my tarnished image for me, then we'll call it quits.'

'But why?' Her brow creased into a frown. 'I mean, why do you suddenly care what people think about you when you never did before?'

He didn't answer for a moment and when he did his voice was reflective. 'Because I'm thinking of throwing my hat into the political ring and my current reputation will do me no favours. If you can make this bad-boy billionaire into a respectable member of polite society, I will reward you very handsomely.'

Emily stared at him. Was he actually *offering her a job*? Asking her to create a squeaky-clean image for him, which would involve her delving into aspects of his life which made her feel ill just thinking about them? She couldn't do it. In fact, she wouldn't do it. You could only ever take a job like this if you were properly impartial and impartiality was the last thing she felt towards the Argentinian billionaire.

She shook her head. 'I don't think you realise how my kind of business operates, Alejandro,' she said. 'I can't suddenly start working exclusively for you—even if I wanted to, which I don't. I have commitments.'

His hand sliced through the air with that same impatient gesture. 'I'm not interested in the detail. I've told you what I want, so make it happen. Leave your job if necessary.'

'Leave my job?' Her lips fell open. 'I'm in partnership with a friend from uni. That's just not possible.'

'Anything is possible, Emily,' he bit out. 'We both know that. We live in a world where a poor illegitimate boy can rise up the greasy pole to have more money than he knows what to do with.'

She shook her head. 'Find someone else, Alejandro. There are plenty of public relations officers who are of an equally high standard who would bite your hand off to get this kind of job.'

'But they aren't you,' he said silkily. 'Are you haggling with me because you want to obtain the highest price for your services—is that what this is all about? In which case, let me tell you something which might influence your opinion.'

He mentioned a sum of money which took her breath away. Emily dug her fingers into the arms of the wicker chair and levered herself up, needing to get away from his distracting gaze as she tried to process the offer he'd just made her. That was a *lot* of money. Walking over to the edge of the veranda, she stared out at the lush Argentinian landscape and the cotton-wool clouds which were billowing up on the horizon.

She knew she ought to refuse because only a fool would accept—given their history. She'd hurt him for no reason other than that she'd been scared. But she had reasons for being tempted by the money—and not just because her embryo PR business could do with a financial cushion. And there was Great-Aunt Jane to think about—her only living relative who Emily kept a tender eye on as often as she could. Because her pension was tiny, wasn't it? She had become one of those old people who were scared of the future because they weren't quite sure if they would have enough money to fund whatever lay ahead. Wouldn't it be great if she could take away some of her worries by presenting her with a generous cheque?

But deep down Emily knew that her eagerness to accept Alejandro's offer was about more than helping care for a dear relative. The truth was that for too long she'd felt as if she was existing on some kind of plateau. As if life was passing her by. These days she rarely dated but when she did, she felt *empty*. As if she'd been carved from stone. And the reason for that was standing right in front of her. Tall, dark and indomitable. The man who made all other men seem as insubstantial as shadows. The man who made the idea of loving someone else seem impossible.

Sometimes she suspected that she'd idealised Alejandro Sabato and allowed time to distort her memory of him, although the reality of seeing him in the flesh was as powerful as it had ever been. But if she'd been guilty of putting him on a pedestal, then surely here was the perfect opportunity to dismantle it. To see for herself the man he really was, rather than the superhero of her young and lovestruck imagination. She could feel the thunder of her heart as she tried to imagine it. Wouldn't daily contact with the arrogant billionaire reinforce all the reasons why it was the best decision to walk away, as well as saving Joya and helping her great-aunt in the process?

She turned back to find him looking at her and the most stupid thing was that all she really wanted was for him to hold her. To cradle her in his strong arms and make her feel truly desired again. Determinedly, she pushed those thoughts away.

'Since I can't see any alternative,' she said slowly, 'I'll take the job.'

Alejandro felt a beat of anger because he'd seen the way her eyes had lit up like a Christmas tree when he'd mentioned the money. It seemed she was just like her mother, he observed bitterly—available to the highest bidder. Yet she wore no outward signs of the wealth she clearly craved. Her clothes were decidedly unsexy and her face bare of make-up. He wondered if she had been disappointed with the laughable legacy left to her by her stepfather and was surprised how much pleasure it gave him to hope so.

'I thought that might sway it,' he remarked, raking his fingers back through the thick tumble of his hair. 'There are very few women who aren't persuaded by the prospect of instant wealth.'

And then he remembered why he was here—not to stand in judgement or to remind himself that she was shallow and avaricious. The real reason was as old as time itself. She had hurt him. Badly. And now it was time to hurt her right back.

He flicked her a smile. 'I'm flying out to Australia for the Melbourne Grand Prix next week and I want you there,' he said silkily.

She nodded as she looked up, her expression composed, but he sensed an inner tension about her which echoed his own. He could see those blue eyes widening. Darkening. He could see the almost surreptitious way that the tip of her tongue slid out to moisten the lush cushion of her lower lip. Soon, he thought, with a beat of anticipation. Soon he would make her realise what she was missing and how stupid she had been to turn her back on him in such a cold and callous manner.

And then he could walk away.

His mouth hardened.

For ever.

CHAPTER THREE

'EMILY, ARE YOU OKAY? I mean, seriously?' Marybeth's voice was full of concern. 'I've never seen you like this before, not in all the years I've known you.'

Slowly Emily turned around to survey her business partner, who'd been her best friend since they'd met during their final year of college. Still reeling from her mother's sudden death, Emily had been floundering when Marybeth Miller had swooped in and taken her under her wing. She'd insisted on bringing Emily back for weekends at her family's rambling farmhouse in north Devon, where Emily had come into contact with the kind of noisy, good-hearted atmosphere she'd never known before. It had been her first experience of teasing siblings and walking for miles in the fresh country air before sitting down to eat enormous hunks of home-made cake, and it had helped her come to terms with her bereavement, though that hadn't been easy.

Her pain had been compounded by other feelings: by guilt and regret—but especially guilt. She kept wondering if she could have done something to stop her mother's inevitable decline. If she could maybe have stopped her taking tranquillisers or shown her that there was a life worth living, even as a divorcee. But alongside the guilt had come a rush of something else and Emily hadn't been able to shake off her relief that she was now liberated from all the emotional trauma of her mother's life. She wondered if it had been that liberation which had prompted her to mail Alejandro a letter, apologising for everything that had happened and offering a cautious olive branch, suggesting that if he was playing in England any time soon, then perhaps they could meet up for a drink. But he hadn't even bothered to reply. And maybe part of her couldn't blame him. Did she really imagine that the proud Argentinian would share a cocktail with her after she'd dumped him so brutally?

'I mean, look at you now—you're *miles* away!' Marybeth was staring at Emily in bemusement. 'And you've got this look on your face, like…'

'Like what?' Emily prompted curiously.

'You're all wired,' said her friend. 'As if someone's turned on a light inside you and you've suddenly come alive. Yet you look scared, too. As if something's waiting just around the corner for you and you don't like what it is.' She paused. 'You know, you don't have to accept this job from this guy Alejandro Sabato.'

Emily gave a hollow laugh. 'What, and turn down the best money and exposure we've ever been offered just because I once stupidly had sex with him?'

Marybeth looked shocked—probably because Emily was never usually that frank. Or maybe it was because she'd lived like a nun for so long that her partner thought she was still a virgin.

'Is that what happened?' Marybeth questioned. 'I mean, I guessed there had been someone.'

Emily blinked. 'You did?'

Marybeth shrugged. 'Of course. You're lovely,'

she said gently. 'But you always clammed up when it came to talking about men and then this really sad look would come over your face, so I didn't like to pry. And whenever you've dated anyone—which doesn't happen often—nobody has come close to capturing your heart, which suggested it must have been badly broken. Is that what happened, Em—with this guy Sabato? Did he break your heart?'

Emily hesitated as she folded another cotton shirt before adding it to the neat and sensible pile already in her suitcase. She never talked about it because it still had the power to hurt and also because she was aware of how badly she'd handled it—in fact, she couldn't have handled it more badly if she'd tried. But maybe she should talk about it. Maybe she needed to make sense of it in her own head, so that she could deal with it competently when she came into contact with him again. 'Alejandro was the housekeeper's son when I lived in Argentina,' she began slowly. 'In the days when my mother was married to Paul Vickery.'

'That's the guy who left you the horse?'

Emily nodded. 'That's the one. Cruel and calculating, but ultimately very rich—at least, he was when I was a child. My mother was completely in thrall to him, mainly because he'd rescued her from a life of poverty as a widow. My father was a fisherman who drowned off the Cornish coast, but even when he was alive, money was scarce. After he died my mother met Paul and felt as if she'd hit the jackpot. She'd found herself a rich husband who gave her a financial security she didn't have to work for. It's one of the reasons why my career has always been so important to me. Why I've been determined never to rely on a man like that.'

She heaved out a sigh. 'And even though he was chronically unfaithful, Paul only had to snap his fingers and she came running, which is what rich men really want women to do—and then they despise them for it. He had a thing about status. A big thing. Socialising in the highest echelons of society was his bag and his stepdaughter mixing with the illegitimate son of the hired help certainly didn't fit into that image, despite the fact that Alej was clearly going to be a big star in the world of polo. It may have been even more basic than that. Alejandro was at his physical peak and poised on the cusp of glory and my stepfather was getting very old by then—so maybe it was that old lion, young lion thing. When he found out I was involved with Alej, he demanded I finish it.'

'So you did?'

It sounded weak to admit it now, but, yes, she'd caved in and done exactly as her stepfather had demanded—mainly because her mother had got down on her knees in that over-the-top way of hers and begged her to. Had sobbed that Paul would never forgive her if she didn't and she couldn't cope with a divorce and going back to being a single mother. The ensuing drama had felt like an embarrassing nightmare and in the end Emily had agreed. But she'd convinced herself it was all for the best and it would save her even more heartbreak further on down the line, because surely to Alej she was nothing more than a brief fling. A teenage love affair which wasn't going anywhere—especially when increasing numbers of women were lining up beside the polo pitch to watch him play and making their availability very plain. Just as she'd told herself she would soon forget him. That the latter part of her assessment had never come true wasn't anyone's fault, particularly not his.

'Yes,' she said. 'I finished it.'

I finished it in the most horrible way possible which still makes me shudder to think about it, which is why I rarely do.

'So why do you think he's chosen you to salvage his image, out of all the PR representatives in the world?' questioned Marybeth slowly.

'He says he wants to go into politics,' Emily answered, her brow furrowing into a thoughtful frown. 'And needs to shed his bad-boy reputation pretty sharpish.'

'And that's it?' Marybeth's eyes glinted. 'That's the only reason he's employing you?'

It was a question Emily didn't want to answer as she snapped her suitcase closed and gave Marybeth a bright smile. 'I guess so. What other reason could there be?'

But she thought about her partner's question all the way to Heathrow airport and through the long flight which followed, which was delayed further by a technical problem on the plane which was supposed to take them from Brunei to Melbourne. Hadn't there been a whisper of revenge underpinning the dogmatic way Alejandro had demanded she go and work for him? Was the unspoken clause that he wanted to capitalise on the undoubted chemistry which still existed between them, or was that just her imagination? Because that was never going to happen, no matter what the provocation. No matter that she still found him the sexiest man she'd ever set eyes on, she wasn't going to tumble into his arms the way she used to do. She didn't dare. Why would she put herself through something like that when the cold glint in Alejandro's eyes made no secret of the fact that he now despised her? All she needed to do was to resurrect his battered public image and earn the money he had promised her. Simple.

It was hot when she arrived in Melbourne—hotter than Emily had expected, though she'd never been to Australia before. She felt grimy and sticky after the long journey but was due to meet Alejandro at the racetrack and reckoned a trip to her hotel to freshen up would make her even later than she already was. So she scurried into a washroom at the airport and did the best she could in the cramped surroundings, but the creases in the clean dress she pulled on were stubbornly refusing to fall out and her cheeks were flushed and shiny.

Passing a news stand, she saw Alejandro's rugged features staring back from the front page of a tabloid underneath the headline *Billionaire's Racy Race Party!*

Digging into her purse for some coins, she tucked the newspaper into her bag and read it during the bus ride to the stadium, hating the way her heart sank as she pored over the feature, thinking how much one of the women photographed entering his hotel resembled his ex-mistress—a fact which hadn't escaped the notice of the journalist. It gave them the perfect opportunity to print an old picture of Colette and Alejandro kissing passionately at the Monaco Grand Prix and Emily couldn't rid herself of the image of the supermodel's long fingers splayed possessively over the Argentinian billionaire's taut bottom.

She was still feeling peculiar when the bus arrived at the race venue in Albert Park, and the constant droning of powerful cars coming from inside the stadium only added to her feelings of disorientation. Her phone started vibrating and she didn't need to see the name to know who it was from, as she squinted at it in the sunshine. The terse message blazing from the screen could have originated from only one person.

Where the hell are you?

Alejandro. Sounding angry and impatient. Was this going to be his default mechanism with her from now on? she wondered. But at least he'd kept his side of the bargain and, just before she'd left England, a batch of photos had arrived, each showing Joya. Now happily rehomed in Alejandro's vast Argentinian ranch, the horse's body had started to fill out and gleam with health as he stood regarding the camera with some of his perky expression of old. Unexpected tears had pricked at Emily's eyes as she'd stared at the images and she'd felt an overwhelming burst of gratitude as she'd boarded the night bus to the airport.

And now it was time for her to keep *her* side of the bargain, despite her misgivings.

She tapped out a reply.

Yes, I had a very pleasant trip—thanks for asking!

Another terse reply shot straight back.

Where are you?

This was going to be fun, thought Emily as her fingers flew over the smooth surface of the screen.

Just going up to the VIP section as instructed. Assume someone will meet me there?

There was no response to this one, so she picked up her suitcase and asked for directions, before heading for the gate where a small but well-heeled throng were congregated. Emily looked around with interest, because she'd never been to a motor-racing event before and it was a lot dressier than she'd imagined. Some of the women were wearing expensive skinny jeans and floaty blouses with discreet diamonds glinting at their ears and wrists, while others were in silk dresses with crazy-high heels. Emily frowned. Maybe Marybeth had been right in insisting that she borrow some fancy clothes for the trip, after all. Surreptitiously, she smoothed down her hair, uncomfortably aware that her battered suitcase was standing out like a sore thumb amid all the soft designer handbags.

Everyone was being ushered through the metal turnstile without fanfare, but as soon as Emily stepped forward, a burly security guard planted himself in front of her.

'Pass?' he said, extending the palm of his hand.

'I should have been left one at the gate.' Emily forced a smile, acutely aware of the beads of sweat which were springing up on her forehead and of a woman in front who had turned round to give her a haughty look. She wanted to exude her usual air of competence but for some reason it seemed to be eluding her. 'By Alejandro Sabato.'

The security man raised his eyebrows. 'Alejandro Sabato? The sponsor?'

'That's right. He's expecting me.'

'Is he now?' The guard could barely keep the smirk from his lips. 'That's what they all say, love. I'm afraid it's more than my job's worth to let you in without a ticket.'

'It's okay, Wesley.' A rich, accented voice filtered through the warm air towards them. 'I can vouch for her.'

The guard's demeanour quickly changed to one of near adulation as Alejandro came through the turnstile, irritation hardening the perfection of his olive-skinned features as he strode towards them. With an impatient movement he gestured for her to move away and Emily was glad to remove herself from the glances they were attracting. Were people bemused by how mismatched the two of them looked? Mightn't she have thought exactly the same if she'd been the outsider?

She wished she could slow down the racing of her heart, just as she wished she could stop her body from prickling with instinctive hunger as she surveyed the man towering over her, with anger glinting from his green eyes. Today he was dressed down in faded denims and a creamy silk shirt, but his casual clothes didn't detract from the unmistakable air of authority and power which radiated from his body. Dark waves of hair were curling onto the collar of his shirt, their unruly profusion somehow at odds with his upright stance and the perfect posture which had always been remarked upon during his riding career. People were taking sneaky photos of him with their phones but he didn't appear to notice.

'You're late,' he accused, as soon as they were out of earshot.

'I know. Sorry about that. It couldn't be helped.'

'Why not? What happened?' he demanded. 'Was the plane delayed?'

'Sort of. There was a tech problem.' Emily shifted the strap of her shoulder bag to stop it rubbing. 'Which delayed the second flight, so the journey took longer than the twenty-eight hours it was supposed to take.'

'More than twenty-eight hours?' he echoed incredulously. 'How is that even possible?'

She wondered if he'd forgotten what it was like to be poor, or to be starting out. If he knew what it was like to consult comparison sites on the web before you took a plane anywhere—or whether he was so used to travelling around in private jets and helicopters that such a mode of transport now seemed completely normal to him. 'I bought the cheapest ticket available, which meant it took a somewhat…um…' she gave a sheepish shrug '…indirect route.'

His eyes narrowed. 'Even though you had a budget which allowed you to travel first class, which I believe was agreed in advance with my assistant?'

'That's right.'

'So?' His eyes bored into her questioningly.

'So I couldn't justify spending that kind of money on a plane ticket and flying to the other side of the world in the lap of luxury, Alejandro. Not when my business is in such a fledgling state and we're still having to budget like crazy because most people don't pay on time. Every penny counts at this stage—that's why we're careful.' She hesitated, and then a smile seemed to spring out of nowhere as she looked at him with gratitude. 'But I wanted to thank you for everything you've done for Joya. He seems so happy now and those pictures of him at your ranch look amazing.'

'It's called an *estancia*,' he snapped.

'Whatever.' Her smile widened. 'But thanks, anyway.'

Alejandro wanted to hang onto his anger but when she looked at him like that it wasn't easy, and it was causing his conscience to stir in an uncharacteristic way, because she looked so damned sweet. But she wasn't sweet, he reminded himself grimly. She was as money-grabbing as her mother. And she was a heartless snob. When she'd walked away from him, she had looked down her pretty nose and given him a shuttered look when he'd asked her why.

You're not the right type of man for me, Alej.

He hadn't known what she'd meant, not at first. He'd been rough and unsophisticated back then. He'd seen the uncomfortable look which had crossed her features. The way she'd licked her lips, like someone being forced to eat cat food. Like a fool he had asked her, unable to believe that Emily—his Emily—could look at him so condescendingly, as if she'd never met him before.

You're illegitimate.

And that matters? he remembered demanding incredulously.

It matters to me.

He'd wanted to tell her that his mother might not wear a wedding ring on her finger, but that his father was someone whose wealth and position could easily eclipse that of her stepfather. But he hadn't done that, because at heart Alejandro Sabato was a proud man. And, in view of what had subsequently happened, thank God he hadn't.

But dwelling on his hurt and his anger wasn't going to get him anywhere—at least, not at this precise moment. Instead, Alejandro pushed away the ugly thoughts as he raked his gaze over her. He had wondered if the intervening years might have given her an air of sophistication, but they certainly hadn't. At the ranch she could have been excused for her plain jeans and T-shirt—but in the VIP section of one of the world's most prestigious race events, she could not.

His mouth thinned into a disapproving line, for he had imagined she would make herself beautiful for him, as women always did. He wondered if this was some kind of subtle rebellion—turning up with her face bare of make-up and wearing a cheap cotton dress. And why was her blonde hair hanging over one shoulder in that thick and wholesome plait, so she looked like some superannuated milkmaid rather than a smooth PR he'd hired to revamp his playboy image?

Yet her drab clothes were doing nothing to dampen his ardour for her. If anything, her prim outfit was heating his blood with a passion he hadn't felt in years and he was having difficulty averting his gaze from her luscious curves, which no plain shift dress could possibly disguise. His throat dried. He resented the physical allure she still seemed to radiate, despite her second-rate appearance. Was she aware that the thin material was brushing tantalisingly against her generous breasts, reminding him all too vividly of the way he used to stroke them until she moaned? Or that her bare legs were making his groin grow exquisitely hard as he wondered what type of panties she was wearing and was filled with a sudden overwhelming desire to discover the answer for himself. Later, he promised himself, with a fierce beat of hunger. Later.

Deliberately, he swivelled his gaze away from her, directing it instead towards the battered suitcase she was clutching. 'And *that*?' he demanded, with soft incredulity.

'It's my suitcase. Obviously.' She tilted a defiant chin. 'I didn't want to be any later than I already was, so I came straight here without checking into my hotel first.'

'Well, you can't stay here, not looking like that.' He fished a shoal of car keys from the back pocket of his jeans and took the case from her. 'My car isn't far away. I'll take you to your hotel so you can change. Or at least iron your dress.'

'I'm very grateful for the sartorial tips, Alejandro. Perhaps you'd like to colour-coordinate my wardrobe for me while I'm here?'

Ignoring her sarcastic comments, he glanced at his gold watch. 'The qualifying session is over and the main race isn't until tomorrow. There's a party on a yacht down in the harbour I need to attend, but that's not until later. Come on. Don't let's waste any more time. Let's go.'

He was so…*bossy*, Emily thought, and part of her wanted to object to his high-handedness. To tell him she'd prefer to start working straight away and check into her hotel later, but that would have been a lie. To be honest, she didn't think she could concentrate on anything right now, especially not on the closely written notes she'd made when he'd first given her the contract. Her brain felt fuzzy and her limbs were as heavy as lead, after being stuck in the middle row of a crowded plane between two women, one of whom had crunched on boiled sweets for the entire flight. Hopefully a quick shower and change of clothes would turn her back into her usual efficient self.

Because she was *good* at her job, she reminded herself fiercely. That was why she and Marybeth had taken the decision to leave the big agency they'd been working at and go it alone. She might be a complete disaster where relationships were concerned, but at least her career was going somewhere. And this was the chance to prove it—to herself and to the world at large. Because if she could single-handedly turn around Alejandro Sabato's bad-boy image, wouldn't that bring in a whole stream of new contracts and catapult their company onto the next level? Wasn't that what she'd been striving for all these years?

So she nodded and smiled at him. 'Okay,' she said politely. 'That'd be good.'

It felt weird having someone carry her bag for her. She'd been on her own for so long that it seemed like a luxury—and a poignant one at that. But deep down she knew it didn't mean anything. Outwardly Alejandro might be acting like a gentleman but there was no denying his underlying hostility towards her, which no acts of chivalry could disguise.

They made their way to a car park, where mouthwateringly expensive vehicles were sitting in gleaming rows. Slinging her suitcase into the boot of one of the most luxurious, he punched out the postcode she'd given him and powered the car out of the park like a restless animal which had just been released for the day.

It quickly became clear that he was driving in an unfamiliar part of the city because he cursed several times in Spanish as they drove past a series of giant business parks before reaching a downmarket residential area, where graffiti was daubed on boarded-up shop windows and litter drifted in slow motion through the streets. Although a relatively short distance away from the racetrack, it seemed like a world away from all the glitz and glamour Emily had glimpsed there. As he pulled upside a motel with dirty windows and two letters missing from the sign, she saw him scowl before slamming his fist against the steering wheel and turning to look at her, undisguised irritation darkening his rugged features.

'Don't tell me,' he said. 'This was the cheapest hotel you could find?'

'Actually, it's five-star—just very cunningly disguised.'

'Cut the sarcasm, Emily,' he snapped, before twisting the key in the ignition again so that the engine powered into renewed life. 'You're not staying here.'

'That's just where you're wrong, Alejandro. I am. This is where I've booked to stay and my room is paid for in advance. I'm perfectly prepared to rough it for a few days and my accommodation is my concern, not yours.' She put her fingers on the door handle. 'Besides, I don't have anywhere else to go.'

'Yes, you do. Don't you dare move. You're not going anywhere.' His no-nonsense tone brooked no argument as he turned the car back towards the city.

'What are you doing?'

'Taking you somewhere which will have easy access to the race ground.'

'I'm not spending all my budget on a fancy hotel—'

'Let me worry about the budget, Emily. Just sit back and enjoy the ride.'

Enjoy the ride? He was *definitely* crazy. Yet somehow…somehow… Emily found herself doing exactly that. She blamed the accumulated jet lag of recent back-to-back flights across the globe for her compliance, because why else would she have settled back into the squishy comfort of the seat, secretly relieved not to have to stay in that ghastly motel, which looked nothing like it had done on the website?

And wasn't she secretly enjoying watching Alej manoeuvre the powerful car through the city streets? It felt like something of a voyeuristic and guilty distraction to observe the thrust of his muscular thighs as he deftly weaved in and out of traffic, and before long he was drawing up outside a beautiful hotel in the historic part of the city. Ornate spires soared up into a cloudless blue sky and window boxes of bright pink flowers added splashes of colour to the gracious façade. Emily glanced up at the sign. Even if her research hadn't flagged up this as one of the most exclusive places to stay in the city—she could have worked that out for herself.

'No way. I can't possibly stay here,' she objected. 'This is one of the best hotels in Melbourne.'

'You have no choice. Everywhere else will be full because of the race.' His voice was underpinned with the steely certainty that here was a man used to getting everything he wanted. 'I have a suite. There's plenty of room. Don't worry, Emily—there's no cause for concern.'

No cause for concern? A low laugh punched its way out of Emily's lungs as she stared at his olive-skinned profile, where once she used to run a gentle fingertip along the shadowed edge of his jutting jaw. Had he become the master of understatement in the intervening years or was he just oblivious to the glaringly obvious? 'You really think I'm going to share a suite with you?'

'What's the problem?' He turned his head to look at

her, his green eyes hard and flinty. 'I know we never made it to the hotel stage in our relationship but surely you've shared accommodation with a man before. And most women manage to rent in mixed houses these days, don't they—without it resulting in some kind of orgy?'

'But we've—'

'Had sex?' he supplied baldly. 'Yeah, in theory we did. Though in reality it was just plenty of foreplay and a single night of romping amid bales of straw before you ran out on me next morning, which hardly qualifies for the deepest and most meaningful relationship of all time. Unless you think I won't be able to stop myself from leaping on you because you're just so damned alluring?'

As he spoke, his gaze was raking over her with undeniable mockery and suddenly Emily felt foolish in her cheap dress and flat sandals. 'I wasn't implying—'

'Yes, you were.' His voice lowered. 'Believe me, Emily—I prefer women who take a little more care with their appearance than you do. But most of all, I like them willing. You, of all people, should know that.'

She could feel her flush deepening and the palms of her hands growing even clammier as she wiped them down the sides of her dress. It was an unkind and unnecessary comment to make. But it was true, wasn't it? She had made it clear that she'd been his for the taking when she'd fallen in love with him. He'd been six years older and had tried to do the honourable thing, but that hadn't deterred her. At the age of seventeen it was as if all the scales had fallen from her eyes. Overnight, it seemed, their platonic friendship had changed and she had looked at him with a hunger she hadn't known before, or since. She had been ready, willing and available whenever the opportunity had arisen. All those snatched and stolen moments had only added an extra layer of excitement to their secret relationship. And then, when he had given her what she'd wanted, she had walked away with nothing but a few cruel words lingering in her wake.

She had done it because she'd been backed into a corner by her stepfather, who had made all kinds of horrible threats.

But hadn't a tiny part of her been relieved to walk away? To be free of all that compulsion and desire and obsession, which had made her fear she was too much like her foolish mother? That she would end up becoming weak and dependent on a man?

'There are two bedrooms,' Alejandro was saying. 'You can have your own space if that's what you want—'

'Of course it's what I want,' she snapped. 'Surely you don't think I'm sharing a room with you?'

'It would be a novel experience,' he observed softly. 'And one I'd be willing to try.'

'In your dreams,' she retorted as a valet approached to open the door for her.

'Yours too, perhaps?' he suggested, with a pointed glance at her hardening nipples.

'Will you please stop making innuendos?'

'I'm not.' He slanted her a mocking smile. 'I'm merely making an observation.'

Pre-empting the approaching valet, Emily opened the car door herself, furious at the accuracy of Alejandro's arrogant words but even more furious at the way she couldn't seem to help her body from responding to him. Suddenly she was aware of a rush of heat which pooled at her groin, but most of all she was aware of the Argentinian's appreciative gaze on her bare legs as she wriggled out of the car.

CHAPTER FOUR

'IT'S HIM! IT'S definitely him! Hey, Alej—can we get a selfie with you?'

Two beautiful young American women with tumbling hair and super-tight denim shorts had spotted their entry into the hotel and were clattering their way across the lobby towards them on gravity-defying shoes.

'No,' snapped Emily. 'Refuse politely.'

Alejandro turned his head towards her, his dark brows raised. 'Why?'

'Because if you're serious about politics, you need to stop people constantly seeing you with gorgeous women fawning all over you. It makes you look like a lightweight and a flirt. Tell them you're expecting a call.'

'But I'm not.'

'Just make an excuse.'

'If you insist,' he said drily.

'I do. And my advice is what you're paying for. Remember?'

'When did you get so insistent, Emily?'

'When I started my own business and recognised the need to assert myself. It's a particularly useful trait when I'm dealing with stubborn men.'

'You don't say?' he mocked.

'Indeed, I do. Now, be polite by all means—if such a concept isn't alien to you—but walk straight past them.'

Without pausing mid-stride, Alejandro called out his apologies to the two women, who pouted prettily as he and Emily made their way towards the elevator. She wondered if she had imagined their look of astonishment as they'd stared at the Argentinian's companion but an unexpected glimpse of herself as they walked past an enormous rose-gold mirror made her realise just how awful she looked.

The doors of the executive elevator slid open and the rapid ride towards the penthouse was just long enough to remind her what real luxury felt like. She hadn't experienced it since her mother's marriage to Paul, when extravagance had been part of her daily life and it had been drummed into her that she must be grateful at all times. Grateful that her stepfather had given her a home—and what a home!

And she had tried. She'd tried so hard. Pretended not to mind those interminable dinners, which had gone on and on and the adults had forgotten she was there. Pretended not to be bored at being dragged around yet another stuffy museum to which her stepfather had donated money in his attempt to ingratiate himself into society. Because wasn't all that preferable to listening to the muffled sobs of her mother and having to play ignorant about where she'd left her bottle of pills?

Sometimes it seemed she'd spent her whole life pretending. She was even pretending now, wasn't she? Trying to make out that she wasn't in the least bit affected by the sexy hunk who was standing on the other side of the elevator.

'We're here.' Alejandro's words shattered her reverie

and Emily followed him into an enormous suite where the first thing she saw—perched on a raised dais—was a white baby grand piano.

Searching round for evidence of more luxury, she quickly found it. Futuristic glass lights in candy shades spilled shafts of colours all over the modern, monochrome furniture. An angular sculpture stood framed against the city sky in one of the vast picture windows. Everything seemed so stark and pristine, which somehow emphasised Alejandro's earthy appeal as he put down her suitcase and walked towards a large desk. His olive skin glowed as he glanced down at a pile of cards and began to flick his way through them. The thick tumble of his hair looked almost blue-black in the sunshine and suddenly Emily found herself wanting to run her fingers through the lustrous waves, just like in the old days. She wanted to press her body up against his and slide her tongue against the roughness of his shadowed jaw. And yet it was dangerous to feel like that. She might be unfulfilled, but at least she was not hung up and obsessing. Not bereft or aching or staring at her phone, waiting for some man who was never going to ring.

She thought how at home he seemed in this lavish setting, he who had been born to abject poverty—and how, ironically, it was her who now felt out of place. And her travel-weary and un-showered state wasn't exactly helping. How could she possibly concentrate on work when she still felt so hot and sticky—especially when Alejandro looked so cool and pristine?

'Perhaps you'd like to point me in the direction of my room?' she suggested. 'I'd like to freshen up before we get down to work.'

'Sure.' He picked up her suitcase. 'Come with me,' he said, observing her instinctively shrinking away as he came close.

Leading her down the wide and spacious corridor towards the two bedrooms, Alejandro wondered when she had become so uptight. He remembered her astride a horse, with the wind in her hair—someone who bore no resemblance to the sensible creature she'd become in her plain clothes. Maybe that was what happened to women when they lost their innocence. Perhaps they lost their softness, too. She was the only virgin he'd ever had so he had nobody to compare her with. Cynically, his mouth twisted. There weren't too many virgins to be found in the world he inhabited.

Flinging open a bedroom door where creamy drapes framed a blue sky, he wished he could just tumble her down on that big white bed and take her without ceremony. Because wouldn't some perfunctory sex rid his mind and body of his damned hunger for her?

'This is it.'

'Wow,' she said softly, glancing at the modern artwork which adorned the walls and appearing to look at everything in the room, except for the bed. She walked over to the window. 'That's some view.'

'Best in the city. Come and find me when you've finished. And don't be long. There's a party on Marcus Hedlund's yacht in the harbour.'

'The Swedish industrialist?'

'The very same. I hope you've come suitably prepared.' His gaze swept over the wilting fabric of her dress. 'These affairs tend to be quite dressy.'

'I know that. I've done my research. Don't worry, Alejandro. I'll try not to let you down.'

The quick tilt of her chin suddenly reminded Alejandro of the daredevil teenager he'd once taught to ride and something unknown and dark twisted deep inside him as he remembered how close they'd once been. Until he reminded himself that the teenager had grown up and become a snobbish replica of her grasping mother. 'I look forward to seeing what miracles you can perform,' he said curtly, before turning away.

Returning to the drawing room, he tried to concentrate on the pile of paperwork awaiting him, but for once he found it impossible to lose himself in his workload. He should have been overjoyed at the fact that he was about to float his highly successful drinks company on the stock market for an eye-watering sum of money. Whoever would have thought that every teenager on the planet would have considered it the height of cool to quaff a cleverly marketed drink which was packed with herbs from his homeland and based on Argentina's favourite drink of *yerba maté*? Or that every business gamble he'd ever taken would confound even his own expectations and lead him to unimaginable riches?

And all this had happened to someone who'd been born in a *villa miseria*—a miserable shack crammed beside hundreds of others in a dirty settlement outside Buenos Aires, with unpaved roads and no sanitation. Even after his mother had managed to shed her past for long enough to get herself a job as a rich Englishman's housekeeper, Alej's education had been almost non-existent. His passion and talent for riding had allowed him to put learning on the back burner and nobody had really cared that he'd skipped school most days. Able to read and write but without a single exam to his name, it had been a matter of pride and perseverance which had later made him devour books and newspapers and educate himself that way.

But his subsequent successes had never managed to fill the void deep inside him, or to lighten the darkness which seemed a fundamental part of his nature. He had been betrayed, first by Emily and then by his mother, and had sometimes wondered if those two key events had scarred him irrevocably, making him the man he had become—someone who functioned efficiently on every level but who never really *felt* anything. He would never know and he didn't really care. His mother was dead now, taking her sordid past to the grave with her, and he had tried with varying degrees of success not to be judgemental about the things she had done.

But Emily was alive, wasn't she? Delicious and luscious and *alive*. Some people said that moving into the future was only possible if you were properly reconciled with your past, and that was something which had so far eluded him. Until now. His mouth tightened. Because that was what he intended to do. To claim her. To enjoy her in a way which had not been possible before. To tie up all the loose ends so there was no chance they could ever become unravelled again.

The sound of soft footsteps broke into his thoughts and he looked up, his groin hardening when he saw Emily standing in the doorway.

He swallowed. A quick glance at his watch showed him that in a little over half an hour she had managed to achieve a remarkable transformation. Her newly washed hair had been piled into a messy updo which gave her a tantalising just-got-out-of-bed look. Escaping strands had already begun to dry dark gold and shiny as they tumbled around her long neck and framed a face which had been delicately touched with make-up.

But it was her outfit which made the most startling difference. Gone was the functional cotton shift and in its place a flirty dress of red silk, a colour he'd never seen her wear before. His throat tightened. Had she deliberately bought it a little on the small side, or was the delicate material supposed to cling to her generous breasts like that, so that he could barely tear his gaze away from them? Bright and bold, it had tiny buttons all the way down the front and fell to just above each shapely knee. Hugging her narrow waist, it flared slightly over her hips and the hot-faced, crumpled creature who had greeted him at the racetrack suddenly became a distant memory.

Alejandro couldn't fault the way she looked and yet something raw and primitive began to throb through his veins as he wondered how many times she had performed this Cinderella scenario in the past. Had she dressed up like this for other men? he thought, with a sharp surge of jealousy. Had they too been busy thinking about how much they'd like to slide their fingers beneath that scarlet hemline to caress her cool thighs, before travelling further upwards to find her melting wetness? A pulse throbbed at his temple. Of course they had. Why wouldn't they, when she'd been the hottest woman he had ever known and had told him that she planned to take as many lovers as possible? That declaration had filled him with an impotent rage for a long time after she'd left and he'd sometimes found himself punching at his pillow in the middle of the night, until he had completely flattened it.

But he doubted any man had pleasured Emily Green

as thoroughly as he was about to do. He wanted to rip the dress from her body and for her panties to follow, but he forced himself to put his desire on ice and to adopt the indifferent mask which both intrigued and infuriated his many lovers.

'Did somebody wave a magic wand?' he questioned carelessly. 'Does it turn back into a sensible cotton dress at midnight?'

She gave a shrug which didn't quite come off. 'If you're referring to my outfit, I borrowed it from my friend, since she goes to a lot more fancy functions than I do.'

Which might explain why the dress was straining so tantalisingly across her breasts that he could see the faint outline of her nipples. He swallowed. 'I see.'

'But we aren't here to discuss my wardrobe choices,' she said, primly nodding her head like a schoolteacher who was about to start a lesson. 'I suggest we get down to work.'

'Of course,' he said. 'Though you could probably use a drink first?'

'Nothing alcoholic!' she responded swiftly.

He gave a low laugh. 'Don't worry, Emily. I wasn't planning on plying you with fine wine. I was offering you water.'

'Oh, right,' she said. 'Well, thanks. Water would be great.'

Emily watched as he got up from the desk, unable to tear her eyes away from him. She'd told him that she wanted to work, but the sight of Alejandro moving across the room made it difficult to concentrate on anything other than his dark beauty and physical grace, as he walked over to a sleek bar of polished black wood.

He added ice to two drinks—yet when he handed her a glass it wasn't coldness she felt but a sizzle of fire as his skin brushed against hers.

She wondered what was the matter with her. She didn't usually have showers which turned into something disturbingly erotic, but that was what had just happened as she'd washed herself in the luxury bathroom. The warm water had failed to remove the prickle of goosebumps as she'd started imagining Alejandro's fingers sliding over her flesh and the corresponding throb of her nipples had made her feel restless as she had towelled herself dry. Yet this was *nothing like* the person she usually was. The prim and efficient woman she'd become. She prided herself on the professionalism which was so important to her and on her ability to think coolly and impartially. So stop focussing on sex and start concentrating on what you're being paid for, she reminded herself.

Sipping at her water, she cleared her throat and put the glass down. 'Right. First of all, I think we need to establish some clear objectives.'

'Some clear objectives?' he echoed, green eyes faintly mocking. 'Perhaps you could be a little more specific.'

'Certainly. We're going to use this high-profile weekend to make people start thinking about you in a different way. But in order for us to work together successfully, I need you to be completely frank with me. You have to answer my questions truthfully, Alejandro. Do you think you can do that?'

'I can try.' He stared at her. 'What exactly do you want to know?'

She jerked her head towards the white baby grand. 'Why the fancy piano?'

'Rock and roll,' he explained with a touch of bemusement, as if her question was a curveball he hadn't been expecting. 'The hotel send up a pianist if any of their guests want to hold an impromptu party.'

'Is that what happened last night?'

He raised his eyebrows. 'Last night?'

'Surely you can remember back to a few hours ago? You say you want to abandon your playboy image in order to pave the way for a possible career in politics, but you aren't exactly going out of your way to help yourself, are you?'

'I don't know what you're talking about.'

'This!' Emily delved deep within her shoulder bag to produce a folded newspaper, which she held in front of him, the splashy headline easily visible. 'I picked this up at the airport and it features a gushing report about the "wild, champagne-fuelled celebration" you held last night. There was even a photo of a very beautiful actress staggering out in the early hours, obviously the worse for wear. If you're going to plan a party, I would advise you to think more carefully about your guest list in future.'

'I didn't plan a party, it just happened.' He shrugged as he met the question in her eyes. 'Two of the other sponsors wanted to see the view from my suite. It's a pretty amazing view—'

'I can see that for myself. Perhaps you could try sticking to the point? It will save us a lot of time if you do.'

He gave a slow smile in response to her sharp words, as if being admonished was something novel. 'And they brought a few people along with them. You know what it's like.'

'Not really, no.'

He seemed undeterred by her stonewalling. 'Apparently a few of the models who are in town for the race gatecrashed a bit later, but I'd gone to bed by then.'

'Alone?' she demanded quickly.

'That sounds like the accusation of a possessive girlfriend,' he observed softly. 'Or what a prosecution lawyer might call a very loaded question.'

'Or a pertinent one?' she returned. 'Just for the record, I read the book your ex-girlfriend wrote—on your recommendation, I might add. According to her, you're very fond of these kinds of parties. And of the type of women who frequent them, often without invitation.'

'And you believed every word of it, I suppose—along with the rest of the world?' His face grew hard and assumed a look of unfettered cynicism. 'Especially the part where she hinted about me enjoying "variety"—which seemed to be the phrase which got most people excited. She made me sound like the worst kind of serial philanderer. She didn't actually mention mirrors on the ceiling and black satin sheets but she might as well have done—although, unfortunately, my lawyers told me there was nothing you could actually put your finger on and call libel.'

'And did you?'

'Did I what, Emily?' he mocked.

'Enjoy…' she licked her lips, wishing she could clear her thoughts of the image of Alejandro making out beneath a mirrored ceiling amid rumpled black satin sheets '…variety?'

'Never.' A note of contempt hardened his voice, matching the sudden forbidding line of his lips. 'I've always enjoyed the attentions of women, but only ever one at a time. And I've never found promiscuity a particularly attractive quality. You of all people should know that.'

Emily flinched, wondering if he'd believed the stupid lie she'd told him. And why shouldn't he have believed it when she'd made it sound so convincing? Hadn't she practised saying it over and over again?

Alej, I don't want to be with you any more. I don't love you any more.

And then, when he had persisted, she had taken the lie one stage further.

It was only ever about sex and I've seen other men in England. Men who are more suitable. Rich, well-bred men I want more than you.

It had been so over the top that she'd half wondered if she'd gone too far and whether he would see through it for the invention it was. But he hadn't. He had believed every word of it and she would never forget the answering look in his eyes. Not for as long as she lived.

But there was a different look in his eyes now because while they'd been talking something had changed. His gaze was no longer icy-cold as it had been the day he'd touched down in his helicopter in Argentina, nor disapproving like when she'd arrived in Melbourne a couple of hours ago. Now it held some of the familiar heat of old as he looked at her, and some of the old hunger, too. It spoke to a feeling inside her. A feeling which had been dead for so long that she'd thought she'd lost it for ever. Or maybe it was just that only Alejandro could ignite it. Only he could make her body seem as if it had fired into vibrant new life.

Against the scarlet silk of her bodice she could feel the ripening thrust of her nipples and, low in her belly, the first sweet rush of awakening, and in those few seconds she longed for him to touch her again. To do those things which used to give her so much pleasure. Most of all, she wanted him to kiss her. To put his arms around her. To make her feel safe and protected.

And that was the feeling which scared her most of all, because you could never rely on a man to provide you with sanctuary. Hadn't that been just about the only thing her mother *had* taught her?

So concentrate, she urged herself fiercely. Don't start thinking like that, and don't start acting in a way which will lead you into trouble. Send out the subliminal message that this is strictly professional and if you start believing it yourself, then Alejandro might believe it, too.

'You're going to need to start protecting your own space a bit more in future,' she advised. 'You can't just let parties *happen.* If things get out of hand it's your image which will be damaged and you need to start guarding it more carefully. Image control, they call it.' She tucked a stray strand of hair behind her ear and subjected him to a cool look. 'We need the world to start thinking of you in a new way, so your reputation as a playboy becomes a thing of the past and in its place comes the sometimes serious, always thoughtful would-be politician.'

'But achieving that is going to be a monumental turnaround, I suppose?' he suggested sardonically.

'I'm not denying it's going to be a challenge, but I have a few ideas.' Feeling more confident now, Emily unzipped her shoulder bag and drew out a plastic-covered folder, keen to prove she'd done her homework. 'I understand your team is going to present you with a special award after tomorrow's race—as a thank-you for all your backing and support and for ploughing so much money into the sport. I think we can use that ceremony as a platform.'

He frowned. 'A platform for what?'

She drew in a deep breath. 'Tell me why you want to go into politics.'

A few seconds elapsed before he began to speak. 'I've been approached by the progressive new party which is riding high in the polls and they are keen for me to represent them. A breath of fresh air blowing through the stale air in the political arena is how they're terming my inclusion.'

'That's the method, Alejandro—not the reason. You haven't told me why you want to do it.'

Alejandro saw the scepticism in her gaze, slightly disconcerted by the thought that she might be more perceptive than he'd given her credit for. He felt a flicker of irritation. Did she see his ambition as nothing more than a stunt—the latest shiny hobby for a man who was bored with life? Was it that which made him want to demonstrate that there was more to him than the cliché? The daredevil sportsman turned billionaire playboy. The shallow, two-dimensional Lothario invented by the press. A wealthy man who cared for nothing but gambling and seduction and expensive toys. Because he was more than that. Much more.

And maybe because it was Emily, he found himself speaking with the kind of candour he might not have used with anyone else. Was that because once she had known him better than anyone? Before the helicopters and the private jets and the homes scattered carelessly around the globe?

'Because there are still people who are born poor and hungry, just as I was,' he husked. 'People condemned to a deprivation which will be repeated through every generation which follows—unless, like me, they're lucky enough to be born with a gift. People who die before their time because decent healthcare isn't available. I want to help to change that,' he finished. 'And politics is a route towards making that happen.'

'That's good. In fact, it's very good,' she commented slowly. 'I think you should say something on those lines when you accept your award tomorrow evening—especially if you can manage to replicate the same degree of passion and conviction.'

Alejandro heard the insinuation, which was highlighted by the look of surprise which had grown on her face while he'd been speaking. Was she suggesting his message was all about delivery, rather than content? That it was more style than substance? Did she believe in the cliché herself? His jaw tightened and suddenly he was angry with himself for caring *what* she thought. Because he didn't have anything to prove. Not to her—of all people.

'You think I'm just a showman, do you, Emily?' he murmured as, without warning, he reached out to cup her chin between his thumb and forefinger so that their gazes were locked on a collision course. That first contact felt like pure, powerful electricity and he waited, wondering if she would push him away. But she didn't. Of course she didn't. Because the chemistry between them hadn't changed, had it? She was as hot for him as she'd ever been. He could see it in the nipples which were thrusting like iron tips against the scarlet silk of her dress, and in the way her lips automatically parted.

He had desired many women in his life but his lust for Emily seemed to be stamped into his very DNA and, even though he despaired of it, his blood was heating at the thought of what he was about to do. He stroked his finger slowly over her cheek. 'You think my words are empty?'

'I…' The word was breathless and the sapphire of her eyes nothing but thin rims against the fathomless black pooling. 'Alejandro…what…what are you doing?'

He could see the pulse which was hammering away beside an errant strand of blonde hair and already he could detect the faint perfume of her sex. If he'd been feeling stronger he might have denied her. Made her wait. Left her high and dry before going to relieve his own frustration, alone in his bedroom, in a way he hadn't done for years. Because wouldn't it make her even hotter if he spun it out? But he couldn't. How could he, when his groin was on fire? When the hard bulge pressing so exquisitely against his jeans felt as if it might explode at any moment?

'Let's pass on the game-playing, shall we, Emily? I'm about to do exactly what you want me to do,' he said, his throat thick and tight. 'In fact, it's the only thing you've ever really wanted me to do, because I sure as hell was never good enough for anything else.'

Emily saw his head lowering towards her in slow motion, giving her all the time in the world to stop him. But she didn't. How could she, when most of what he said was true? Because yes, she wanted him. She'd never really stopped wanting him—not through all the arid years since last he'd held her like this. Because Alejandro Sabato possessed a power which he wielded over her like some dark and erotic spell. He could make her hot for him. Wet for him. Instantly.

She shuddered when at last he bent his head to kiss her because it had been a long time since anyone had kissed her, and never like this. Only Alej could kiss like this. His tongue slid inside her mouth and the intimacy of that fed her spiralling hunger as she looped her arms around his neck. And then she was close. Close enough to feel the sudden hard jerk of his erection pressing against her.

'Alej,' she whispered against his mouth and this time he didn't object to the familiar use of his name.

His response was to stroke his fingertip down her neck, drifting a slow line to her cleavage—before slipping it inside her dress to cup her straining breast. And still she didn't object. How could she, when he was tracing a tantalising circle over one rock-hard nipple which was thrusting eagerly against his finger? He deepened the kiss and she writhed against him. Hungrily. Restlessly. And then, without warning, he scooped her up into his arms and carried her over to a huge black leather sofa before depositing her on top of it. She was on *fire*…so eager for him to touch her again that she didn't care about the implications of being horizontal. All she could think about was how much she wanted him in her arms and she groaned with pleasure as he lay down on top of her, his mouth reclaiming hers with an urgency as flattering as it was irresistible.

Her eyes closed as she gave herself up to sensation and suddenly it was nothing *but* sensation.

The honeyed beat of blood in her veins.

The throbbing heat between her legs and exquisite peaking of her breasts.

'Mmm…' he said as he continued his expert caress of one puckered nipple, through her bra. 'I had forgotten just how delicious these were and now I want to see them again for myself.'

Each word was punctuated by the swift undoing of each tiny button, his fingers operating with a dexterity which spoke of vast experience. And even though that should have daunted her, Emily felt powerless to protest—especially when the air felt so deliciously cool against her heated skin. Or maybe it was because he forestalled any such protest by the highly effective method of using his other hand to inch up beneath the hemline of her dress. The breath shuddered from her lungs. It had been eight years since anyone had touched her like this and it felt as if she had tumbled into paradise.

But he seemed momentarily surprised as the sides of her dress flapped open to reveal her bra.

'Oh, my,' he breathed.

'Is something wrong?' she questioned dazedly, opening her eyes to see him studying her breasts with rapt attention.

He shrugged as he tested the elastic of one flesh-coloured strap and it pinged rather inefficiently against her skin. 'This doesn't exactly fulfil the promise of the sexy dress.'

That was definite censure she could hear in his voice. Was he criticising the T-shirt bra she wore beneath all her clothes to give her a smooth line as well as contain her too-large breasts? 'It's practical,' she defended.

'I'm sure it is. It is also a little plain.' He gave a lazy smile as he resumed his teasing ministrations. 'Don't the other men in your life demand you wear pretty lingerie from time to time?'

'What other men?' she supplied, her over-stimulated body playing havoc with her thought processes, especially when he was stroking her nipple like that.

'I'm not going to flatter myself I'm the only one, particularly after your parting words to me,' he whispered against her neck. 'Or is your air of gauche innocence just a perk you provide to all your clients?'

It took a few moments for his meaning to register and when it did, the implication was so insulting that it completely took her breath away. 'A *perk*?'

He shrugged. 'Why not? It happens.'

Emily stared at him incredulously before pushing his hand away and slithering out from beneath him to scramble to her feet. Her hands were shaking with rage as she tugged the flapping halves of her dress together and began to rebutton it, glaring at him where he lay, like some dark and indolent panther. 'You really think I would behave like that with just…*anyone*? That I would do this kind of thing with *clients*?'

Unperturbed by her accusation, he got up, raking his fingers back through the tumble of his hair, before tugging down his shirt and tucking it into his jeans. 'I don't know,' he said coldly. 'Discrimination was never your strong point, Emily. When you left you told me you were going to enjoy other men and I'm assuming you did.'

Because it had been the only way she could ensure he would let her go. The only way she could guarantee he wouldn't test her resolve.

But what was the point of raking all that up now and revisiting a past which was surely best left forgotten?

Even if he *was* looking at her as if she were nothing but a cheap tramp who put out for anyone who happened to turn her on. She wasn't here to parade her virtue or seek his good opinion of her. And wouldn't it make it easier to deal with the attraction which still burned between them if on one level he continued to despise her? She smoothed her dress down over her hips, and only when she was confident that her image was restored did she lift her gaze to his.

'I'm not quite sure how that happened,' she said, in a voice which sounded unnaturally calm.

'You want me to describe for you how hormones work?' he drawled.

Ignoring his sarcasm, Emily made her voice sound bright, like the one she'd used all those times when she'd been trying to rouse her mother from the deepest of sleeps. It was a note of determination, but it was also one of survival. Even if it didn't always work—you still had to give it a try. 'And we're going to forget that it ever did happen. Do you understand that, Alejandro?'

He gave a low laugh. 'Oh, I understand more than you think, *querida*, but I'm afraid it's not that easy. Because you want me, Emily. You might wish you didn't, but you do. You want me so badly I can almost *taste* it and, beneath that vampy borrowed dress, I'm willing to bet my entire fortune that your panties are wet.' His eyes glittered. 'The truth is that I'm excited about having sex with you and am counting down the hours until you're honest enough to admit you feel exactly the same way.'

CHAPTER FIVE

THE COCKTAIL PARTY was a crush—a glitzy affair on board an enormous yacht moored in Melbourne's exclusive harbour, filled with socialites and celebrities who had gathered in the city for the big race. The luxury craft bobbed against a backdrop of glittering skyscrapers, an internationally famous rap artist was playing at the far end of the deck and trays of drinks were being circulated by young and very beautiful serving staff who looked like off-duty actors. Very quickly Alejandro was surrounded by a cluster of what looked like adoring fans, leaving Emily standing at the shadowed edge of the exalted golden circle which grew around him.

In truth she'd wanted to skip this party, especially after that disturbing interlude on the sofa. The fact that they'd been so intimate and the fact that she had very nearly succumbed to having sex with him had left her needing to put some very necessary space between her and Alejandro. She didn't think she could bear to keep encountering his mocking green gaze, which was enough to start her heart racing as she remembered his fingers sliding so tantalisingly over her breasts and her thighs.

But it had been about more than the physical. It had

been the other stuff, which was way more disturbing. She'd felt connected to him on another level. As if he was the only one who could tap that cold, dark place deep inside her and fill her with warmth and life. Was that being fanciful? Of course it was. She mustn't start inventing fairy tales about him when the reality was apparent, if only she had the courage to face up to it. She was just a frustrated and lonely woman who hadn't been touched like that since she was barely eighteen years old and, in the intervening time, her body must have been simmering away with frustration. It was just a bitter irony that the only man she'd ever cared for was also the man she'd deliberately wounded because she'd been too young and confused to see any other way out.

She had to let it go. She had to or she wouldn't be able to complete the job tasked to her and her professional pride and reputation would be dented. She wanted Alej to see her as someone other than a sexual pushover. Which was why she'd coolly suggested he attend the cocktail party on his own while she tried to claw back some of the hours lost to jet lag. But he had refused point-blank.

'Me stroking your breasts before you deciding you don't want to play along any more doesn't qualify you for dispensation from the job you're being paid to do,' he had drawled. 'You're the official face of my sober new image, Emily, and you're coming to the party with me. You can catch up on your sleep tomorrow, before the race.'

She hated the way he talked about sex so...*casually*...as if it was nothing more than an enjoyable bodily function which could just be enjoyed without much thought or deliberation. Maybe that was how men like him thought of it. When women flung themselves so eagerly at Alej Sabato—herself included—why wouldn't he think of them as anything but sexual fodder? But she had found herself unable to argue with his logic. You couldn't really cite being overly attracted to your boss as a reason for not doing your job properly, could you?

Nonetheless, it had been with a heavy heart that she'd put a few final tweaks to her dishevelled appearance and joined him in the back of the chauffeur-driven car which had brought them down to the harbour. And now she was cast in her favourite role of observer, watching the comings and goings of the glittering guests as she stood in a shadowed corner.

She noticed that, although the party was attended by lots of the hunky drivers who were competing in the race the following day, it was the charismatic Alejandro who captured all the attention. Everyone wanted to talk to him, she realised. She spotted a famous Hollywood actress making her way across the deck to push her way through the small crowd gathered in front of him, her famous fall of blonde hair blowing softly in the early evening breeze. Emily screwed up her nose. Kate Palmer, yes, that was her name—a woman who'd won two BAFTA awards, amongst others. And wasn't that a top-selling novelist surreptitiously sneaking a selfie with him, despite Emily's stern instructions that such casual interactions must stop if he wanted to be taken seriously?

She told herself it was professional pique which was making her so cross that he was ignoring her advice but the truth was a little more sinister. Because a dark rush of jealousy was clenching at her heart, making her want to rush over to the glittering group and to grab

Alej possessively by the arm and to announce that he'd been making love to *her* earlier.

'Must be frustrating.'

A voice made Emily break her gaze from the oddly uncomfortable sight of Alejandro saying something which made the award-winning actress dissolve into instant laughter. Reluctantly she turned her head to study the tanned features of the tall man who had positioned himself beside her, his fair hair and open face making him seem the Argentinian's very antithesis.

'What must?' she asked.

The man shrugged. 'Dating someone like that, who attracts women like moths to the flame. He's famous for it. Or should I say infamous? I saw you come in with him,' he said, by way of an explanation Emily hadn't asked for.

'I'm not dating him,' said Emily slowly.

'No? Well, that's the best news I've heard all evening.' His blue eyes lit up and he extended his hand. 'Marcus Hedlund.'

'Emily Green,' she said as she shook it.

'Happy to meet you, Emily Green. You know, I'm looking for someone who might be interested in sailing away for a year and a day.' He smiled. 'And I've always had a thing about a woman in a red dress. Could I interest you in the position?'

'That's a terribly kind offer,' said Emily sweetly. 'But I'm afraid I'm not in a position to sail anywhere right now—and I'm a terrible sailor anyway.'

'I could teach you. We Swedes make great teachers—didn't you know that?'

Emily smiled back in spite of herself. 'I'm afraid I'm beyond teaching.'

'Nobody is beyond teaching.' Marcus plucked two glasses of champagne from a passing waitress and handed one to Emily and, although she had diligently stuck to fizzy water all evening, she couldn't resist a sip of the fine wine.

'So, back to Sabato,' he continued. 'You're saying he's just…?'

'Just wondering why you're monopolising my newest member of staff,' interjected a voice of steel, and Emily looked up to see that Alejandro had extricated himself from his adoring audience and was standing in front of them, surveying her and Marcus with an unfathomable look darkening his green eyes.

'You were ignoring her, so I stepped in,' said Marcus, giving an unabashed shrug. 'I was simply being chivalrous.'

'Is that what you call it?' queried Alejandro drily. 'Surely you have plenty of women to choose from, Marcus—especially when you own a yacht this size.'

'Not when you're in the vicinity, man. And surely you must know by now that it's not the size of someone's yacht which interests them. Nice to meet you, Emily.' Marcus grinned. 'Don't waste your time falling for him.'

'I don't think there's much chance of that happening,' Emily answered crisply, watching as the Swede raised his glass in a mocking toast and sauntered across the deck, before turning her attention to Alejandro. 'Were you listening to a word I said to you earlier?' she questioned exasperatedly.

He raised his eyebrows. 'Surely I'm the one who should be feeling aggrieved, since I've just found you flirting with one of my oldest friends.'

'I shall flirt with whoever I please. You seem to have no qualms about doing the same. And please don't try to change the subject, Alejandro. I'm serious.'

He could see that. She had assumed a disapproving expression, which seemed at odds with the woman who had briefly come to life like a firecracker in his arms a couple of hours ago. In her he had seen glimpses of the old Emily, who would thrill to his touch just as he would thrill to hers.

But he hadn't really known her at all back then, had he? He'd attributed to her all kinds of qualities she didn't possess, probably because she'd been an innocent virgin who had made him feel old-fashioned and protective towards her. She had destroyed his idealism with a few cruel words and, because of his dalliance with her, his mother had been summarily dismissed from her job.

He felt a beat of anger as he remembered his impotent rage when he'd heard about his mother's sacking, but anger was a pointless emotion. Desire was something he was better equipped to deal with. And revenge, of course. A primitive reaction but a very satisfying one, nonetheless. He hid his flicker of anticipation behind a bland mask of social concern.

'Would you like some food?' he questioned.

'No, thanks. I'm allergic to caviar. I'm going to head back to the hotel and do a little work before getting an early night.'

'I'll come with you.'

'No, Alejandro,' she said, in a low voice. 'You stay on here. People will be disappointed if you leave now. You're obviously the guest of honour and you don't need me hanging around. Besides, that actress you were talking to has been staring at you with moony eyes for the last five minutes.'

His eyes narrowed. 'I thought you told me women were off limits?'

'Women in the *plural*, not the singular! If you…' She drew in a deep breath and seemed to be having difficulty finding the right words. 'If you've decided you want to enter into a normal relationship with someone, that would be…fine. In fact, it would be more than fine and I can't see that having an actress as a consort would act as a deterrent to your political ambition. It's hardly mould-breaking, is it?'

'So you're giving me your consent to date her?'

Her mouth flattened. 'You don't need my consent to date anyone. You're as much of a free agent as I am. Just try not to make too much noise if you decide to bring her back to the suite tonight, will you? I'll take your car to the hotel and send the driver straight back. Goodnight.'

With that, she was gone, giving him a brief smile as she turned to leave, and Alej was left feeling distinctly outmanoeuvred as he stared at her retreating form. Shiny strands of dark blonde hair were dangling at the back of her neck and her skirt was a scarlet sheen as it swished enticingly against her bottom.

The actress was heading towards him but he barely noticed her—he was too outraged by Emily's liberal attitude as a myriad previously unknown and buttoned-up prejudices came flooding to the forefront of his mind. Was she really giving him the thumbs-up to bring another woman to his bed tonight, when he had been doing some fairly intimate things to *her* a few hours earlier? Especially when she was sleeping just a few yards down the corridor? His mouth hardened with disapproval. Was that the type of free-love world she operated in these days?

'Alej?'

It was the classically trained voice of Kate Palmer, her short Grecian-style dress showing a lot of honed and gleaming thigh. Slanting him a slow smile, she ran her fingers through her defining fall of hair with the deliberate nonchalance of someone who spent much of her life being watched.

'I wondered where you were.'

'Standing right here,' he said. 'As you see.'

'Do you fancy going on somewhere else?' she questioned, just a fraction too casually. 'I've been invited to a party in Kooyong and we were all thinking of going on to the casino later. Should be a good crowd.'

Alej studied her. She had the twin cachet of beauty and fame and most men wouldn't have thought twice about accepting an offer he suspected she didn't have to make very often. His indifference towards her wasn't feigned and yet it infuriated him that all he could think about was Emily and the insouciant way she'd left him standing there. Was she playing games with him, he wondered—or did she still get off with the kind of foreplay which threatened to drive a man insane?

He realised that the actress was still looking at him with confident expectation and curved his mouth into a regretful smile—because who was to say he mightn't take her up on her offer sometime in the future?

'Not tonight, I'm afraid. Early night for me,' he explained. 'It's the big race tomorrow.'

She quickly recovered her obvious disappointment

and slanted him another smile. 'Of course. Good luck. Isn't one of your drivers in pole position?'

His heart wasn't in it but he forced himself to continue the predictable conversation about his team's chances, giving her time to beat a dignified retreat before he left the bobbing yacht and went in search of his car. The city was alive with a pre-race buzz of excitement and people were spilling out of bars and restaurants, but all Alej was aware of during the journey back to the hotel was the insidious invasion of desire. It heated his blood and licked at his skin. It was making him distinctly uncomfortable as his trousers strained over the throbbing hardness at his groin. His mouth was dry and his heart was racing as he entered the hotel and when the elevator deposited him in the penthouse suite, he found himself hoping against hope that Emily hadn't gone to bed.

She hadn't.

She was lying on the black leather sofa and she was fast asleep. His heart missed a beat. She'd changed from the borrowed red party frock and slipped into a pair of wide yoga pants and a sleeveless vest, against which her breasts rose and fell in time with her steady breathing. Before her a half-drunk cup of herb tea stood next to her computer and the closely written notebook she'd been referring to earlier. She'd let down her hair, so that it surrounded her head like a flaxen pillow, and it was that more than anything which had Alej transfixed as he stood in the doorway, feeling like a voyeur, not just to her, but to the past they had once shared.

Because she used to wear her hair flowing down her back like that when she'd been seventeen, when he used to run his fingers wonderingly through the lustrous thickness, as if it were pure, spun gold, blending into the pillow they'd made of the hay bale. He thought about just going to bed and leaving her there—except that she'd wake up cold and uncomfortable and she wouldn't be able to work unless she was properly rested. At least, that was what he convinced himself was his motive as he began to move towards her. As he glanced down at the table he could see she'd been drawing grids and a big triangle, around which different letters were scattered so that it looked like one of those mathematical equations he'd thankfully been spared due to his lack of schooling. Right in the centre of the page the letter *M* was written, with a big red circle around it and a series of question marks beside it.

'Emily?' he said softly.

'Alej!' Her eyelashes fluttered open and she stirred, rubbing her fist over her eyes. 'Sorry. I must have fallen asleep. Obviously.' She yawned. 'What time is it?'

She flicked him a heavy-lidded gaze and once again he felt his heart contract, because hadn't she looked at him like that plenty of times before, in that sleepy, trusting way? Those times when she'd made him feel he could conquer the world. That everything she needed, he could provide for her. But his body had been the only thing she'd wanted, he reminded himself savagely. And maybe it still was.

'It's still early,' he said evenly.

'Oh.' She struggled up into a sitting position. 'Is the party over?'

But Alej didn't want to make polite small talk. He didn't want to pretend he felt nothing as he looked down at her blonde and ruffled beauty. 'Were those other men you left me for as good as me, Emily?' he questioned suddenly.

'I'm sorry?'

'You heard me.'

She blinked at him and he could see a faint colour begin to wash over her pale cheeks. 'What on earth has brought all this on?'

'Seriously. I want to know. Were they as big as me? Did they make you come as easily as I did?'

She was frowning now, half in confusion and half with something else. Something which made her tongue slide out of her mouth to moisten her lips. 'Alej. Are you out of your mind? What on earth has brought all this on? Stop it,' she whispered.

'But you don't want me to stop it, Emily. You never did. That much hasn't changed.'

His green eyes were burning into her, making her skin feel as if it were on fire, and Emily knew she should get straight off that sofa and head for the sanctuary of her bedroom. But somehow she couldn't seem to bring herself to move—because the trouble was that he was right. She *didn't* want him to stop—she wanted him to carry on talking dirty to her all night long and looking at her in that hungry way, as if he wanted to ravish her. The blunt sexual boasts were turning her on, as she guessed they were supposed to, and the warning narrative spinning around her head wasn't strong enough to withstand the increasingly urgent demands of her body.

And suddenly Emily had no real desire to fight them. Why would she when she'd been living without physical contact for so long? When most times she felt more like a piece of stone rather than a flesh-and-blood woman. Had abstinence brought her any pleasure or felt even a little bit worthwhile? No way. It had served only to make her isolated—but then, she'd always felt like that. She'd always been the person on the outside who was looking in. The daughter who was nothing but a burden to a socially ambitious mother and then the stepdaughter who had got in the way. Alej had been the only person who had ever made her feel as if she mattered.

He was smiling now. That slow killer smile which always used to get her. She hadn't been able to resist it then and it seemed she couldn't resist it now.

Feeling like someone caught up in a dark spell, Emily obeyed the Argentinian's wordless command, and opened her arms to him.

CHAPTER SIX

'Guau!' The word escaped from Alej's lips like a murmured curse as he sank on top of Emily's soft and eager body and felt the first contact of her breasts. He could feel the hard thrust of her nipples pinpointing into his chest as he pulled her closer, his hands sliding down to reacquaint themselves with her legs. Blood pooled into his groin as he stroked her thighs through the soft cotton of her yoga pants.

'Alej,' she moaned as if she was asking him a question, but he didn't press her to elaborate because it was pretty obvious what she wanted—judging from the urgent way she was circling her hips against the rocky pole of his erection like some kind of wildcat on heat.

Once again the thought of another man doing this to her filled him with a blind rage but, ruthlessly, he drove it from his mind. Because anger and jealousy would detract from his purpose and all he needed to think about was this one thing. Of losing himself deep inside her and riding her to fulfilment. Ridding himself of this damned fever which had lain dormant inside him for too long and been brought to a head when he'd seen her standing with the Argentinian sun bouncing off her blonde hair and her arms around a mangy horse's neck.

He'd thought that time might have diluted his reaction to her and when he saw her again he would feel nothing but indifference. But he had been wrong. Badly wrong. Because every night since that recent meeting he had dreamt of her. Had imagined doing this to her. Touching every inch of her curvy frame and then plunging into her tight wetness—long and hard and deep. He wanted sex and nothing more, but first he needed to assess whether she wanted the same.

'Que quieres?' he demanded roughly.

She shook the head which was slumped against his shoulder, as if words were beyond her, but Alej asked again. He needed to ask it, even if the idea of her refusal was unendurable. But he would endure it. Hadn't he endured more than most men would have to face in a lifetime? Reaching to turn her face towards his, her shuddered breath warm against his fingers, he asked again, this time in English. 'What do you want, Emily?'

'You!' she burst out, as if an inner floodgate had opened inside her. 'I want you!'

It felt like a triumph, but only a momentary one because the exquisite ache between his legs was warning Alej that he needed to keep his wits about him or this would be over too quickly. Already he wanted to explode like a teenage boy on his first time and that wasn't going to happen, for he had waited too long to squander a single second of this.

His mouth found her neck, the tip of his tongue trailing a feather-light path along its surface, which quickly had her wriggling with pleasure. His groin bucked as she circled her hips against him with urgent hunger, which made his heart race. He had forgotten just how responsive she was. How her receptive body thrilled to just about anything he did to her. Maybe that was because the two of them had taken foreplay to a whole new level and then redefined it. There had been long months of denying themselves that final penetration and when they had…

Against her neck, his lips hardened.

When they had…

Bitterness rushed through him but he forced himself to shelve it because nothing was going to detract from this. He could feel her moving against him, turning her head towards his face in silent plea. She wanted him to kiss her, he knew that. But he didn't want to kiss her—at least, not there. He didn't want to do anything which might masquerade as true affection and he certainly wasn't going to give her the pleasure of imagining he felt anything for her other than lust. Because he didn't. The only thing he wanted from Emily Green was her body. Her sweet and tempting body.

With a low growl he got off the sofa and then bent down to pick her up in his arms. She was heavier than she looked but he liked that. He liked the solidity of her firm flesh as he carried her through the enormous room, past the white piano and colourful displays of flowers. Past the giant picture windows with their views over the Melbourne rooftops and the skyscrapers which were glittering like jewels in the night.

'Where…where are we going?' she gasped.

'Where do you think we're going? To discuss some of your "clear objectives"?' he growled sarcastically. 'I'm taking you to bed.'

Her eyes were huge and dark as she stared up at him. 'We've never…we've never actually been to bed before,' she whispered.

It was both the right thing and the wrong thing to say. It filled him first with fury and then with intent. Because he had only ever been good enough for the stable, hadn't he? Hidden away like some guilty secret amid the spiky bales of straw. Played with as if he were a puppet. She'd had him on the end of a string and whenever she had tugged it, he'd come running, hadn't he? The low-born illegitimate son of a servant who had been punching well above his weight by romancing the rich man's stepdaughter. Well, the tables had most definitely turned, he thought grimly, as he planted his foot in the centre of the door and shoved it open with a forceful kick.

'No, we haven't. And right here just happens to be about the biggest and most luxurious bed you can imagine,' he said as the door swung shut silently behind them and he carried her towards the snowy-covered king-size. 'Don't they say the best things in life are worth waiting for?'

A trickle of apprehension ran down Emily's spine as Alejandro's words washed over her like dark silk and she wondered if it was just her imagination or whether they were underpinned with danger. For one terrifying moment of clarity she wondered how she had allowed this situation to arise—just as she wondered if there was still a chance to come to her senses and put a stop to it. But the truth was that she didn't want to, even if such a thing were possible. Because by then he had laid her down on top of the bedcover and was peeling off her vest top and the last of her misgivings were dissolved by the sweet touch of his fingers against her bare skin.

The sexual hunger which he had ignited earlier now began to build to an unbearable pitch as he touched her.

Like somebody with a bad fever, she was trembling uncontrollably as he began to explore her skin, murmuring something in Spanish which she'd never heard him say before. Was she imagining that it sounded almost like *anger*? But by then he was sliding down her yoga pants so she was lying there in just her bra and knickers. Almost thoughtfully he ran his finger around the dip of her navel, circling it ever so slowly before moving it down towards her sensible cotton pants. To make it easy for him, Emily parted her thighs and felt herself stiffen with growing excitement.

'Oh,' she said.

'Oh, what?' he mimicked lazily as he whispered his fingertip lightly over the already damp gusset.

Her heart started punching loudly in her chest and she felt almost bashful as hot colour flooded her cheeks. But this wasn't the time or the place for shyness, she told herself. It wasn't as if they'd never done this before. But the weird thing was that, although she'd been more intimate with him than with any other man, the fact remained that right now he seemed like a very sexy stranger and it was making her a little bit apprehensive.

Stop thinking like that, she urged herself. Concentrate on the pleasure he's giving you. 'That feels so good,' she managed, because surely that was the sort of thing she should be saying.

'Does it?' She could hear the smile in his voice. 'I haven't even started yet, Emily.'

'I'd forgotten…'

'What?' he prompted softly, his finger still teasing her with those unbearable feather-light little touches.

As her eyelids fluttered helplessly to a close, Emily thought about telling him the unvarnished truth. She'd forgotten how he could make every inch of her body feel like a newly discovered erogenous zone. She'd forgotten because she'd made herself forget—along with all the other X-rated memories of the things they'd done together. Like the time he'd once made her come with his fingertip stroking the crotch of her jeans, instantly arousing her despite the barrier of the thick denim—and she had felt so deliciously grown-up and decadent as she'd stood shuddering in a darkened corner of the stable. She'd filed away those recollections because they seemed to have belonged to another time and another person. They certainly bore no resemblance to the sexually barren woman she had become.

'I don't remember,' she breathed.

'What a pity,' he mocked. 'I was waiting with bated breath.'

He stopped touching her and stepped away from the bed to begin removing his own clothes and, although Emily was aware that she was behaving passively, somehow she felt powerless to respond in any other way. Because wasn't she afraid he'd discover that he was the only man she'd ever had sex with? Wouldn't that slightly laughable admission display her vulnerability and leave her open to being hurt? Wouldn't it be like handing him a great big fistful of power, when he already had much more than her? So she said nothing and lay back on the bedcovers, watching him. And, oh, he was definitely worth watching.

She'd only ever seen him removing casual and dusty clothes, either jodhpurs or jeans, not an immaculate lightweight suit which must have cost a small fortune. But the end result was the same—it didn't matter if he wore denim or silk, it was the body beneath which was the ultimate jewel. Shrugging off his jacket, he unbuttoned his silk shirt to reveal his honed and gleaming chest, and Emily's heart pounded with delighted recognition as she ran her gaze hungrily over it.

Could any man be as beautiful as Alejandro Sabato? she wondered longingly. His limbs were long and strong and his washboard abs reminded her of the disciplined way he'd always lived. The way he'd exercised his hard body until it was coated with sweat. Her gaze moved further down as he unzipped his suit trousers, letting them fall to the ground before kicking off his suede moccasins, so that he was left standing in nothing but a pair of dark and silky boxer shorts. And how could she look anywhere other than at the tantalising line of dark hair which ran downwards, drawing her attention to the rocky bulge at his crotch?

Did he see where she was looking? Was that why he stroked his fingertips over the steely outline of his erection with deliberate provocation, so that she bit her lip with frustrated voyeurism as colour flooded into her cheeks?

'Frustrated, Emily?' he questioned softly, but there was a definite touch of cruelty and control edging his question.

A number of answers sprang to Emily's mind, though it was difficult to concentrate on anything when she was being confronted by such a glorious sight. She could have asked him not to tease her. Not to use his expertise and mastery to make her feel even more inexperienced than she was. But she needed to grab back some control. She was no longer a nearly eighteen-year-old virgin whose whole world revolved around a dashing young polo player she'd known since she was twelve, but a woman of twenty-six. If she was going to have sex with Alejandro—which she certainly was, or else she wouldn't have been lying here naked and aching while watching him undress—then shouldn't it be on as level a playing field as possible?

So she levered herself up onto her elbows, noticing the way his gaze swivelled to the bounce of her breasts as she did so, before fixing him with a steady look. She thought about all those films she'd seen—where confident women smiled, as if it was perfectly normal to have sex and to say exactly what it was you were feeling inside. Or not feeling. Concentrate on the sensation, she told herself—and leave emotion out of it.

'Yes, I'm a little bit frustrated. Surely you must be, too,' she answered, with the flicker of a smile as she removed her bra and pants with hands which weren't as still as she would have liked them to be. 'So why don't you hurry up and get over here?'

That shocked him. Of course it did. She suspected he was a little bit old-fashioned at heart and she would never have said anything like that before—not in a million years. She watched his face momentarily darken before he dropped his shorts, walking towards her with supreme confidence in his aroused nakedness, in a way she doubted any other man could match.

'You mean like this?' he questioned as he lowered himself down on her.

'Yes,' she breathed. 'I mean exactly like that.'

'Are you going to tell me how best you like it?'

'I'll…' The word came out in a gasp. 'I'll leave that to you.'

Alej positioned himself so that his weight was on his elbows, putting him in a perfect position to see the darkness of her sapphire eyes. Her lips were parting and their moist gleam was enticing but still he couldn't bring himself to kiss her. So instead he ran the tip of his tongue down her neck and then to her chest, before making a moist path along the hollow between her breasts. He could taste the salt of her sweat and she moaned a little as he moved his head to concentrate on one pert mound, teasing the nipple until it was rose-dark and puckered before turning his attention to the other breast.

'That's…'

'What?' he prompted huskily as the word was bitten off by her teeth digging into her bottom lip.

'Amazing,' she breathed.

'I should hope so.' He smiled before sliding his tongue over her belly and as he sensed her growing frustration, that somehow pleased him. Restlessly, she tried to lift her hips in impatient demand but he stilled her by teasing light circles over her skin before tiptoeing his fingers down towards the soft bush at her groin. Her little moans had stopped and he could tell she was holding her breath, wanting him to touch her where she most wanted to be touched. For a while he teased her some more by holding off and when his middle finger alighted on her sweet spot and began to strum, she almost shot off the bed, convulsively clutching him by the shoulders. And as her nails dug into his flesh, Alej felt a brief flare of something he couldn't define. Maybe it was his own little bit of rebellion which made him wonder how she would deal with it if he calmly removed himself from her body and told her he'd changed his mind.

But he couldn't. Even though she had betrayed him and treated him like dirt. Even though hers had been the first act in a chain of events which was to darken his life for ever, he couldn't pull back. Even if he were about to die, he couldn't think of anywhere else he'd rather be right now, with the warm, potent scent of sex in the air, and the only sound their shuddered breathing as he felt himself grow so hard that he wanted to explode. He'd planned to make her come every which way—first with his finger and then with his mouth. He'd planned to further increase his desire by making himself wait before finally thrusting into her molten heat and driving up to the very hilt of her, but he could see now that wasn't going to be a possibility. He wanted her now.

'Oh!'

She made a single syllable of disappointment as he withdrew his finger from her sticky heat.

'Always so impatient,' he observed.

Her teeth were digging into her lower lip again and now there was anxious query in her sapphire eyes, as if she'd suddenly realised he'd been having second thoughts. 'Alej?'

He paused for just long enough to make her anxiety real before he relented. 'Don't worry, *querida*,' he whispered. 'I'll be right back. But first I need to get some protection.'

She nodded. 'Of course.'

As he removed himself from the bed, Emily was overcome with a rush of remorse and shame. What was the matter with her? Was Alej aware that if he hadn't intervened she would have happily taken him unprotected into her body, desperate to feel his unsheathed hardness inside her? How insane would that have been—if she'd ended up pregnant with Alej's child? Yet the idea didn't fill her with the horror it surely should have done. Instead she got a frighteningly vivid image of herself cradling a black-haired baby in her arms and she experienced a pang of something which felt like wistfulness. Or regret.

It was only when he turned his back on her to dig into the pocket of his suit trousers that she noticed the scar which snaked across his back—a livid zigzag, dark red and angry against the olive skin. It was the only disfigurement on an otherwise perfect physique but it was big enough to make her gasp out loud.

He must have heard her because he turned around—the glint of the foil condom matching the sudden forbidding glint of his eyes.

'Oh, Alej. Whatever happened to your back?' she whispered.

'I don't want to talk about it. Especially not right now.'

'But it's—'

'I *said*, I don't want to talk about it. Do you want me to repeat it in Spanish?'

The harsh note of finality in his voice was deterrent enough, but by then he was back beside her and suddenly the scar was forgotten. Everything was forgotten and her attention was inevitably drawn to other things as he opened the foil with exaggerated care before stroking it onto the erection which was nudging hard against his belly. A wave of something like shyness washed over her as she saw how aroused he was and Emily's heart warred with her mind about what it was she was expecting from this. Her body had certainly been brought to life and already she felt poised on an erotic knife-edge, where the slightest thing would send her hurtling over the edge. But something was missing. Something she couldn't put her finger on.

'Now,' murmured Alejandro as he moved over her and she could feel his hardness pressing against her. 'Where were we?'

She was running her fingertips hungrily over his bare back, her fingertips encountering the raised surface of the zigzagging scar for the first time. But he shifted his position slightly and she said nothing more about the disfigurement, concentrating instead on his husky question. 'I'm not…sure,' she answered.

'Then how about I remind you, Princesa?'

It was a long time since he'd called her that but this time the nickname was underpinned with a harshness which had never been there before, which in any other circumstance might have made Emily think twice about what was about to happen. But it was already too late. He was licking her breasts and her blood was pulsing warm and thick as she felt the experienced flick of his fingers against her clitoris. She heard him murmur his approval and then her thighs were spreading open as if no power in the world could stop them and he was entering her. He was pushing deep inside the slickness which awaited him and filling her completely. Emily moaned and instantly he stilled, his eyes narrowed in question.

'It's good?'

Wordlessly, she nodded. Of course it was. It was better than good. Better than anything she'd ever experienced—but it was a shock, too. Alejandro had always been big—not that she had anyone to compare him to, of course—but their first time together had been so loaded with emotion that she hadn't had time to appreciate it properly in the way she could now. But she couldn't tell him that. She didn't want to stir up bad feelings about the past and neither did she want to confess to another possibility—that her body had become unaccommodating and tight in all the intervening years, because it had been so starved of pleasure.

So she put her hands on his shoulders and sucked in a deep breath. 'Is it good for you, too?'

'Oh, Emily. You have no idea,' he groaned in response. 'Especially when you play the part of breathless little innocent so effectively. Aren't you a little old to be cast in the role of disingenuous virgin?'

For a moment she scented more danger. He thought she was playing games, or acting a part? That this was just a cynical approach she was adopting to inject a little excitement into their lovemaking? She wanted to tell him the truth—that this was so beautiful that deep down she *did* feel as innocent as the first time she'd lain with him. But she guessed he would dismiss such an idealistic sentiment and, anyway, her thoughts were blotted out by his next potent thrust.

At first his movements were slow—as if he was determined to emphasise how utterly he filled her—and Emily was taken aback by how intimate it felt. One flesh, she found herself thinking. Was that why those stupid tears began to prick at the backs of her eyes, forcing her to blink them away before he saw them? Why she turned her face to search for his kiss, only to realise that he was far more intent on bending his dark head to lick at her nipple? But then his movements grew more rapid as he shafted up deep inside her and all her doubts were put on the back burner because suddenly Emily was rediscovering sex—big time. His body was hard and powerful. His skin felt like satin against her fingers and she was like a woman possessed as she writhed beneath him, moaning things like, 'Please...' and, 'Oh, yes...' and, 'Yes, that... *That.*'

'You mean like that?' he clarified, withdrawing almost completely before driving up deep inside her again.

'Yes...yes...' she breathed. 'Exactly like that.'

And then it happened, almost without her expecting it—that heady rush of promise which morphed into perfect bliss as her world exploded into countless dazzling stars. Emily clung to him, crying out helplessly as her body spasmed around him before she heard his own shuddered moan and felt his driving jerks as he spilled his seed inside her. Spent, he collapsed on top of her and those next few moments were the closest thing to sanctuary she'd felt in a long time. For a while she just lay there, cocooned in his strong arms, feeling as if she were floating on some warm and rippling sea until Alejandro's words shot into her thoughts and scattered them like a spray gun.

'I certainly wasn't expecting it to be quite so easy,' he remarked.

'Easy?' she echoed, wondering if she might have misheard him.

'Mmm...' He turned onto his side and stared at her, his green gaze smoky and assessing. 'But I'd forgotten how hot you were. Hotter than any other woman I've ever had.'

Emily didn't answer straight away. You don't have to answer, she told herself. You're not on some game show with the clock ticking away. You can take as much time as you want. All the time you need to get your head around the fact that you have just *slept with your boss.*

Unwrapping his arm from where it was coiled so

comfortably around her waist, Emily rolled away from him. It would be tempting to jump up from the bed. To grab her clothes and rush from the room—maybe even slamming the door behind her so that it echoed through the vast penthouse suite. But that wouldn't be the behaviour of someone who was mature and responsible, would it? It was difficult to come back from something as dramatic as that, and didn't they need to move on—or not—from what had just happened? He thought she was easy—and could she really blame him? So why not go along with that? Let him think she was sexually rapacious, just as he was. Especially since the alternative was to wail and wonder why she'd done such a stupid thing, which ran the risk of making her look both reckless and indiscriminate.

So she fanned her face exaggeratedly with her hand. 'Thanks.'

He looked momentarily perplexed. 'Thanks?'

'Mmm… It's always nice to be described as hot,' she remarked blandly, seeing his face inexplicably darken in response. 'Quite literally in this case. Boiling hot, actually—despite the air conditioning. Any chance you could rustle us up a glass of water, Alej?'

He looked outraged—there was no other word for it—but Emily told herself she didn't care. What good would it do her if she fell back into his arms and told him that she was only ever hot with him? Such an admission would show weakness and she'd already made herself weak enough in his eyes.

But despite his obvious disapproval of her question, he nonetheless accommodated her wishes, sauntering out of the bedroom in all his glorious nakedness and giving her time to snap the light on and scramble back into her clothes. He seemed unsurprised to find her fully dressed when he returned minutes later with the requested water and—rather disturbingly—the notebook she'd been scribbling in earlier, just before her jet-lagged state had caused her to pass out on the sofa. He yawned and positioned himself back on the bed, waiting until she had gulped down half a glass of water before holding the notebook aloft.

'What's this?' he questioned, his finger jabbing at the grid diagrams she had drawn earlier.

She shrugged. 'It's life-coach stuff I use when I'm working with new clients. You know. All about reality and perception and fixed ideas. I'm guessing you probably don't want a complete breakdown of the meanings?'

'You're right. I don't.'

'Mainly it's about what it is possible to change in your life,' she elaborated, as still he continued to look at her enquiringly.

'And the *M*?'

There was a pause as Emily felt her cheeks growing warm. 'You're contemplating a massive change and you probably need to simplify your life. Stop jet-setting quite so much and make more of a base in Argentina, especially as that's going to be your home when you go into politics.'

'I asked about the *M*,' he emphasised silkily. 'Which you have circled and underlined several times.'

The hotness in her cheeks increased. 'Part of your "problem"—which plenty of men wouldn't actually define as a problem—'

'Get to the point, Emily.'

She drew in a deep breath and watched his gaze

flicker to the wobble of her breasts. 'Is the woman thing.'

'The woman thing?'

She nodded. 'That's what lets you down every time. Not just the book Colette wrote, which was probably motivated by bitterness that you didn't marry her. But also the way you seem to attract women like a magnet. Like Marcus said earlier—you can't seem to help it. The online edition of one of the Australian tabloids is even carrying a photo of you taken with Kate Palmer tonight—there must have been a long-lens photographer at the harbour. And the author who took a surreptitious selfie at the same party has already put it up on her social-media page—and she's got over thirty-one thousand followers.'

'None of this is new,' he pointed out.

'No, but it only fuels your reputation as a commitment-phobe who plays the field like mad—and those are not the kind of qualities which ordinary people want from the person who is representing them.' Somehow she met his bright green gaze without flinching. 'The *M* stands for marriage. You need a wife, Alej. And before you look at me that way, why not? Would-be politicians have been making judicious marriages since the beginning of time. It would be an instant badge of commitment and respectability which would only help your career.'

'But I don't want to get married,' he observed caustically. 'I never did. Not with Colette. Not with anyone.'

She shrugged. 'And that's your dilemma.'

Yes.

His dilemma.

Or maybe not.

From his vantage point on top of the rumpled bedclothes, Alej studied the woman with whom he'd just had the best sex he could remember, and yet here she was calmly discussing his marriage to someone else. A wave of something like bitterness ran through him. Was she really such a hard-hearted bitch that she could coolly advocate he go and find himself a wife and not really *care*? Did he mean so little to her? *Of course he did. Nothing new there, either.* Yet the irony of the situation didn't escape him because deep down he knew that if she'd displayed sadness and resentment at the thought of him marrying someone else, she wouldn't have seen him for dust.

But maybe *Emily* was exactly what he needed. For now, at least. He'd thought she'd cared for him all those years ago but he'd been wrong, just as he'd been wrong about so many things. But back then she had been barely eighteen with the world at her feet. She must have believed anything was possible and had since discovered that it was not. Because surely it hadn't been her life's ambition to end up running some crummy little business and living in a tiny London apartment. Didn't she miss the riches she had grown up with while she lived in Argentina and the kind of lifestyle which came as part of the whole package?

Even more pertinently, wouldn't she have learnt by now that no other man came close to him when it came to giving her physical pleasure? Her gushing and instant response whenever he touched her would seem to indicate so. Wouldn't marriage add a deliciously dark element to the revenge he was determined to extract from her? Wouldn't it ensure she would never really forget him, because what woman ever forgot the man who slid a golden ring onto her finger?

'I think you could be right, Emily,' he said, easing himself up on the bank of squashed pillows and slanting her a slow smile. 'I need a temporary bride—and you are the obvious candidate.'

CHAPTER SEVEN

THERE WAS A moment of stillness, when time seemed to be suspended as Emily stared at Alej in astonishment. Her nails dug into the bed sheet. He had just asked her to marry him! The hunky Argentinian billionaire had just asked her to be his bride! And wasn't it weird how easily the mind could distort reality and allow fantasy to take over for a few disbelieving seconds? Why else would a rush of joy have flooded through her body at the thought of being joined with the man she had once loved so fiercely? The man who could still make her feel more alive than anyone else. Who, even now, could take her into his arms and make her dissolve with longing.

Until she reminded herself that this was no romantic moonlit proposal, inspired by his certainty that they were meant for each other and he couldn't live without her. This was a cold and calculated public-relations exercise. A marriage made not in heaven, but within the scribbled pages of a moleskin notebook—by her!

She prayed that she'd managed to hide her initial delight because if Alej had any idea how much the idea had thrilled her, it would put her in a poor bargaining position. But she didn't have to bargain with him, she reminded herself. She was a free agent. An employee.

And yes, she'd just had sex with him, but so what? She certainly didn't have to marry him.

'Is that a joke?' she questioned as coolly as she could, though her heart was still crashing against her ribcage and she found herself wondering if he'd be able to notice its thundering movement beneath her vest.

'You know it isn't.'

She stared up at him—sprawled there unashamedly, his naked olive body outlined against the white covers. His eyes were bright, his jaw much darker than usual, and he exuded the air of a man who was physically satisfied. He looked utterly delectable and completely sexy—but she wasn't going to think about that. She couldn't afford to. 'You must realise that I can't possibly marry you, Alej.'

'Why not?' he said.

'Because...because it's a crazy idea.' She shook her head, trying to inject some conviction into her voice as she found herself fantasising about a big white dress and a bunch of scented flowers the size of a rugby ball. What was the *matter* with her? She got up off the bed, mainly to protect herself from the allure of his proximity. 'Crazy,' she repeated.

Outside, the moon was gleaming silver over the Melbourne skyscrapers and the sense that she was living in some strange kind of parallel universe descended on her again. As if she would ever take part in a marriage of convenience to a man she'd once been in love with! Wouldn't that be like playing a kind of high-stakes emotional Russian roulette, with her the guaranteed loser?

She drank some more water and then walked over to the window, still trying to get her head around what had happened. The sex had been amazing, but something had been missing during that erotic encounter which had definitely been there before. Something in him. It had taken a while for her to work out what it was, and the answer had arrived in a heart-sinking moment of understanding. Because he hadn't been like the loving and tender Alej of old. He had been like a machine, not a man. A warm, breathing machine who could bestow inordinate amounts of pleasure—but a machine nonetheless.

And she was most definitely not a machine. She had never felt so vibrantly and deliciously *alive* and the reason for that was because Alej had awoken something in her. Something which thrilled her because she'd thought she'd lost it for ever—the ability to feel emotional intensity and physical pleasure. But her reaction scared her, too. Because wasn't it dangerous to feel those things, when the man involved had a heart of ice?

'Before you give me all the reasons why you shouldn't,' he said, 'let me list some of the reasons why you should.'

She sank down into a cross-legged position on a white leather window seat and stared at him. 'Go ahead.'

'I will pay you a lot of money to be my wife,' he said tonelessly. 'For a limited period, of course.'

'Of course you will, Alej. You're a very rich man.'

She could see in his green eyes a flicker of scorn, and his lips twisted as he spoke.

'Don't tell me the thought of a seven-figure sum doesn't turn you on, Emily?'

It was a vulgar statement, which made her wonder what kind of circles he'd been mixing in. The same kind as her mother, probably, she reflected painfully. The ones where women made no secret of adoring diamonds and fast cars and luxury yachts anchored in city harbours. *Did he think she was cut from the same cloth as the woman who had birthed her?* 'Money often creates more problems than it solves,' she suggested.

'An admirable sentiment. Though one I find difficult to believe and only ever expressed by people who don't have any.' He paused, his green eyes glinting. 'If the money offends you, then give it to charity—nobody is stopping you from being altruistic. Think about it, Emily,' he urged silkily.

So she did. She thought about being able to help Great-Aunt Jane. To *really* help the woman who had sacrificed so much for Emily's mother and been given barely a word of thanks in return. The last time her mother had entered rehab to try to conquer her tranquilliser addiction, it had been Emily's great-aunt who had somehow managed to scrabble together enough money to pick up the bill. At the time it had been doable—just—because Jane had been working as a legal secretary, but now she was existing on a tiny pension and getting frailer by the day. Wouldn't it be *great* to free her from the worry of future medical bills incurred by the inevitability of aging? To not just present her with a one-off cheque, but enough money to look after her for the rest of her days.

Emily bit her lip as she thought about being able to take a proper holiday herself—her first in years, because she'd been ploughing all her time and any spare money into the business. She could wear a floppy hat and sarong and finally get to read the stack of books stashed away by her bed back home. There would probably even be enough to pay off some of her mortgage. Wouldn't it be good to cut herself a bit of slack for once?

But none of these considerations addressed the way she felt about Alej, because she recognised that marriage would be a velvet-lined trap, which would pose all kinds of hidden dangers. She'd just had sex with him and she couldn't seem to control her reaction whenever he laid a finger on her. So what if her feelings for him intensified? What if she found herself falling in love with him all over again? She couldn't do it. For sanity's sake, she must refuse.

'No, Alej.'

He gave a slow smile. 'Before you give me your final answer, perhaps it is time for me to be blunt—as you English sometimes say.'

'That remark is usually the forerunner to some kind of insult.'

'Or a home truth, perhaps?' He ran a lazy finger reflectively along the sensual outline of his lips. 'You are—how old, now?'

She wanted to tell him that he knew exactly how old she was, but maybe he didn't. Maybe she was crediting herself with more importance in his memory than she really had and he'd simply forgotten. 'Twenty-six.' His eyes were boring into her. Was it that which made her elaborate, like a child trying to make themselves seem more mature? 'Nearly twenty-seven, actually.'

He nodded. 'And there has been no engagement? No close brushes with marriage?'

Her heart squeezed because his interrogation felt painful for all kinds of reasons. It made her feel like a failure and it made her feel like a bit of a freak. 'No.'

'Ever lived with anyone?'

'No again.'

'In that case, I will be doing you an enormous favour, Emily.'

She screwed up her face in genuine confusion. 'How do you work that one out?'

Did she imagine the flicker of pleasure which lifted the corners of his lips and the glint of triumph which sparked in the depths of his green eyes?

'A man who has never married is seen as something of a catch. As sexy and elusive,' he murmured. 'Unfortunately, it is not the same for a woman since she loses her appeal with each year that passes.'

It was a good thing she wasn't still holding her glass of water because Emily honestly thought she might have hurled it at his patronising head. But at least his outrageous comment propelled her out of the numbness caused by his shock proposal of marriage. 'Did you decide to throw all the feminist textbooks onto a bonfire of your own arrogance?' she hissed at him, the serenity of her yoga pose forgotten. 'Or are you just going out of your way to insult me—as I suspected from the beginning?'

'Please don't shoot the messenger. I am merely telling it how it is,' he said calmly, with an expansive shrug of his broad, bare shoulders. He pillowed his ruffled black head back against crossed arms and studied her reflectively. 'But if you were a divorcee,' he mused, 'and a rich one, to boot…that would immediately make you attractive to all kinds of men. Which means you'd have a lot more chance of finding yourself a suitable partner in the future.'

Even though she knew her reaction was deeply irrational, Emily found herself hurt by the things he was saying. But why shouldn't he talk about her long-term future so objectively and with no role for him to play in it, when that was the reality? Yes, he'd had sex with her and, yes, he was offering her a bizarre kind of marriage—but he wasn't doing it because he had *feelings* for her. And although she could see the undoubted benefits of him taking a temporary bride—hadn't she suggested it herself?—she sensed he wasn't telling her the whole story.

'I'm getting a strong suspicion that your desire to bed me and wed me might be motivated more by revenge than a quest for respectability,' she said slowly.

Alej almost smiled, until he reminded himself that her sometimes uncanny ability to read his mind was something he should be wary of. It was certainly nothing to admire. Yet her words rang true, didn't they? A marriage of convenience would undoubtedly put paid to the rather tedious description of playboy, which always followed him around. But more than that, it would place her uniquely in his control. They would be living together and sleeping together. What greater opportunity would there be for him to have his delicious fill of her before casting her aside, as once she had done to him? 'It is true that my feelings towards you are mixed, Emily.'

'Because I was the only woman to have ever walked away?' she guessed.

'You think my ego overrides all other considerations?'

'Possibly.'

'I cannot deny your words and yet it is a little more… complex than that, *querida*.' There was a pause. 'You never really gave me a reason for your sudden change of mind, did you, Emily? You went from screaming ecstatically in my arms to condescending ice maiden within the space of hours. You walked away from me as if we were strangers who had just met. You gave me your virginity, then you told me that you didn't love me and that you wanted other men. And you never really explained why.'

There was a pause while Emily's mind spun with possibilities and she stared down at the swirly patterns on her trousers, unwilling to meet his piercing gaze. Surely it was best to just brush his question aside and leave the past where it should be. But then she wondered who she was trying to protect—surely not a man who had ruled her mother's life with a rod of steel before leaving his stepdaughter a sick horse as a final mark of contempt. And wasn't there a part of Emily which wanted to redeem herself in Alej's eyes—who wanted him to stop looking at her with that thinly veiled scorn?

'My stepfather threatened me,' she said slowly as she lifted her gaze to his. 'He told me he would never forgive me if I continued to see you.'

He gave a bitter laugh, shaking his head so that the dark waves of hair dangled around his neck. 'And, of course, he was such a worthwhile individual that you desperately needed his approval? Forgive me if I don't buy that, Emily, when I know how much you hated and feared him. Perhaps you were more concerned he would cut off all your money.'

She sucked in a deep breath as she lifted her gaze to him. Had she stupidly underestimated his intelligence? That he would just suck up any story she was prepared to give him? 'No, you're right. It wasn't just that,' she admitted and she swallowed the lump which had risen in her throat. 'My mother begged me to listen to him and to do as he said, because he threatened to divorce her if I got involved with someone like you.'

'Someone like me?' he repeated. 'What exactly does that mean?'

The lump in her throat wasn't shifting but Emily knew she couldn't avoid the question burning from his green eyes. 'You were poor and had no father and that didn't sit well with his inflated ideas of his place in society. My mother was terrified of what her life without him would be.'

'Without his wealth, you mean?' he suggested softly.

Emily bit her lip. No, not just his wealth—although that had obviously been a big attraction. But her mother had been one of those women for whom a life was not complete without a man. Her first husband had been poor and after being widowed, she had devoted all her energy to finding a rich replacement and, when she'd succeeded, had clung onto him like a limpet.

And didn't it frighten Emily to think she might have inherited that sapping trait of mindless dependence? She'd been acutely aware of loving Alej back then, in a way which could never have been reciprocated—because what hope was there for a relationship between a man on the brink of a glittering international career and a teenager who was barely out of school? Wasn't that another factor which had convinced her it would be better in the long run if she let him go, because that way she would avoid all the inevitable pain when he stopped caring about her? Once again, she dropped her gaze, not wanting him to see the fear in her eyes.

'Something like that,' she said.

Alej stiffened. She was lying about something, he just didn't know what—lying in that smooth, natural way which came so easily to women. But, in a way, didn't her duplicity bolster his intention to wed her? His mouth twisted. Wouldn't it give him a kick to make a mockery out of the whole damned institution of marriage, while allowing him to enjoy legal sex with the woman who could turn him on like nobody else?

'But they divorced anyway, didn't they?' he questioned.

She swallowed. 'Yes.'

'And your mother died soon afterwards?'

She paused for a moment, recounting the facts like bullet points—as if she was determined to avoid having to answer any more questions about it. 'Yes. In a house fire. I was away at university and unable to visit her as often as I'd done before. She'd taken tranquillisers—more than usual—and obviously didn't put out her cigarette properly. She didn't hear the smoke alarm go off and by the time the fire brigade arrived, it was too late. They said she wouldn't have known anything.' For a long time afterwards she had been plagued by guilt. Guilt that she'd been unable to save her mother. And guilt at the relief she'd felt on being freed from the burden of care.

He spoke softly in Spanish, sympathising with her for her loss, and she inclined her head in acceptance.

'Thank you,' she said.

But Alej did not allow the momentary air of reflection to detract him from his purpose as he forged on with his proposal. 'Of course, if you married me—'

She shook her head. 'Alej, let it go. It's not going to happen. Why would it?'

'Why, for sex and for money, of course,' he continued softly. 'Those are the main reasons why women marry rich and eligible men, aren't they? We're just being a little more open about it than most.'

'And what about…' she hesitated before plucking up enough courage to ask it '…what about love?'

'What about it? I think it's overrated.' He saw something die in her eyes and felt a warm rush of pleasure. 'Overused,' he continued, with harsh emphasis. 'And even if you feel it for a while—it's soon over.'

'But there are other kinds of love,' she objected. 'The kind which endures. What about the love a mother has for her child?'

Alej felt his skin grow cold. 'You think your mother was such a shining example of maternal love, do you, Emily?'

She shook her head. 'I'm not naïve enough to think that, no. But maybe your mother—'

'Let's just change the subject, shall we?' he interrupted. 'I thought we were talking about my marriage to you.'

'We were. And I've made my feelings on the subject clear.'

He got out of bed and he could see suspicion vying with desire as he walked over to the window seat and pulled her to her feet. And as soon as she was in his arms, all that instant chemistry was back. The moment they touched—even though he was naked and she was fully dressed—he became fired up with lust.

'Would you like me to change your mind for you?'

'That's not…fair,' she mumbled unconvincingly as he began to stroke his finger over her neck beneath the thick fall of unbrushed hair.

'I think you would,' he murmured. 'That's the feeling I'm getting, loud and clear.'

'We're…we're standing right in front of the window.'

'It's reflective from the outside,' he growled. 'Nobody can see in.'

He silenced any further words with his mouth, finding her lips with an urgent kind of hunger, achingly aware of the low groan which seemed to come from deep inside him. She kissed with a passion which made him silently curse and wonder how she could make him feel this way. Like it was the first time all over again. As if he'd never had sex with anyone else. His groin grew rock-hard and he closed his heart to further analysis. It was what it was. Why knock it before he had fully exploited it?

His hands on her hips, he backed her towards the nearest wall and wondered if this might bring her to her senses. If she'd tell him to get his hands off her and announce she was going to break her contract, because they couldn't keep having indiscriminate sex like this, as boss and employee. And didn't part of him want that? Wouldn't he have respected her more if she'd done that—shown some fire and spirit and strength—if she'd morphed back into the pure virgin he'd once known and respected? But she didn't. She did what every woman who ever came near him did. Flung her arms around his neck and positioned herself with an effortless tilt of her pelvis, so that the removal of her trousers became almost seamless.

Her panties slid to the floor and she bucked as he touched her. He wanted to explode as he moved his hand away from her wet heat to fetch another condom, but the action wasn't made any easier by the frantic way Emily was circling her hips. With a swift, delaying kiss he pushed her away and walked over to find what he was looking for, tearing open the foil as he reached her again. Bending his head to her peaking nipple, he slid one hand between her thighs. He wanted to instruct her to put the rubber on for him, but already he seemed so close to coming that he suspected her trembling fingers might end it all too quickly and the risk of *that* was something he wouldn't tolerate.

It seemed to take for ever, but at last he was able to push deep inside her and the loud groan he heard reverberating around the high-ceilinged room was all his. He rocked into her—over and over—and it was hard and fast and elemental. He heard her choked sob as she began to come but his own orgasm was upon him almost immediately. Swamped by the pulsing tide of pleasure and fatigued by the lethargy which instantly swept over him, he slumped against her, his breath fanning her neck. Long seconds passed—or it might have been minutes—until he had the strength to lift his head to study her. To brush away her ruffled hair as he bent his lips to her ear.

'So. Are you going to marry me, Emily?'

Emily told herself to say no. To protect herself from his powerful allure and from her own weakness and susceptibility to him. But no words came. Only a stupid rush of pleasure at the thought of being his wife. Something painful twisted deep inside her, because she realised that she had walked straight into a trap of her own making. She'd proposed a marriage of convenience because she'd thought it could help advance his political aspirations and, now that the chips were down, she couldn't bear the thought of some other woman wearing his ring.

So could she risk marrying him, despite the fact that once she'd loved him and she suspected that a lot of that love was still there? Because if she agreed to become his bride it was imperative she keep that fact secret, or she would be at a tactical disadvantage. Far better to focus on the material advantages of becoming Señora Sabato and allow Alej to think she was motivated by nothing more threatening than avarice.

'I guess it's too good an offer to turn down,' she said, injecting her voice with a deliberate note of greed.

As if on cue, a cold light flared in his green eyes. 'Of course it is.'

'How much are you offering me?' she continued, forcing herself to play the game. 'How much do you think I'm worth?'

'The two things are not necessarily the same.' A hard light came into his eyes as, slowly, he told her just how much he was prepared to pay.

Emily swallowed, the game momentarily forgotten. 'Gosh,' she said faintly. 'I guess only an idiot would refuse that kind of money.'

'Or someone with principles, perhaps—which have clearly bypassed you along the way,' he responded cuttingly. 'What kind of a wedding do you want, Emily?'

The kind where the groom is looking at me with love, not with a mixture of scorn and lust. The kind which is destined to last for ever.

But Emily pushed the hopeless thoughts away and shrugged, determined not to communicate the sudden hopeless ache in her heart. 'If we're going to go through with a meaningless ceremony, we might as well do it in style,' she said briskly. 'I mean, I think a church service would be a step too far, but there's no reason why we can't go the whole hog with a white dress and flowers and all the attendant razzmatazz. That's the kind of story which the press love—and this is all about publicity, isn't it? And in the meantime…' She cleared her throat. 'We really ought to have an engagement ring to add credibility.'

He nodded. 'Have a look online in the morning and choose something you like the look of.'

'Online?' she repeated dully.

'Sure. There must be some sort of design you've always lusted after. Carat size no obstacle, of course. We should be able to take delivery of it before the big race tomorrow, so that you can show it off to the world.'

Emily's heart pounded. His words were the antithesis of romance but she told herself to be grateful for that. Because nothing could have emphasised better that this was simply a marriage of convenience than Alej's emotionless statement about buying her engagement ring online.

CHAPTER EIGHT

THERE WERE FLOWERS EVERYWHERE. Massed white roses and tiny pale-blue forget-me-nots, which Emily quickly realised were the colours of the Argentinian flag. It was a nice touch from the Vinoly Hotel, she acknowledged—a luxury South American–owned hotel in London which Alej had taken over for the weekend and where their wedding was shortly to take place.

She stared into the mirror at the unlikely vision of herself in a wedding dress, because, despite her groom's sarcastic words about choosing the kind of engagement ring she'd always lusted after, she'd never had daydreams about what she might wear on such a day. There had been one very glaring omission to wedding-day dreams because it had been impossible to imagine such a day without Alej, which had obviously been a strictly forbidden fantasy. But fantasy had somehow become reality and a huge yellow-diamond engagement ring was sparkling at her finger, while a waterfall of tulle was held in place by a fragrant crown of creamy roses. Behind her stood Marybeth, though still with concern criss-crossing her face.

'Are you sure?' questioned her only bridesmaid, for

the hundredth time. 'It's not too late to back out. I mean, are you absolutely sure you're doing the right thing?'

Of course she wasn't. But Emily certainly couldn't blame her friend for her repeated questioning. Wouldn't she have done exactly the same if the situation had been reversed? Brushing her fingertip over one of the antique roses in her bouquet, she forced a smile. 'Why wouldn't I be?'

'Because it's been so fast—'

'I know. But we were lovers years ago.'

'Yeah. So you said. But *marriage*? Especially when you seemed so unsure about even *taking* the job. And now this. A big, fancy wedding in front of the Argentinian ambassador and all. It's such a big step. Do you…?' Marybeth shifted a little awkwardly on her mauve satin ballet pumps 'Do you love him, Emily?'

Emily felt her heart twist. She didn't want to answer this—not to herself and certainly not to her closest girlfriend. Because who wasn't to say that the churning emotions she'd been experiencing for weeks weren't just the result of hormones—of her body finally being sexually satisfied after all the arid years since Alej had last made love to her? Yet because she could see the fear on Marybeth's face, she found herself uttering soothing words, which happened to be rooted in truth.

'I…care for him,' she said.

'Okay…' said Marybeth, a little doubtfully. 'Well, that's certainly an improvement on what you were saying about him before you went to Oz. Better get going, then—and get this party started!'

But Emily's nerves felt jangled as she made her way towards the grand function room, despite her smooth words of assurance. She hadn't seen Alej since the day after his shock proposal and had since been beset by a growing fear that he might have changed his mind and simply not shown up. It was only when she'd peeped out of her hotel window that morning, and seen a whole fleet of black limousines arriving, that she'd realised he wasn't planning on reneging on his intention to make her his wife—and she'd been taken aback by the relief which had washed over her.

In order to arrange a fancy wedding at such short notice, she had flown back from Melbourne alone, after Alej's team had—in true fairy-tale tradition—won themselves a podium place at the city's Grand Prix. Afterwards there had been fireworks and champagne and a party which had gone on all night, during which he had announced their surprise engagement to an already febrile press. And amid all the excitement of reporting that one of the world's biggest commitment-phobes was finally taking the plunge into matrimony, Emily realised that her new fiancé's political intentions had very definitely been put on the back burner.

But he had shrugged almost carelessly when she had pointed this out. 'A couple of weeks won't make any difference.'

'Maybe not.' Her voice had grown thoughtful. 'We could announce it while we're on honeymoon. It will be a good press release, especially if we pick a day when there isn't much news around.'

There had been an odd note in his voice. 'You think of everything, don't you, Emily?'

'That's what you're paying me for.'

His voice had mocked her. 'No, *querida*. I'm paying you for a lot more than that.'

It was an observation which caused her some disquiet

and one she didn't want to reflect on for too long—but then she'd had a lot of practice at pushing unwanted thoughts away. Life was strange, she thought as the doors of the grand salon swam into view. Hard to believe that in a few minutes' time she would be Alej's wife—something she'd longed for in those far-off days as an impressionable teenager. But this was nothing more than a complex game they were playing—and she should forget that at her peril.

The sound of a string quartet greeted her as one of Alej's hunky polo-playing friends pushed open the ornate doors and as everyone turned to look at her, for a split second, she felt beset by more nerves. She wondered if Alej's friends were judging her and wondering why his standards had fallen so far below his usual diet of supermodels and heiresses. Yet wasn't another part of her secretly wishing this was the real thing, instead of being the ultimate public relations gesture?

But then she saw him waiting for her beneath an arch of flowers and felt her heart hitch beneath the silk-satin of her gown, because he looked utterly gorgeous. The most gorgeous man in the room. Wearing a suit more formal than anything she'd ever seen him in before and, with a couple of centimetres clipped from his ruffled black hair, he appeared to be a more sombre version of the man she'd known in previous guises. His new air of gravitas was slightly unsettling, emphasising again that this was simply a different mask he was wearing. Yet the moment he took her hand in his, all her determination to keep emotion at bay drained away and her heart gave a great big leap of longing.

I don't want to love him, she thought desperately. *I don't want to be hurt by him.*

'You look beautiful,' he said.

It was said presumably to add credibility, but nonetheless his words made Emily glow as she handed her bouquet to Marybeth. 'Thank you,' she said, hiding her excitement behind a calm smile.

The ceremony passed without event and only afterwards did Emily realise she'd been on tenterhooks throughout the entire proceedings. Had she been afraid that his supermodel ex would burst through the doors and try to put a stop to it, like in some dramatic Hollywood film? There was a hush as Alejandro made his vows, his eyes fixed on hers with an expression of desire underpinned with something darker. Something which made her senses scream out a nameless warning, despite the sensual ache which was already starting low in her belly. Because wasn't that hostility she could see flickering in the depths of his steady green gaze?

Afterwards, a starry reception spilled over into an adjoining function room, filled with politicians, actors and even members of the British royal family, with whom Alej used to play polo, back in the day. She thought how easily he mixed in such an elevated section of society and how her own guest list was far more modest—though Marybeth's family certainly made up for any paucity in numbers with their noise and laughter. And then the music began to play for the first dance and, as Alej took her hand and everyone turned towards them, Emily felt as if she was walking onto a giant stage.

Because you are. Because this is all make-believe and none of it is real.

But in that moment it *felt* real as Alej laced his warm

fingers in hers and led her onto the dance floor. As achingly familiar strains filtered into her ears, she wondered if he was deliberately torturing her with a song she hadn't heard for many years.

'What made you choose this?' she questioned, the silk of her wedding gown whispering over the marble floor as she tried and failed to erase the blissful memories of those hot, Argentinian nights.

'You used to love it.'

She shifted awkwardly but, annoyingly, it only seemed to decrease the space between them. 'Maybe I did, but not…not any more.'

'No. Your tastes are more sophisticated these days, perhaps?'

'It's not that.' She drew in a deep breath. 'We're not the same people any more, Alej. It doesn't seem appropriate, somehow.'

'What would you rather they played?' He spun her round, his eyes glinting hard and green. '"Money, Money, Money"?'

She didn't react to the taunt. 'Let's try to keep the hostilities to a minimum for the duration of the reception, shall we?'

'Then try smiling, Princesa. Instead of looking as if you're standing on the edge of a deep precipice.'

'And if I told you that was exactly how I felt?'

His eyes bored into her. 'And why might that be?'

She hesitated. 'Because I'm finding this all harder than I imagined it would be.'

'Why?'

'I don't *know*!'

Three beats of music followed and Alej tightened his fingers around her waist, because it was the first time she'd let that cool mask of composure slip and inexplicably he found himself wanting to see what was behind it. 'Do you miss your family?' he questioned suddenly. 'Do you wish your mother was here today?'

She tilted her head back and he could see her throat constrict, and the tiny pearl which hung from the end of a fine gold chain quivered at her neck.

'Yes,' she admitted, her voice breaking a little, her free hand reaching up to touch the necklace. 'It's stupid, but I do. She was a terrible mother in many ways but she was still my mother.'

'Is that her necklace?'

She nodded. 'My father bought it for her before they were married. She hardly ever wore it—said it was too cheap—but I love it. Far more than any of those flashy jewels which Paul bought her and which she ended up pawning anyway.'

Alej felt a wave of something approaching sympathy until he quickly reined it back in. He didn't *want* to feel sympathy for her. He wanted to feel only the things he could deal with—like lust and anger and the hot, sweet release of fulfilment. Because she'd never given a *damn* about him and his family, had she? Never even stopped to find out what had happened to his mother. His lying, cheating mother, but—as she herself had just said—his mother all the same. His mouth twisted. Of course she hadn't. Because the little people were invisible to people like Emily. She might have affected to despise her snobbish stepfather, but maybe she'd absorbed more of his values than she'd been aware of.

He put his lips close to her neck, his voice growing husky. 'I'm bored with dancing and bored with people watching our every move. How soon before we can escape so that I can consummate this marriage of ours, because I am aching for you, Emily? Can you feel how much?'

'We can't…' Her words tailed off as he slid his thigh between hers. 'We can't just leave the reception early in order to go to bed.'

'Why not?'

'Because that's not playing the game we're supposed to be playing,' she said sternly, her voice taking on a note of firmness. 'We have to at least *look* as if we love each other, even if it isn't true—otherwise the marriage will appear to be a stunt instead of looking authentic, and that could easily backfire on you.'

'So how would you like me to manifest my "love" towards you, Emily?' he taunted, pleased to see her cheeks flush a deep pink in response to his swirling movement, which was making his hardened pelvis thrust against the slippery silk of her wedding gown.

'We could try having a conversation, rather than making out on the dance floor.'

He bit back a reluctant smile. 'What do you want to talk about?'

Her fingers curled against his chest, her hand a pale starfish against the dark material of his suit jacket, and he found himself covering it with his own.

'What we're going to do for our honeymoon, for a start.'

With an effort, he dragged his thoughts away from the sensation of her breasts pushing against his torso, which was resulting in a punishing hardness in his groin. 'I told you,' he said. 'We take my plane wherever you want to go and stay in five-star luxury along the way.'

'Not the best idea.' She shook her head. 'I think that will be counter-productive.'

'Meaning?'

'It will continue to make you look like some aimless playboy with more money than he knows what to do with and no general purpose in life.'

'You may or may not be aware that wherever in the world I am, I work—and I work hard,' he said coldly. 'It is possible to do such things remotely these days.'

'I know it is. But there will be no real focus for me, will there?' She shrugged and seemed to find it difficult to meet his eyes. 'It'll just be all about…sex.'

'It's a honeymoon, Emily,' he pointed out.

'But not a real one,' she reminded him sharply.

'Are you telling me you're unhappy about the idea of having wall-to-wall sex? That's certainly not the impression you've given me so far.'

'That's not what I'm saying at all. But I'm still going to be working for you—and when we decide to call time on the marriage, I want to have achieved what I set out to achieve. Call it professional pride, if you like.' She waited until the Argentinian ambassador had danced past them with a complicated sashay of his hips. 'Do you remember my original brief to you in Melbourne?'

'I've scarcely thought of anything else,' he said sardonically.

'When we talked about simplifying your life, you decided to sell off your home in France because, if you're planning to be based in Argentina, it makes no sense for you to have a base in Paris. So couldn't we…couldn't we use the honeymoon to go there—and afterwards maybe go to your *estancia*?'

'Why?'

Because although I know it's a kind of madness, I want to see some of the different facets of your life. I want to glimpse the private man behind the glossy façade. I want to see your homes—not just the fancy and impersonal five-star hotels you seem to spend your life in.

But Emily had no intention of revealing her foolish thoughts to him, so instead she gave a careless shrug. 'It might be an idea to choose whichever sentimental items you want to keep before your Parisian apartment goes on the market. It might be very satisfying to tidy your life up like that.'

'I can think of only one thing which will satisfy me right now,' he growled. 'And it has nothing to do with the marketing of property and everything to do with the removal of your clothes.'

'Alej Sabato! You are outrageous!'

But he paid her half-hearted protest no heed, dancing her smoothly out of the ballroom and into the discreet elevator, which had exclusive access to the hotel's newly designed honeymoon suite. The elevator doors had barely slid shut before he pushed her up against a rose-tinted mirror, his hand sliding inside the bodice of her wedding gown as he started to kiss her.

'People will notice we've gone,' she gasped against his urgent mouth, as, blindly, he jabbed at the top-floor button with his finger.

'Who cares? We're married, Emily. This is legal.'

There was champagne on ice and roses everywhere but the moment their suite door swung closed, their only focus was on pulling at each other's clothes. His suit hit the deck and her wedding dress lay abandoned on the carpet and soon they were naked on the great big honeymoon bed—save for the coronet of roses still pinned in her hair.

Emily could see her wedding ring glinting gold as Alejandro pulled her into his arms, his eyes a blaze of green as he began to plunder her mouth once more. 'Oh,' she said breathlessly, as his hand slid searchingly over every naked curve, his unsteady survey of her flesh making it feel as if he were discovering her by touch alone. As if it were an eternity since they'd lain together rather than a matter of days. His name trembled on her lips. 'Alej.'

'Shh…'

Afterwards she was glad he had quietened her because hadn't she felt a compelling urge to tell him how much she'd missed him during their days apart—and if she started indulging in that kind of revelation, who knew where it might end? So she kissed him hard instead, mounting her own survey of the flat planes of his magnificent physique—perfect save for the jagged scar on his back, which he had refused to discuss. Her orgasm came quickly—powerfully intense as it racked through her body in a way which made her feel momentarily helpless. Did her choked mewl of fulfilment touch something inside him? Was that why his arms tightened around her and he buried his face in her hair before groaning out his own shuddering pleasure?

She must have fallen asleep, because when she opened her eyes again, it was to see early stars already beginning to pepper the sky outside the un-shuttered windows. Still sleepy and caught in the half-world between wakefulness and slumber, her mind drifted around tantalising pathways. Was it possible they could make this marriage work? she wondered fleetingly. Could they compromise somehow? Forget about the bad stuff and concentrate on the good stuff and learn to love one another all over again?

'Are you awake?' she whispered.

'I am now.' Alej rolled over and studied her. Awake and already hard and wanting more—for that was the effect she had on him. *The effect she'd always had on him.* He ran his fingers over her pale and quivering body, watching her nipples harden as he scratched his nails lightly over the soft fuzz of hair at her groin, before dipping his head to it.

'Alej?' she said, in a voice which sounded slurred although he knew she had drunk nothing stronger than water at the reception.

'I'm not in the mood for conversation right now,' he ground out.

He parted her thighs gently and began to minister to her with his mouth, hearing her moan as he slowly licked her damp folds. He flicked the tip of his tongue against her tight bud, enjoying her unique taste and the way her nails scrabbled helplessly at the petal-strewn duvet as he quickened the movement. And in a moment of disturbing clarity, he realised he had only ever done this with her. It had been just one of the myriad ways they had pleasured each other without the actual act of penetration, when she had been so young. The memory of that had stayed stubbornly with him and the thought of laying his mouth so intimately against another woman had repulsed him. Yet even that simple fact had maddened him, for he saw it as a weakness and unwanted dependence upon the woman who had rejected him. He wanted to draw his mouth away in order to frustrate her but instead he found himself revelling in the taste of her. Musk and honey, he thought achingly, and he hardened as she began convulsing against his lips.

There was another condom close by but, although he was rock-hard and eager to enter her, something held him back. Instead, he watched until her shuddered breathing had steadied itself and then her eyelids fluttered open, as if she had suddenly become aware that his gaze was on her. He saw the trace of uncertainty which crossed her face and for some reason that gave him pleasure as he lay back against the bed and, with a careless flick of his hand, indicated the throbbing hardness at his groin.

'Now you,' he said softly. 'Your turn.'

Still dazed after her orgasm, Emily felt suddenly wary about what he wanted her to do, yet surely that was completely illogical. After all, she'd done it many times in the past—not just in the stables but outside in the lush pastures, where the fresh Argentinian air had helped provide her with a liberating sense of freedom. But back then they had been *close*. Young and passionate—with none of all the bad history or hangups which had stood between them like a barrier ever since. Suddenly she felt almost *shy* about what he wanted her to do—and she needed to lose that attitude quickly. She was a grown-up, she reminded herself. And now a wife.

So she wriggled down the bed to position her head close to his groin, running light fingertips over his erect shaft and registering the instinctive shudder which racked through his body as she did so. Up and down, her thumb and forefinger moved with feather-light touch, revelling in the sensation of his silk-encased hardness. She continued with this stealthy rhythm until she saw his eyelids flutter to a close, and only when she was sure she wasn't being observed did she bend her head to him. He moaned as she took him into her mouth and already she could feel the sticky wetness on his tip as she began to suck him.

'Emily,' he groaned, tangling his fingers into her hair and dislodging a stray clip from her bridal headdress, which he plucked out and tossed to the floor.

She danced her tongue over him, tracing little patterns over his pulsing stiffness, enjoying the way he thrust his pelvis towards her, as if silently begging for relief. But Alej didn't beg, she reminded herself. He'd told her that a long time ago. She opened her mouth wider because he had suddenly tensed and she felt a rush of something like triumph as he flooded into her mouth. She revelled in the salty taste of him as she raised her head and drew the tip of her tongue over her lips to catch a drop she must have missed, realising that he was watching her intently.

But it wasn't satisfaction she could read in the suddenly stony depths of his eyes, but a dark anger she'd never seen there before. She blinked at him in confusion, feeling out of her depth. 'You didn't enjoy that?'

'Don't ask disingenuous questions. You know damned well I did.'

Her confusion deepened. 'Then why aren't you smiling?'

'Because I have something on my mind. Do you want to know what it is?'

Actually, she didn't, because she suspected she

wasn't going to like it—but she wasn't a child who could simply run away from things which might be hard to hear. 'Go ahead,' she said quietly.

Crossing his arms behind his head, he pillowed his head on his elbows. 'I'd forgotten just how good you were at doing that. But as you were licking and sucking me with such beautiful precision, I couldn't help but wonder how many other men you have administered to in such a way.'

Administered to in such a way? Emily recoiled with something like indignation. He was making her sound like some sort of perverted nurse! 'You're asking me to tell you how many men I've slept with?' she questioned.

He looked momentarily surprised at her candour before quickly recovering himself, but Emily reminded herself that Alej Sabato didn't have the monopoly on being 'blunt'. And wasn't this something which needed to come out anyway? Hadn't it troubled her for a long time that the erroneous picture she'd once painted of herself was one she deeply regretted?

His voice was harsh. 'That's exactly what I'm asking you.'

'None,' she said flatly.

He shifted his position slightly, his eyes narrowing. 'Excuse me?'

'None,' she repeated. 'Would you like me to say it in Spanish for you? *Ninguno!* You're the only man I've ever given oral sex to! The only man I've ever been intimate with! The only one! Do you understand? I told you I wanted to have sex with other men because it was the only way I could guarantee you wouldn't come after me. I knew it would disgust you and I was right. But I did it because I thought it was for the best all round.

I honestly didn't think we had any kind of future together, Alej.'

Alej sat up, his heart pounding as the meaning of her words sank into his disbelieving ears. She hadn't slept with another man in eight long years? Could she be speaking the truth? His gaze swept over her. Her cheeks were flushed, her long fair hair ruffled from where he'd been running his fingers through it and her lips darkened by the pressure of his kisses. On the one hand he was pleased—of course he was—because the thought of her so intimately touching another man was like plunging a dagger deep into his heart.

But on the other…

Anger began to well up inside him, like the slow swell of the ocean when a storm was approaching. Because wasn't this the greatest sin of all—the one committed by every woman he had ever known?

'So when you told me that you wanted other men,' he questioned, his voice unsteady, 'that you had seen other, more *suitable* men…'

She shook her head as his words tailed off. 'It wasn't true. You were the only man I ever wanted,' she breathed. 'The only one I could ever contemplate being intimate with. You still are.'

Alej felt a punch of primitive satisfaction but forced himself to ignore it, because sexual exclusivity wasn't really what he was focused on, no matter how much it pleased him to realise that he was the only one. Because she was missing the point completely. She was looking at him as if he should be pleased. As if she'd just given him some kind of gift instead of reinforcing the most bitter truth of all. And the most stupid thing of all was why he had thought she was any different from all the rest.

Because all women lied, didn't they? His mother had lied to him and then Colette had lied *about* him, but, for some reason, the falsehoods which had sprung from Emily's lips had been the hardest of all to bear.

And still he didn't know what to believe.

'So were you lying to me then?' he questioned softly. 'Or are you lying to me now?'

CHAPTER NINE

THEY FLEW TO France the very next morning, to Alej's apartment in the eighth arrondissement—a sprawling affair at the top of an historic building, situated on a famous street, opposite an equally famous hotel. In the distance the River Seine glinted in the sunshine, and nearby the trees in the Tuileries Garden provided a leafy canopy for wandering young lovers.

But not for her and Alej, Emily reflected a couple of days later, as she looked around at the lavish but unlived-in surroundings of her husband's Parisian home. They might have been photographed together walking around the city's famously romantic spots, but it had all been for show. A sham. Just like their marriage.

It made her shudder to think she'd been naively wondering if maybe they could make a go of their marriage, but never again would she be guilty of allowing herself to believe in such an illusion. Why would she when, in Alej's eyes, she had committed the cardinal sin of lying and he could not—or would not—forgive her for the transgression she had owned up to on the first night of their honeymoon. The memory of it still jarred. It sat like a black cloud on her horizon. He'd accused her of being a liar and she had no defence against his words because they had been true. She *had* pretended not to care for him and to want other men. But when she'd tried to explain her reasons—maybe even to express all the love and fear which had motivated her actions—his clipped command had cut her short.

'A lie is just that, Emily,' he had drawled. 'There can be no justification. And women lie as easily as breathing. Fact.'

She tried not to care and to throw herself into the role she was being paid for, because surely that should now be her priority. She liaised with his assistant about their travel plans and arranged an in-depth interview with one of France's most respected journals, in which Alejandro talked with passion about polo. About how the sport had rescued him from poverty and that he wanted more children to benefit from similar opportunities.

Sitting in on the interview, Emily had been confused about why he wasn't promoting his burgeoning political career, but didn't dare butt in and prompt him, though she might have done if it had been anyone else. And when the interviewer suddenly asked whether he planned on having children himself now that he was married, Alej had glanced up at Emily, his gaze hard and impenetrable.

'No plans at present,' he had replied smoothly.

And Emily had despaired at the stab of pain which shafted through her as she'd heard those words, as once again she'd found herself longing to hold a baby against her breast and to suckle the child of Alej Sabato. Dragging her thoughts back to the present, she turned away from the window, away from the glitter of the upmarket shops and the silver gleam of the river. What a hopeless fool she was.

Only at night did her new husband let his guard down, when an unspoken truce left no room for anything other than mutual delight under cover of darkness. But even then Emily wasn't safe from her own stupid, see-sawing emotions. Because when they were naked and he was kissing her and moaning out his pleasure, it was all too easy to get carried away. To imagine he felt something other than carnal desire for her. But he didn't. He couldn't have made that plainer. She was his temporary wife who served a dual purpose in life. Who provided him with respectability and sex. And wouldn't she have been a hypocrite if she had refused the latter through some kind of warped principle, when she enjoyed it just as much as he did?

They spent several days in the city, trawling through his personal effects while Alej selected items he wished to keep, but there were surprisingly few. A scale model of one of his racing cars. A bronze sculpture of his first polo pony and a framed paparazzi photo of the US president sipping from a can of MiMaté. Everything else—the contemporary furniture, the stunning artwork and a small library of rare edition books—he had dismissed with a careless flick of his fingers.

'Get rid of them. I don't want them.'

'Is there anything of Colette's here, which she might have forgotten to take?' She cleared her throat and forged on. 'Perhaps she…she might want to come and pick something up?'

His smile was knowing, as if he was perfectly aware that her question was a thinly disguised method of gathering information. For a moment she wondered if he was about to withhold it, but, with a look of mockery, he supplied it.

'Colette never actually lived here, even though she liked to make out she did. There's nothing of hers here and little else that interests me. So auction it all off. The money raised can go to my charitable foundation.'

Emily supposed it was an admirable way to dispose of his past, if a little cold-blooded.

'And in case you're wondering,' he continued silkily, 'Colette now lives in New York, so it's unlikely you're going to run into her along the Avenue Montaigne.'

Emily found herself expelling a huge sigh of relief because she'd actually been dreading bumping into the glamorous supermodel. Was it that or the fact that their time in Paris was drawing to a close which made her suddenly dare to try to open up some further lines of communication between them? Or because they'd gone to bed soon after lunch and his defences were down? He had seemed very much like the Alej of old as he had explored her body and lazily kissed every inch of her skin and she had found herself revelling in their old familiarity and wishing she could deepen it.

She could hear the sound of the shower being turned off and minutes later he walked into the bedroom, a white towel wrapped around his narrow hips and tiny droplets of water highlighting the honed perfection of his olive skin. She watched his reflection in the mirror. The liquorice-black tendrils of his hair were damp, his buttocks were paler than the dark skin above and below—and wasn't it predictable that she could feel her body instantly respond, despite the fact that they'd been having non-stop sex all afternoon?

He opened the wardrobe door, giving her a perfect view of that livid scar on his back—a scar he now seemed comfortable about letting her see, though there had still been no explanation about how he'd acquired it. But everyone had scars, Emily realised suddenly. Just not all of them were visible.

In a couple of hours' time they were meeting a friend of his from way back, an Italian businessman named Salvatore di Luca who was bringing along his latest girlfriend—a neuroscientist who happened to look like an underwear model—which was probably why Emily had allowed Alej to buy her a dress from the Chanel shop, which was situated just along the street from his apartment. She was wearing it now and the deceptively simple cut of the fine black silk was ridiculously flattering, as were the killer heels which were sitting beside the door to be put on at the last possible moment. But her appearance was the last thing on her mind. Suddenly she knew that she wasn't prepared to be fobbed off with throwaway answers any more. She didn't care if this relationship of theirs wasn't destined to last—why *shouldn't* she learn as much as she could about the man with whom she was temporarily spending her life?

She waited until he was almost dressed, because his nakedness was distracting, and then she turned from where she'd been seated at the dressing table, applying a light slick of lipstick.

'Are you ever going to tell me how you got that scar?' she questioned.

He shrugged as he tugged up the zip on his suit trousers. 'I told you I didn't want to talk about it.'

'I know you did. But I do.'

His eyes narrowed. 'Why?'

'Because we're about to have dinner with one of your oldest friends and, unless you want him to guess this is a sham marriage, it might be better if you didn't come over as a complete stranger to me.'

'And telling you how I got this thing will help?'

'I think so. It might help explain some of a past which you seem determined to keep hidden.'

He turned around, the movement seeming slow, his green eyes hard and flinty as they surveyed her.

'Please, Alej,' she added quietly.

There was a pause. A long pause. And then he gave a long and ragged sigh. 'I was attacked,' he said finally. 'By a man with a razor. Or, to be more accurate—by several men.'

He saw her flinch, as if a steel blade had penetrated *her* tender flesh. Her fingers flew up to her lips in shock and she looked about eighteen again.

'Oh, my God,' she breathed. 'What happened?'

He wondered afterwards what made him continue with his story because he'd never told anyone else. Was it the afterglow of the delicious sex they'd recently shared? Or because living with someone was way more intimate than he'd anticipated, with the inevitable erosion of all the barriers you tried to erect around yourself?

Or maybe it was simply because it was Emily and she had always been the one to burrow beneath his skin.

And suddenly he was right back there. A different time and a different place. And a very different man. He unlocked the memory and it floated free.

'I'd been playing in Argentina and my team had won the last match of the season, as we were expected to do,' he began slowly. 'I even scored the winning goal.'

'That must have been a good feeling,' she said.

He gave a bitter laugh. 'Not really. I'd been approached to fix that match, but, like every other time it had happened, I'd refused.' There was a pause as he looked at her. 'But the offer still left a bad taste in my mouth and it added to my growing disenchantment with some aspects of the sport.'

She nodded, but she didn't speak. She was an astute woman, he acknowledged—one who had learned to use silence to her own advantage. Because he could have stopped the story there. Told her he'd had a few drinks and got into a fight but didn't bother reporting it because he didn't want the negative press of some barroom brawl. Explained how he'd found a backstreet medic to suture it for him on the quiet—hence the resulting scar. All these things were true, and Alej was a man with a powerful aversion to lies. But there had been other reasons for him not wanting the truth behind the brawl to emerge, hadn't there? He wondered if it was the soft expression in Emily's deep blue eyes which made him want to confide in her, or the sudden realisation that some secrets were so dark that they had the power to eat away at your very soul, if you let them.

'I was in a bar,' he continued. 'A rough, simple kind of place not far from where I'd grown up, where a man can go unbothered and drink his beer in peace.' But it hadn't been like that. Word had got out that he was there and someone had come to find him. The oily thug in the cheap suit Alej had recognised instantly. His face had been ugly with anger, his words uglier still. 'I was approached by a man,' he said, his eyes fixed unblinkingly on Emily's face. 'The same guy who'd tried to get me to fix the match. He blamed me for refusing and for all the money he'd lost as a result. And then he told me that my mother was nothing but a cheap hooker and that he'd "had" her.'

She flinched again, but this time a dull red flush stained her cheeks and he saw the way she clenched her hands into tiny fists. 'How dare he say that?'

He almost smiled at the fervour of her instant denial because hadn't he felt exactly the same, when for a few foolish and naïve moments he'd thought the man was lying? 'He even tried to explain how and where, in very graphic detail, and that's when I hit him.'

'Good! I'm glad you hit him. He deserved it!'

Another sigh left Alej's lungs. The crack of bone and the pliant dip of giving flesh had satisfied him, but only for a moment. Nothing ever lasted for longer than a moment, he reflected bitterly. 'And that's when two of his gorillas came charging in, picked me up and carried me out of there and nobody tried to stop them. And behind that bar, in a dark and stinking alley, they each took turns to trace patterns on my back with a rusty blade, so I would never forget them.'

'Oh, Alej.' She jumped to her feet and scooted towards him, the earnestness on her face seeming at odds with the unusual glamour of her new black dress as she put her arms around him. 'Get off,' he bit out from between gritted teeth as he tried to shake her away.

But still she held him, rubbing at his shoulders as if he had just come in, frozen from the snow. 'No, I won't get off,' she said fiercely. 'You let me touch you whenever we're having sex—well, maybe I want to touch you now, when you need my sympathy.'

'I don't need your damned sympathy,' he growled, dislodging himself from her grip at last, despite her objections.

'I'll be the judge of that. Please, Alej. Tell me what happened.'

He walked over to the window and watched as an enormous vintage Rolls-Royce pulled up outside the Ritz hotel opposite. 'I left polo the very next day.'

'Why?' she questioned quietly.

He didn't answer for a moment and when he did his words sounded as if they'd been dipped in some corrosive liquid. 'Like I said, I'd been growing disenchanted for some time and the blade attack was the last straw. The cuts those men inflicted on me took a long time to heal—which meant it would be even longer before I could get back to match fitness. And I'd had a severe life shock in learning that my mother was a prostitute. I needed something different to think about. A new direction. And so I left the sport which had devoured my every waking thought for as long as I could remember and went into business instead.'

'And no one stopped to question why?'

She was a public relations officer, Alej reminded himself—of course that would be the first thing she thought of. He turned away from the window and stared at her. 'No. There were no more matches and it was nearly Christmas. I took myself off to the Caribbean to recover and people just thought I was recuperating. It was while I was there that I got an email from the guy who had come up with the idea of the MiMaté drink, asking if I wanted to invest some money in his venture, and, seamlessly, my business career was born.' His mouth twisted. 'And ironically I discovered that fame—or notoriety—still had me in its clutches. That making vast amounts of money breeds its own kind of celebrity.'

'And that was the end of it?' she persisted. 'You weren't scared of being attacked again?'

He shook his head. 'I took courses in martial arts. I learned how to protect myself. Put it this way—I never went into a backstreet bar ever again.'

'And did you talk to your mother?' she questioned slowly. 'About the accusations?'

She was looking puzzled and Alej wondered if she guessed he was holding something back or whether he was crediting her with more astuteness than she actually possessed. But even though he was still questioning his sanity in having started all this, he knew he was going to complete the story. Because wasn't it a relief to let it out at last—like a bitter and poisonous mix which had been living inside him for too long, before finally bubbling to the surface?

'No. It isn't an easy subject to bring up, when you stop to think about it. So I just buried it. Deep.' His voice was rough as he pushed out the words from lungs which suddenly felt dry. 'You see, after my mother was sacked by your stepfather, she never worked again. I'd bought her a little house in the country and she grew vegetables and for a while she seemed almost happy. But then she was diagnosed with lung cancer. She had a full-time carer living with her, and I used to visit her regularly.' He paused and then nodded. 'And even though I'd told myself countless times it couldn't possibly be true, I couldn't shake off the look on that man's face when he told me about her. I kept telling myself it was none of my business. That how she had lived her life was nothing to do with me. I planned to say nothing and then, the day before she died, she turned to me and said, "You know, don't you?"'

He saw incomprehension and then shock on Emily's face. 'She guessed?'

He nodded.

'What did you say?' she breathed.

'I asked her what she meant.'

You know what I mean, son. Her failing voice had come out as a reedy rasp. *I've seen the empty expression in your eyes whenever you look at me that was never there before. Did you find out that I worked the streets when you were a little boy?*

'And?'

He'd almost forgotten Emily was there. Alej's vision cleared as he met her sapphire gaze. 'What could I say? What could I tell her, other than the truth, when the truth was the only thing I could hold onto? And then she told me everything.' His lips hardened as he spoke and suddenly he got an acrid taste in his mouth. He walked from the bedroom into the dining room, aware of Emily following him, before going over to the antique cabinet which would shortly be sold at auction and pouring two fingers of whisky into a crystal tumbler. He swallowed a fiery mouthful before holding his glass aloft. 'Want one?'

She shook her head. 'No, thanks. I want you to carry on with your story.'

He gave a bitter smile as he put the glass down on the gleaming wood. 'Hers was a not unusual tale and in many ways, I wasn't making a moral judgement. You don't have to stand on a street corner to sell sex for money—I know women who would promise pretty much anything if they thought they were going to get a diamond necklace out of it. But this was a very different version of reality from the one I'd been given when I was growing up.'

Her voice was tentative. 'Surely you wouldn't have expected her to tell you the truth when you were a little boy?'

'Of course not. I could understand why she would keep her prostitution a secret. She wasn't the first young woman who would use her body to pay the bills and she certainly won't be the last,' he bit out. 'But not why she felt the need to lie about the circumstances of my conception and about my father. When we moved from the favela and she found a job as housekeeper to your stepfather, she told me we wouldn't be there long. She explained that my father was a rich and powerful man and one day he would return and rescue us and take us away from a life of servitude and we would live together happily on the acres of the pampas he called home.'

'And you believed her?'

'Of course I did! Children tend to believe what their mothers tell them. And we both know what good liars women can be, don't we, Emily?' There was a pause as he flicked her a cynical look. 'But she saved the best for last. The dramatic deathbed declaration which can never be challenged once the final breath has been taken. There was no rich and powerful papa. No father at all, as it happened—just a former client of hers, an itinerant rogue who used to beat her up.' He swallowed. 'But still she let him keep coming back for more. He was nothing but a thief and a con man who spent most of his time in prison and was killed by wrapping his motorbike round a tree—but not before making her pregnant with another child.'

'Oh, Alej. That's terrible,' said Emily dazedly, blinking her eyelids rapidly as if she was trying to hold back tears. 'I'm so sorry.'

He gave another bitter smile. 'Funny, isn't it? I always regretted being an only child, except then I discovered I wasn't. That I have a younger brother. A child she had no hope of supporting, so she did what any self-respecting mother would do and sold him.'

'What was that you said?' Her voice sounded as if it were coming from a long way away as she stared at him in disbelief. 'Are you telling me your mother had another baby and she *sold it*?'

His jaw firmed. 'That's exactly what I'm telling you.'

'Oh, Alej—'

'No,' he said bitterly. 'Please spare me the kindness and compassion—the trembling lips and big, wet eyes. That's not why I told you. And that's it. That's the story. There is no more.'

'There must be.' She walked over to the drinks cabinet and stood next to him, the delicate silk of her black dress making a soft, whispering sound and the faint scent of summer flowers drifting in the air as she reached him. 'You have a brother, Alej. It may not be the ideal scenario—but that's a wonderful thing, surely? You've got a sibling—which is more than I do. Someone whose gene pool you share. Someone you can have a unique relationship with. Have you managed to find him?'

'No.' Even Alej could hear how cold his voice sounded as he answered her question, but it wasn't nearly as cold as his heart. 'I haven't found him because I haven't bothered looking for him. He was sold to a woman in America and that's all I know.'

'But surely you—'

'There is no "surely" about it,' he ground out. 'I'm too old to believe in fairy stories, Emily. Do you really think I would track him down, so that we could have some great big family reunion? Do you honestly think he knows the background of the woman who gave birth to him? Even if he does, do you imagine that's something he's ever going to want to celebrate?'

Emily didn't answer. Not straight away. Her head was too busy buzzing with the emotional repercussions of his shocking revelation. But one thing quickly became apparent—like the agitated and muddy water of a pond which finally grew still, so you were able to see the stones on the bottom. No wonder Alej was so cold and mistrusting. No wonder he thought all women lied. Because in his experience, they did. She'd told him lies herself, hadn't she? Big, powerful lies. She'd told him she didn't want him. That she'd wanted other men. She'd said that because she was scared—scared of her own feelings and her mother's unpredictable behaviour. Scared of being hurt and scared of the future.

Even now, she'd only given him half the truth, hadn't she? She had been too much of a coward to take that final step and to tell him what was deep in her heart. And didn't he need to hear that, now, when he was at his most vulnerable? When he must be aching and hurting deep inside, despite the proud expression on his face.

'I also need to tell you something, Alej.'

He withered her with a sardonic look. 'Don't tell me your mother was a hooker, too?'

She didn't respond to the jibe. 'When I told you on our wedding day there had been no other man—'

'It had conveniently slipped your mind that you might have forgotten to mention one or two?' he suggested.

She blanked his harsh sarcasm, because of course he would lash out at her—wouldn't anyone have lashed out in the circumstances? But he hadn't yet made sense of his past, she realised—and maybe in a way, she had been guilty of the same. 'No. There has been no other man because…' she swallowed '…because nobody ever came close to you. And what I felt for you, I've… I've never felt for anyone else.'

She didn't know what kind of reaction she had been expecting from this tentative revelation but it certainly wasn't the one she got. All his icy composure had vanished and his face now blazed with sudden fury. 'Is this pity you dole out to me now, Emily?' he demanded savagely, angry green fire spitting from the depths of his eyes. 'You think that because I have revealed my shameful parentage to you, I will grab at any crumb of affection which comes my way? That the illegitimate son of a hooker and a thief will be grateful for anything he can get?'

She saw his pain and his anger and thanked whichever self-protective instinct had stopped her from coming right out and telling him she loved him. And wouldn't logic rather than emotion serve her better than anything else right now? 'I don't care about your past!' she said quietly. 'I don't care who your father was or what your mother did.'

His face was a mask. 'I didn't tell you because I wanted your affirmation,' he said coolly. 'I only told you because you asked.'

CHAPTER TEN

'THE THING IS, ALEJ—if you're serious about going into politics, there are a couple of issues you really need to consider first.'

Alej glanced up from the financial journal which was dancing unintelligibly before his eyes. Emily was standing on the other side of the room, pulling on a pair of silk panties, her curvy body illuminated by the morning sunlight, which was turning her hair to pure gold. He swallowed down the lust which was rising up inside him, a lust which seemed permanently outside his control. Last night before dinner he'd told her his dirty secret, expecting…what? He wasn't sure—but it certainly hadn't been her steadfast acceptance of the grim facts about his parentage as they'd come spilling out of him like dark poison.

He felt his gut twist. He'd thought that knowledge of his past would drive her away. That he'd see her face contort with disgust, no matter how much she tried to keep it hidden. But instead she had remained calm. There had been no recriminations. No hurt expression at the way he had snapped at her. She'd just slid her feet into her new shoes and they'd gone out for dinner with Salvatore di Luca and his girlfriend and Emily had settled easily into her role of glowing newly-wed. She'd acted as if he hadn't told her the sordid truth about his past, which had only reinforced his prejudices about her. Because maybe now she knew the whole truth about him, she imagined she was in a stronger bargaining position. His jaw tightened. Had she been seduced by the private jets and luxury hotels, the jewels and designer clothes he had provided for her—and decided she didn't want to give them up without a fight? Was her love of material comfort greater than discovering that her husband was the son of a violent drunk and a prostitute?

Yet when they'd had sex last night, she'd been as tender as ever he'd known her. She had held him tightly afterwards, her long fingers gently stroking through his hair in a way which had felt delicious. Dangerously delicious. He had pulled away from her afterwards and had lain there staring mutinously at the darkened ceiling. Was all that tenderness born out of compassion? he had wondered bitterly. Did she really think he needed her *sympathy*?

'Alej?' she was saying. 'Have you been listening to a word I've been saying?'

He shrugged. 'It's not particularly easy to concentrate on anything when you're doing a reverse striptease in front of me,' he drawled.

She was zipping up the sleek cream dress, which had also come from the Chanel shop, and he could see the sudden look of courage which crossed her face—as if she was about to say something he didn't want to hear. 'If you're serious about going into politics,' she said quietly, 'aren't you worried that some of the stuff about your mother will come out?'

Half regretting his impetuousness in telling her, Alej

shook his head. 'Why should it? It never has before, not even when I announced I was leaving polo.' His jaw tightened. 'I suspect most of her clients will be dead by now and those who aren't are hardly going to boast about consorting with a prostitute, are they? Even if they do make the connection.'

'But it might,' she persisted. 'Especially if you're entering politics, when every aspect of your past will be dragged into the daylight and raked over.'

He shifted uncomfortably. 'That's just a risk I'm going to have to take.'

'Unless you take control of it,' she suggested.

His eyes narrowed. 'Meaning, what?'

She seemed to choose her words with care. 'None of us should be defined by the things our parents have done. You are a good man, Alej, and you do good things. You have a charitable foundation—'

'Like I told you before, I'm not asking for your affirmation,' he said harshly.

'And rather than living with the fear of disclosure,' she continued firmly, 'I want you to think about making some kind of announcement. If the information about your past comes from you, then it loses some of its power. I'm not suggesting you do it straight away—just think about it when you're about to launch your campaign.'

Once again Alej felt the sharp prick of conscience. He wished she would stop being so damned reasonable, because with each second that passed he was reminded of what had made him fall for her in the first place. Her softness. Her understanding. Her enthusiasm. But that was then, he reminded himself grimly, and this was now. It wasn't going to be easy to do what he had to do and the longer this quasi-marriage went on, the harder it became. But he couldn't give her up. Not yet. There was still too much of her soft sensuality for him to experience before that day came around. He swallowed. So maybe he should take her back to Argentina—to where it all began. To be alone with her and enjoy her over and over again, until his appetite was finally sated. Wouldn't there be a delicious sense of irony to complete the circle that way?

Pushing back the rumpled sheet, he got out of bed. 'I'm having new flight plans drawn up with my pilot,' he said.

'Oh?'

'We're heading for Argentina,' he supplied coolly.

Pausing mid-brush of her hair, she turned round from the mirror and blinked at him. 'Already?'

He shrugged. 'Why not? We're done here in Paris. Make sure you're packed and ready to go. We'll be leaving this afternoon.'

Emily turned away, determined to hide her hurt at his cold and commanding tone, just as she had hidden it yesterday when he had rejected her attempts to comfort him after he'd told her about his mother. But what had she expected—that a man so deeply scarred and traumatised by his terrible past would turn around and let her get close, just like that? Was she really that naïve?

But she refused to do what she suspected Alej wanted her to do—to war with him just because he seemed determined to pick a fight. Because she couldn't do that. She deeply regretted her past lies and the part she'd played in increasing his suspicion of women, and surely the only way she could make amends was to demonstrate her support for him in a quiet and caring way.

So she was determinedly upbeat on the way to the airfield to Alej's jet, and grateful for the large bedroom on board, which meant she was able to sleep for most of the night flight to Buenos Aires in the vast king-size bed. But Alej didn't join her and every time her eyelids fluttered open it was to find her husband sitting working on his laptop, seemingly oblivious to the hours which were creeping away. As morning broke in a firework explosion of coral and golden sunrise, she saw that he'd fallen asleep in the chair.

Sliding out of bed, she padded over to kiss his forehead and he awoke with a start, his gaze briefly disorientated before he seemed to gather his wits about himself. And not just his wits. He was hard for her and seemingly ready and so was she and she gave silent thanks that the plane's crew had their own private quarters at the other end of the giant aircraft as he ripped off her little satin teddy. Pausing only to unzip himself and push his trousers down far enough to free himself, he impaled her completely before kissing away her startled gasp of pleasure as he bounced her up and down on his lap. Was *this* all she meant to him? she wondered, just before she succumbed to the pulsing tide of pleasure which beckoned.

She was showered and dressed by the time their plane touched down—the faint flush of her cheeks and bright eyes the only outward sign of their lovemaking, though inside, her heart was pounding like mad. A chauffeur-driven car was waiting to take them to Alej's *estancia* and Emily drank in the sight of the Argentinian countryside. Last time she had been here, it had been for a brief and flying visit—jolted by running into Alej again and marred by Joya's ill health. This time it was different. Her head might be all over the place but in many ways she had found a curious kind of contentment, because didn't she actually *enjoy* her husband's company, as well as being completely bamboozled by the things he did to her in bed?

She was lost in her own thoughts when Alej pointed out the soaring shape of a distinctive mountain.

'They say it resembles the shape of a reclining woman. There's the curve of her breast and the—'

'I don't need a lesson in anatomy,' she cut in quickly.

'Well, any time you change your mind about that, I'm prepared to help you, Emily,' he taunted softly.

Blushing, she cleared her throat, aware of the chauffeur's dark gaze in the driving mirror and wondering if he spoke any English. 'So what made you buy a place out here?' she said, with a deliberate change of subject, as the luxury four-wheel drive began to descend into a green valley.

There was a pause before he spoke. 'If you look down there you can see exactly why.'

Emily blinked and then her eyes widened. She could. Nestled in a glorious dip and surrounded by beautiful mountains, she watched horses grazing happily in the lush emerald pastures, and the silver ribbon of a winding river as it meandered along. As the car bumped its way up the track towards the simply built wood-and-stone building, Emily felt her heart wrench with a powerful kind of longing. Because before her she could see something which she'd never really had. Something which felt like home.

The breath caught in her throat. 'Oh, Alej,' she said. 'It's beautiful.'

It was even more beautiful inside. Not eye-wateringly sumptuous like the apartment in Paris, but it had an air of quiet comfort, which was equally luxurious. The solid-looking furniture was designed to be used, not looked at, and the views from the giant windows were to die for. There were big skies with gusting clouds and rich, fertile soil with bags of space to run around in. Stupidly, she suddenly imagined children here, making joyful shouts as they played or rode their little ponies…

'The staff live in a house a little way down the track,' he explained, his deep voice butting into her suddenly painful thoughts. 'They leave me everything I need and only come if I call them, which isn't often, because this is a place for solitude—not people.' He nodded towards the kitchen. 'I'll make some coffee. You might want to take a trip upstairs. I've left a wedding present for you in the bedroom.'

She stared at him in surprise before a mild stab of panic hit her. 'I haven't bought you anything.'

But he had already turned away. 'It doesn't matter. Go and see if you like it.'

Emily's heart was pounding as she ran upstairs and quickly found the master bedroom, which commanded the best views of all. And lying on the bed were a number of garments, which made her stop in her tracks. An exquisite pair of jodhpurs, a cream shirt of finest silk and a pair of brown riding boots in leather as soft as melted butter. And all in exactly her size. She didn't see the note at first, written in Alej's distinctive writing, and as she did she felt her heart clench with something like hope.

Put these on.

Her fingers were trembling as she did just that, not daring to dream that his gesture might mean what she wanted it to mean. Because the other night in bed—in those quiet and intimate moments after the heady hunger of sex had been satisfied—hadn't she told him that, yes, she missed riding, but that living and working in London made the pastime difficult. Just as she'd told him how much she missed the sweeping majesty of his homeland—and how it had been there, for the first time in her life, that she'd felt truly free. Had her words reminded him of the connection they'd once shared? Despite his immense power and wealth, was it possible that he yearned to recapture some of that connection—or at least discover if such a thing were feasible?

She pulled on the soft leather boots and ran back downstairs to where the pungent aroma of strong coffee was wafting from the kitchen. Alej turned to watch her final descent, his eyes narrowing with a look she'd never seen there before, and didn't some imperceptible flicker in their verdant depths send a brief shiver tracking down her spine? She sucked in a deep breath, desperate to know what had prompted such a thoughtful gesture but terrified of saying the wrong thing.

'Thank you,' she said simply, because she couldn't really go wrong with that, could she?

He nodded as his gaze skated over her. 'You look… amazing.' He nodded towards the steaming pot, his words uneven. 'Help yourself to some coffee while I go and change. I thought we could ride out together. I have two horses saddled up and ready in the stables. That's if you're not too tired after the trip?'

Emily shook her head, unable to stem her rising feeling of anticipation. 'Not tired at all,' she said eagerly.

'I'm tired of being cooped up inside and it's a long time since I was in the saddle.'

She drank her coffee and waited for Alej. He reappeared soon enough in jodhpurs which clung to his narrow hips and a shirt as fine as hers, which outlined the shadowy musculature of his torso, and Emily had to fight the urge to touch him. He led her out to the stables, where she saw a gleaming black stallion and beautiful golden mare, all saddled up and waiting to go, and her heart leapt with excitement at the thought of riding again after so many years. And then the groom appeared from within the gloom of the stable and his face was one she seemed to recognise. It was like a flashback, she thought—as past and present became confusingly combined, because he reminded her of her stepfather's elderly groom, Tomas.

'It's Tomas's son, Gaspar,' explained Alej, as if he had read her mind. 'He and his wife work for me now.'

Gaspar smiled and greeted her in Spanish before going back into the stable and when he returned, he was leading an old bay horse who began to whinny with pleasure as it came trotting across the yard towards her. Emily felt the prick of tears in her eyes as she threw her arms around his dear, familiar neck.

'Joya!' she said, burying her face in his well-groomed mane, and for a moment she thought she might cry. 'Oh, Joya. You look so…so *well*.' She lifted her face to meet Alej's hard green gaze, her voice shaky with gratitude. 'How can I ever thank you, Alej?'

His smile was brief as he shook his head, the firming of his mouth non-committal. 'No thanks are needed. I take pleasure myself in witnessing Joya's recovery, although, as he is too old for you to ride, you must be content with this palomino. Now let me see if you can remember what to do before I join you,' he said as he helped her up onto the saddle.

At first, Emily felt nervous and then exhilarated as she mounted the beautiful golden horse, but the main feeling which dominated was one of safety. Safe beneath Alej's watchful gaze, with his hand firmly on the rein as she trotted around the paddock. And wasn't it amazing how quickly it all came back—with confidence flowing through her by the second as she went through her paces? It wasn't long before Alej jumped on his own horse and Emily felt momentarily winded as she watched him ride. Because here was poetry in motion, she thought hungrily. Here was his skill and his gift perfectly demonstrated in a masterclass of strength and symmetry, as he put the stallion through his paces.

They rode for an hour and Emily would have gone further, but Alej shook his head.

'Don't be greedy,' he said, his eyes as green as the lines of grass which bounded the silver river. 'That's enough for one day.'

So she dismounted, hot and a little sweaty, and as she did so she thought about what else she was greedy for. Her senses had been stimulated by the ride and now she wanted to make love. She wanted it with an urgency which never failed to take her by surprise, but today it felt more intense than usual. And once the groom had taken the horses and they had returned to the house, Emily reached for the man who had been a part of her life since she was twelve years old.

For the next couple of weeks, it was as if she'd found the life she'd always been secretly looking for. A simple life and a good life. Up early and out on the horses before being quickly swallowed up by the sweeping landscape as they breathed in the fresh, Argentinian air. They ate al fresco and dangled their feet into the clear waters of the river and lit fires and barbecued fish. And whenever the opportunity arose, they explored each other's bodies—and each time was so intense that it was sometimes difficult for Emily to bite back the words of love she was longing to whisper in his ear.

Give it time, she urged herself, as he slid his rocky thigh between hers. Don't rush it. Let things settle, and heal, and who's to say what could grow between us if we nurture it? Maybe Alej wanted the same as her, though it was impossible to know what he was thinking or feeling and she didn't dare ask him and risk shattering the magic which seemed to have sprung up between them.

Afterwards, she found herself wondering how long that false state of affairs might have continued. How long it would have taken her to discover the horrible truth, if Tomas and Rosa hadn't decided to visit their only son, Gaspar. At the end of their two-day stay, Emily insisted on cooking them lunch, followed by *yerba maté* and sweet *alfajores* biscuits served on the veranda and, shortly before they left, she took Tomas down to the stables to see Joya.

'He is happy here,' the elderly groom pronounced, a huge grin splitting his creased face as the ancient bay came up to nuzzle him.

'Very happy,' Emily agreed.

'As are you.'

She wasn't going to deny it, not even to herself. And maybe the smile on her face told its own story. 'Yes,' she said quietly. 'I am.'

'Just as I am to see Señor Sabato settled and married at last,' said Tomas quietly, before giving a rueful shrug. 'And to think that if he hadn't decided to come to your stepfather's house that day, it might never have happened.'

Emily was in such a dreamy state that it took a moment or two for Tomas's words to sink in and when they did, she couldn't work out what he was talking about. 'But you were the one who emailed Alej,' she said.

'No, no,' Tomas negated, with a shake of his head. 'Señor Sabato contacted *me* first, to find out what time you would be visiting Joya.'

It didn't seem to make any sense at all and yet it made perfect sense. Or should that be *imperfect* sense? Emily wondered bitterly as an icy shiver ran down her spine.

It took every bit of concentration she had to say her farewells to Tomas and Rosa and to wait until she and Alej had returned to the house, before she dared confront him. And wasn't there a part of her which didn't *want* to confront him? Which wanted to carry on exactly as they were, no matter how false a situation it might be? She waited until he had pulled a beer from the fridge—declining the one he offered her.

'Tomas told me something strange today, just before he left,' she began slowly.

He flicked the top off the bottle, taking a long swallow before fixing her with his hard, green gaze. 'Oh?'

She licked her lips. 'He told me that he didn't contact you to ask for help with Joya. That you were the one who got in touch first.'

He raised his dark brows. 'And?'

'Why did you do that, Alej?' Her brow furrowed. 'Why were you the one who instigated the meeting?'

'Because I wanted to see you again.'

Still she clutched at straws—but then, wasn't it natural to grab at anything you could, when it felt as if you were drowning? 'To hire me, you mean? To use my PR skills to salvage your reputation and enhance your political ambition?' she added, just in case she hadn't made herself clear.

There was a pause. A long pause which suddenly felt like a shotgun being loaded.

'But I don't have any political ambition,' he said slowly.

Emily gazed at him with a feeling of desperation, as if they were both looking at the same picture on the wall but each seeing something different. As if she could see a boat and he could see a tree. 'Of course you do,' she said briskly.

'I don't,' he said simply.

'But you said—'

'I told you that to get what I wanted.'

'To get what you wanted,' she repeated, like someone learning a new language. She shook her head. 'You've lost me, I'm afraid. I haven't got a clue what you're talking about, Alej.'

'Then maybe I should tell you.'

'Maybe you should.'

Alej drank another mouthful of beer, leaning back against one of the worktops, his gaze fixed on the sudden stillness of her pale face. A shaft of guilt pierced at him, but he forced himself to disregard it. Why should he feel guilty? She'd treated him like a stud. Hell, she was *still* treating him like a stud. Even if the last few weeks had been good, the only reason she was here was because he'd offered her money and because he turned her on.

So tell her. Tell her just how gullible she's been.

'It started back in March, when I heard you were in town for the reading of your stepfather's will,' he began softly. 'And I can't deny I was curious.'

Not just curious. The very mention of her name had stirred up all kinds of stuff inside him—stuff he'd thought he'd forgotten. Stuff he'd wanted to forget. Anger and resentment and bitterness, too. But most of all—when he had clicked onto the photo on the internet and seen her smiling face and golden hair—he had felt lust. That same powerful lust which had always overwhelmed him whenever he saw her. He remembered the kick to his heart and the way his mouth had dried as he'd stared at the sapphire glitter of her eyes.

'Okay,' she said cautiously, but her voice was still filled with confusion. 'You were curious. That figures.'

He shrugged, his fine silk shirt whispering against his torso. 'I saw your photo and I was intrigued. I decided I wanted to see you again. I'm sure you can imagine why.' He paused as he flicked her a look. 'So I had to work out a way of doing that.'

'Please tell me I'm not hearing this, Alej,' she said quietly.

'Oh, but you are,' he said, steeling his heart to the sudden tremble of her lips. 'I read that you were part-owner of a modest PR agency and figured you would probably find it difficult to turn down an obscenely well-paid project if it was offered to you on a plate. And so I decided to employ you, but first I had to work out a good reason for doing so. I was known for my playboy lifestyle and avoidance of commitment—but neither of those things had ever impacted negatively on my career before. So I decided I needed a new career, one where image *did* matter—and that's when Alejandro Sabato, the would-be politician, was born.'

Her lips opened into an expression of disbelief. 'You mean…you mean you never intended to run for office?'

He put the half-empty beer bottle down on the counter. 'Never. Politicians have never been my favourite people. Oh, I've been approached often enough in the past to get involved, but I've always preferred to channel my energies and money directly into my charitable foundations. The politician is just the middleman who takes his cut along the way.'

She walked over to the window and stared out in silence. 'And the marriage?' she questioned eventually, her back still to him. 'What was the point of that?'

'It guaranteed that you would stay for as long as I wanted you,' he said. 'In fact, I quite enjoyed watching your enthusiasm as you planned it all, reinforcing my opinion that all women are suckers for a wedding. And on a practical level, a marriage of convenience meant I could rid myself of the tiresome playboy handle, once and for all.'

She turned around then and her cheeks were even paler than before, making her eyes look like two huge sapphires which dominated her face. 'So you were lying to me all the time?'

He didn't flinch at her accusation. Why should he? Yet the clench of his heart was uncomfortable—as uncomfortable as acknowledging the pain which was glittering from her big blue eyes. 'Yes, I was lying,' he grated. 'Now you know how it feels.'

Emily didn't move from the window as a flood of

conflicting emotions rushed through her, making her feel faint and light-headed. There was hurt, of course there was. Bitter hurt. And she felt foolish, too—for having walked straight into his cruel trap to get her into his bed and wreak some sort of revenge on her.

But she'd gone willingly, hadn't she? There had been no coercion on his part, and that chemistry of old had exploded as if they'd never been apart. Only this time, their relationship had been on a deeper level than before. Or so she'd thought. It hadn't just been about first love and sexual awakening. He'd confided to her about his mother. He'd laid his soul bare for her to see all the darkness there. And yes, he had lied—but he was right: she had done exactly the same. Did it matter? she wondered suddenly. Could their lies have simply cancelled each other out so that they could forget all about them and start over?

And then she shook her head as if to clear it, wondering if she was in danger of going completely mad. Because of *course* it mattered. She'd told him lies because she'd been young and scared and had been backed into a corner. She hadn't cold-bloodedly worked out some torturous form of revenge, as Alej had done. He'd plotted to get her back into his bed but he'd played with her emotions, too. All these days here when she had been lulling herself into a sweet and romantic dream about a tentative future—while Alej must have been quietly laughing at how stupid she was.

Had he let his defences down in order to manipulate her—to try to get her to fall in love with him all over again?

And hadn't he succeeded?

'You bastard,' she hissed, and suddenly it felt as if

something had broken inside her. As if her determination to do the right thing and say the right thing had all crumbled away. What a *dupe* she had been, she thought disgustedly. Hadn't she learnt the hard way that you could never rely on a man for your happiness? That her independent life and career was the only reliable path to contentment? There might not have been anyone since Alej—but neither had there been this tearing pain which made her heart feel as if it were splintering into a thousand tiny pieces. 'I may have been guilty of telling lies, but not of cold-blooded emotional manipulation,' she raged. 'And at least I had youth on my side. What was your excuse? Because you know what? I actually feel sorry for you, Alej.'

'Sorry for me?' he questioned furiously. 'This from the woman who married me purely for money?'

'What other reason would I have for wanting to marry you when you're so closed up and cold and don't dare to ever trust anyone?' she retorted. 'You're just stuck in some empty loop where all you can see is the negative. You can't seem to shake off the past and appreciate what you have right now. Well, thank goodness I saw this side to you before I—'

'Before you what, Emily?'

She shook her head, aware that she had almost given herself away, because she sure as hell wasn't going to feed his already massive ego by telling him she loved him. Because surely now her main goal must be to eradicate him from her mind, and from her life. 'None of your damned business! You know what I suggest you do? That you go and find your blood brother. You find him and meet with him—because that's something which might help you make sense of your past, since nothing else has worked. Oh, and you can keep *these*!'

She twisted the yellow-diamond engagement ring and the matching studded wedding band from her finger and threw them on the table, where they landed with a clatter. 'And in the meantime, I'd like a car to take me to the airport where I intend getting the first scheduled flight back to England. And don't even think about putting me on your private jet, Alej—because there's no way I'm setting foot on it.'

CHAPTER ELEVEN

IT WAS THE dullest day Emily could remember, but then she'd been particularly sensitive to adverse weather conditions of late. When you spent a lot of your leisure time staring out of the window, you tended to notice things like spattering raindrops and fog so thick that it looked as if the world were permanently shrouded in a grey blanket. Maybe she should be grateful that the world wasn't all bright and sunny. Imagine if the sun were shining and the sky bright blue—wouldn't that only emphasise just how dark her world was and how broken her heart?

She just missed him. So much. She hadn't factored that in when she'd stormed from the Argentinian billionaire's *estancia*, barely even gritting out a goodbye when the car had arrived to take her to the airport. And in the intervening weeks there had been nothing. No email, no phone call—not even a letter from his lawyer, announcing that he wanted a divorce. He probably wasn't even going to bother asking for a divorce, she thought gloomily. He could get one automatically in a couple of years on grounds of desertion and, in the meantime, his marital status might stop other women from trying to rush him to the altar.

Being an estranged husband would only add to his inestimable appeal.

She kept repeating to herself that she would get over it sometime soon. And that surely his lies and manipulation were reasons enough to make her despise him? But somehow it didn't seem to work like that. Instead, she found herself remembering the way he had kissed her and the things he had told her. Things he'd never confided to another soul. Didn't that mean anything? No, it didn't, she reminded herself sternly. It meant nothing at all. It was game-playing Alej at his best—the politician who never was! The man who'd done his best to whittle away at her defences and manipulate her emotions.

Only her finances were giving her reasons to be cheerful—and on many different levels. She wondered if Alej had expected her to refuse the massive fee he'd paid to marry her—in which case, he was going to be disappointed! Ignoring Great-Aunt Jane's protests, Emily was using most of the money to help secure her elderly relative's new home in sheltered housing accommodation—and the peace of mind this gave them both was incalculable.

And business was suddenly doing very well indeed. She and Marybeth had acquired a steady stream of new clients, which had meant they'd had to take on an extra member of staff—a hard-working young woman called Sophie, who fitted in immediately. It wouldn't have taken a genius to work out that their new, super-cool reputation had come about as a result of mixing with a certain billionaire Argentinian. This naturally attracted lots of interest, yet somehow Emily's polite but detached attitude managed to stop the most avid questioners in their tracks. So that when someone inevitably enquired where her husband was, she would reply, 'He's away on business at the moment,' while daring anyone to ask more.

And nobody did. At least, not until Emily walked into the office one morning and Marybeth looked up at her with narrowed eyes.

'You haven't worn your wedding ring since you got back.'

'That's right.'

'Want to talk about it?'

'Nope.'

She didn't want to be one of those women who rehashed the whole heartbreak of a broken relationship to her friend, thus forcing herself to relive it, over and over again. And she didn't want Marybeth calling Alej names, because she was the only one who was allowed to do that. She had given it her best shot—that she had failed was down to the people they both were and the things which had happened to them. Her lies about wanting to sleep with other men had made him seek a primitive kind of revenge. Between them, they'd both helped destroy any possibility of a happy future together—even if Alej had shown any genuine signs of wanting one. Which he hadn't, Emily reminded herself painfully. He had let her go and was probably supremely happy about it. Even worse—she swallowed, trying to get rid of the rawness which had risen in her throat—he might even be back on the circuit, seducing and allowing himself to be seduced by the most beautiful women the world had to offer. Women he would never really trust, because his trust had been breached and his attitude warped by the lies he'd been told by his mother and by Colette. And by her.

But she knew she couldn't sit around pining for him for the rest of her life. She had to get out there and start living—even if her heart was hurting. She had to. She wasn't going to be like her mother, growing increasingly dependent on a bottle of tranquillisers to take the edge off a reality she didn't like. She had loved and lost, but it happened. It was all part of life.

'So what are you going to do now?' Marybeth was saying.

She looked at her friend rather sheepishly. 'I've started riding again. I realised how much I'd missed it.'

'You're joking?'

'Do I look like I'm joking? I can afford one lesson a week—I mean, it's not like I'm the biggest consumer in the world. There are actually riding stables in Hyde Park, which aren't as expensive as I thought.'

'Good for you.' Marybeth gave her a sly look. 'And I guess that means you'll get to wear those sexy new riding clothes you brought back from your honeymoon.'

The cold wind whipped around him and the rain was lashing so heavily that the short journey from limousine to apartment block meant Alej was as soaked as if he'd just been out sailing on rough seas. He scrolled down the list of names beside each corresponding doorbell until he came to the one which said Emily Green, and then jammed his thumb on the doorbell.

The silence which ensued was so drawn-out that he began to wonder if she was out, despite the assurances of a member of his London office, who had reported back that she'd finally arrived home from work. He glanced at his watch. He supposed she could be asleep already—but at *nine o'clock*?

And then he heard her voice through the intercom. Her soft and beautiful voice.

'Hello?'

'Emily. It's me.'

He supposed she didn't have to ask who, since everyone told him his accent was distinctive, but he wasn't anticipating the long silence which followed, before a strained voice asked a question so low that he had to dip his head forward in order to hear.

'What do you want?'

He wanted to feel her arms around him and his lips on hers, her soft body wrapping itself around him—that was what he wanted. But he wasn't really in an ideal bargaining position to state his demands, and certainly not from out here. 'It's raining and it's cold, Emily—'

'I don't need a meteorological report, thank you. If you don't like it then go back to Argentina—I believe the weather's more reliable there!'

'I'm not going anywhere until I've spoken to you.' He put his mouth close to the intercom. 'Now, we can do this one of two ways. You can let me in by pressing the buzzer or I can use a rather more unconventional means to grant entry, and if that involves kicking this door down then that's exactly what I'm going to do.'

'You wouldn't dare do that!' He could hear the bravado in her voice.

'You want to bet?'

The buzzer sounded and he pushed on the door quickly before it locked him out again, stepping inside to be bathed by the harsh light of the fluorescent strips overhead. Ignoring the elevator, he took the stairs two at a time until he arrived at her front door to find it slightly ajar. Cautiously, he pushed his way inside before shutting it quietly and heading towards the room from which light was streaming onto the wooden floor in the hallway. She was standing in a small sitting room, her back to him, staring out at the diamond glitter of the city lights in the night sky. She must have heard him enter but she spoke without turning round.

'Why are you here, Alej? What do you want?'

'I want to see your face so that I can talk to you.'

'Tough. You can talk to me this way.'

'Emily, please.' His voice dipped. 'What are you trying to hide?'

She turned around then and his pulse thrummed as he thought how different she seemed from the woman he'd said goodbye to just a few weeks earlier. Even in that short time her body seemed more honed and her cheekbones appeared sharpened as they cast shadows over her pale skin. And she'd had her hair cut. Not short, he registered, with grim relief, but the few inches which had been lopped off the flowing golden locks and the new, blunt-cut style made her look slightly aloof and very contemporary.

'I'm not trying to hide anything, but I see no need for further communication with you, Alej,' she said stiffly. 'So say what it is you came to say and then leave me in peace to get on with the rest of my life.'

Those last few words made him realise how much he had hurt her—more than he'd ever imagined. And, even more importantly, that he had no desire ever to do so again. But would she believe him if he told her that? Did he have any right to *expect* her to believe him after the things he had done? He walked across the room towards her. 'Please don't back away,' he said.

'I don't want you near me.'

'Okay.' That hurt, but he took it because he suspected he deserved it, sucking a breath which felt hot and ragged. And suddenly all the words he'd been composing in his head on the flight over seemed to form themselves into just three. 'I'm sorry, Emily.'

Her eyes looked very dark and very bright. 'Sorry for what? That you got found out? That Tomas rumbled you and let me in on your little secret sooner than you intended? Which makes me wonder just how long you were going to keep up the pretence of wanting to go into politics, Alej. Long enough for the thrill of having sex with me to wear off, I suppose?'

'In theory, yes—'

'You absolute b—'

'But in practice that day was never going to come around because I could never tire of you, Emily.' His fervent words cut through her fury. 'How could I, when I love you?'

She shook her head so that her hair swung in a pale and silky arc around her shoulders. 'Don't you *dare* come out with things you don't mean!' she said fiercely.

'You really think I would lie about something like that?' he questioned. 'When I've always loved you—even though I've spent a long time trying to deny it to myself. It's why your lies hurt me more than any of the others. Fabrications came to my mother as easily as breathing, which wasn't really surprising, given her history. And Colette's lies meant nothing, not really. My relationship with her was never intended to be anything other than a no-strings affair. She was the one who wanted more. Who was prepared to write that vicious book about me when I wouldn't—or couldn't—give her what she wanted.' He took another step towards her and this time she didn't stop him. 'Can we start over?' he said simply. 'Will you be my wife in every sense of the word, Emily? Will you let me love you and cherish you, for as long as we both shall live?'

Emily looked into his bright green eyes and felt a quiver of hope begin to shimmer over her skin, but still she was wary because she was scared. Scared of what would happen if she let herself believe that what he said was real. Scared of hurt and scared of pain. 'What made you come here today?'

Briefly, he closed his eyes and sighed as he opened them again. 'You forgot your necklace.'

She blinked. 'My necklace?'

He dug into his pocket and withdrew a battered box Emily instantly recognised, just as she did the fine gold chain and tiny pearl which lay inside—the necklace which had belonged to her mother.

'I rang up the office to speak to you and Marybeth told me you were helping your great-aunt move,' he continued. 'I remember you telling me that she didn't have a lot of money and so I put two and two together and guessed you'd used the payment I made when you married me.'

'And you were surprised I hadn't used it for my own greedy gain?' she said sarcastically.

'Hardly.' His lips curved into a sardonic smile. 'The contemptuous way you slung your wedding and engagement rings across the table was pretty indicative that you aren't one of the world's gold-diggers, no matter how much I initially wanted you to be. But the real reason I rang was that you'd changed your phone number and I wanted to talk to you and tell you how much I missed you. Wrong tense,' he corrected acidly. 'Miss you. Every second, every hour and every day. And I want to know whether we can try again. Whether you can forgive me for what I did and give us another chance.'

Emily saw the conviction which was blazing from his green eyes and could feel her heart racing as she hovered on the knife-edge of uncertainty. She knew what would be the safest option. To send him on his way, because love inevitably brought with it the potential for pain and if she stayed single she would be spared that. Oh, she might get bored or lonely—but she wouldn't be leaving herself open to the possibility of feeling as if someone had ripped her heart right out of her chest with jagged fingernails.

But that was a decision she was never going to make. It was a no-brainer, really. She loved him. Totally. She always had and always would. 'Of course I can,' she whispered shakily.

His quizzical green gaze met hers. 'Why?'

It was a seminal moment and Emily realised that she held the balance of power as she looked into his beloved face, which for once held a trace of insecurity, but the thought was lost the moment she went into his waiting arms because weren't they equals?

'Because I love you too, Alej. My darling, darling Alej,' she whispered. 'You are my man—you always were and you always will be. The only man for me.' She hesitated. 'And you aren't the only one to have made mistakes. I was wrong to let my mother and my stepfather pressure me into giving you up and it's something I've regretted ever since because—'

But he silenced her with his kiss and as the kiss deepened, the hurt and the pain began to dissolve. She was shaking with emotion and desire as he drew his head away, his hand skating slowly down the side of her face. 'Do you think you might like to show me where you sleep?' he questioned unsteadily.

'I think I might,' she answered, almost shyly.

It was much later, when they were lying in her rather cramped bed, wrapped in each other's arms, that she traced her finger over the outline of his lips. 'What about your brother, Alej? Did you find him? Did you even try?'

'Yes, I tried,' he said, turning his face towards hers. 'I've had a team of investigators working on it and every avenue they've explored, they've come up with a blank. But we will find him, Emily. Of that I am certain.' His voice grew husky. 'But now, can we talk of other things? Because I have something I need to do.'

Emily blinked as he got out of bed and fished around in the pocket of his jacket and pulled out another leather box—this one much less battered than the one which had belonged to her mother. And then he was getting down on one knee and prising open the lid and there, sitting on a bed of dark velvet, reposed a huge sapphire, surrounded by a glittering oval of diamonds. It was as if he had captured the dark ocean and poured it into the sparkling gem which almost blinded her.

'What's this?' she breathed.

'Your engagement ring.'

'But I've already got one. The yellow diamond?'

'Which I told you to choose from the internet,' he agreed darkly, as he slid the ring onto her trembling finger. 'Bad karma. So I picked this ring myself—mainly because the sapphire matches your beautiful eyes and because the diamonds are as bright as your spirit.'

It sat snugly on her finger but Emily paid it little heed for her attention was drawn by the far more beautiful image of the man who was kneeling before her. 'Oh, Alej,' she breathed, tugging at his shoulders to drag him back into bed, so that she could put her arms tightly around his neck and hug him. 'I love it, but not nearly as much as I love you—and if you don't kiss me very quickly I think I'm going to explode!'

EPILOGUE

'AND I AM very proud to declare this riding centre open,' Emily said. Her Spanish was now almost fluent again—but she guessed that was the beauty of having undergone an intensive course to brush up on the beautiful language she'd once excelled at.

There was a thunder of applause as the great and the good of Argentina greeted her declaration with prolonged applause and the children in the front few rows wriggled impatiently, eager to get out and start riding some of the fine horses which were waiting for them in the stables. Emily smiled as she sat down in her chair in the front row and waited for her husband to speak.

Today was the official opening of the riding school for disadvantaged children which she and Alej had established—right next to his brand-new polo school, which was situated just outside Buenos Aires. It was probably the single most rewarding thing Emily had ever been involved with and when she'd mentioned this to Alej, he'd told her he felt exactly the same. In fact, he was planning to involve himself with both schemes on a fairly regular basis, allowing his business empire to be run by the top people he had on his payroll, until the day came when he had a son or daughter of his own to take over when the time came, if they wanted to.

'You were great today,' Alej murmured once the celebrations were finally concluded and they were settled in the car which was taking them home.

Emily looked across at him, and smiled, thinking how stunning he looked in that charcoal-grey suit, with the top two buttons of his shirt undone to reveal a glimpse of olive skin.

'So were you,' she breathed.

'*Querida*, do you think we'll ever get bored with this mutual lovefest?' he drawled.

A glow of satisfaction rippled through her as she shook her head. 'Not in this lifetime.'

They were heading for Alej's *estancia*, to that simple stone-and-wood building by green pastures and a silver river, which had felt like home from the first time she'd seen it and still did. They had settled in Argentina as soon as they could, after the night Alej had turned up in London—wet from the rain and his face filled with something like vulnerability—before declaring his love for her. Emily had sold her small apartment and given the proceeds to the new riding school, so that it was as much her venture as Alej's. She'd also sold her share in the business to Sophie, who was proving a super-efficient replacement.

'A little too efficient,' Emily had confided ruefully to Marybeth, just before she'd left for her new life. 'You won't miss me at all.'

'Oh, I'll miss you, all right,' Marybeth had said, her voice sounding suddenly choked. 'But I'm coming out to stay with you after Christmas, don't forget.'

'As if. I'm laying on some Argentinian hunks specially for you!'

With Alej's arm around her shoulders, the journey to the *estancia* was smooth and surprisingly fast and once they had dismissed the chauffeur, it was just the two of them—with a free evening ahead. And once she'd been outside to check on Joya, Emily returned happily to the house.

'What shall we do now?' she questioned.

'Guess,' said Alej softly as he began to unbutton her dress.

She nuzzled at his neck and nipped the lobe of his ear like a tiny animal and he laughed and carried her upstairs, despite her protests. 'You won't always be able to carry me, you know!' she exclaimed as he proceeded to lay her down on the bed.

'Yes, I will,' he vowed as he continued to undress her.

Emily didn't bother correcting him. At least, not then, when she was so involved in helping him out of his own clothes, and her heart was thundering by the time she felt his naked skin against hers. But as he stroked her body with his usual rapt and detailed fascination, his fingers halted in their slow circumference of her breast, and he frowned.

'Something is different about you, *querida*.'

Did he know her so well? She guessed he did. But she simply smiled and said nothing.

His brow creased with concentration as his fingertip circled the other breast. 'Are you?' he persisted, and the expression on his face when she nodded was one she would carry in her heart for the rest of her days.

'*Sí,*' she whispered. 'I'm having your baby, Alej.'

She could see his throat constrict. 'How far gone are you?'

'Just six weeks. But we were so busy with the move that I didn't notice at first.'

His gaze was much brighter than usual as he brought his mouth down to brush over hers, his deep sigh of contentment warm against her. *'Te amo,'* he said, somehow both fierce and gentle, all at the same time. '*Te amo*, Emily.'

And when he entered her, with breathtaking eroticism and infinite tenderness, Emily cried out with love and with joy and, very soon, with fulfilment.

For a long time afterwards she lay there trembling in his arms, her head pillowed on the rapid rise and fall of his chest, while he stroked her hair.

'It happened sooner than I thought,' she said reflectively.

He gave a low laugh. 'Judging by the amount of times we've been having sex, I'm surprised it hasn't happened sooner.'

'But we might not have been able to have children at all,' she ventured.

'Then we would have adopted. Or fostered.'

'Yes.' Her voice was still thoughtful. 'But I still think we've been very lucky.'

His fingers tangled in the silken tumble of her hair, Alej looked up at the ceiling. Yes, she was right. Very lucky—that he had followed his instincts and sought her out, and that both their hearts had been big enough to forgive and to try again.

With his wife's gentle persuasion he had managed to forgive his mother for what she had done, and to let all the bad memories go. Because one day he wanted to tell his children about a woman who had sometimes sung when she was planting vegetables and who made the best *yerba maté* of anyone he knew. Because nobody was all bad, he'd realised—just as nobody was all good. The only faint shadow in his life was his lack of success in locating his sibling, but at least now he had discovered a name.

Lucas.

Lucas.

His heart clenched. Strange to think he had a brother. That someone, somewhere in the world shared his gene pool.

'Shall I get us something to drink?' asked Emily, her soft voice breaking into his thoughts.

He shook his head. 'You will do no such thing. From now on I will be waiting on you hand and foot, *bella*.'

'I'm not an invalid, Alej,' she scolded softly.

'No, you are my wife and the mother of my child.' He turned her face towards him. 'My beautiful Emily, who has taught me the meaning of love.'

'As you have me,' she said shakily. 'Just as you've taught me so much else besides. About acceptance and forgiveness. About strength in the face of adversity. And I love you too, Alej. I love you so very much.'

His arms tightened around her and the pounding of his heart threatened to deafen him. And as the setting sun turned the river into a ribbon of bright coral, Alej tilted Emily's chin so he could kiss her again.

* * * * *

HIS TWO ROYAL SECRETS

CAITLIN CREWS

For Flo, my favorite twin.

CHAPTER ONE

"THE ONLY THING that matters is the line," Crown Prince Ares's dark and intimidating father told him when he was little more than five.

At that age, Ares had no idea what his father meant. He didn't know what line his father was referring to or what bearing it could possibly have on him anyway. At five, Ares had been primarily concerned with how many hours a day he could spend roaring about the palace grounds, out of sight of his nanny, who was forever trying to make him "act like a gentleman."

But he had learned, already and painfully, never to question his father.

The king was always right. If the king was wrong, you were mistaken.

By the time he was ten, Prince Ares knew exactly what line his father was referring to, and was already sick to death of hearing about his own blood.

It was only blood. No one cared if he skinned his knee, but it was clearly very important that he listen to lectures about *the purpose* of that blood. Its dignity. Its import.

When it was still the same blood that welled up

in any scrape Ares might get while doing things he shouldn't around the palace. Things his old nanny liked to tell him were responsible for her gray hair.

"You do not matter," his father would rant during Ares's scheduled appointments with him. "You are merely a link in a noble chain, nothing more!"

The king was forever flinging brandy and various decanters this way and that in his private compartments as he worked his temper into a lather. Ares did not enjoy these appointments, not that anyone had asked him.

And Ares had been schooled repeatedly not to move when his father raged. To sit straight, keep his eyes averted, and refrain from any fidgeting or reacting. At ten, he found this to be a kind of torture.

"He likes a moving target, child," his mother would tell him, her voice cracking as she sat with him, her hands cool against his face and her eyes kind. "You must work on keeping your posture perfect, and never betray your emotions by so much as a flick of an eyelash."

"What would happen if *I* threw something at the wall?"

The queen's smile was always so sad. "Don't do that, Ares. Please."

Ares came to think of it as something of a game. He pretended to be a statue, like the ones that would be made of him someday to grace the King's Gallery that had stood in the Grand Hall of the Northern Palace since—or so the story went—the islands that made up the kingdom of Atilia rose up from the sea. Marble and gold, with a fancy plaque listing his accomplishments.

"Our line has held the crown of Atilia for centuries,"

his father would thunder, while Ares would think, *I am stone*. "And now it rests entirely in your hands. You, a weakling, who I can hardly credit sprung from my own loins."

Stone straight through, Ares would tell himself, his eyes on the windows and the sea outside.

By the time Ares was a teenager, he had perfected the art of sitting deathly still in his father's presence. Perfected it and also complicated it, because he was an adolescent and more certain by the day that he had not one drop of the old king's blood in him—because he hated him too much to be related to him.

"You must never, ever say such things out loud," his mother told him, her voice as exhausted as her gaze was serious. "You must never give anyone in your father's court leave to doubt your parentage, Ares. Promise me."

He had promised, of course. Ares would have promised his mother anything.

Still, sometimes the crown prince was not in a mood to play statues. Sometimes he preferred to stare back at his father with as much insolence as he could muster, wordlessly daring the increasingly old and stooped king to throw something at him. Instead of at the stone walls of the palace, as he usually did.

"You are nothing but a disappointment to me," the king thundered at every appointment—which, thankfully, occurred only a handful of times a year now that Ares was dispatched to boarding schools all over Europe. "Why should I be cursed with such a weak and insolent heir?"

Which, naturally, only encouraged Ares to live down to the worst expectations his father had of him.

Ares accordingly…enjoyed himself. Recklessly, heedlessly, and thoroughly.

Europe was an ample playground, and he made friends in all the desperately pedigreed boarding schools he was eventually kicked out of. Together he and his bored, wealthy friends would traipse about the Continent, from the Alps to the beaches, and back again. From underground clubs in Berlin to parties on superyachts somewhere out there in all that Mediterranean splendor.

"You are a man now," his father told him bitterly when he turned twenty-one. "Chronologically."

By the law of their island kingdom, twenty-one was the age at which the heir to the throne was formally acknowledged as the Crown Prince and Heir Apparent to the Kingdom. Ares's investiture cemented his place in the line of succession, and further, that of his own heirs.

It was more of the same bloodline nonsense. Ares cared even less about it now than he had when he was five. These days, Ares was far more interested in his social life. And what antics he could engage in now he had access to his own vast fortune.

"Never fear, Father," he replied after the ceremony. "I have no plans to appall you any less now I am officially and for all time your heir apparent."

"You've sown enough wild oats to blanket the planet twice over," the king growled at him.

Ares did not bother to contradict him. First, because it would be a lie. He had indeed. And second, because the hypocrisy might choke him. King Damascus was well-known for his own years of sowing, such as it were.

And unlike Ares, his father had been betrothed to his mother since the day of her birth.

It was yet one more reason to hate the man.

"You say that as if it is a bad thing," he said instead, no longer playing games of statues in his father's private rooms.

He was a man grown now, or so everybody told him. He was heir to the kingdom and now would be expected to carry out duties in the name of the crown he would wear one day. He stood by the windows in his father's compartments and looked out over the sloping hills and crystal blue sea.

This would always be Atilia to him. The murmur of the ocean waves. The soft, sweet scent of flowers on the breeze. The Ionian Sea spread out before him.

Not the king and his penchant for smashing things and causing as much distress as he could at the slightest provocation.

"It is time for you to marry," his father intoned.

Ares turned, laughing, and then laughed harder when he saw his father was serious. "You cannot imagine I will be amenable to such a thing. Can you?"

"I have no interest in suffering through the sort of twenties you will inflict upon me. And upon this kingdom."

"And yet suffer you must," Ares replied with a soft menace that was as close as he'd ever come to taking a swing at his father or his king. "I have no intention of marrying."

His father broke a decanter that day that had been in the family since the 1700s. It burst to pieces slightly to the left of Ares, though he hadn't moved a muscle. He'd only stared back at the old man.

But it had broken something in Ares nonetheless.

It wasn't the shards of priceless crystal raining down on his traditional regalia. It wasn't his father's temper, which Ares found little more than tedious at this point.

It was the whole…show. The titles, the land, the bloodline. It all meant more to his father than he ever had. He hadn't been raised by his parents, he'd been monitored by a succession of servants and paraded in front of his father only every now and again. And only when everyone could be certain his behavior was perfect.

Or tolerable, at any rate.

He couldn't help thinking that really, he would prefer not to be a prince at all. And if he had no choice in that, well, there was no need to participate in passing the mantle of blood and nonsense on to the next generation. Ares had no intention of marrying. No interest in it.

But he was adamantly opposed to having children.

He couldn't help but think it was the bloodline itself that had made his father a monster, coupled with the crown. And he was a monster primarily to his son. He was cold to Ares's mother, but it was Ares who got splintered decanters and rage.

Ares had no intention of passing that rage along to his own children. Ever.

"You should not rile your father so," his mother said years later, after Ares had indulged in yet another conversation with the king about his marital prospects. He was twenty-six. "We shall have to start importing decanters from the Southern Palace."

Atilia was an ancient island kingdom in the Ionian Sea. The Northern Island was the most geographically north of the islands that made up the kingdom and was where the business of the country took place. The Northern Palace was accordingly the more stately residence of the royal family. The Southern Palace, on the most southern edge of the most southern island in the kingdom, was about relaxation, not matters of state. Beaches and ease and what breathing room a man could have when the weight of the kingdom sat on his shoulders.

Not that Ares intended to hoist up that weight himself, but still, he preferred the south. It was where he'd been enjoying a few weeks of recuperation after a long goodwill tour before his father had issued his summons. Because clearly too much time had passed between unpleasant conversations about Ares and the bloodline.

"I can't control what riles the man," Ares replied, dryly. "If I could, the last twenty-six years would have been markedly different. And there would be a great many more breakable objects left unattended about the palace, I imagine."

His mother had smiled at him the way she did, soft and sad. Ares always assumed it was because she couldn't save him from his father. She couldn't make the king treat the prince the way he treated her—with icy disinterest. "It is not the worst thing in the world to start turning your thoughts toward the next generation."

"I don't have it in me," Ares told her then. The conviction had been growing in him for years, by then. He studied his mother, and her drawn, dear face. "If you are an advertisement for the institution of marriage, or what one must bear to become queen of these islands, I cannot say that I am greatly inspired to foist this dubious pleasure on anyone."

That was true, but what was more true was that Ares enjoyed his life. He kept a home of sorts in Saracen House, a separate, palatial estate that was part of the palace complex on the Northern Island. But he was never there. He preferred the energy of Berlin. The hustle and rush of London. The mad, thrumming energy of New York City.

Or, really, any place his father was not.

And besides, Ares had yet to meet a woman he wanted for more than a night or two. Much less a lifetime of bloodlines and pomp, tradition and circumstance. He very much doubted the woman who could make him reconsider existed.

Nor was he particularly upset about this lack.

"I see how you are looking at me," his mother chided him. She sat as she always did, upright and elegant, on the chaise in her favorite room of the palace where the sunlight stood in for happiness. Or so it had always seemed to Ares. "And I'm not so old, thank you, that I cannot remember the excitement of youth and the certainty that I could predict the twists and turns of my own life."

"I hope you're not planning to give me any details of the excitement of your youth," Ares said. "Particularly as I was under the impression you spent most of it in a convent."

The queen's smile hinted at secrets, and made Ares glad. He liked to think his mother had more to reflect on in her life than his father and the glacial coldness he knew their marriage contained.

"You must find a wife of similar background," his mother told him quietly. "You are to be the king, Ares. Whatever your marriage is like, whatever bargains you and your spouse make with each other, she must be a queen without stain. So, too, must your issue be without blemish. Do you understand what I'm saying to you?"

He did. But understanding did not equal obedience.

"That I should put off marrying as long as possible," Ares said, and grinned at her. "I am more than happy to oblige."

Ares was halfway through his thirties when his mother died suddenly, lost to a quick-moving cancer she'd thought was a bout of the flu. And Ares was still reeling, still mourning when his father called him back to the Northern Palace some months after the funeral.

"You must know that it was your mother's dearest wish that you married," the king growled, his hand clenched around a crystal glass like it was a weapon. "The bloodline is your most sacred duty, Ares. The time for games is past."

But as it happened, Ares was even less a fan of his bloodline than he had been before. Something he would have thought impossible.

His mother had left him all her papers, which included the journals she had kept since she was a girl. Ares, missing her in the bleak months after her passing, had lost himself in those journals. He wanted to hoard every memory he had of her. He wanted to feel close to her again.

Instead, he learned the truth about his parents. Or about his father, rather, and the royal marriage. Once Ares had been born, they had tried for a spare until the doctors had made it clear that the queen could likely not have any more children. The king hadn't missed a beat. He'd openly flaunted his mistresses.

All those ladies of the court who had cooed at Ares when he was young. All those noblewomen he'd been instructed never to speak with in private. How had he missed their true role?

His father had broken his mother's heart.

Over and over again, every time he took a new woman to his bed.

And Ares had never been overly fond of the king. But this made it worse. This made him hate his father, deeply and irrevocably.

"You betrayed my mother casually and constantly," he said now, his own hands in fists because he did not require a weapon. And wanted only an excuse. "Yet you imagine you can speak to her dearest wishes now she has passed? Do you dare?"

The king rolled his eyes. "I grow weary of coddling you and your refusal to do what is required of you."

"If you're so interested in your bloodline," Ares told him now, "I suggest you expand it on your own, as you seem so predisposed to do. You do not need me to do your dirty work for you. And let me be perfectly clear on this. I will not do it."

His father sneered. "Why am I not surprised? Once a weakling, always a weakling. You would even give away your throne."

But Ares didn't think of it as giving away a throne—

and one he'd never wanted anyway. He was ensuring not only his freedom, but the freedom of any potential children he might have had. He was making certain no child of his would be raised in that cold palace of lies.

And he refused to treat a woman the way his father had treated his mother.

Ever.

His father married again, quickly, to a woman younger than Ares. Ares caused a scandal by refusing to attend the wedding.

The kingdom was in turmoil. The royal advisors were beside themselves.

"The throne has a stain upon it," cried the most senior advisor, Sir Bartholomew. He'd come all the way to New York City to plead his case before Ares, who had refused to grace a room that also contained the king since that last, dark conversation with his father. "The kingdom is reeling. Your father has installed his mistress and dares to call her his queen. And he has claimed that any issue he gets upon her will supersede you to the throne. You cannot allow this, Highness!"

"How can I prevent it?" Ares asked.

He lived halfway across the planet. He spent his time carrying out his royal duties and running the charity he'd started in his mother's name and still enjoying his life as best he could. The tabloids loved him. The more they hated his father, the more they adored what they'd called his flaws as a younger man.

Ares had no intention of submitting himself to his father's court. He had no interest whatsoever in playing the royal game.

"You must return to Atilia," Sir Bartholomew cried,

there in the penthouse suite of the hotel Ares called home in Manhattan. "You must marry and begin your own family at once. It is only because your father continues to refer to you as the Playboy Prince that the people feel stuck with his terrible choices. If only you would return and show the people a better way forward—"

"I'm not the king you seek," Ares told him quietly. Distinctly. And the older man paled. "I will never be that king. I have no intention of carrying on this twisted, polluted bloodline beyond my own lifetime. If my father would like to inflict it on more unwary children, I can do nothing but offer them my condolences as they come of age."

Ares thought of his mother after his advisors left, as he often did. What he would not give for another moment or two of her counsel. That sad smile of hers, her gentle touch.

Her quiet humor that he knew, now, only he had ever witnessed.

You must marry, he could hear her voice say, as if she still sat before him, elegant and kind.

And he missed his mother. Ares understood he always would.

But he had no intention of following the same path his parents had.

He would die first.

His phone was buzzing in his pocket, and he knew it was more invitations to more of the parties he liked to attend and act as if he was a normal man, not the heir to all this pain and hurt and poison. He eyed the face in his mirror that he hated to admit resembled the King's, not hers.

Ares straightened his shoulders until his posture was as perfect as she would have liked it, on the off chance she could still see him, somehow. He liked to imagine she could still see him.

And then he strode off to lose himself in the Manhattan night.

CHAPTER TWO

Five months later

"PREGNANT?"

Pia Alexandrina San Giacomo Combe gazed back at her older brother, Matteo, with as much equanimity as she could muster.

She'd practiced this look in the mirror. For a good month or two already, and she still wasn't sure she'd gotten it right.

"That's what I said, Matteo," she forced herself to say, in a very calm, composed, matter-of-fact sort of way.

She'd practiced that, too.

"You cannot be serious," her brother blustered, a look of sheer horror on his face.

But Pia was standing before the wide desk in the library of the ancient manor house that had been in her father's side of the family since that early, hardy Combe ancestor had clawed his way out of the textile mills and built it. Or she thought that was how the story went, having always preferred to tune out most of the lectures about the grand history of both sides of her family. Because her parents had so dearly loved to lecture *at* each other, as if their histories were engaged in a twisted battle for supremacy.

And because she was standing there before her brother, wearing a dress that fit her more tightly than she might have liked—in all that unrelenting funereal black that Pia had been draped in for the past six weeks since their mother had died—she could feel it when Matteo's disbelieving stare landed on her belly.

Her belly, which, despite Pia's best attempt to pretend none of this was happening, was protruding. Sticking right out, whether she liked it or not.

There was no way around it.

Her mother, of course, had noticed that Pia was getting "chunky" in the week or so before she'd died. And Pia had learned a long, long time ago exactly what weight she needed to maintain to avoid the acid side of her mother's tongue. Her mother had seen the instant Pia had exceeded that weight, the way she had when Pia had been a rather moonfaced and shy young girl. To the ounce.

Puppy fat is for poor girls with no prospects, the legendary Alexandrina San Giacomo had said to her woebegone twelve-year-old daughter, her magnificent face calm—which made it worse. *You are a San Giacomo. San Giacomos do not have chipmunk cheeks. I suggest you step away from the sweets.*

After that Pia had been so determined to, if not live up to her mother's impossible standard of effortless grace and beauty, at least escape her scathing put-downs. She'd dieted religiously throughout her teens, yet her cheeks had steadfastly refused to slim down, until one morning she'd woken up, aged twenty-two, and they'd gone.

Sadly, she'd taken her fateful trip to New York City shortly thereafter.

And Pia couldn't say why her mother had done what she had done. She couldn't definitively state that it was because she'd discovered her unmarried daughter was pregnant, and on the verge of causing the kind of scandal that was usually her mother's province. Hadn't Alexandrina spent the bulk of Pia's childhood beating it into her—not literally, thankfully, though Alexandrina's tongue was its own mallet—that Pia was to walk the straight and narrow? That Pia was to make certain she remained peerless and without blemish? That Pia needed to be, above all things, Snow White—pure as the driven snow or Alexandrina would know the reason why.

The truth was, Alexandrina hadn't much liked the reason why.

Pia couldn't say that the news that she was not only not at all innocent any longer, but pregnant by a stranger whose name she didn't know, had made her mother decide to overindulge more than usual, as she had. And with such tragic results.

But she couldn't say that wasn't the reason, either.

And now it was six weeks later. Alexandrina had died and left their little family—and her planetful of admirers—in a state of despair. And then her father—brash and larger-than-life Eddie Combe, who Pia had thought was surely immortal—had collapsed with a heart attack three days ago and died that same night. And Pia was certain, now.

This was all her fault.

"You are serious," Matteo said, darkly.

She tried to keep her face calm and expressionless, as her mother always had, particularly when she was at her most awful. "I'm afraid so."

Matteo looked as if he had glass in his mouth. "You are aware, I feel certain, that we are moments away from our father's funeral?"

Pia decided that wasn't a real question. She waited instead of answering it, her hands folded in front of her as if she could stand there all day. She gazed past her brother and out at the Yorkshire countryside arrayed outside the windows, green hills beneath the gunmetal sky. Matteo, his gray eyes more dark and brooding than the stormy sky behind him, glared at her.

But when he spoke again, she had the impression he was trying his best to be kind.

"You look pregnant, Pia."

As if she might have missed that. "I do."

"There will be press at this funeral service. Paparazzi everywhere we turn. There was no avoiding them six weeks ago and it will be even more intense today. You must know what kind of commotion a visible pregnancy will cause."

To his credit, he sounded as if he was *trying* to talk without clenching his jaw like that.

"What do you suggest I do?" Pia asked the question quietly, as if it hadn't kept her up since the night her father had died. If she didn't attend the funeral, would that be worse than if she did?

"How the hell did this happen?" Matteo growled.

Pia had always considered herself close to her

brother. It was only the two of them, after all, caught up some ten years apart in the middle of their parents' famously tempestuous, always dramatic love story. Eddie Combe had been known as much for his tendency to take a swing at his business competitors as for his business itself, Combe Industries, that was the direct result of those tough Combes who'd climbed out of the mills.

Meanwhile, Alexandrina San Giacomo had been the most beautiful woman in the world. That was what they'd called her since she'd been all of eighteen. At her funeral, pop stars had sung elegies, the world had watched the televised version to weep along and post pictures of their black armbands, and rarely a day had passed since without Pia encountering some or other remembrance of Alexandrina that called her *La Bellissima, the angel of our time.*

And that was the more restrained lot.

Their parents' love story had transfixed a generation. Pia had always been transported by it herself, especially as her experience of their love came with the shouting matches, the broken crockery followed by Those Noises behind locked doors, and their utter and complete fixation on each other at all times. No matter who else was in the room.

Matteo, darkly handsome, broodingly intense, and excruciatingly dedicated to his role as the last San Giacomo heir as well as his father's successor in the family business, was precisely the sort of child one might expect to come from such a union.

Pia, by contrast, had been hidden away for most of her life, which she had always assumed was a direct consequence of her chipmunk cheeks. She'd been packed off to a convent, then a finishing school, while everyone in the family had gone to extreme and excessive links to keep her out of the public eye.

They all claimed it was to protect her, but she knew better. She was too awkward. Too chunky. The most beautiful woman in the world could not have an embarrassing, tragic daughter, could she? Alexandrina had been a swan by any measure. Pia was, sadly, still very much the ugly duckling in comparison, and she'd resigned herself to that.

Or she'd tried, very hard, to resign herself to that.

"Did you…ask me how it happened?" She stared at her brother now, feeling the wholly inappropriate urge to let out a laugh. Only her brother's likely reaction to such a thing kept her from it. "Not that you fling it about, or anything, but I was fairly certain you…already knew."

"Thank you for making light of the situation, Pia," Matteo snapped, that glass in his mouth getting the better of him. "I'm glad this is all a joke to you. Our father's funeral starts within the hour. You don't think you could have given me some advance warning about—" his gaze raked over her, and made her cheeks heat with shame "—this?"

"I thought I should do it in person," Pia said. That was true. What was also true was that she really hadn't wanted to do it at all. "And you've been down in London since—" But she didn't want to discuss their mother's death. "And I knew you would be coming up here for the funeral anyway, so I thought, why not wait until I saw you."

And Pia was nearly twenty-three years old. She

might have been protected to the point of smothering her whole life, but she was still a woman grown. So why did she find herself acting like a stammering child when her older brother glared at her?

"This is a disaster," he growled, as if she'd missed that. "This is not a game."

"You're not the one who can't wear most of the clothes in your wardrobe, Matteo," she replied. Airily, because what else could she do? "I don't think you need to tell me how real this is."

He stared at her, shaking his head. And Pia had tried so hard to put a brave face on all this. But the truth was, she was ashamed. She could feel that heat in her cheeks, and everywhere else, too.

And the way Matteo looked at her then, as if he was so disappointed in her it hurt, Pia was very much afraid that she would stay ashamed forever more.

"I'm sorry," she said quietly.

"Who is the father?"

But that only made that sickening shame inside her worse.

"Dad asked me that, too," she said, instead of answering the question.

Because the answer was so…squalid. Humiliating, really. Oh, she'd thought it was so delightful before. She finally had a secret! She was a modern woman at last, like everyone else she knew! She'd stepped smartly into her own future, seized the day—or the night, to be more precise—and had stopped keeping herself like some kind of vestal virgin, forever on the shelf, because for some reason her scandal-ridden family seemed united in their desire to keep her from making the mistakes they had.

Everything was fun and games until the morning sickness hit, she had discovered.

Matteo's glare darkened, which should have been impossible. "Dad knew about this?"

"Both Mum and Dad knew about it," Pia said, her voice small.

Of all the things she couldn't believe, what newly lived inside of her was really the least of it. She didn't understand how the world could continue turning without her parents in it. Her mother had been like the sky above, even in the quiet of her own sitting room. That vast and given to sudden storms. Her father had been like a volcano. Big and imposing, and always *this close* to eruption.

How could they both be gone?

And how could she live with the sure knowledge that she was what had killed them, one way or another?

Her hand crept over her belly, then froze when she saw Matteo's dark gaze follow the movement. A new wave of shame swept over her.

"What..." Matteo shook his head as if he couldn't take all the information in. As if he could make it go away by scowling at it. Or her. "What on earth did they say?"

"About what you'd expect." Pia tried to straighten her shoulders and stand taller, because Alexandrina had always told her it made a girl look a size smaller. "Mum wanted to make sure I knew that it was better to have a boy, as girls will steal your beauty." She opted not to mention the awkward moment that had followed that pronouncement, as Pia and her mother had stared at each other, neither one of them pointing out the obvious. That Pia had clearly done nothing of the kind. Her brother blinked, and she pushed on. "While Dad said, and I quote, 'I should have known you'd turn out to be nothing more than a common tart.'"

She even approximated their father's growl of a voice, with that broad hint of Yorkshire he'd played up, the better to discomfit those who thought they were his betters.

For a moment, Pia and Matteo stared at each other.

Pia felt her stomach turn over, and not with leftover morning sickness. But with disloyalty. Her parents had always had it in them to be awful. Temper tantrums were one of their primary forms of communication. They had always been capable of saying terrible things, usually did, and then went to great lengths to make up for it—usually not by saying anything directly, but with whirlwind trips to far-flung places. Or sudden bouts of affection and sweetness.

They had been disappointed in her. Pia knew that. But if they'd lived, the temper would have given way to something kinder, no matter what they'd said to her in the heat of their initial reactions. She should have said that, too. She should have made it clear she knew they would both have softened.

But it felt too late. For them, certainly.

And for her, the child who had always disappointed them.

Pia could hear the sound of movement in the house outside the library. The staff was getting ready for the gathering that would happen after the service and burial. When all their father's captain-of-industry contemporaries and associates—as Eddie Combe hadn't trafficked in friends—would clutter up the house, pretending they missed him. And all of Europe's heads of state would send their emissaries, because Eddie Combe might have come from the dark mills of Yorkshire, but he had married a San Giacomo. San Giacomos had been Venetian royalty in their time. At least one of their ancestors had been a prince. And that meant that the crème de la crème of Europe was bound to pay their respects today, no matter how little they had cared for Eddie personally.

Pia wanted no part of any of this. And not only because she was terribly afraid that she would cause a commotion simply by appearing in her…state. But because she still couldn't believe her parents were gone. Not when she hadn't had enough time to watch them come round. Not when she'd never know if this time, she'd disappointed them *too much* or if they'd soften the way they usually did. It seemed premature to mourn them.

And deeply unfair that she was expected to do it in public, as if she was part of a show for others to watch and judge.

"Do you not know who was responsible for getting you in this condition?" Matteo asked. Icily. "Or are you simply choosing not to name him?"

And maybe Pia was a little more emotionally fragile than she realized. Because that rubbed her the wrong way.

"I think you'll find that I'm responsible for getting myself into this condition," she replied. "I wasn't attacked, if that's what you mean. Nothing was done to me that I didn't enthusiastically participate in. I'm not a damsel in distress, Matteo."

There was a part of her that might have liked the fact she was pregnant—had it not horrified everyone who knew her. Pia had always wanted a family. Not the one she had, but a real family. The sort that she imagined everyone else had.

Matteo was studying her, and she could almost see the machinery working in his head. "That trip you took to New York. That was it, wasn't it?"

"If you mean the graduation trip I took to celebrate finally completing college, then yes." And oh, how she'd fought for that. It had been Matteo who had finally stepped forward and bluntly told their parents that Pia deserved as much of a chance as anyone to live her own adult life. Her cheeks burned all the brighter. Because she was imagining what he must be thinking of her now. "We had a lovely week in New York. It turns out, I happened to come back home with a little bit extra—"

"I don't understand. You…?"

There was the sound of footsteps beyond the door, and darker clouds began to pull together over the hills in the distance. And Pia stared back at her brother, her cheeks so hot they hurt.

"You don't understand?" she asked him. "Really? I've certainly seen your face and photographs with different women in the tabloids, yet you remain unmarried. How can this be?"

"Pia."

"If you're going to act like we're Victorian, Matteo,

I should have every right to ask about the state of your virtue. Shouldn't I?"

"I beg your pardon. *I* am not in the habit of having intimate relations with women that I do not know."

"Well. Okay, then." She drew herself up even straighter. "I guess I'm just a whore."

"I doubt that very much," Matteo growled.

But the word stayed in her head, pounding like a drum, because the doors to the library were tossed open then. The staff that Matteo had kept at bay came flooding in, his erstwhile assistant was there to whisper in his ear, and it was time to do their sad duty.

And she knew their father had thought exactly that of her, at least for that moment. He'd looked at her—really looked at her, for a change, because Eddie Combe had usually preferred to keep his attention on himself—only three days before his heart attack. And called her a common tart to her face.

She kept telling herself that wasn't cause and effect. That the heart attack hadn't had anything to do with her condition. And that, if he'd had more time, he would have found her in the next days or weeks and gruffly offer some sort of olive branch.

Yet as she rode down in her brother's car, tucked there in the back with him while he tended to the business of running the family company and his assistant Lauren handled calls for him, she accepted that she couldn't know for sure. How could she?

The last thing Pia knew Eddie had thought about her was that she was a whore. He'd said so. And then in a matter of days, he was dead.

Her mother had called her fat, which wasn't anything new. Then again, that was the worst thing Alexandrina could think to call another woman, and she hadn't yet cycled through to the usual affection before she'd passed.

Either way, Matteo and Pia were orphans now.

And Pia was still terribly afraid it was her fault.

But she snuck her hand over her belly because whether it was or wasn't her fault, that didn't extend to the next generation. She wouldn't allow it.

The funeral service was simple and surprisingly touching. It made Eddie seem far more approachable than he had in life, and Pia wondered if she would understand the man more as time went on. If her memories would mellow him into more of a father figure, lingering on his gruff affection. Or if he would always be that volcanic presence in her mind. The one that had thought his only daughter was a trollop right before he'd died.

The ride back up the hill toward the Combe estate was somber, and Pia was glad, in a fierce sort of way, that it was a moody day. The dark clouds threatened, though the rain held off, and they stood in a bit of a brisk, unpleasant wind as Eddie's casket was lowered into the ground in the family plot.

The vicar, who Eddie had hated in life, though had requested in his will in some attempt to torture the holy man from beyond, murmured a prayer. Pia kept her eyes on the casket that was all that remained of her father—of her childhood—until she could no longer see it.

And somehow kept her tears at bay. Because there were too many cameras. And how many times had Alexandrina lectured her about red eyes and a puffy face?

It hit her again. That Alexandrina was gone. That Eddie was gone. That nothing was ever going to be the same.

Then Matteo's hand was on her back and they moved away from the grave site to form the necessary receiving line for those who might or might not make it back to the small reception at the house. It was times like these that her years in finishing school came in handy. Pia was infinitely capable of shaking hands and making meaningful eye contact with every royal in Europe without noticing them at all.

"May I offer my condolences on the part of the Kingdom of Atilia and His Majesty King Damascus, my father?"

Something about that voice kicked at her.

Pia's hand was already extended. And even as she focused on the man standing before her, his hand enveloped hers.

And she knew that sudden burst of flame. She knew the shiver that worked its way from the nape of her neck down to pool at the base of her spine.

Her eyes jerked up and met his.

As expected, his gaze was green, shot through with gold. And as shocked as hers.

Pia panicked. How could this be happening? The last time she'd seen this man, he had been sprawled out, asleep, in a penthouse suite high above Manhattan. She had gathered her things, feeling powerful and shaken at once by her daring and all the things he'd taught her, and had tiptoed away.

She'd never imagined she would see him again.

"You," he said, almost wonderingly. "New York."

And part of her was warming, in instant response to the way his mouth curved in one corner. As if Pia was a good memory, as he had been for her. At least at first.

Before the morning sickness had sent her to the doctor to discuss the flu she couldn't kick.

But Pia couldn't indulge in memories, good or bad, because she was standing next to her brother. And he was focusing that dark scowl of his on the man still holding Pia's hand.

"New York?" Matteo asked. Demanded, more like. "Did you say you know my sister from New York?"

"Matteo. Stop."

But the man, still smiling slightly, seemed unaware of the danger he was in. "I met your sister in Manhattan some months ago," he said, amiably enough. He smiled at Pia. "Do you go there often?"

"*Miss Combe*, my *younger* sister, has been there once," Matteo growled. "And guess what? She picked up a souvenir."

"I beg your pardon?"

The man frowned. But in that way very important men did, as if inviting everyone around them to apologize for opportuning them.

"My sister is six months pregnant," Matteo bit out.

Pia had the sense that she was in some kind of slow-motion car accident. The sort she'd seen in movies a thousand times. She could almost hear the scraping of the metal, the screech of the tires. Yet everything before her seemed to move in tiny, sticky increments. She watched her brother ball up his fists and step closer to the man. The man—who had told her his name was Eric, though she doubted that was real—did not back up.

And they both turned and stared at Pia as if she was some kind of roadside curiosity.

"If your sister is or isn't pregnant, that is no concern of mine," the man said.

Far less amiably.

Just in case Pia had wondered if it was possible to feel worse about all of this. Look at that! It was. She rubbed at her chest as if that could make her heart stop pounding the way it was. Or at least, ache less.

"Pia," Matteo said, dark and furious. "Is this the man?"

"Have you forgotten where we are?" she managed to ask, though she was barely able to breathe.

"It's a simple question," her brother bit off.

"Once again, the state of your sister's womb has nothing to do with me," the man said.

And he wasn't just *a man*.

If Pia had been going to throw away a lifetime of doing the right thing and making the correct choice over any old man, she would have done it years ago. *This* man was beautiful. Those gorgeous eyes and silky dark hair, a jawline to inspire the unwary into song and poetry, and shoulders to make a girl cry. *This* man had walked into the party where Pia had already been feeling awkward and out of place, and it was as if a light shone upon him. It was as if his bones were like other people's, but sat in him differently. Making him languid. Easy.

His smile had been all of that, plus heat, when he'd aimed it at her, there beneath some modern art installation that looked to Pia's eye like an exclamation point. In bronze.

But best of all, this man hadn't had any idea who she was.

She could always tell. It was the way they said her name. It was a certain gleam in their eyes. But he'd had none of it.

He'd liked her. Just her.

Just Pia.

She'd planned to hold on to that. She'd *wanted* to hold on to that. But it seemed that would be one more thing she didn't get to have.

"Thank you so much for asking about my private life, Matteo," she said to her brother now. In a decent impression of her mother's iciest tone, which came more naturally than she'd expected. "But as a matter of fact, I have only ever had sex with one person."

Then she looked at the man before her, and her memories wouldn't do her any good, so she cast them aside. No matter how beautiful he was. "And I regret to inform you, but that one person was you."

But that didn't have the effect she expected it to have.

Because all the beautiful man before her did was laugh.

At her, if she wasn't mistaken.

"Like hell," he said.

And that was when Matteo punched him.

Right in the face.

CHAPTER THREE

ONE MOMENT ARES was standing straight up, looking one of his past indulgences in the face.

He'd laughed, of course. What could he do but laugh?

Because the truth was, Ares hadn't forgotten her. He hadn't forgotten the way her gray eyes had lit up when she'd looked at him. He hadn't forgotten her smile, shy and delighted in turn. And he certainly hadn't forgotten her taste.

He might even have toyed with the notion of what it would be like to seek her out for another taste, now and again over the past few months—

The next moment he was on the ground, and it took him a moment to understand that the Combe heir had punched him.

Hard.

Not only that, he'd chosen to do so in full view of the paparazzi, all of whom swooped in closer like the locusts they were at the sight. They took picture after picture and held up cameras to record every last detail of the Crown Prince of Atilia's inelegant sprawl across the wet grass in the middle of a funeral.

Ares glared up at the man who had laid him out.

He wanted—badly—to respond in kind, but restrained himself. Because he might not want to be king, but he was still a prince, whether he liked it or not. And princes did not swing on bereaved commoners, no matter the provocation. Moreover, he preferred to control the stories that appeared about him, especially when the press on his father was so dire these days.

He couldn't change the fact this man had hit him. But he could opt not to react in a manner that would only make it all worse.

He climbed back to his feet far more gracefully than he'd gone down. He brushed himself off, his gaze on the man scowling at him in case he started swinging again, then put his hand to his lip. When he drew it away, he noted darkly that there was blood.

Because of course there was blood.

Because everything was about his damned blood. Hadn't his father told him so a thousand times before Ares had turned seven?

Ares noticed movement in his periphery and held up his hand before his security detail handled the situation in a manner that would only make it worse. He glared at the Combe heir, whose name he hadn't bothered to learn as he'd run over his notes on his way here today.

That seemed like a significant oversight, in retrospect.

"You understand that I am the Crown Prince of Atilia, do you not?" he asked coolly instead. "Attacking me is considered an act of war."

"That doesn't frighten me," the other man retorted.

"What should frighten both of you is that this entire conversation is being recorded," Pia hissed at the pair of them.

And that was the thing. He could remember *her* name. Pia.

Such a little name when she had hit him with a good deal more force than her brother had just now.

And the hits kept coming today.

A closer look showed Ares what he should have noticed from the start. That she'd thickened around the middle. And she was a tiny thing—easy enough, if a man had a decent imagination and the necessary strength, to pick up and move around as he liked, and Ares certainly had liked—and her bump was clearly noticeable. Huge, in fact.

It was very clearly…exactly what it was.

But what it could not be was his.

"I have never in my life had unprotected sex," Ares said with as much regal hauteur as he could manage.

The Combe heir looked enraged. Pia only shook her head, her gaze darting around to their audience before returning to her brother.

"If you two want to roll about in the dirt, flinging your toxic masculinity about like bad cologne, I cannot stop you," she said, half under her breath. "But I refuse to become fodder for the tabloids for the first time in my life because of your bad decisions."

And she turned around and marched off, as if it wasn't already too late.

When Ares looked around he could see the speculation on every face within view. Because there had been a punch, and now Pia was leaving, and it didn't take a mathematician to put her belly and him together.

But it was impossible.

"I suggest you follow my sister up to the house," her brother growled at him.

"Or you will do what?" Ares asked, every inch of him the product of at least a millennia of royal breeding. "Punch something again? You do not tell me where I go or do not, Mr. Combe."

"Watch me."

Ares laughed again, more for the benefit of their audience than because he found any of this funny. Or even tolerable.

And then, because he couldn't see another option, he turned and made his way up the long drive that led from the family plot toward the big, hulking house that sat there at the top of the hill. But he took his time, chatting merrily with other guests, as if he was at a party instead of a funeral. As if he didn't have what he suspected was the beginnings of a fat lip.

And as if he hadn't been accused of impregnating a woman by her overprotective older brother, in full view of too many cameras.

He could leave, he knew. No one would keep him here, no matter what Pia's brother imagined. His security detail would whisk him away at a moment's notice.

But Pia's condition was not his doing—could not be his doing—and he felt compelled to make that clear.

He walked inside the manor house, wondering, not for the first time, how it was these northern Europeans could tolerate their stuffy, dark houses. The palaces of Atilia were built to celebrate the islands they graced. The sea was all around, and invited in, so it murmured through every archway. It was there, shimmering, just around every corner.

He asked after Pia in the grand entryway and was shown into the sort of library that made him think of all the headmasters' offices he'd found himself in during his school days. Usually en route to his latest expulsion.

She was standing at the window, staring out at the miserable British countryside, wet and cold. But what he noticed was her back was too straight.

And he didn't know why she would claim that he was the one who'd impregnated her, but it was hard to remember that as he looked at her from behind.

Because he remembered that night.

It had been their second round, or perhaps their third. He had woken to find her standing by the window, wrapped in a sheet from the thoroughly destroyed bed, her fingers against the glass. Manhattan had gleamed and glittered all around. Ares had gone to her as if drawn there by some kind of magnet. He'd brushed aside the weight of her dark, silken hair and put his mouth to the nape of her neck.

He could still remember the heated, broken sound she'd made. Just as he could remember the chill of the glass beneath his palm when he'd braced himself there and taken her from behind—

He shook himself out of that now. Especially when his body responded with as much enthusiasm as he remembered from that night.

"I'm not the father of your baby," he said, his voice grittier than it should have been when he knew he hadn't done this.

"When I realized I was pregnant, I tried to find you,

of course." Pia didn't turn around. She stayed where she was, her back to him and her arms crossed above her swollen belly. He couldn't stop staring at it, as if he'd never seen a pregnant woman before. "It's a decent thing to do, after all. But no matter who I asked, which was its own embarrassment, no one could remember any 'Eric' at that party."

"And because I lied about my name, you think it appropriate to lie yourself? About something far more serious?"

She let out a small sound, like a sigh, but she still didn't turn to face him.

"When I couldn't find anyone by the name of Eric, I thought that was fair enough. Not ideal, but *fine*. I would do it by myself. As women have been doing since the dawn of time. But that's easier to make yourself believe when no one knows. When you haven't yet told your whole family that yes, you had a one-night stand in New York City. And you don't know the name of the man you had that one-night stand with. But guess what? You're pregnant by him anyway."

"It is not my baby."

"But I withstood the shame," she said, her shoulders shifting. Straightening. "I'm figuring out how to withstand it, anyway. I never expected to see you again."

"Clearly not." Ares could hear the darkness in his voice. The fury. "Or you would not dare tell such a lie."

She turned then, and her face was calm. Serene, even. That was like a slap.

Until he noticed the way her gray eyes burned.

"And the funny thing about shame is that I keep thinking there must be a maximum amount any one person can bear," she told him. "I keep thinking I must be full up. But no. I never am."

Something twisted in him at that, but Ares ignored it.

"You cannot wander around telling people that you're having my child," he thundered at her. "This doesn't seem to be penetrating. It's morally questionable at best, no matter who the man is. But if you claim you carry *my* child, what you are announcing is that you are, in fact, carrying the heir to the Atilian throne. Do you realize what that means?"

Pia looked pale. "Why would I realize that—or anything about you? I didn't know who you were until fifteen minutes ago. Much less that you were a *prince. Are* a prince. A *prince*, for God's sake."

A man who had renounced his claim to a throne should not have found the way she said that so...confronting.

Ares pushed on. "Now you know. You need to retract your claim. Immediately."

"Are you denying that we slept together?" she asked, her voice shaky.

"We did very little sleeping, as I recall. But I don't see what that has to do with anything."

"I've only ever slept with one man," she threw out there. "You."

Or so it seemed to Ares as it sat there, bristling in the center of the library floor.

The implications of that statement roared in him.

But Pia was still talking. "If you are not the father, we have a far larger problem on our hands." She even smiled, which made the roaring in him worse. "Shall I contact the Vatican to notify them of the second immaculate conception? Or will you?"

Ares stared back at her as that scathing question hung in the air between them, too, joining in with all the rest of the noise. The roar of it. And it wasn't until that moment that he realized that for all he liked to think of himself as an independent creature, in no way beholden to crown or kingdom unless he wanted to be, he really was a prince straight through.

Because he was wholly unaccustomed to being addressed in such a manner.

It had never occurred to him before this moment how very few people in his life dared address him with anything but the utmost respect. Yet today he had been punched in the face. And was now being spoken to in a manner he could only call flippant.

Pia swallowed as he stared at her, and then wrung her hands in a manner that suggested she was not, perhaps, as sanguine as she appeared.

Ares didn't much like what it said about him that he found that…almost comforting.

"Happily," she said in a low voice, "it doesn't matter whether you believe me or not. There is a selection of tests to choose from to determine paternity, both before and after birth."

"It is not a question of whether or not I believe you."

"I'm not sure I blame you," she said, as if he hadn't spoken. Another new experience for Ares. Especially as she sounded as if she was attempting to be *generous*. "I can see how such a thing would be difficult to believe if I was…like you."

Ares's brow rose and he suspected he looked like all those pictures of his lofty, patrician, infinitely regal ancestors. "Like me?"

"I doubt you remember the particulars of our night. Or me. And why would you? You must have such adventures all the time."

He might have been caught on the back foot since he'd arrived in Yorkshire this afternoon, but he wasn't foolish enough to answer that question.

"Here is what I don't understand," he said instead, as a sort of low, heated pounding started up in his chest, then arrowed out into his limbs. His sex. "You claim you were innocent before that night. Why? You're not a child."

"Do children prize chastity? Or is it their natural state?"

"I could not say if they prize it or do not," he growled. "I know I never did. I shrugged it off at the first opportunity. I was under the impression that was the entire purpose of the boarding schools I attended." He prowled toward her, keeping his eyes fast on hers. "Were you locked away in a convent, Pia?"

Something like humor flashed across her face. "Yes."

That startled him. He came to a stop before her. "An actual convent? Complete with nuns?"

"Of course with nuns. It couldn't very well be a convent without nuns, could it?"

"What on earth were you doing in a convent?"

She looked wry. "Protecting and defending my honor and holding fast to my chastity, of course. What else?"

"And what? The moment you walked through the convent doors into the big, bad world, you decided the time was ripe to rid yourself of that pesky hymen? With the first man you laid eyes upon?"

He ignored the other thing in him, dark and male,

that didn't like that idea. Because Ares was not accustomed to being *any man*, indistinguishable from the rest. Notable only because he was male.

"First I went to finishing school," Pia said, and for all that her eyes were too big, and her face was pale, Ares noticed that she didn't back down. "There I learned excruciatingly important things. A bit of political science and economics to pepper my banquet conversation, and how best to talk about books to make myself seem important and intellectual, yet approachable. I learned how to dance graciously, as befits a hostess and guest at any gathering. I learned the various degrees of curtsies, and when to employ them. I was meant to be a kind of weapon, you understand."

"I do not understand." But he was too close to her now. He couldn't seem to pull his eyes away from her. There was not one part of him that wanted to, for that matter, and he remembered that magnetic pull, that night. How could it still affect him? "But I'm feeling the effects of your bombshell, nonetheless."

"I graduated six months ago," Pia said quietly, her chin lifting as she held his gaze. "My friends and I decided to take a trip to New York to celebrate. One of my friends knew the person who was throwing that particular party. And there you were. See? There's nothing nefarious."

"Save the fact that I have had what I could only term an epic amount of sex in my lifetime, *cara*," he said, almost drawling the words. "But no one has ever turned up claiming I left them pregnant."

"I didn't actually 'turn up.' You did. Here. At my father's funeral." Her gray eyes glittered. "But by all means, let's brush that aside and continue to talk about your feelings."

"It is not a question of feelings," he said, through his teeth. "It is a question of what is possible and what is not."

She lifted a shoulder, then dropped it. "There is only one possible way I could have gotten pregnant. Because there was only the one night. And only the one man."

"But I do not—"

"Please." Those big, gray eyes implored him, though the hand she held up was rather more of a demand. "There's no point arguing about this. Why don't you give me your details and I'll arrange a test. No point discussing it further until then, is there?"

"Pia. You cannot imagine that I will simply wander off into the ether, can you?" He didn't know what possessed him. One moment he merely stood there a foot or so away from her. And in the next, his hands were on her delicate shoulders, holding her there as if she'd tried to walk away. When he should have wanted that. "Or is that what you want me to do?"

A strange expression moved over her face, darkening her eyes. That wry twist to her lips was back, and deeper this time.

"That's a question you need to ask yourself, I think," she said softly. "In the absence of a test, who's to say who the father is? I certainly won't say a thing, no matter who asks."

That dropped through Ares like a stone. A heavy weight, sharp and cold and jagged, sinking deep inside him.

He could turn around and leave, right now. His lip would heal. The tabloids would speculate, but then, they always did. If he didn't feed them, surely the stories would die away.

And he could carry on as he'd always intended. As he'd planned.

But despite himself, he thought of his mother.

Of how disappointed she would be in him if she were here.

Nothing had been more important to the queen than her family. Him. All she had ever wanted for him was a wife. A child.

He could shrug off his father's obsession with bloodlines without a second thought, and had. He'd shrugged off his father as easily.

But never his mother.

Never.

He realized his hands were still wrapped around Pia's shoulders. Her head was tipped back, and that belly of hers was between them.

And he wanted nothing to do with this. He wanted to turn back time, refuse to come to this funeral, or go back further and make sure he was nowhere near that party in Manhattan that night.

Even if that would have meant missing out on that taste of her that haunted him still, loathe as he was to admit it.

"There are two things you must know about me," he told her gruffly, as if he was making vows. "First, I have no intention of marrying. My father, the king, would love nothing more than to knock me out of the line of succession entirely. And I have done my best to help him with that, as it is preferable to playing his little games. And second, but just as important, I had no intention of ever having children."

"Is this the royal version of congratulations?" she asked, but her voice quivered. He could feel it inside him, like shame. "It needs a little work."

"I want no part of this," he told her, dark and sure. "But I will do my duty. One way or another."

Ares wasn't sure what he meant by that. All he could seem to concentrate on was that he'd moved too close to her without meaning to. His mouth hovered worryingly close to hers. He could so easily tilt himself forward and help himself to those lips of hers, impossibly sweet and soft and *right there*—

But Pia twisted her shoulders and stepped back, out of his grip. He could have held her fast, and knew full well he shouldn't have felt a sense of heroism that he hadn't. And then he felt something far worse crawl through him as her hands went to cover her belly.

As if she was protecting her child from him.

His child, if what she said was true.

"I haven't asked you for anything," she said, very distinctly. Quiet, but sure. "Including your reluctant, begrudging sense of duty, thank you very much."

The door behind them opened, and Ares turned, astonished that anyone would dare interrupt him.

It was a day for astonishment, it seemed.

"Your Highness," the head of his security detail said, bowing his head apologetically. "I'm afraid there is a situation with the paparazzi. We must go."

CHAPTER FOUR

PIA FELT AS IF she had whiplash. Everything had been in hideous slow motion at her father's graveside, but now, it was as if events were tumbling of their own accord. A glance out the window showed the scrum of reporters, all shouting and shoving. Her gut felt much the same.

She felt as if she was a train on a broken track, careening out of control.

Though she knew better. There was no train. Events weren't carrying on of their own volition. And while she might feel out of control, that didn't make it so.

It was him.

Prince Ares.

His name was not Eric. It had never been Eric. And now that she knew who he was, she couldn't quite imagine how she'd believed he was just…some guy. That he was royal appeared stamped deep into him, today. How had she missed it in New York? It was the way he stood. It was the way he lifted that imperious brow of his. It was the way he assumed command, instantly.

He drew her back from the window. He barked out an order to his guard, then returned his considerable attention to her, green and gold and grave.

How had she convinced herself there was anything *regular* about this man at all?

"We cannot get to the bottom of this here," he told her in a tone that matched the expression on his face. And made everything in her careen about all the more. "You will have to come with me."

"Come with you?" she repeated, dazed. "What do you mean? Where?"

But Ares did not wait for her acquiescence. Perhaps he assumed it wasn't necessary. Perhaps, where he came from, agreement with his every whim and desire was the law of the land. He certainly acted as if it was. He strode off, his long legs eating up the floor of the library in only a few strides. And then he stopped at the door, turning back to her with that astonished, arrogant look of his.

"Pia. That is your name, is it not?"

In case she'd forgotten that every single part of this situation shamed her and humiliated her.

"It is, yes," she said, threading her fingers together and making herself smile the way she'd been taught. Serene and smooth. "And in all the confusion and violence, I believe I missed your formal introduction. You are…?"

She watched that hit him, like a slap. He blinked as if it had never occurred to him that any person alive might not know precisely who he was—suggesting that he'd thought she was only pretending not to know him in New York.

Pia should have been more sympathetic. After all, she knew what it was like to be known, often when she would have preferred to be anonymous. She knew what it was like to have an inescapable family identity that followed her around and often preceded her. And possibly, if she had been a better sort of person, she wouldn't have taken such enjoyment in watching Ares's struggle.

Alas.

"I am His Royal Highness, Crown Prince Ares of Atilia. Duke of this, Earl of that. But no need to address me by my full title. Ares will do."

He certainly didn't appear the least bit ashamed that he could have spent a night like that with someone and not know their name. Pia resolved she should feel no shame herself.

And while she couldn't quite get there, she could certainly fake it. She lifted her chin and tried to exude a sunniness she didn't quite feel.

"It's lovely to meet you, at last," she said. "But you should know that I have no intention of going off somewhere with you. I did just meet you, after all."

And she remembered every scandalous searingly hot detail of the night she'd spent with him. She had seen all kinds of expressions cross his face. She had seen him laugh, go tense and hot, shatter.

But she had never seen him look *dangerous* until now.

"You do not understand, so allow me to enlighten you." His voice was almost as striking as that expression on his face. Dark. Powerful. Nothing lazy or offhand about him, and his green eyes blazed. "You have made a claim to the throne of the kingdom of Atilia. If what you say is true, you are pregnant with my child."

"What does it matter?" she asked, with a brazen sort of calmness she did not feel. "You said you have no intention of marrying. And so what if you have illegitimate children? Don't all kings litter them about, here and there, down through the history books?"

His perfect, sculpted lips thinned and if possible, his gaze grew hotter. And more dangerous. "Atilia is an ancient kingdom, bound by ancient rules. I cannot imagine you truly want a lesson in our laws and customs regarding succession."

"I'm certain I didn't ask for a lesson in anything."

He ignored that. Or didn't care, more likely. "Legitimate issue takes precedence over illegitimate issue. But only if they are male."

"What a shock."

"I am next in line to the throne. Any legitimate child of mine would ascend that throne after me. In the absence of children, a line of succession would move on. Either to any children my father's second wife produces, or to my cousin. If any children I have are illegitimate, they would precede my father's second round of children only if my father had girls."

"That is a fascinating history lesson. Thank you." She smiled at him still, though it felt more…fixed, somehow. "An alternative would be for you to go away. And never tell anyone. I will do the same. And we will never again talk about *issue*."

Or anything else, she thought stoutly. And waited to feel relief rush in.

But instead, she felt something far more bittersweet flood her, though she couldn't quite name it.

"I'm afraid it is much too late for that, Pia," Ares said, with that quiet power of his that shook through her no matter how solid she told herself she was. "Because speculation already exists. Reporters clamor outside even now. What they cannot learn for certain, they will make up to suit themselves."

"You must know the folly of living your life by what the tabloids say," she chided him. Gently.

"I never have."

"Wonderful." She smiled. "Then no need to start now."

"You said yourself that you have never appeared in the tabloids before. There is no reason to throw yourself in the midst of a nasty little scrum of them, like a bone to pick."

If Pia didn't know better, she might have been tempted to think he was trying to protect her.

"More than that, there were reporters who heard you make your claim," Ares said. He shook his head. "Do you know nothing of the history of this planet? Wars have been fought for much less than a claim to a throne."

"You talk about war a lot," she said, and felt herself flush when his gaze turned considering. "In case you were unaware."

"I am a prince. One of my main roles in this life is preventing wars from ever taking place. One way to do that is to conduct my private affairs *in private*." He inclined his head, though Pia was aware it was a command and not a sign of obedience or surrender. "My car awaits."

"And if I refuse to get into it with you?"

"I have a security detail who will put you in the vehicle, no matter your protests. But you know this." Again, that dark, considering look that seemed to peel her open. "Is that what you want? Plausible deniability?"

For a moment, Pia didn't know what she wanted. She

felt the way she had when her doctor had come into the exam room and told her the news. Pia had been fairly certain she was dying of something. All those strange cramps. The fact that she kept getting sick. She was certain something was eating her away from the inside out.

It had never occurred to her that she could be pregnant. The word itself hadn't made sense.

She'd made the doctor repeat herself three times.

Looking at Ares, here in the library of Combe Manor where she had spent so much of her childhood, was much the same.

That train kept jumping the tracks and hurtling away into the messy night, no matter how still she stood or how gracefully she tried to hold herself together.

But she could hear her brother's clipped tone from the other side of the door, issuing his own orders. She'd seen that scrum of ravenous reporters out in front of the house, clamoring for a comment and ready to pounce.

"Let me tell you what sort of life you will lead," her mother had said in the days following her graduation from finishing school, right here in this very same manor house, stuffed full of pictures of all the battle-hardened Combes who had charged out of their circumstances and had *made something of themselves*, no matter what.

Pia knew she was meant to feel deeply proud of them all. When instead, all that desperate clawing for purchase made her feel…tired. And unequal to the task.

"Am I supposed to know what to do with my life?" Pia had asked. "I can't seem to make up my mind."

"It's not for you to decide, dear girl," said her mother, who only called Pia *dear* when she was in one of her less affectionate moods. Pia had sat straighter, waiting for the inevitable other shoe to fall. "Your father has gone to a tremendous amount of trouble to make you into the perfect heiress. Biddable and sweet enough. Reasonably accomplished in the classic sense of the term. And very, very wealthy, of course."

It had seemed wiser not to say anything. Pia had sat there at the breakfast table off the kitchen where her mother drank her hot water and lemon, murmured about how refreshed she felt with each sip, and raised her brows at Pia's slice of toast with a bit of creamery butter.

Which was to say, it was a normal breakfast at Combe Manor. Pia could have drunk the hot lemon water herself, but she'd long ago learned that it was better to disappoint her mother as early in the day as possible, so there could be no grand expectations over the course of the day she would then fail to meet.

Alexandrina had let her gaze sweep over her daughter as if she was sizing her up for market. "You will work in some or other worthy charity that we will vet, of course. You will dedicate yourself to your good works for a year, perhaps two. Then I imagine your father will suggest a suitor. He might even allow you to pick one. From a preselected group, of course."

"You make it sound as if he plans to marry me off."

Pia had spent much of her life despairing over the fact that while she had the same dark hair and gray eyes as her mother, Alexandrina's all…came together. She was simply beautiful, always, no matter what. It was a fact, not a to-do list. Pia had the raw material, but she was put together wrong. No matter how hard she tried to glide about, exuding effortless beauty.

"Dear girl, your brother will run the business," Alexandrina had replied, as if Pia had said something amusing. "He is already in line to do so. You are here to be decorative, or if not precisely decorative—" the look she'd slid at her daughter had been a knife, true, but Pia had been so used to the cut of it she hadn't reacted at all "—you can be *useful*. How will you accomplish this, do you think?"

Pia hadn't had an answer for her. Her accomplishments, such as they were, had always been a serene collection of tidy, unobjectionable nouns. She'd no idea how one launched off into a verb.

"What did you do?" she asked her mother instead.

She already knew the story, of course. Her father liked to belt it out at cocktail parties. Alexandrina had been set to marry some stuffy old title of her father's choosing, but then she'd met Eddie. First they'd made headlines. Then they'd made history, uniting the brash, upstart Combe fortune with the traditional gentility of the San Giacomos.

Pia rather doubted that an epic love story was in the cards for her. Epic love was the sort of thing that *just happened* to women like her mother, and led to decades of *true love*. Which in the San Giacomo/Combe family had always meant operatic battles, intense reunions, and a revolving door of scandals and sins. Pia had always thought that, really, she'd be quite happy to find herself *reasonably content*.

"You and I are not the same," Alexandrina had said softly that day, something making her gray eyes glitter. "And I can see that you think I'm being cruel to you. I am not."

"Of course not," Pia had agreed, staring at her plate and wishing she could truly rebel and order a stack of toast instead of her one, lonely slice. But she only dared antagonize her mother—who despaired over Pia's sturdy figure, inherited from the Combe side of the family and suitable for factory work, not fashion—so far. "I don't think that at all."

"We have wrapped you up in cotton wool as a gift, Pia," Alexandrina had intoned. "Always remember that."

Pia remembered it, all right. She'd decided she wanted no part of any cotton wool, so she'd charged right out and shed it in New York. Enough with *nouns*, she'd thought. She wanted to be about *verbs*, for a change.

And look what that had got her.

"You look as if you're mulling over a very important decision," Ares said, still watching her from the door. "But you must realize that you have no choice here."

"It's out of the frying pan, into the fire."

Pia hadn't meant to say that out loud. But there it was, dancing between them.

Ares didn't reply with words. He only inclined his head in that way of his, that she already knew was him at his most *royal*. Too royal to live, really.

And Pia thought of her father, blustering and brash Eddie Combe, who had called her names and then died. She would never see him smile at her again. She would never stand there while he blustered and bullied, then softened. He would never pat her on the head the way he had when she was small and tell her things like, *Buck up, girl. Combes don't cry.*

But another thing her father had said, so famously

that the vicar had quoted him in the service today, was that if the worst was coming, you might as well walk into it like a man rather than waiting for it to come at you as it pleased.

Control the conversation, Eddie liked to say. And had said, often.

And then did.

Pia told herself that was why she moved then, walking across library floor as if she was doing the bidding of her unexpected prince. That was why she followed after him, ignoring her brother and their guests as his staff led them through the manor house, down and around to the servants' entrance, far away from the mess of reporters out front. That was why she got into the car that waited for them there, meekly and obediently, and sat next to Prince Ares as he drove her away.

It wasn't capitulation, she assured herself. She was *controlling the conversation.*

And it certainly had nothing at all to do with the way looking at those green eyes of his made her heart thump wildly in her chest.

Or that melting feeling everywhere else.

CHAPTER FIVE

PIA REGRETTED HER impulsiveness the moment the car started moving.

She regretted it as they left Combe Manor behind, taking the little-used back road off the hill and leaving the paparazzi—and her brother, and her entire life—behind them.

Pia told herself she was only getting a few tests. That she wasn't leaving anything, not for long. That this would all be perfectly fine once she and Ares were on the same page and plans were made for the future.

But she couldn't shake the sense of foreboding that squatted on her, there on the smooth leather seats of the royal town car.

The car swept them off to a private airfield, and Pia dutifully trooped up the stairs into the jet that waited there, assuming that the prince would take them off to London. Where there were doctors aplenty who could administer the necessary tests, and give him the answers she already had, but he needed to see on official letterhead of some sort or another.

She told herself that she didn't mind that he needed proof. After all, wasn't that at the crux of all this? He didn't know her. She didn't know him. That would perhaps suggest that they shouldn't have slept together, but they had, and it was only to be expected that he would require proof. Even if he really had been just some guy named Eric.

But the sound of the jet engines lulled her to sleep, and when Pia woke again because the air pressure was making her ears pop, she felt as if she'd been sleeping for a very long time.

"Where are we?" she asked sleepily, because a glance out the window into the dark didn't show the mess of lights she would expect above a city like London.

Ares sat across from her on one of the royal jet's low, gold-embossed leather couches.

"We will be landing shortly," he said, without looking up from his tablet.

Pia always forgot that her body had changed, and kept changing. She went to sit upright and struggled a bit, certain that she looked as ungainly and inelegant as she felt.

"Yes, but where?" she asked, hoping her businesslike tone would divert attention away from what her mother would have called her *persistent ungainliness.* "That can't be London, can it?"

Down below the plane, there were great expanses of darkness, and a few lights. They were headed toward the light, but it was far too contained to be a city.

"It is not London," Ares said, something in his voice making her turn her head around to look at him directly. "It is the kingdom of Atilia. My home, after a fashion. I'm taking you to the Southern Palace."

"But… Why on earth would you take me…?"

"Where did you imagine I would take you?"

He considered her, and she became *aware*—in a hot rush that made her cheeks flare into red—that they were, for all intents and purposes, alone in this compartment of his plane. His security detail had stayed in the main bit, while Ares had escorted her here and closed the door. She had no idea how she had possibly slept so deeply when Ares was right here, taking up all the oxygen.

And that was all before she started thinking about the ways this man could *take* her.

Not to mention the ways he already had.

"I assumed, reasonably enough, that we would pop down to London."

"London is far too exposed. Here in the islands I can control who sees you and me together, what conclusions they might draw, and so on. And I can have my own doctors administer any tests."

"I didn't bring anything," Pia protested. And when that aristocratic brow of his rose, as if she wasn't making any sense, she felt her face get hotter. She cleared her throat. "Like a passport."

"I am the Crown Prince," Ares said dryly. "I do not suffer bureaucracy."

"Because you are the bureaucracy?"

She regretted that. Especially when all he did was fix that overtly calm green gaze on her, making her want to squirm about in her seat. She refrained. Barely.

"And after I take all the tests you need me to take?" She blinked a few times, trying to clear her head. And the sleep from her eyes. "My life is in England."

"If by some chance you are truly carrying my child

and the unexpected heir to the kingdom of Atilia," he said, with something far too complicated to be simple temper in his voice, "then you can be certain that life as you know it has changed irrevocably."

"Well, of course it has," Pia said. Crossly, she could admit. "But it has nothing to do with you. Impending motherhood generally changes a girl, I think you'll find. It's fairly universal."

The jet was dropping closer to those lights below, and Pia felt something like panic clawing at her. Maybe that was why she didn't wait for him to answer her.

"You can't spirit me away to an island and keep me there, Ares," she said instead. But if she was looking for some kind of softness on his face, there was none to be found. He could as easily have been carved from marble. "You know that, don't you? That's all well and good in the average fairy tale, but this is real life."

"I keep trying to explain to you who I am," Ares said quietly. Almost apologetically, which made every hair on her body feel as if it stood on its end. Because he was the least apologetic creature she had ever met. "I have never been a good prince, it is true, but I'm a prince nonetheless. And we have entered my kingdom, where my word is law. I am afraid that you will discover that I can do as I like."

"But—"

"Call it a fairy tale if you like, *cara mia*," he murmured. "If it helps."

It did not help.

That panic continued to claw at her as the jet landed. As Pia was marched off—escorted, she supposed, and politely, but it all felt rather more kidnap-ish than it had before—and bundled into yet another gleaming car. This time they were driven along a precipitous coastal road that hugged the looming hills on one side and dropped off toward the sea on the other. They skirted around the side of the island, until they came upon what looked to Pia like a perfect fairy-tale castle.

Just in case she didn't already feel as if she'd stumbled into the pages of a storybook already.

It rose as if from a pop-up children's book, blazing with light as it sat up over the sea on a jutting bit of hillside. It even had turrets.

"What is this place?" she managed to ask, half-convinced she was still dreaming.

"It is the Southern Palace, as I said," Ares said from beside her in the car's wide backseat. "If, as I suspect, you are merely pregnant yet not with any child of mine, you will stay here only as long as it takes you to sign the appropriate legal documentation that asserts you have no claim to the throne of my kingdom. And never will."

"I don't want your throne. Or your kingdom."

"Then it will all go very quickly." He turned then, the light from the palace as they approached the first wall beaming into the car and making him gleam. Making him even more beautiful, which was unhelpful. "But if, by some miracle, what you say is true? Then allow me to be the first to welcome you to your new home, Pia. You can expect to be here for some time."

"Once again," she said, working hard to keep her voice calm when she felt nothing but that panic inside her, shredding her, "you might be a prince and this might be your kingdom—"

"There is no *might*, Pia. I am who I say I am."

"Well, *Eric*," she replied, glaring at him, "you cannot actually kidnap women and hold them captive in your palace, no matter who you say you are. I think you'll find it's generally frowned upon."

Ares settled back in his seat as the car slipped into some kind of courtyard, then continued under a grand archway that led deeper beneath the palace. And if he was bothered by the name she'd used—the name he'd given her in New York—he didn't show it.

"You are welcome to register a complaint," he said after a moment, as if he'd taken some time to consider the matter. "In this case, your only recourse would be the king."

And he let out a laugh at that, which was not exactly encouraging.

Still, Pia kept glaring at him. "Is he more reasonable than you? He would have to be, I'd think. You could take me to him right now."

Ares laughed again. "My father is not a safe space," he assured her. "For you, or anyone else."

The car finally came to a stop. And Pia couldn't help the sense of doom that washed over her then. It was that same clawing panic, and something more. Something that made her heart ache.

Ares exited the vehicle with an athletic grace Pia would have preferred not to notice, nodding at the guards who waited there.

Her heart in her throat, Pia followed him, climbing out of the car to find herself in yet another courtyard. She was surrounded on all sides by thick castle walls. Far above was the night sky, riddled with stars. And it had never occurred to her before that there could only really be turrets where there were steep walls all around. That turrets belonged to fortresses, like this one.

But there were no walls steeper and more formidable than the man who stood there, watching her much too intensely as she looked around at her lovely, remote, fairy-tale prison.

Ares. Her prince.

Her jailer.

And whether he was prepared to accept it or not, the man who'd gotten her pregnant.

"I don't want to be here," she told him. But quietly.

"I do not want women wandering about the planet, telling people that I have left them pregnant when I have taken great care never to do such a thing," he replied, almost too easily. "Life does not often give us what we want, Pia."

"If you insist on keeping me here for the moment, I want an exit strategy. I want to know how and when and—"

"If I were you," Ares said, his voice low, "I would be very careful about making any demands."

He moved one finger, and a smartly dressed woman appeared before them as if by magic. "This is Marbella. She will be your chief aide. If you have any questions, you may address them to her."

And he didn't wait for her answer. He simply strode off, princely and remote, his footsteps echoing against the stone until they disappeared.

Pia watched him go, much longer than she should have, and then turned to face the woman who waited at her side.

If she expected a friendly chat, or even a smile, she was disappointed. The other woman bowed slightly, then beckoned Pia to follow her as she set off in a completely different direction into the palace. Each room they passed was more fanciful than the last. Everything was open, airy. Though it was dark, Pia could still sense the ocean all around them. The seething. The whispering. As if it was just there, around the next corner, out of reach—

Marbella led her down a very long corridor that opened up this way and that into galleries and salons, all of them lit up and done in bright, cheerful sort of colors that she imagined did nothing but encourage the sun to linger.

"Who lives here?" she asked after they'd walked a while.

"The Southern Palace has been the preferred retreat of the royal family for centuries, madam," Marbella replied with severe formality. "His Highness is the only member of the family who uses it with any regularity these days, though even he has not been here in some time."

"Does that mean no one else is here?" She thought about what he had said by the car. "Is the king here?"

She thought the other woman stiffened, but that seemed unlikely, given how straight she already stood. "His Majesty resides and remains in the Northern Palace, madam."

Pia nodded sagely, as if she knew the first thing about Atilia, its geography, or its palaces.

Marbella led her on until they reached a beautiful suite of rooms that was to be Pia's for the duration.

Pia did not ask how long that duration was expected to last.

Inside her suite, she found a selection of clothes laid out for her use, that she supposed had to have been flown in from somewhere. She flushed, trying to imagine how Ares had come by the measurements. Had he measured her while she slept? Or did he simply…remember her? And had only added a bit of pregnancy weight to his estimate?

It was amazing how red her face could get at the slightest provocation.

She was grateful when the other woman retreated, leaving her to a glorious set of rooms that she suspected overlooked the water, not that it mattered. A prison was a prison, surely, no matter the view.

Pia took out her phone, was delighted to find she had service, and quickly pulled up what she could find on the kingdom of Atilia. And better still, the Southern Palace.

The palace where she sat was on the southernmost island of the kingdom. What population there was here was spread out across the island in the small villages dotting it. The palace, on the other hand, had been carved out of the side of the mountain as a kind of folly for a long-ago queen. It looked like a fairy-tale castle, but it was, as Pia had felt when she'd looked around, a nearly inviable fortress. There was the Ionian Sea in front and a mountain in back, with only one road in and out.

If anything, she'd been underplaying what was happening here.

The man who had impregnated her was a prince. She

had hardly had time to take that on board. But in case she'd had any doubt, the castle put it to rest. Everything he'd said to her was true.

Ares was a prince. *The* prince. And he had every intention of holding her here.

Until and unless he felt like letting her go.

She was still in her funeral garb when the doctors came, an hour or so later. They'd set up their own makeshift exam room in the palace, and Pia thought about fighting it. Because she, after all, knew what the test was going to say. Surely there had to be a way to keep this from happening. She could refuse to submit herself to the examination…

But she knew without asking, or trying, that there was little point. Ares would keep her here either way until he had his answers. No matter what those answers were.

That runaway train barreled across uneven ground, far off the track, hurtling Pia right along with it.

And the funeral garb felt fitting, really, as she sat in one of the many brightly lit sitting rooms with Ares after the doctors were done with her, awaiting the results.

He stood by one of the open, arched windows that were really doors, looking out at the dark expanse of the ocean. The air this far south was thicker. It insinuated itself against her skin like a caress—but she told herself it was only the humidity. She sat, very primly, on the sofa and tried to keep herself calm.

She *tried.*

The door opened after what seemed like several eternities. Possibly more. All passed in the same tense silence.

Ares turned and the doctor bowed low. "Congratulations, Your Highness," the man said. "You are indeed the father."

Pia couldn't seem to look away from Ares's face. That arrested expression. Something cold and bleak in his gaze.

It made her heart flip over, then sink.

But the doctor wasn't finished. Because of course he wasn't finished. Pia braced herself.

"They are both male," the doctor said.

There was a short, electric pause.

"Both?" Ares asked, his voice a slap.

Neither the doctor nor Ares so much as glanced at Pia, and still she felt as exposed and vulnerable as if she'd been stripped naked and pinned to the wall.

"*Both?*" Ares asked again.

And the words Pia knew were coming sounded to her like bullets when they came, as inevitable and terrible as they'd been when she'd heard them for the first time.

"Yes, Your Highness." The doctor bowed lower. "It is my great honor to inform you that you have been blessed with twins."

CHAPTER SIX

THERE WAS NOTHING but white noise in Ares's head.

A long, sort of flat-line noise that he was fairly certain signaled his own end.

For what else could it be?

Twins.

Twin boys.

He couldn't make the words make any sense. The doctor retreated and Ares stared at Pia as if he could see through that black dress she wore. As if he could see inside of her, where there were *twins*. Boys.

Sons.

Ares's head pounded like a terrible hangover, when he couldn't recall the last time he'd drank to excess. His throat felt dry and scratchy, as if he'd caught a virus and was on the verge of tipping over into misery. He thought it was possible that he shook, too, though he couldn't tell whether that was in him or around him—and he couldn't seem to catch his breath long enough to truly make the determination.

What did it matter what shook? She was carrying twins.

His twins. His sons. *His.*

When he finally raised his gaze from her belly and

the impossibility—*two* impossibilities—she carried even now, Pia was still sitting there on the ancient settee that had stood precisely where it was now as long as anyone could remember. Her legs were demurely crossed at the ankles. Her hands were folded neatly in her lap. She gazed back at him, her eyes big and gray and solemn, and fixed on him in a manner that made him…restless.

"Some people might be offended by your reaction," she said quietly, into all that white noise and shake inside him. "But I'm not. My own reaction to the news was very much the same."

"Twins," he managed to say, though his tongue felt tied in knots. "*Twins.*"

She had the grace to look faintly abashed. "You claimed you couldn't have impregnated me with one baby. You were certain. I didn't see what throwing the reality that it was twins into the mix would accomplish."

Ares couldn't argue with that, which made him even more… Whatever he was. He ran a hand over his face, wincing when his palm hit his lip. He'd already forgotten that her older brother had punched him. Matteo, he'd learned on the flight, when he'd finally read the informational one-sheet his aides had prepared for him before the funeral. Matteo Combe, president and CEO of Combe Industries…though the tabloids were having a field day with the punch he'd thrown, even calling him unfit for his own office.

It seemed quaint, almost. A remnant of a former life.

A life where Ares could not possibly have been facing down the fact he'd gotten a woman pregnant. With *twins*.

"Well," Pia said, a bit too brightly. "Perhaps you had better explain to me how you think this imprisonment is going to work."

"How far along are you?" he heard himself ask.

She blinked, then tilted her head slightly to one side.

"I remember you, Pia," Ares retorted, his voice tight. "But I failed to mark that particular night down in my diary."

"Six months," she replied, the lack of inflection in her voice an indictment all its own.

But he was more focused on the span of time. Six months. It made his head swim. And it meant…

"So you will… That is to say, we will…"

He couldn't say the words out loud. Was he sweating?

"In a few months," she said. "But babies are tricky. They do what they like. And I'm told twins tend to come sooner rather than later."

"In the history of this kingdom, there have never been twins."

She dared to look amused. "Ever? Really? In the course of how many thousands of years?"

He thought his growl might have been audible, then. "In the royal family, I should say. There have only ever been single births."

"They say it skips a generation," she offered, helpfully. She studied him for a moment. "My father's aunts were twins."

"Twins," Ares said again.

As if, were he to say the word enough, it would change things, somehow.

Pia stood then, then smoothed out the front of her dress, though it required no smoothing.

"I don't think we're going to have a conversation with much sense in it tonight," she said quietly. Kindly, even, which made him want to…do things. "I suppose that even if you released me on the spot, there would be no leaving here before morning. Why don't we talk about this then. When you've slept on the news and let it settle a bit."

"What do you imagine there is to talk about?" Ares scarcely sounded like himself. "You have… This has…"

"Yes," she said, sounding faintly amused in a way he didn't care for. At all. "You've caught me. I schemed to get pregnant. And to get pregnant with twins, no less. I hunted you down, cold-bloodedly used you to do my evil will, and then, as a coup de grâce, I went away and never contacted you again. Because secretly I knew that my father would drop dead and you would show up at his funeral—"

"I am trying very hard not to blame you for this," Ares told her, and his voice, like the rest of him, was tight and taut and not him at all.

She gave the distinct impression of laughing at him without actually doing so. "That's very kind of you. Because as I recall, we were both there. Unless you'd like to pretend that you, in fact, are a twin and *Eric* is the real father?"

Ares wished that *Eric* was a real person, so he could knock him out.

"I don't understand how this is possible," he said. Possibly not for the first—or fifth—time. "I am a man who enjoys sex, I grant you. But I had no intention of procreating. Ever. I have never been anything less than scrupulous about protection."

She made a sympathetic noise, though she didn't look the least bit sympathetic. "Did you have a vasectomy, then?"

It seemed that Pia was the one delivering knockout blows tonight.

"I did not," Ares said. Stiffly.

"As it turns out, a vasectomy is only 99.9 percent effective. People do still get pregnant after them, though it's rare."

"I've just said I never had one." And he had stopped explaining himself decades ago, yet he felt the strangest urge to leap to his own defense now. "I suppose I might have gotten round to it, eventually."

The fact he'd been so adamantly opposed to procreating and yet hadn't taken steps to ensure he couldn't seemed, now, like the very height of foolishness. What had he been thinking? He had been so certain his blood was poisoned, given the example his father had always set of what happened when their long line of royals met the crown. He had been so clear about the fact he wouldn't risk poisoning any children himself, to end the misery with him. And yet…

"I've had a few months to research protection in a panic, as I, too, failed to understand how this happened," Pia told him in the same calmly informative way that made his teeth grind together. "And as it turns out, as they told us in the convent, the only version of protection that is one hundred percent effective is abstinence."

She even smiled faintly as she said that. And something in Ares turned over, bright with temper.

"Do you think this is entertaining?" he demanded,

his voice hardly more than a growl. "I understand that you didn't plan this. Yet it has happened anyway, apparently. And you have had months to come to terms with it. To make your little jokes about abstinence. But my world ended tonight, Pia."

And he watched, in that sickening mix of dismay and shame, and fury, too, as she slid her hands down over her belly as if she wanted to protect her children.

From him.

Ares shouldn't have cared about something like that.

But it turned out, he did.

"You're not the only person whose world ended today," she threw at him. "In case you've forgotten, you didn't discover this news at a garden party. That was my father's funeral. And thank you for asking, but both of my parents, in fact, were less than thrilled about this. I had the distinct pleasure of telling them that I got pregnant from a tawdry one-night stand with a total stranger. That went over very well. My father called me a tart."

"How can you possibly be a tart if the only man you've ever slept with is me?" Ares asked, and had no idea what that *thing* was that roared about in him. Almost as if he wanted to defend this woman against her own, dead father.

"I think it was the unmarried, pregnant, and no idea who the father was part that got to him," Pia replied. "But then he died a few days later, so I didn't get a chance to follow up on that."

But Ares was still stuck on the fact that she had never touched another man.

Something kicked in him. Something that wasn't

the fact he had *children* coming, like it or not. *Twins.* Something that wasn't all the ramifications of that he couldn't quite face. Not quite yet.

Something that felt a good deal more primitive.

He moved toward her, watching the way her eyes widened. But better still was that little kick of awareness he could see flicker in all that solemn gray.

"No man but me," he said.

"Yes," she said, her voice shakier and much less calm than it had been a moment before. "That is correct."

"You didn't tell me that night."

"Well. You know." Her face was red. Even the tips of her ears were red. "It didn't seem relevant."

He prowled even closer.

"You went to an actual convent. Then a finishing school. And straight after that, you found me in an otherwise forgettable party in Manhattan."

She looked as if she wanted to make a break for it, but stood fast. "That is the sum total of my life thus far, yes. Lucky me."

"I remember you, Pia," he said, his voice low and much too dark, and her eyes widened in response.

But he couldn't seem to help that. Just as he couldn't seem to help himself from reaching out and taking her chin in his hand.

As if she was his.

He expected her to jerk her face away from his hold, but she didn't. And he watched, mesmerized—fascinated—as her pulse went wild in her neck.

Her breathing grew labored. But what intrigued Ares was that he could feel her, inside him. He could feel the kick. The heat. Like touching her was sticking his fingers into an electrical socket, sending sparks showering through him.

"I remember you," he said again, intent and sure, and threaded through with all that electricity. "You flowed over me like water. No hesitation, no concern."

"Perhaps I was significantly drunk," she said, her voice tart, but he could see the softness in her gaze. The melting heat.

"No," he said, remembering. "You were not."

"Perhaps that's what it's always like. I assumed it was. All that…" Her cheeks pinkened even further. "Flowing."

"No," Ares said again, though he sounded too hot, too dark. "That is not what it's like. Not normally."

It had all seemed easy, to his recollection. As if they had been meant to meet like that, then come together in such a glorious, heedless rush. She had arched into his hands as if she'd done it a thousand times before. He'd found her mouth and the place where she was greediest, then tasted both. Her cries had broken over him as if it was a dance they'd practiced a hundred times. More. She had felt explosive in his hands. A glorious, greedy burst of light and sensation.

But more than that, he'd thought when he'd first surged deep inside her and she'd shaken all around him, familiar.

The word that had echoed in his head then was the reason he'd made no effort to seek her out afterward, no matter how often he'd thought of her since.

Home.

Ares, of course, had no home. He'd walked away from his kingdom and had no intention of assuming his throne. Any home he'd had, he'd buried with his mother.

Homes were for other men. Men who deserved them.

Men who were not poisoned with the blood of the Atilian royal family.

He ordered himself to drop his hand. To step back. To put more distance between him and this woman who had shaken him months ago, and here, now, might as well have been a full-scale tsunami.

But he didn't let go the way he knew he should. And instead of stepping back, he moved forward.

"Perhaps we should test it," he said.

"Test what?" She frowned at him. "The last time we tested something I ended up pregnant. With twins."

"Remind me how that happened," he dared her, low and dark.

And it didn't make any sense. He shouldn't want to be anywhere near her, not when his worst nightmare was playing out before him, inside her—

But he couldn't seem to help himself.

Ares bent and pressed his mouth to hers.

And the heat kicked through him, wild and hot. It lit him up, reminding him of that night in Manhattan while it stormed through him, new and mad.

He wasn't satisfied with the press of lips, so he angled his head, taking the kiss deeper. Making it dangerous. Making it clear how easy it had been to go from a conversation at a party to that very long night that had resulted in…this.

He pulled her to him, sliding his hands over her shoulders, then down her back.

And she kissed him back, meeting the thrust of his

tongue. She pressed against him as if she, too, wanted to get closer. Her hands came up and found his chest, and he could feel her belly between them, pushing into him, and that, surely, should have woken him up from the spell—

But instead, Ares kissed her deeper. Harder.

He slid his hands between them and felt the insistent mound of her belly himself.

Her belly. His babies.

And she was the one who wrenched her mouth from his then.

Everything was jumbled around inside of Ares. He had never put his hands on a pregnant woman's belly before. He'd certainly never done so with the knowledge that the babes within were *his*.

It should have disgusted him. He'd always been so revolted at the very idea of fathering a child.

Or maybe it was his own father who had revolted him, now he considered it.

And this was Pia, with her wide eyes, and that generous mouth that drove him crazy. Her taste was in his mouth again, making him wild. Making him hard. Making him feel like someone else entirely.

Someone who put his hands on a woman's belly, understood what he felt there were his own sons—*sons*—and felt a deep, possessive thrill at the notion—

What the hell was happening to him?

All of it was wrong. It was as if he'd been taken over by a different man. A stranger. And yet Ares didn't step away. He didn't even drop his hands. He felt that possessiveness in his chest. His sex.

"I don't think this is the answer to the situation we're

in," Pia said, though her voice wasn't any steadier than he felt. "I think sex has already caused enough trouble, don't you?"

"I don't know that there are any answers," Ares replied. "We might as well console ourselves with the one thing we appear to be so good at."

"I…don't know how to respond to that. I don't have any context."

"Then you'll have to take my word for it." He moved his hands over her bump, telling himself it meant nothing. That he was relearning her shape, that was all. That the fact his palms could not contain her belly, much less the lives within it, didn't matter to him at all. "We are very, very good at it."

And something shifted in him, turning over too fast. Ares found he could no longer tell what, precisely, he meant by that. He was talking about sex, surely. Wasn't he?

But Pia was clearly not inclined to parse the nuances. She stepped back further, almost running into the settee behind her in her haste. And he couldn't deny that there was something in him that took immense satisfaction in the fact that he affected her in this way.

Because no one else had ever touched her. Only him.

That primitive thing inside him, heretofore wholly unknown to him, stirred again.

Her lips were swollen from his kiss. Her body was swollen with not one, but two of his children.

And he might not want to accept what that meant. He might find all of this impossible and bewildering in turn, no matter what the doctor had said. But Ares couldn't deny that the sight of her, lushly fertile and entirely his, made him…

Deeply, darkly triumphant, on a level he hadn't known existed.

"No," she said, very distinctly.

"No?"

"Whatever that look on your face is. Whatever it is, no. I want no part of it."

"But all bets are off now, are they not?" He felt…ferocious. "I am a man who never planned to have children, yet you are carrying two, and they are mine. Who knows what else we think we cannot have, or do not want, that will happen here against our will?"

"I have no intention of spending the next few months trapped here," she told him, in that same sober, serious way. "You now know that you're the father of these babies. *My* babies. I'm glad. That wasn't a secret I meant to keep from you in the first place. But now that you know, there's no need for all these…" She looked around the room, and waved her hand as if to take it all in, and the whole of the palace besides. "All these royal shenanigans."

Ares had never felt the weight of the Atilian crown more than he did in the moment she dismissed it, and so easily.

"Here's the problem, Pia," he said, feeling as growly and uneven as he sounded. "I cannot decide what to do with you."

"I don't recall signing myself over into your care. You don't decide what happens to me. I do."

"You are a quandary," he told her, and the things that roared inside him were loud again. They competed with each other. They were made of furor and fang, and over and over again, they drew blood. That damned blood of his. "I have to decide how to proceed."

"Terrific. You go ahead and think on that to your heart's content. Meanwhile, I'll fly straight back to England and carry on with my life, shall I?"

"That's not going to happen." When she scowled at him, he laughed. Because what was there to do but laugh at the very notion that either one of them could wander back to their normal lives now? Or ever? "I think perhaps, *cara*, it is not I who am being unreasonable."

"Says the man who kidnapped me."

"You say you wish to go back to England. Where would you go?"

Pia's frown deepened. "Home. Obviously."

"The paparazzi already have their teeth in this story. Your brother is fielding calls for his resignation after his display of violence and I'm certain that the palace will already have received a thousand queries about whether or not his pregnant sister is the reason he belted me. Do you think they'll magically leave you alone?"

"They always have before," she said, and for the first time, he understood how very sheltered she'd been. It should have appalled him, surely. But instead, he had the strangest urge to shelter her.

"Convents and finishing schools do not capture the public's imagination the way a scandal does," he told her. "Or the world would be a very different place."

"We can still deny it." She sounded almost…desperate. "Matteo is a Combe. Combes are always punching people. What's a prince in the mix?"

"I think you know better."

"I don't see why anyone has to know about this if we don't tell them," she argued. "It's always seemed to me that the people the tabloids hound the most are the ones who court the attention. If we don't court it, surely they'll move on to something else."

"Pia. Remember, please, that I am not some debutante's gelded date, on hand to waltz on command at her coming-out ball. I am the Crown Prince of this kingdom, for my sins. The very hint that any woman's baby could be mine will send my people into a frenzy."

She shook her head, her face pale again. "What does that matter? You told me that you don't want children and don't want a wife. Frenzy or not."

"I don't."

"So there's no point to any of these conversations, is there?"

"What I want and what I plan to do with what has happened are two different things, I think," he said.

He wasn't sure why her reluctance made his temper kick at him. Only that it did.

And he stared her down until she lowered her eyes, there in the palace his ancestors had built while the blue blood he hated—and yet shared with all those who had stood here before him—stormed in his veins.

It made him feel alive, like it or not. It made him *want*.

It made him wonder how this was going to end.

"If I were you," Ares told her, all princely command, "I would resign myself to it."

CHAPTER SEVEN

Pia had no intention of resigning herself to anything, thank you, and especially not her own kidnapping.

Sure, she'd gotten into his car and onto his plane of her own free will. It had seemed vastly preferable to the baying press outside Combe Manor. But she hadn't expected to come here. That had to count against him. She was determined it did.

She broke away from that room where she'd felt as if Ares was holding her in his grip, where her mouth still throbbed from his kisses—God help her, that man could *kiss*—and hurtled herself out into the palace corridors. It took her longer than it should have to find her way back to her suite, and by the time she made it she was tired, emotional, and shaking.

Pia told herself she was peckish, that was all. Because once the morning sickness had stopped, she'd become ravenous. And hadn't stopped.

Her aide met her inside her rooms and quickly produced a lavish spread for Pia to choose from. And she wanted so desperately to be the sort of unwilling captive who could turn up her nose at anything she was offered. Not to mention, weren't there too many tales about unwary virgins who were lured into treacherous places they could have left—if only they hadn't eaten there?

"Lucky that you're no virgin, then," she muttered to herself as she helped herself to a heaping plate of seconds.

But after the palace staff had swept all evidence of her private feast away, Pia stayed where she was. She sat up straight in the most uncomfortable chair in her outermost sitting room. She channeled her many years of being taught manners by unimpressed nuns, sat so she wouldn't drift off to sleep, and waited.

The hours ticked past. The night wore on.

And when she decided it was late enough that even infamous playboy princes—not that she'd worn down her phone battery by Googling him exhaustively—had taken themselves off to bed, if only because there was precious little other entertainment to be had here on the southern tip of the middle of nowhere, she stood. She stretched her protesting limbs, let herself out of her room again, and resolved that she would walk out of this palace if necessary.

It took her a while to find her way through the maze of halls and corridors again, and she got lost more than once. But eventually she found herself on the ground level, where she set about looking for a door that led outside—instead of into yet another courtyard.

Unfortunately, there were courtyards everywhere, as if every member of the royal family who'd ever spent time here had built their own.

There were courtyards that opened up to the sky and others that were really more like squares beneath the floor above. There were courtyards that opened into the sea itself, but Pia couldn't seem to find one that led to that road she knew they had taken in. She kept getting turned around. She thought she was retracing her steps when she turned a corner and yelped because someone was *right there.*

"Imagine my surprise," Ares said darkly, "to be roused from my slumber by my staff, and told that the palace was not under attack, but that one of my guests—my only guest—was creeping about the place like a criminal."

"I'm not creeping anywhere and I'm certainly not a criminal," Pia threw at him.

And only then did she take in what he was wearing.

Or more to the point, *not* wearing.

Because the Crown Prince of Atilia stood there before her wearing nothing but a pair of loose black trousers, slung low on his hips as if to suggest that he had been sleeping naked and had tossed them on when he came to find her.

And everything else was just…him.

Those wide, smoothly muscled shoulders. That broad chest that narrowed to lean hips. Ares kept himself in excellent physical condition—she hadn't built that up in her fantasies since New York, it turned out—all rangy muscles and that loose-limbed elegance he wore so easily.

He wasn't the only one who remembered that night in Manhattan. She did, too. How she had crawled over him in sheer, greedy delight. How she had tasted him, tempting them both nearly past endurance. How she had filled her mouth with salt and man and the dark heat that rose between them still.

Here. Now.

"Why aren't you dressed?"

She all but shrieked out the question, half in a gasp, and knew even as it escaped her lips that she'd revealed herself. That she'd given herself away.

Completely.

"Why, pray, would I be dressed?" he asked mildly, though his green eyes glittered there, in the deserted hall. "Perhaps you have not noticed, Pia, but it is the middle of the night. Why are you still dressed as you were hours before? And more to the point, why are you lurking about as if you are casing the place? Are you?"

Pia didn't know what came over her. One moment, she'd had a clear sense of purpose. Of direction. Or intention, anyway, no matter if she couldn't quite find her way.

And then in the next, Ares was standing before her half-dressed. And she was still trapped here in this fairy-tale fortress. And she was an orphan and a mother, both at the same time. And all of that seemed to crash into her.

As if that damned runaway train had looped around and plowed straight into her, flattening her.

Her face crumpled, no matter how hard she fought to keep it smooth. Unbothered. And as she fought off the huge sob that seemed to roll out of her, then on top of her like a great weight, she saw Ares's expression… change.

Pia kept thinking that she'd reached the absolute outer limit of the shame that any one person could feel. She kept thinking there could be no further depths to plumb.

And then something else happened.

She tried to cover her face, because she couldn't stand the fact that he was *right there*, watching her as she quite literally fell apart in front of him.

But his hands were on her, brushing her shoulders and then shifting. Before she knew what was happening he was lifting her up, hauling her high against his chest.

"Don't be foolish," she sobbed at him, her hands still over her face. "I'm hugely pregnant. You'll give yourself a hernia."

"Pia," Ares said in the most regal voice she'd heard from him yet. "Please be so good as to shut up."

She obeyed him. Or she tried, anyway, but she couldn't keep the sobs inside. And later she would find herself appalled and humiliated that she'd so easily surrendered. To her emotions, to him. To everything. But here, now, she tipped her head forward, rested against his shoulder, and let the tears come.

Later she would regret this, she was sure of it.

But for a while, there was only the width and strength of his shoulder, holding her steady as he moved. There was the scent of him, clean and male, with a hint of something else. Soap, perhaps. Cologne, maybe. She couldn't quite tell, but she knew that scent. She remembered it. And it soothed her.

She didn't understand why he should be capable of calming her when no one else ever had. When her life was filled, in fact, with people and places and things that did the exact opposite of calming her. But she didn't have it in her, just then, to fight him.

Not when he was so strong, and so warm, and when

his arms wrapped around her as if she was light and sweet and beautiful. As if he could carry her forever, and would.

And when he finally set her down again, she had to bite her own tongue to keep from protesting.

She wiped at her face, then looked around, and it took her longer than it should have to recognize that she was in a bathroom. A huge, suitably palatial bathroom, that was. If she wasn't mistaken, he had taken her back to her own rooms.

And she sat there, feeling limp and fragile with the force of her own feelings—none of which she could name—as the Crown Prince of Atilia filled her bath. She sat where he'd put her, there on the wide lip of the oversize tub. And she watched him, vaguely astonished that His Royal Highness knew how to go about such a mundane task.

The beauty of her convent education was that she and the rest of the girls from wealthy families who could afford to go there had been taught how to function like regular people. It was one of the convent's primary missions, in fact.

"You do realize I have servants to do this, don't you?" one of the girls in Pia's year had thrown at Mother Superior one morning as they'd all been scrubbing the floors of their dormitory.

"My dear child," Mother Superior had replied, in that mild voice that made them all wince, "you are being taught basic chores not for you, though you can certainly benefit from learning them, but for those servants. In the perhaps vain notion that a dose of empathy might allow you to inhabit your place in this world with more consideration for others."

That had stuck with Pia, along with the punishment Mother Superior had levied against their entire class for the rest of the semester—that was, scrubbing the whole of the great hall. On their hands and knees.

Now she sat in a palace with a man she barely knew but would have sworn didn't lift a single finger if someone else could do it for him. A prince who'd given her twins and spirited her away from her life—twice, now. And she wondered who'd taught him the same lesson.

And then wondered what was wrong with her that she wanted, so desperately, to believe that he was capable of something like empathy. Because that might make him into the father she knew he didn't want to become.

Why do you want him to be a father? she asked herself, harshly enough that she could have been one of her own parents. *You can raise these babies perfectly well on your own. You don't need him.*

That was true. She knew that was true. And still, Pia watched Ares sprinkle bath salts over the hot water as if this was church. Then she didn't know what to feel when he came back to her, there on the edge of the tub set in an alcove with the sea outside.

"I think it is time you took off this shroud you are wearing, *cara mia*," he said in a low voice.

Pia looked down. She knew she hadn't changed her clothes, but she hadn't really processed the fact that she was still wearing that same black dress, severe and solemn and not remotely comfortable, that she'd worn to her father's funeral. And then to his grave.

She raised her gaze to Ares. "I don't think I want to."

Something moved over his face. He crouched down before her so he was on eye level with her. His arms were on either side of her legs, caging her there against the tub, and she thought that on some level, she should hate her heart for the way it beat so hard when he was close. She really should.

Ares shifted, moving back on his heels, but he did not rise. And his eyes were green and gold and that, too, felt like betrayal.

"I understand," he said, astonishing her anew.

Pia wanted to believe that, too. With a fervor that boded ill for her.

A faint smile moved over his mouth as he saw her expression. "When my mother died she lay in state, as is the custom here. And then my father and I walked through the streets as we transported her to her final resting place. I wore the typical regalia of my station, a uniform I have never found comfortable in the least. And yet, when it was over, when I was out of the public eye and back in my private rooms, I found I couldn't bear to move. I couldn't bear to change out of that uniform." His gaze seemed particularly green then. "Because I knew that doing so would indicate that I was moving on in some way."

"You loved your mother very much."

"I did. Did you not love your father? Or your own mother?"

He moved a hand to rest it on her thigh, and Pia was…astounded. She could feel the heat of him, all that power and strength, and be aware of him as a man. But she could also find that grip of his comforting, apparently.

She felt too many things to choose one, much less name it.

"There is no right answer," Ares said. "I had an excellent relationship with my mother. I have no relationship with my father. Parents are complicated."

And Pia was sure she wasn't the only one of them who was painfully aware that they were soon to be parents themselves. That they could inflict God knew what on their own children.

It was an unbearable intimacy to share with a man who was as good as a stranger.

"My parents had children only as an afterthought," she heard herself blurt out.

Anything to stop thinking about herself and Ares as terrible parents. Or any kind of parents.

What she'd said was true, of course. She'd read articles that had said as much, and less nicely. But she had never said it out loud herself before. And in a way, it felt like grief to hear her own voice, speaking that truth.

But somehow, she wanted to keep going. "Or at least, *I* was an afterthought. I suppose they always planned to have my brother. The heir of my father's dynastic dreams, et cetera."

She stared down at Ares's hand, and wanted to slide her own on top of his more than she wanted to breathe. She would never know how she kept her hands to herself. Or how she pushed on when she wasn't sure how or why she was speaking in the first place.

"When they focused on me at all, I think they saw me as a project," she told Ares as the scent of the lavender bath salts filled the room. "I don't honestly know that they were capable of loving anything but one another. I don't mean that in a bad way. I loved them both, I think. But it was always bound up in the ways I disappointed them."

His green eyes were grave. "How could you possibly be a disappointment?"

Pia didn't know how to answer him. And she knew that the reason for that was ego, nothing more. Pride. She didn't want to tell this man what he should have been able to see with his own two eyes.

And would, now. Now that he knew who she was. And therefore knew who her mother was. It was one thing to be herself, Pia knew. She could do that. It was when she was compared to Alexandrina that people felt the most let down.

Her parents most of all.

But she couldn't bring herself to point that out to Ares. She didn't have it in her.

"I'm glad I'm having boys," she said instead. "I think that must be easier."

Whatever light she'd seen in his gaze shuttered then. He moved his hand, which struck Pia as yet another tragedy she was unprepared to face, and reached into the water behind her.

He tested the temperature, then moved back, rising to his feet in a lithe rush that was nothing short of dazzling, with all that muscle and grace.

"You should get in," he told her, sounding distant and royal again. "Then I suggest you get some sleep. I cannot promise you that grief goes anywhere, but the sooner you start the process of moving on, the sooner you'll get to the part that's easier. Eventually, you'll find it hurts a lot less than it did."

"I think that must feel like losing them all over again," Pia said, without thinking.

Arés's gaze was too hot, too arrested as it snapped to hers.

"It does," he bit out.

And he left her there, sitting in her funeral dress on the side of a hot bath, wondering how and why he'd made drawing her bath feel like a gift. And why she wanted nothing more than to sink into it, fully clothed, and lie there until she stopped *feeling.*

When she stood, she felt unsteady on her feet. She found herself crying all over again as she pulled the dress off, then folded it neatly, placing it much too carefully on one of the nearby counters.

As if it was precious to her when really, she wanted to burn it. She had worn it twice in six weeks' time. She would never wear it again.

And when she sank down in the bath, and lost herself in the silken embrace of hot water, lavender, and steam, she let the tears fall until they stopped of their own volition. Pia didn't know who she cried for. The mother who had never loved her the way Pia had wished so desperately she would. The father who had viewed her as something to barter, or an amusement, but never a real person.

Or this new life she'd stumbled into, whether she wanted it or not. The babies she carried, the prince who had fathered them, and the terrifying, unknown future that loomed ahead of them all.

She cried herself dry, and only then did she rise up from the tub, towel herself off, and take herself into the vast, airy confection of a four-poster bed that waited in the bedroom. She crawled into the center of the bed, turned over onto her side to find the only position where she could be remotely comfortable, and wrapped one arm around her belly.

"I promise you this," she murmured out loud to the twin lives inside of her. "I will never barter you away. I will tell you I love you every single day of your lives. And you will never, ever find yourself wondering on the day of my death if you grieve because you miss me—or because you don't."

And still murmuring vows to the sons she would bear within a few short months, but treat better if it killed her, Pia finally fell asleep.

CHAPTER EIGHT

Ares had no idea what was happening to him as each day bled into the next, then a week slipped by. Then another.

And he and Pia stayed suspended in the same waiting game.

It was easy enough to make the Southern Palace his base of operations. So easy, in fact, that he couldn't quite remember why it had been so important to him to live apart from Atilia in the first place.

He flew in and out, from one royal engagement to another. And despite the barrage of scandalmongering headlines about him and Matteo Combe—and the expectant state of the Combe heiress the world had ignored until the funeral—his actual life was the same as it had been before. Did it matter what he called his base when he flew everywhere anyway?

Ares assured himself that nothing had changed. Nothing but his location.

Except he noticed that he found himself almost eager to return to the palace at the end of each engagement.

Almost as if he couldn't truly be easy until he'd seen Pia again.

If she had cried again after that first night, she never showed it. Nor did she make further attempts to break out of the castle, which was a relief if only because it prevented Ares from sharing parts of himself when he never, ever did such things.

The reports Ares received about her in his absence were always glowing. She was unfailingly polite and kind to all members of the staff. She went on walks, around and around the many courtyards, and at low tide, down to the beach, where she was known to spend time on the rocks, staring out toward the horizon. She never tried to lose her security detail. She seemed perfectly happy to have regular checkups with the doctor.

Her only request had been a laptop computer, which Ares had been more than happy to provide, particularly as it gave him leave to monitor what she did.

After all, he had never promised her privacy.

And that was how he discovered that what Pia did with her time was write an online column for one of those internet magazines that Ares had always personally believed were the scourge of the earth. He found this discovery so astounding that he sat with it for nearly a full week before it occurred to him to do anything about it.

One night, after he'd flown back from some or other formal charity event in mainland Europe, he found her curled up in what the staff had informed him was her favorite room of the palace. It was known as the Queen's Sitting Room, in the ancient wing, and had been built to accommodate a queen who had loved the ocean, her books and needlework, and liked to sit where she could look out all day while the business of the court carried on elsewhere. During the day the light cascaded in through the arched windows. At night, light made to look like candles blazed from every surface while the waves surged against the rocks outside.

Ares moved soundlessly into the room, not sure what to do with the wall of sensation and something perilously close to longing that slammed into him the moment he saw her.

Every moment he saw her, if he was honest.

Pia sat cross-legged on the chaise pointed toward the windows, a pillow over her lap—or what lap she had, with her huge, pregnant belly in the way. She was frowning down as she typed, worrying her bottom lip between her teeth, and Ares was only a man.

And it had been a long time indeed since he had taken a woman, now that he thought about it. Too long. Months.

Ares found he didn't actually want to scour his memory, because he was terribly afraid that Pia really had haunted him. That he might not have touched another woman since that night in New York.

He didn't want to consider that possibility, so he considered her instead.

His gaze traced the elegant line of Pia's neck, and the little wisps of dark hair that had tumbled down from the knot at the top of her head. He leaned against the doorjamb, letting his gaze drift lower. Her breasts swelled against the loose top she wore and he remembered covering them with his hands in New York. Now he wondered if they would spill over from his palms, so generous had they become. His mouth watered.

And there was something about her lush, swollen

belly that got to him, no matter how he tried to pretend otherwise.

There was something about the fact that she carried his babies, that she was big and round by his doing, that made something dark and primitive wind around and around inside him until he was tight like a coil.

He didn't know how he felt about becoming a father, but that had nothing to do with his appreciation of what he had done to her body. Or how she seemed to take to it so easily, so naturally, like one of the ancient goddesses that the locals claimed had first lived here on the site where the palace stood.

He shook himself, bemused at the direction of his own thoughts.

"When did you become an advice columnist?" he asked her, unaware until he spoke that his voice had gone all…gravelly.

But he couldn't worry about that when he had the distinct pleasure of watching Pia jolt in surprise. She whipped her head around, and then Ares's pleasure turned to a deeper joy as her cheeks reddened.

The way they always did when she saw him.

As if she couldn't keep herself from flushing pink and deeper red, which made him wonder if she was pink and red all over.

The possibilities made him ache.

"How do you…?" she began.

But her voice trailed off. She looked down at the laptop before her, and Ares braced himself for her temper. For the outburst that was almost surely coming.

He had to wonder if he'd asked the question specifically to provoke her.

If he'd lowered himself to such games.

But when Pia looked at Ares again, her gray gaze was resigned. "You're monitoring this laptop. Of course you are. I don't know why I didn't assume you were from the start."

Ares inclined his head slightly. "For security purposes, naturally. This is a royal palace."

"And because you're nosy." Her gaze stayed steady. "You want to know things about me without having to ask."

He could see that moment shimmer between them, Pia in her funeral dress on the side of that tub and him too close and much too open, and he was sure she could, too. But she didn't say anything.

"You could be in league with the tabloid reporters who swarmed us in Yorkshire," Ares said mildly instead. "You could have been planted by my enemies."

"Do you actually have enemies?" Pia asked, her voice even more mild than his. It scraped at him. "Or is this a part of those many wars you appear to be waging, though no one is waging them back at you?"

Ares leaned one shoulder against the doorjamb, crossed his arms, and regarded her sternly. "I suppose you could say I am my own war."

He certainly hadn't meant to say that. He didn't even know where the words had come from. Only that once they were out there, he couldn't deny the stark truth of them.

Or the acrid taste they left behind in his mouth.

It was like the first night she'd been here and that bizarre urge he'd had to *tend to her*. Ares wasn't certain he had *tended to* another person in the whole of his life, save his own mother in her final days. He hardly knew her. He knew the urge even less. It felt as if he'd been hit on the head and had only come to—and back into himself—when she'd reminded him of the fact that she was having sons.

His sons.

Every time he thought less of the sweet ripeness of her body and more about what that ripeness would result in, it hit him in the same way. Hard. Debilitating.

A full-on body blow.

"If you are your own war, you are lucky, Ares. That means you can call it off at any time." She closed the laptop and set it aside, her gray gaze on him. "You can have an armistice whenever you like."

"It is not quite that easy."

But he sounded more uncertain of that than he should have.

"Why are you spying on me?" she asked him, direct and to the point, that gaze still firm on his.

And if her voice had been sharp, or accusing, Ares would have known what to do. He could have handled it with a dose of royal arrogance, or that edgy thing in him that was always too close to the surface when he was in Atilia. Or near her.

Instead, he felt something like…outgunned.

"I would not call it spying," he replied, after a moment, but the words didn't seem to fit right in his mouth. "I told you. There were security concerns."

"Yes," she said, lifting up that chin of hers again. "I write a column. It's silly, really. There are lots of people who go through life without having to suffer through a finishing school. After all, its only real purpose is to make a person—and let's not kid ourselves, it's always a female person—so scrupulously well mannered that she could be a queen, if necessary."

Something powerful seemed to roar between them at that.

But Ares refused to acknowledge it. And Pia's cheeks only got redder.

"Hypothetically speaking, of course," she hurried to say. She looked away then, and Ares wondered if he was reddening, too, deep inside. "There's that story of the Queen of England at some dinner party. They'd set out finger bowls and the guest of honor picked his up and drank from it, which ought to have humiliated him. And would have, if he'd known. Everyone froze, not sure what to do in the face of such a breach of etiquette. But what did the queen do? She reached over, picked up her own finger bowl, and downed it like a shot. I don't know if that's true, but I like to think it is."

"Because you like to advise your readers to drink the contents of the finger bowls they encounter?" Ares asked. Darkly.

He felt…not himself, already. But even more so when Pia only gazed at him so calmly that he felt as if he'd turned into some kind of beast where he stood, misshapen and overlarge.

"Figuratively speaking," she replied. "I pretend to talk about good manners in my column. But really what I'm talking about is how to be kind."

"Kindness is overrated," Ares heard himself growl.

But Pia only shook her head. "No. It's really not."

"I admire these lofty sentiments, I do," Ares said in that same dark tone, all beast and very little prince. "But if you know that I have been monitoring what you do on that laptop, you must also know that I'm aware you monetize those columns of yours."

If he expected that to get to her, he was disappointed when all she did was smile. Patiently. In a manner that made him want to…break things.

Or get his hands on all that round, tempting lushness.

"No one knows it's me, do they?" That smile of hers was so bland it bordered on offensive. "I can assure you, no one wants to hear from poor little rich girl Pia Combe about how to be a better person."

"You have been writing this column for years. Since your second year of university, if my math is correct." He knew that it was.

"Well, there's only so much finishing a girl can do," Pia said lightly. Airily. She didn't actually wave her hand through the air dismissively, but it felt as if she had. "I thought it was a more reasonable outlet than some of the other ones my friends took up. Unsuitable men, for example. Or tempting scandal and often fate itself in all sorts of disreputable nightclubs. Unfortunate substances. A little column I never expected anyone to read seemed rather tame in comparison, but then, I have always been the little brown sparrow in a family of nothing but brightly plumed parrots. It felt very me."

Ares scowled at her. "I have absolutely no idea why you are suddenly talking about birds. Much less *plumage*."

"I know who I am. That's all I'm saying."

"You certainly don't need the money," Ares said, as if he'd caught her involved in some kind of con.

"I don't keep the money," she said, making a face as

if he was the one drinking out of finger bowls at formal banquets. "It's not a lot, or not by the standards I imagine you're used to, but I give it away. There are always needy people trying to raise money for various causes, and I like to give where I can. Without any strings."

"You could do that with the interest off a single month of your trust fund, one assumes."

"I could. But I was raised by Eddie Combe, who liked to rant and rave about the value of an honest day's work. I'm not pretending to work in any mines, but there's something to be said about earning my own money and spending it how I like." Her gaze searched his. "In fairness, I suppose crown princes aren't generally encouraged to do such things."

"There are some kingdoms that exult in the sight of their royals getting dirty with the common folk, but Atilia is not one of them," Ares said. "My mother spent time in the Royal Hospital, but ministering to the ill was about as far as the country was willing to let her go."

Thinking of his mother didn't bring the stab of grief it normally did. Possibly because he kept thinking that his mother would have loved Pia unreservedly. Ares could almost see them together, sitting in this very room, passing that laptop back and forth and discussing who next to help.

He found he was clenching his jaw so hard he was surprised he didn't snap a tooth.

"If you can help, you should," Pia said quietly, so much an echo of his childhood that Ares had to blink to make certain he wasn't sitting with his mother again, letting her quiet goodness cancel out his father's latest tantrum.

"I had no idea when I met you in New York that you were such a saint," he heard himself growl then.

Pia blinked, then flushed a deeper shade of red, and he felt as if he'd slapped her. That made him feel monstrous again. A cartoon beast, all fur and fury.

But he couldn't seem to stop himself from making every one of these moments with her…worse.

"Did you not?" she asked, lightly enough, though her gaze had gone cool. Wary. "I felt certain I was wearing my halo."

"I don't recall you wearing anything at all."

And that electric thing was back, bright and hot between them. Ares could feel his pulse thick and hot in his temples. In his chest.

In his greedy, hungry sex.

"I sit here every day," she said, though her voice was scratchier than it had been a moment before and there was a light in her eyes that made his pulse…worse. He decided to take that as a kind of victory. "I read a lot of tabloid takedowns. Alternate reality versions of me. Versions where I cold-bloodedly trapped a prince with my uterus. Then pitted said prince against my own brother, using my unborn child as collateral. I spend a lot of time wondering how it's possible that a person who never appeared in a single scandalous story before, ever, could attract the hatred of so many so fast."

"Is this about to veer into sparrows and parrots again?"

"I already feel stripped naked, is what I'm trying to tell you." Pia swallowed, hard. "It's bad enough that every time I pick up my phone or open a search engine I'm treated to more side-by-side comparisons between me and my mother, who, you may have heard, is still widely held to be the most beautiful woman who ever lived. I don't need you to come in here and taunt me."

"Taunt you?"

Ares hadn't expected that. Just as he didn't see it coming when Pia rose to her feet, betraying a gracefulness he felt certain she didn't know she possessed—but he could feel. All over him like a caress. She picked up the laptop and clutched it to her chest, then looked at him as if he was still very much that cartoon monster.

"I don't know what you want from me," she said, so quietly that it felt like condemnation. As if she could see the poison in his blood from where she stood. "I don't think you know either, which is the only reason why I'm tolerating this."

"This palace, renowned the world over for its beauty and never made available to the public. A life of ease, waited upon hand and foot. This is what you feel you must 'tolerate.'"

"You didn't liberate me from a gutter," Pia said, in that same quiet, deliberate way. "I'm not dazzled by your material possessions. I can see quite clearly that this is a prison no matter how lovely the furnishings might be."

What Ares didn't understand was why he felt as if he was in prison, too, when he was the one who came and went as he pleased.

"Consider this a grace period," she told him, very much as if she was the one with the control here. "I had months to get used to the fact that I was pregnant with twins. It wouldn't be fair of me not to accord you the same span of time to come around to the notion. But the clock is ticking, Ares. You can't keep me here forever and even if you could, there will soon be three of us."

"I would not challenge me if I were you." And his voice was a dark ribbon of sound he hardly recognized.

"You will have to make a decision," Pia replied as if she couldn't see the threat in him. Or didn't care. "Or do you think that I will have these babies locked away here, and then raise them like this, isolated from the world? As if we don't exist? You may be ashamed of them. Of me. But I am not."

"I never said I was ashamed."

She drew herself up, which only made him more aware of her lushness.

"Your indecision might keep me here," she said, as if she hadn't heard him. "I might even like it, as it keeps me from having to have unpleasant conversations with my older brother and everyone else who is suddenly dying to know my personal business."

She moved toward him then, the laptop in one arm and the other one wrapped over her belly.

"Pia—" he began, as if her name in his mouth didn't remind him too much of her taste. As if he didn't *ache*.

"But you will not lock these babies away from the world, Ares. They will not be victims to your indecision. Do you understand me?" And he had never seen that expression on her face before. Fierce. Sure. *Maternal*, something in him whispered. "My children will walk in the sun. They will be loved. They will not be hidden away like someone's dirty secret, and I don't care if it is in a palace. I won't have it."

And he wanted to stop her. He wanted to somehow

talk his way through the great mess inside of him, but he found himself frozen solid.

Unable to do anything but stand there, more monster than man.

And Ares wasn't sure that ratio was moving in his favor as she swept past him and disappeared down the hall.

Leaving him to feel the true weight of this palace he'd made a prison, as surely as if he'd fitted it with bars.

Ares had learned a long time ago not to read tabloid interpretations of his life, but he still found himself flipping idly through the worst of them on his tablet the next day as he flew to the Northern Island for the grand dedication of something or other.

A bank, perhaps. A monument.

He didn't care about that. Because the tabloids were filled with base speculation and nasty insinuation. Nothing new, but Ares found it clawed at him in a whole new way when the subject was Pia instead of him.

His own face was everywhere, with shots of him laid out on the ground and the bloody lip Matteo Combe had given him.

Matteo had been taken to task by his own Board of Directors, who were muttering about a no-confidence vote. They'd even gone so far as to sic an anger management specialist on him for a time, which Ares couldn't help but find amusing.

But there was nothing amusing about the things they almost but not quite called Pia. Because instead of fading away with nothing new to add to the story, it seemed the tabloids had only gotten bolder in their coverage during the time he and Pia had been in the Southern Palace.

Playboy Prince's pregnancy scandal! the headlines screamed.

Ares supposed he should count himself lucky that no one had dared mention the tabloids to his face.

He was congratulating himself on that as he stood in the grand, marble lobby of the Royal Bank of Atilia that was being dedicated to the King, where he was meant to say a few words. But there was a change in the crowd, suddenly, as he prepared himself to speak. He could feel it in the air. The ripple effect. The whispering and the gasping, followed by deep bows and curtsies all around.

Ares swore beneath his breath.

But he knew that he betrayed not a single emotion on his face when his father came in all his considerable state to stand beside him. Ares turned, as was required, and performed his own bow to his monarch.

"Prince Ares," the King said by way of greeting, and only because people were watching and would likely expect him to greet his only son.

"I did not expect to see you here, Your Majesty," Ares said beneath his breath as they stood for a rousing go at the Atilian national anthem. And he should not have seen his father, because it was well-known amongst the palace staff that the crown prince and the king preferred never to be in each other's company. "My secretary must have made a mistake."

"There was a mistake, all right," King Damascus retorted, making no attempt to hide his glare and no matter that the crowd was on the "*long may our king in grace and wisdom preside*" part of the song. "It's about time you and I have a word."

Ares could think of very little he would like less.

But they were in public. There was the brief ceremony to get through, made ten times worse by the presence of his father and all the extra pomp and circumstance that went along with the presence of the King of Atilia at such a banal event. And when it was done, he had no choice but to exit several steps behind his father as custom dictated, then follow him as commanded.

Because a son could rebel against his father. But Ares's father was also his king, and what the king decreed was law.

The old man insisted that they return to the Northern Palace, where Ares had made it a point not to set foot since his mother had died.

He knew his father was well aware of this.

But King Damascus wanted to draw it out, because he was as sadistic now as he had ever been. He marched Ares straight back to that private sitting room of his, where he had been lecturing Ares in between bouts of temper for as long as Ares could remember.

This time, Ares took the seat his father indicated and lounged in it. Not insolent, necessarily, but not reverent, either.

"This feels nostalgic," he said after the silence had dragged on too long.

"I'm glad you think so," the king said. "I feel nauseated, myself."

Ares smiled. Thinly. "Shall I contact your staff, sir? Do you require medical attention?"

The king moved to his personal bar, and Ares watched with a certain sense of resignation as his father poured himself a drink from yet another crystal decanter that Ares imagined would soon be in broken shards all over the stone floor. He did not offer Ares a drink, because he was still as petty as ever.

"Do you want to explain to me why your pregnant little piece is all over every paper?" the king demanded.

Ares wasn't sure what, precisely, it was that surged in him then. But he knew it was violent. Dark and furious, and aimed at his father.

Which he knew was treason.

But he didn't care.

"I beg your pardon, Your Majesty," he said icily. "You must surely be referring to yourself. I have no 'piece,' as you put it."

"You told me this would never happen," his father snarled at him. "You *promised* me, or I would have married you off years ago."

"Nature will do what it will do, father," Ares said, with a great flippancy he in no way felt about Pia or the babies she carried. "I don't understand your concern. I am not married. There is no actual scandal, there are only tabloids making noise."

"Was it noise that knocked you flat?"

Ares made himself stay where he was, seated and unthreatening. "That was a misunderstanding, nothing more."

"Do not expect my permission to marry her," his father said, and though he grew smaller and more wizened every time Ares saw him, that glare of his was as baleful as ever. "Do not think that the fact she is a

San Giacomo in any way makes up for all that peasant blood in her."

"I will remind you, sire," Ares said, acidly, "that I do not require your permission to marry. You struck down that law yourself, the better to make way for your own mistress."

"You mean your queen," his father growled. "Her Majesty Queen Caprice to the likes of you, and I warn you, I will tolerate no disrespect."

Ares forced himself to lounge back in his chair, though he wanted to be the one to start breaking things, this time. "And what of our great and glorious Queen Caprice? My understanding was that her chief attraction was her supposed fertility. Yet I've seen no sign that she is expecting your heirs."

"Watch yourself, boy."

"One is tempted to conclude that the reason you sired but one disappointing child was your fault. Not my mother's, as has been commonly agreed."

He meant: *by you and your doctors.*

"Is that your goal? You think that if you start having illegitimate children it will make you the better man?" His father laughed, but in that angry way of his that allowed for no actual humor. "On the contrary, Ares, all it does is remind the kingdom what a waste of space you are. A profligate playboy, governed by his base appetites. I should thank you for doing me a favor."

Ares stared back at this man that he had feared and hated for most of his life. Here in this room, where he had been threatened, belittled, and shouted at more times than he could count. Here where he had made decisions based entirely on how not to be the man facing him.

And he could cite chapter and verse about the things he didn't want. The man he didn't wish to become. The blood in him he hated, that had run hot just now, so desperately did he want to respond to the sneering violence in his father's voice in kind.

But he had other weapons.

You are always in a war, Pia had said.

And Ares supposed that was true. He had always been in *this* war. He had been dropped in it at birth.

But all that meant was that he knew how best to aim, then take fire, at the man who had taught him how to fight—never realizing, apparently, that in so doing he betrayed his own weaknesses.

"Did I not tell you the good news?" he asked his father mildly. Almost kindly. "Pia has made me the happiest man alive. She has agreed to be my wife. I know you—and the kingdom—will extend us your deepest congratulations."

And the first wedding gift he received was the splintering sound of his father's decanter against the castle wall. It was such a touch of nostalgia he very nearly came over all emotional as he took his leave.

And it was not until he was on his plane, heading back toward the Southern Palace, that it dawned on Ares that he would have to figure out how best to share these glad tidings with the woman he had yet to ask to be the wife he'd never wanted.

CHAPTER NINE

ONE THING PIA'S childhood had taught her, like it or not, was that a person could get used to anything.

No matter how outrageous or absurd things seemed, and no matter how certain she was that they might, in fact, kill her—they never did.

She had gotten used to her parents' excesses. The further removed she got from the operatic marriage of Eddie Combe and Alexandrina San Giacomo, the more she started to think of them as eccentrics, somehow unable to behave in any way other than the way they had. In a decade or so, she was sure, she would find herself nostalgic for her parents, their tempestuous relationship, and all those endless, theatrical fights she'd found so difficult to live through while growing up with them.

So, too, was Pia becoming used to her life in her very own prison of a palace.

She felt like Rapunzel, locked away in her little tower, visited by nothing and no one—save the man who came to her, mostly at night, and made her head spin around and around without laying so much as a finger on her.

Pia spent her days writing columns about fussy manners as stand-ins for deeper emotions, reading revolting things about herself in the tabloids—then vowing to stop reading revolting things about herself in the tabloids—and repeating the same thing over and over.

Her nights were punctuated by unpredictable glimpses of Ares.

Would he appear in the doorway as the shadows grew long, not there one moment and then a great, brooding presence in her peripheral vision the next? Would he ask her to join him for a drink with a guarded look in his green eyes and the suggestion of a banked fire in the way he held his big body? Would she agree, then sip at fizzy water as he swirled stronger spirits in a tumbler, the silence thick and layered between them? Or would they go a few rounds of conversation that always seemed so…fraught?

Pia never knew. She only knew that she looked forward to Ares's appearances with an unseemly amount of anticipation. And missed him when his duties kept him away.

She could admit to herself, when she wasn't making arch remarks about her prison tower, that she had always been a person better suited to life outside the glare of media attention and tabloid speculation. That night in New York had been the one and only time she'd tried to…be someone else.

Maybe, she told herself dourly in a voice that sounded a bit too much like one of Alexandrina's mild rebukes, *the reason Ares cannot bear to spend more than a few moments in your company, and no matter that you are carrying his children, is because he sees only that terrible lie when he looks at you.*

She didn't like to think about that. But how could she not? Pia was not beautiful. She was nothing like her mother. A man like Ares could have anyone, and had. Why would he want to be tethered for the rest of his life to *her*?

Pia had thought she'd come to terms with her looks—or lack thereof—a long time ago. It was a natural consequence of being Alexandrina San Giacomo's only daughter. She had been destined to be a disappointment from the day she was born.

But she hadn't marinated on that sad fact in a long time. Apparently, being hugely pregnant and mostly alone, locked up in a castle like an embarrassment that needed to be hidden away from the light, got into a girl's head. And stayed there, hunkering down and breathing fire, whether she liked it or not.

"I will make sure that *our* branch of the family is better," she promised her babies every day, shifting around on her favorite chaise as the boys kicked at her. With more and more vigor as the days rolled by and they grew inside her. "I promise."

Pia was well into her seventh month of pregnancy when she discovered that her family had more branches than she knew.

Because it turned out that she and Matteo had another brother.

A half brother, Dominik, that their mother had given away when she was a teenager, long before she'd become an icon.

A scandalous little fact about her mother—her family—that Pia discovered by reading a tabloid.

"Did you know about this?" Pia asked Matteo in

disbelief, reaching him on some business trip somewhere. When she knew he did, as the papers seemed to suggest that the new brother was dating Matteo's personal assistant—who had always returned Pia's calls before, yet was failing to do so at present. "How long have you known *we have another relative* and not told me?"

"It's not as if you've been available, Pia," Matteo said, and she would have said it was impossible for him to sound any colder than he already did. But he proved her wrong.

"I think by 'available' you mean, 'sitting in a room you might accidentally enter,'" Pia said, with a little more asperity than she normally showed her brother. Or anyone. "When the common definition also includes this device I'm calling you on right now. It's very handy for the sharing of important news, like brand-new family members appearing full grown. Or even to say hello."

"If you wish to be kept up-to-date on everyday concerns, you would have to actually make that known," Matteo retorted. "Instead of running away from your own father's funeral and hiding out somewhere."

Pia had never thought of herself as a particular heir to the famous Combe temper. But she was so angry then, and possibly something else that she didn't know how to name, that the rest of the conversation stayed something of a blur to her.

And when she hung up, all she could think about was her mother.

Vain, beautiful, magnetic, impossible, deliriously compelling Alexandrina, who Pia had always wanted so desperately to please. And who Pia had always failed to please.

And who Pia had always thought had locked her away in that convent out of shame. Spite, perhaps. Or simple disinterest in a daughter who was so much less.

It had never occurred to her that when her mother told her that wrapping her up in cotton wool was a gift, Alexandrina had meant it. Just as it had never crossed Pia's mind that her mother's life could ever have been anything less than perfect. Or if not perfect, exactly as she'd wanted it.

Pia hardly knew how to think about a different Alexandrina. A woman who was…a person. A woman who had carried a child, just as Pia was doing now, and had given it away. An act of grace or shame, sorrow or hope, that Pia literally could not imagine living through herself.

Thinking of Alexandrina so young, and faced with such a tough decision…knocked Pia's world off balance. The Alexandrina she'd known was so smooth and polished. Even when she fought with Eddie. And had certainly not been harboring any deep hurts.

And maybe that was the hardest part of grief. It was always changing. Growing, expanding, shifting to fit whatever little pockets it found.

She had to assume it would always be that way.

And she was still sorting through what it meant to have a brother she didn't know—who, for all she knew, might want nothing to do with the family that had abandoned him long ago—when she looked up to find her very own Prince Not Quite Charming standing there in the doorway. The way he liked to do.

"How long have you been standing there?" she asked, her hands on her belly, still caught up in those confronting thoughts about her mother.

"What does it matter?" he asked, brooding and dark.

Pia forced a smile she didn't feel. "I've resigned myself to the cyber spying. It's your laptop and I have nothing to hide. Look through it at will if you feel you must. But I don't understand why it's necessary for you to lurk about your own palace like this."

"I do not lurk." His voice was even darker then, and there was a considering sort of gleam in his green gaze. "It is not my fault you are unobservant when it comes to your surroundings."

"Well, Ares—" she began, hotly.

But he held up a hand before she could continue down one of their familiar little paths that always led to the same place. Parry, retreat, regroup—and parry again. Back and forth they would go, until it was difficult to tell who struck whom. And who left the most marks.

"Come dine with me," he said, to her shock.

That did not usually happen. Ares was usually out for dinner, at this or that ball that Pia could follow on social media or in the papers the next day—not that she did such a thing. As that might be interpreted as too much interest in the man.

And maybe it was the novelty that had her biting her own tongue. She shifted, standing up—which took leveraging herself off the arm of the chaise these days—and then crossing to him.

He held out his hand as she approached. And Pia took it.

And it was as if the balance shifted. Or her world, still off its axis, tilted even more sharply. It felt as if the floors beneath her feet suddenly slanted terrifically, leaving her head spinning.

It wasn't just his touch. Or it wasn't only that. It was that solemn look, grave and intent, in those green eyes of his. Pia was sure she hadn't seen him look at her like that since…

But she didn't dare say it. She didn't dare think it.

And as Ares took her hand, then led her down the halls of the palace, she was buffeted by the memories of what happened between them that night in New York. When he had taken her hand like this and led her out of that party, and then all these restless things inside her had shifted into heat. Fire.

All that longing and need, greed and revelation.

It all kept washing over her, memory after memory.

He led her to the wing of the palace she knew was set aside for his exclusive use, and into a private dining room. It could have comfortably fit a crowd, but the table was set up to feel intimate, with a view over the ocean as the last of the sunset spread pink and orange over the horizon. Pia couldn't help thinking about the fact that they had skipped this part in New York. The sit down, have a meal, and learn about each other part.

This felt…remedial and precious, at once.

She found she was afraid to break the silence.

"I'm surprised you're here," she made herself say because it was best to rip the bandage off and dive straight in—another one of her father's favorite sayings. "Your social calendar is always so full."

"I canceled it."

"You mean, tonight's engagement?"

"All of it," Ares said.

And then did not expand on that statement at all.

The staff swept in, laying out the first course, but Pia hardly noticed it. And the babies must have sensed her agitation—or maybe it was anticipation, or something far more insidious, like longing—and as she rubbed her hand over her belly, she received a volley of kicks.

She must have sighed a little, because when she looked up, Ares was frowning at her. Not from down the length of a banquet table, but from much, much closer. Within reach.

"Is something happening?" he asked.

Aside from the hand he'd offered her tonight, Ares hadn't touched her since her first night here. And even then, it seemed to her that he had gone out of his way to avoid touching her belly. Yet when she looked at him now, he had the oddest expression on his face.

There was no doubt that he was focusing all his attention on her. On her belly, to be more precise, where her hand rubbed at the tiny little foot inside.

"One of them is kicking," she told him. "Which means the other one will likely join in any second now and make it a football match."

Ares looked as astonished as he did uncertain then. "Now? As you sit there?"

"Do you...? Do you want to feel it yourself?" Pia offered, surprised by the vulnerability she heard in her own voice.

And worse, the hope.

Ares rose from his chair, rounding the corner of the table that separated them. Then, without skipping a beat, he slid down before her. And there was a look on his face that she had never seen before. His green eyes were dark.

Pia smiled. “Give me your hands.”

She didn’t wait for him to offer them. She reached over, took his hands in hers, and brought them firmly against her belly.

And, sure enough, the moment his hands slid into place over her bump, two different sets of feet reacted.

Pia watched Ares’s face. The jolt of surprise. The understanding of what he was feeling beneath his palms.

And then, like a dose of pure sunshine, the wonder.

“Does it hurt?” he asked, his voice hushed.

“Sometimes it’s uncomfortable,” she said softly. “Or surprising. Or if one of them stretches out and presses their feet up against my ribs, that aches.”

He shifted, coming down on his knees before her chair, and his hands were suddenly everywhere. Moving all over her bump, as if testing it. Learning its shape.

And the more he ran his hands over her, the more Pia liked it. And in a way that had nothing at all to do with their babies or any kicking. She felt the shift in her like a flame leaping into life, from coals she’d imagined were cold.

It turned out they were only smoldering.

When Ares looked up at her again, there was a gleaming heat in his gaze that she recognized. Oh, how she recognized it. How she *felt* it.

“Pia,” he said, his voice low. Hot.

And an unmistakable invitation.

Pia couldn’t take this. Not for another moment. Ares

was so close, his hands on her, that look of marvel and need on his beautiful face.

How could she do anything but melt? And as she melted and ran hot, that liquid greed bloomed inside her, low in her belly and deep between her legs.

Where only Ares had ever touched her.

His gaze searched hers.

Did she whisper his name? Or did it live in her already? Always?

Whichever it was, it made Pia lose her head completely. She leaned forward, slid her hands to hold his face, and then settled her mouth to his as if she might die then and there if she couldn't taste him again.

She felt him groan, low and deep, as if it came from the depths of him. She felt his big, athletic body shake slightly, as if from the force of the same wild sensation that swept through her, too.

And then his mouth opened beneath hers and he took control.

And when he kissed her, Pia forgot that she wasn't beautiful.

When Ares kissed her, Pia felt as if she was made entirely of glory. Light and lovely, sweet and right, strung out on the heaven in his every touch. All that hot perfection.

Ares moved closer, one hand curling around her neck as if to guide her where he wanted her. The other stayed put on her belly.

She felt untethered by her own need, and anchored at the same time.

He made her feel like she could fly. Like this was flying.

Ares kissed her and he kissed her, and Pia didn't know which one of them was trying harder to move closer. To take the kiss deeper. She was frustrated that he wasn't closer. She wanted his skin on hers, his hands on her bare flesh.

She *wanted*.

Ares groaned again, then shifted back. His mouth curved at the sound of protest she made, and he pulled her up from her chair. He set her briefly on her feet, but only briefly, because he moved then to lift her into his arms.

And here she was absurdly pregnant, yet he was still making her feel as if she weighed nothing at all.

"Ares, you can't—"

"So help me God, Pia," Ares growled down at her. "If you're about to tell me that I cannot lift you when I have very clearly already done so, I will be tempted to drop you over the side of the balcony."

And she didn't think he was likely to do that.

But she didn't finish her sentence, either.

He bore her outside, onto the balcony he had just mentioned, wide and open. He lay her down on a wide, low chaise, and followed her. Then stretched out beside her so they were finally—*finally*—touching, head to toe.

And that was almost too much.

But Ares took her mouth again, and they both groaned at the heat. The mad, glorious kick of hunger.

He kissed her and he kissed her, and she kissed him back with all the longing and need she'd kept inside her all this time. All that delirious fire that he stoked in her.

Only him.

Ares was dressed for one of his royal engagements, but he pulled back to shrug out of his jacket and his shirt, giving Pia access to those wide shoulders of his and better yet, his mouthwatering chest.

She took instant advantage, moving her hands over him and letting herself exult in his strength. His heat.

Each and every perfect ridge and tempting hollow.

And everything was too hot. Too good.

He found her breasts, so plump and big now. And he made such a deep, male sound of approval as he filled his hands with them that Pia forgot to be self-conscious. He pushed up the loose blouse she wore and freed her breasts from the front clasp of her bra.

Then he bent his head to take a nipple into his mouth.

And the sensation was so intense, so wild and overwhelming. It shot through her, a molten hot line from her nipple to her hungry sex, that Pia felt herself pull too tight—

Then she simply shattered, there and then.

Ares let out a laugh of dark delight that shivered its way through Pia like a new, bright flame. Then he moved to her other nipple, taking it into his mouth in the same greedy, demanding way. She tried to breathe. She tried to fight it off, but he only sucked a little harder—

And that was it. She went tumbling from one peak to the next, and broke apart all over again.

"I can't believe how sensitive you are now," he murmured, his mouth on her belly. "Let's test it, shall we?"

Then—slowly, carefully, ruthlessly—he stripped her of the loose, easy clothes she wore.

And Pia was too busy falling to pieces, and gasping

for breath, and crying out his name, to think about the things that would have torn her apart at any other time. Her size, for example. How fat she must look. How different than before.

But she was too busy losing herself in Ares's mouth. Beneath his clever, wicked hands.

She didn't notice when he stripped out of the rest of his clothes, too, because his hands found their way between her legs, teasing her slick flesh until she broke apart again.

And again.

And then, finally, Ares went and knelt before the chaise, pulling her to the edge and opening her legs wide. He held himself there, moving between her thighs. Only then did he find her soft, wet heat with the hardest part of him.

His gaze lifted to hers. Pia held her breath. And Ares pushed his way inside.

Slowly. Carefully.

Almost as if this was sacred. Beautiful.

As if she was.

"Pia," he murmured, as if her name was a prayer.

And then he set about his devotions, one perfect thrust after the next.

And she was already coming apart. She was already in pieces. Over and over again, as if the pleasure was a wave and she was caught in the undertow, tossed and tumbling and wild with it.

She lost count of how many times he brought her to that glorious cliff and tossed her over, only to catch her on the way down and do it all again.

It was too much, and it was beautiful and perfect,

and Pia never wanted to go without it—without him, without *this*—again.

She heard a distant sound and realized that she was saying those things out loud, but she didn't have it in her to mind that, either. Not when she was captured in that undertow, lost in the whirl of it.

Pia shook and she shook, she came down a little only to feel him surge deep inside her again, and she shook even more.

Until she thought she might become the shaking.

And finally, when he hit his own cliff, Ares gathered her to him. He dropped his head into the crook of her neck and called out her name as he shattered at last.

And she understood, now, Pia thought in a kind of wonder when she surfaced to find herself tucked up on that chaise, Ares having crawled up next to her like a kind of warm, gloriously male blanket.

It had been so hard, after New York, to understand why she'd behaved the way she had there. Why she'd done those things, and so easily and carelessly when that wasn't her. That wasn't how she behaved.

But she got it now. It was this. It was Ares.

It was extraordinary.

He was remarkable.

And it was no wonder that she had never been the same since.

She found herself running her fingers up and down her belly, in the absent way she often did, and she smiled when Ares did it, too, from beside her. Tracing patterns this way and that.

Introducing himself, she thought when one baby kicked.

Letting them know who he was, she thought when the other followed suit.

"Pia," Ares said, in that low, marvelous voice of his that she loved to feel roll over her like the sweet, thick breeze from the sea before them. "You are the mother of my sons."

"That's me," she said softly, and her smile trembled a bit on her mouth. "Like it or not."

He looked up from her belly, leveling all that green intensity on her. His expression was grave. "I want you to marry me."

It was an order. A royal command.

And what surprised Pia was how deeply, how passionately she wanted to obey him.

But what did she know about marriage? Nothing but what she'd seen growing up. And certainly nothing that let her imagine two people so unevenly matched could make it work. She'd watched her parents' marriage explode time and time again, sometimes in the same evening. She'd watched it fall apart a thousand times, though they'd stayed together. She'd watched the games they played with and at each other, and the pieces they'd carved from each other that she didn't think they'd ever gotten back.

And Eddie and Alexandrina had been a love story for the ages.

Pia didn't see any reason why she should subject her babies to a far grimmer, far less exalted version of her parents' marriage. All the struggle and pain and yet none of the love.

How could she subject herself to that? And worse

still, how could she make her babies grow up like that? Hadn't it been hard enough for her?

She lay there on the balcony with the sea as their witness, naked and replete, still spinning in all that sensation and sweet hunger. She reached over and slid her hand over Ares's, holding him to her.

And she said no.

"No." She said it distinctly. "I won't marry you. But you are the father to my sons, Ares. That won't change. We don't have to be married. We can just...be parents."

He was quiet for a long, taut moment.

"And how do you think that will work when I take the throne?" he asked mildly, though Pia wasn't fooled by his almost offhand tone. "Will the two princes have alternate weekends with their father, the King of Atilia, and then spend the rest of the time in some godforsaken Yorkshire village?"

"We'll figure it out, one way or another." Pia made herself smile at him, though it felt like a risk when his green eyes were so dark. "With or without my beloved, godforsaken Yorkshire."

Ares rolled to his feet. Then he reached down and pulled her up from the chaise, letting her stand there before him as the night air danced over them.

And as Pia longed for more.

"I mean to have you as my wife," he told her, starkly.

"No," she said again, and felt something hitch in her as she said it, as if the longing was tangled up on itself. "No, you don't. You want to marry me for the babies, but it has nothing to do with *me*. You don't want *me* for a wife. You want your babies' mother."

"Why can't I want both?"

"No," she said again. Calmly and firmly, despite that tumult inside her that she feared was something even more embarrassing.

Like stark, desperate yearning, despite everything.

And Pia expected him to argue. To rage, perhaps, the way her father would have. Or go dark and broody, the way she'd seen him do before.

But Ares only smiled.

CHAPTER TEN

PIA DIDN'T KNOW what she'd expected. Perhaps she thought that having been rejected, Ares would go off somewhere. Lick his wounds with his favorite whiskey. Pretend the conversation had never happened.

Instead, he helped her dress, pulling the softly elegant knits into place. Then he ushered her back into the dining room and took his time helping her into her seat. He sat—too close to her—at the entirely too intimate table, and they…had a perfectly civilized dinner.

Complete with finger bowls at the end.

"And if I drink mine?" she dared ask him. "Will you do the appropriate thing as host? All to make me feel comfortable?"

But this was why Pia wrote columns about seemingly insignificant things like whether or not to send thank-you notes—yes, always—and whether one should flout convention in matters such as the wearing of white in the off-season—of course, if you can pull it off.

Because it was never about the finger bowls. It was about taking care of other people.

It was about whether or not she felt safe with him when Pia didn't know if she'd ever been safe in her life.

Or how she could possibly know the difference when she didn't know what such a thing felt like.

"Marry me," Ares replied, his green gaze tight on hers. Because he was relentless and he clearly didn't mind her knowing it. "And you will see exactly what kind of host I am."

Pia did not drink from her finger bowl. And she was shaken all over again, if in a markedly different fashion, by the fact Ares hadn't let it go. If he was chastened or upset by her refusal, he didn't seem to show it.

After dinner, he escorted her out into the hallway, but when she turned to make her way back toward her wing of the palace, he held fast to her arm.

"I think not," he said quietly. "We have only just begun to take the edge off, have we not?"

"The edge?" Pia repeated because she didn't dare imagine that he meant what she thought he did. What her body certainly hoped he did, as it shivered everywhere, inside and out, when she was sure she shouldn't have been able to feel a thing. Not when she'd felt too much already.

"*Cara mia*, it has been much too long since New York. My hunger for you has yet to be quenched."

Maybe she should have argued. Held fast to some or other standard…but Pia wanted him more than she wanted to fight him.

All she did was nod. Once.

Ares did not do a good job of hiding his sharp, hot grin then. He led her to his vast suite of rooms, instead. And he laid her out on his massive bed, clearly made for kings, and crawled up over her to learn every inch of her body all over again.

And when she was writhing, and out of her head once more, he turned her over. He settled her on her hands and knees, so he could slide into her from behind.

That time, she screamed his name when she burst apart.

Every time she burst apart.

And that was only the beginning of his campaign.

He had all her things moved into his rooms and when she objected, merely lifted an arrogant brow.

"I do not wish to traipse down a mile of palace corridors when I could more easily turn over and find you in my bed, Pia," he told her. Loftily.

And maybe Pia was weak. But she liked sleeping in his bed. And she liked it even more when he turned over and woke her up.

He still maintained his schedule of events. Royal necessities that meant he was always trotting off to this or that.

But he came home more than he had before.

And Pia laughed at herself when she realized that was the word she used now. *Home.* To describe this mad, fairy-tale palace where she was locked away from the world.

Or maybe, something inside her suggested, *this is where you get to retreat from the world.*

When had her prison begun to feel like a *retreat*?

She found she stopped looking at the tabloids, particularly as they now starred both of her brothers and their various romantic entanglements. It wasn't only that she didn't want the nasty, gossipy version of her family in her head. It was more that she liked focusing on her own life.

Because she had a life, for once. She was growing brand-new humans inside her. She was carrying on with her writing. And she had Ares, after a fashion.

He taught her things it was impossible to learn in a single night.

And if her giant, pregnant body was any kind of hindrance, he never showed it. He seemed perfectly capable of coming up with new, improved ways to make sure they were both comfortable while they explored each other.

Sometimes he talked. He made dark, delicious promises, then followed through on each and every one of them.

Other times, he was dark, silent, and impossibly beautiful as he moved over her, in her.

One afternoon, after he had made her sob, scream, and then beg a bit for good measure, Ares sprawled beside her. The bed was big, wide, and rumpled beneath them. Up above, the ceiling fan turned lazily, keeping the air moving. Pia could hear the ever-present sound of the ocean outside, crashing over the rocks and surging against the shore.

And Ares was hot and beautiful, all leashed power and male grace as he lay there beside her, his fingers laced with hers.

No matter what happened, Pia knew she would always remember this moment. When she'd almost forgot her body entirely, or could only seem to remember what he could do to it.

Beautiful, something in her whispered. *He makes you feel beautiful.*

"Marry me," he said, the way he always did. He had

asked her to marry him so many times now that she thought it had lost its power. Almost. Now it was just a thing he said.

Pass the salt, please. Marry me.

Pia laughed. "You know I can't."

"I know no such thing."

She sighed, shifting in an attempt to get comfortable. "You were very clear that you wanted no wife. No children. And the children were a surprise to us both, but I think we will do very well now that we've adjusted to it all. But why add marriage to the mix?"

"I remember seeing your parents at a ball," Ares said into the quiet of the room, with only the ocean outside as accompaniment. "It was perhaps ten years ago now. It was a ghastly sort of state affair, bristling with diplomats and career socialites."

As he always did, now, Ares moved his hand over her belly. Finding one baby's head, and the other's pair of feet. Saying hello to his sons. Pia had grown used to the patterns he drew there. The way she sometimes drifted off to sleep and woke to find Ares crooning nonsense to her belly.

She hardly dared admit how that made her feel. Riddled with hope. Laced through with sweetness. So full of impossible, unwieldy emotion, she felt it was one more part of her set to burst. At any moment.

"I never knew my parents to subject themselves to anything grim or ghastly," Pia said, trying to rally when everything felt too emotional these days. She was in her eighth month, and twins were usually early. Her time with them as part of her was almost over. And so, too, was her time with Ares nearing its natural conclusion.

She could feel it with every breath. "They much preferred to be the life of the liveliest parties they could find."

"I imagine it was a business affair for your father," Ares said. "There were stultifying speeches, as there always are. Much self-congratulation. Then the dancing began. There were the usual awkward couplings of diplomats, their wives, and so on. These things are typically excruciating. But then your parents took the floor."

Pia thought she knew where this was going. She smiled, settling more fully on her side. "My parents loved to dance."

"That was instantly apparent. I don't know anything about their marriage, or not anything that wasn't twisted to sell papers, but I did see them dance. I saw the way they looked at each other."

"Not only as if there was no one else in the room," Pia said softly, remembering. "But as if no one else existed at all."

"My own parents did not dance unless it was strictly necessary for reasons of highest protocol," Ares told her, propping himself up on one elbow and regarding her, an odd sort of gleam in his green eyes that made them seem burnished with gold. "And when they did, they did their best never to gaze at each other at all. I watched them dance at the same ball ten years ago and I imagine it was perfectly clear to everyone in the room how little esteem they held for each other."

"Did they not…?" Pia didn't quite know how to phrase the question.

Ares let out a laugh, but it was tinged with bitterness. "My father liked to indulge his temper. When it was aimed at me, he liked to throw things against walls. I am only grateful that he contained that rage to me alone and never aimed it at my mother." He shook his head. "They say he is a decent enough ruler, but he was a cold, unfeeling husband and is a terrible father."

"You don't have to talk about this," Pia said quietly, when she thought he wouldn't go on.

Ares's eyes glittered. "My mother provided him with the requisite heir, thus securing the bloodline and the kingdom, which was all he cared about. Once that was accomplished, he felt perfectly justified in pursuing his extracurricular interests. Without caring overmuch if that might hurt her feelings. In fact, I think I can say with perfect honesty that I have never known my father to care about anyone's feelings. Ever."

Pia tried to pull up pictures of the king of Atilia and his late queen in her head. And more, tried to think of them as people instead of pictures anyone could look at.

"Your father cheated on your mother?" she asked.

"Constantly." Ares smiled, but it was little more than the sharp edge of his teeth. "And enthusiastically. Quantity over quality, if my sources are correct."

Pia let out a breath, and directed her attention to the place where their hands were still linked.

"I think my parents cheated on each other as well," she told him, though she'd never admitted that out loud before. No matter what the papers said. "I know they loved each other, madly and wildly. Everyone knows that. But part of that kind of love is all about hurting each other. I think the glory was in the coming back together, so they always seemed to look for new ways to break apart."

Ares lifted her hand and brought it to his mouth. He pressed his lips against her knuckles and Pia's heart instantly careened around inside of her chest. Fizzy and mad, as if they weren't already naked. As if they hadn't already spent hours making each other moan.

His gaze was intent on hers. "I never wanted to marry because I watched a royal Atilian marriage play out right in front of me. My father was a brute, always. And my mother was always so sad. I never wanted that for any woman bound to me, whether by duty or desire."

He reached over and brushed her hair back from her face, and Pia didn't want to see the look on his then. It was…too open. Too complicated.

It made her heart pick up its pace.

"But I am willing to take the chance that you and I can make something different, between us. Something better, Pia."

She shook her head at him, afraid that if she investigated any further she would discover that the lump in her throat and the glassiness in her eyes could tip over too quickly into tears. And would.

Because she kept telling herself that he was joking. Or if not *joking*, precisely, saying these things she'd always wanted to hear because he thought he could convince her that way. Not because he actually believed them.

But the trouble was, she *wanted* to believe him. And the more of these sorts of things he said, the more she wanted to believe.

When she knew better.

"Ares," she began.

"We are magic in bed, Pia," he said, in a voice as

intense as the way he looked at her. "That is how we came to be here in the first place. Is the worst thing in the world to think we might as well make it official?"

"You're the one who gave me a lesson in the lines of Atilian succession." She wanted to roll out of the bed and storm away. But it took her too long to do such things—or anything—these days. So she settled for rolling away from him, and pushing herself up into sitting position.

And as she did, she was suddenly too aware of how naked she was. How huge her breasts had become. How misshapen her belly was, sticking so far out, with her belly button protruding.

"Yes," Ares was saying, watching her. "I'm concerned about the lines of succession. Should I not be? I told you the day of your father's funeral that it was no small thing to claim you carry my child. That hasn't changed. If anything, the closer we get to your due date, the more serious the matter becomes."

"Because all of a sudden now you care deeply about these things?"

"I may not have set out to make myself heirs." And there was something granite in his voice. In the gaze he leveled on her. It made something deep inside her start to tremble. "But they exist. They will be here sooner rather than later. And I would prefer it if they had access to all the rights and privileges their position as my heirs allows them."

"Why?" She was rubbing her belly, and made herself stop. "You felt one way about all of this, then you interacted with your father and everything changed. It's hard not to think you simply want to defy him."

His expression changed, and she wondered if he'd thought she didn't know. That she hadn't seen the pictures of the two of them—*King Damascus Takes Errant Heir to Task!* the papers had cackled—and seen the dark look on Ares's face.

"What do you think will happen?" he asked her, and she thought she hated it most when he sounded so *patient*. So *reasonable*.

"Do you need me to explain to you where babies come from, Ares?" she asked him, proud that she kept her voice calm.

"The world already believes you are pregnant with at least one of my children," he replied, only that cool gleam in his eyes indicating that he was even aware of the question she'd asked. "Let us say, for the sake of argument, that I let you go right now. And you set out into the world, footloose and fancy-free as you claim to want. You're lucky enough not to be impoverished, which means you will no doubt be capable of raising these babies just fine on your own."

"I've been making this argument for months."

"But the world will continue to think they are mine, no matter what lies we tell or lengths we take to conceal that truth. And what then?"

"What do you mean, 'what then?' Rumors are just rumors—"

"Rumors are rumors, yes. But thrones are thrones, *cara mia*." And she didn't know what that note in his voice was then. Or that look in his eyes. Only that it made her tremble—again. "And we may have grown progressive in these latter days. We prefer to have our fights in ballot boxes rather than in the streets or on poppy fields. But that does not change the fact that you will be raising two boys with a direct claim to the throne of Atilia. I understand that means nothing to you, but I assure you—it will not only mean something to my people, it will mean even more to whoever succeeds me."

"Succeeds you?" She didn't understand.

"I will take the throne, and then I will die," Ares said, with certain matter-of-factness that made her want to scream. Or do *something* to protest the ruthless inevitability in his voice. "And whoever comes next, whether it be a cousin or whatever issue my father manages to rustle up in his waning years, your boys will be out there. Some will inevitably claim that one of them is the rightful king. And do you know what will happen then?"

"Let me guess," Pia said, more sharply than she intended, surely. But she couldn't seem to pull herself back. "Another war."

"The blood of Atilia runs in my veins," Ares told her, his voice low and insistent. "It is poison. It is war and it is pain. And I am sorry to be the bearer of this news, but it is in you, too, now. It is in those boys. It is who we are."

"I don't know what any of that means." But she had moved herself back as she spoke, so she was sitting up against the headboard. And she was watching him as if he might snap at any moment, and then God only knew what might happen. Or what she might do. "Of course there's nothing in your blood. Royalty is not a virus."

"I beg to differ," Ares said, with a short sort of laugh, bitter and dark. "Royalty is power, nothing more and nothing less. And power infects. It could be that some successor seeks you out, and tries to neutralize any threat that your boys present. That is horrifying enough to contemplate."

That he had already contemplated that stung Pia. When she hadn't. She hadn't thought much beyond her pregnancy. She had been too busy settling here in this palace of his. She had been too focused on her hopeless little heart.

She was already a bad mother and her children weren't born yet.

"But there is also another possibility," Ares said in that same powerfully mild way that was wreaking havoc on her. "Who knows who our sons will grow up to become? Either one of them might decide that they deserve their birthright. What do you plan to do then?"

Pia's heart clattered around in her chest. And all she could seem to do was beat herself up for the possibilities she hadn't considered.

She tried to shake it off—because she could beat herself up on her own time. She didn't have to do it when Ares was watching her like this, close and very nearly *ferocious*. "So your position is that we should marry, and that will somehow...prevent your sons from taking the throne? Or prevent someone else from taking it? Or prevent...something else? I'm not following you."

"Pia—"

"And I've already told you that I won't restrict your access from them. I mean that. But a marriage between you and me isn't about them. It's about me."

She hated the fact that her voice cracked on that last word. That it gave her away so completely. That it showed him things she didn't want him to know.

"Pia," he said again, even more calmly than before.

And this time, she didn't care how hard it was. She got herself to the edge of the bed, and shoved herself off. She had to stand still for a moment, her hand on the small of her back, and she almost burst into tears because she wanted to storm away. But there was no *storming* in her current state. There was only waddling. And she already felt bad enough. She certainly didn't need to *waddle* in front of him. Naked.

She grabbed at the coverlet that had been kicked to the foot of the bed. It was something spun from gold and unicorn dust, or so it appeared, like everything else in this place. Pia wrapped it around herself like a makeshift dress.

And she didn't understand how she had let all this happen.

It was as if she hadn't quite been paying attention. There had been all that mind-altering sex to distract her. And the exquisite sweetness of their nights together made her forget herself during the day. He'd moved her into his rooms and she'd just…let it happen. She hadn't put up so much as a token protest. In fact, it hadn't occurred to her to protest.

She'd been enjoying herself too much.

And now she was in her eighth month of this pregnancy. She was enormous. And she couldn't tell if she was finding it hard to breathe because she was emotional, or because she had two babies pressed up hard against…everything.

But she knew that she'd miscalculated. Greatly. She had more than miscalculated.

Because what she couldn't tell him was that while he

had been indulging himself, and playing whatever game this was with her, she had been doing something far more dangerous. He had been playing a long game, trying to get her to marry him for his own suspect reasons.

But Pia had been falling in love.

And she had to bite back a little sob as that word poured through her, so bright and hot she was shocked he couldn't *see* it.

She couldn't think of anything more stupid. Or embarrassing. But it was true. She had fallen in love with Ares. If she was honest, she suspected that it had happened at first sight at that party in New York. Because she had never been affected by any other man.

But one look at Ares and she'd wandered off with him, happily. Then she'd gotten herself wildly, irrevocably knocked up. And to add insult to injury, as was apparently her specialty, she'd gone off with him again at her own father's funeral.

She'd let him lock her up here. And sure, she had a thousand excuses for herself. There were guards. There was only one road out and it was closely watched. But the truth was, she hadn't tried very hard to get away from him after that first night.

Pia had told herself she was nesting. That was what pregnant women did—every article she found online said so. She wrote columns about trusting one's gut and how best to handle awkward social interactions, while all the while she was handling her relationship with this man just about as badly as it was possible to do.

Because Ares might have decided he wanted something other than what he'd told her he wanted at the start, but it didn't matter. Because any way she looked at it, what he really wanted was his sons without the trouble of custody agreements. Which was fair enough.

But it felt even more brutal now that he didn't want *her*.

He would have sex with her. Extremely good sex, if what he said was true about this wild, greedy thing they shared. But he didn't love her. He couldn't love her. He hadn't been looking for *her* when he'd found her at Combe Manor that day. He'd been on one of his royal engagements, doing his duty to the family.

When Pia knew, thanks to her father, that when a man loved a woman he could not rest. He would seek her out, no matter what damage it did. *No matter what.*

It was long past time Pia faced the facts here, no matter how little she liked them.

"I don't understand why everything changed," she said to him, trying to keep her panic tamped down. And worse, that bright beacon of a word she couldn't say and a thing she shouldn't feel. "You were very certain about the things you didn't want."

"It's not a question about what I want," Ares said, his green gaze hooded. "It's a question of what is right."

He was still on the bed, lounging there in that seemingly careless way of his. And it made her heart kick at her. *He* did, even now.

She tightened her grip on the coverlet. "Because somehow, what is right involves war in the blood and something about poison. Oh, yes, and infectious power."

"I want to make you my queen," Ares said, and he no longer sounded quite so mild. "Do you not understand that part of it?"

"I understand it," Pia heard herself say, though she hardly recognized her own voice. "That's the problem."

She turned her head away, not sure what might be written all over her face then. What he might see. She wrapped the coverlet even tighter around her, bitterly aware that the only thing she could wrap around herself at all these days was a piece of fabric that had been made to stretch across a bed. A very large bed.

Her throat ached, but she made herself speak anyway. "I'm the size of the barn. But even if I were not, you and I both know what I look like on any normal day."

There was only silence, and Pia was forced to turn back and look at him.

Ares only gazed back at her, a baffled sort of look on his gorgeous face.

Pia made a frustrated sound. "I'm not a queen!"

"You are a queen if you marry a king. It is really that simple."

"The very idea is laughable, Ares. Do you understand me?" Her voice sounded like a sob. But she couldn't seem to stop herself. She couldn't do a single thing to avert this horror as it happened. "People would *laugh*."

CHAPTER ELEVEN

FOR A MOMENT there was nothing but the echo of Pia's raw words hanging there between them.

She wanted to snatch them back with her own two hands. Her fingers twitched as if they might try, all on their own.

"Now I am the one not following you." Ares looked bemused and haughty at once, every inch of him royal as he lay there on the bed as if he was entirely at his ease. Perhaps he was. "People would laugh why, exactly?"

Pia was shaking. Everywhere. She wrapped her hand around the nearest bedpost, hoping it would steady her. Hoping something would, when the floor seemed so treacherous beneath her. She couldn't believe he was going to make her say it out loud. And worse, she couldn't tell if he was taunting her.

"A man like you is on a certain level," she said, pulling herself up as straight as she could, despite the weight of her belly. And the far greater weight of her shame. "You must be aware of this."

"You mean that I am the Crown Prince? Yes, Pia. I am aware of it. It is the sort of thing they tend to tell you from a very young age."

"I don't mean the fact that you're a prince, although that's part of it. I mean… You." She waved her hand in his direction. Trying to take in all of it, all of *him*, as he lounged there. Golden, rangy and athletic, as if someone had come in and carved a god from marble and breathed life into the stone. "You are a beautiful man. You are meant to find a beautiful wife. No one would accept a queen like me for a man like you."

Ares stared at her for a long while. As the panic and worry inside her intensified, she focused on strange things. Like the muscle in his jaw that clenched, seemingly of its own volition. Or the way his green eyes seemed darker. More dangerous.

"I will take it that what you are telling me is that you do not believe you are beautiful," he said. Eventually.

Pia made herself smile, though she was terribly afraid that the humiliation of this might take her out at the knees. Or maybe she only hoped it would.

"My mother was widely held to be the most beautiful woman in the world. Yes, she had her issues. She was not always kind, or good. Or even polite. And judging by the pills and the alcohol she took at the end, she was also not very happy." She blew out a breath, and hoped he couldn't hear how it shook. "My brother thinks it was deliberate, but I don't. For a while I thought maybe I pushed her to it, and my father, too, having fallen pregnant the way I did. But now I think it was an accident, because the one thing I know about Alexandrina San Giacomo is that she had no intention of going out with a whimper."

Alexandrina had been an opera heroine, always. Any death scene she'd planned would have been long-winded, theatrical, and would have required a vast audience. Most important, she would have needed to make certain she stayed beautiful throughout.

Pia didn't know when her certainty that she was to blame had…shifted. She suspected it had to do with spending all this time with Ares. All she knew for certain was that somehow, it had been a long while since she'd felt personal guilt about her parents' deaths. One had been an accident. The other had been inevitable. Her pregnancy had nothing to do with either.

Which didn't make it any easier.

She remembered that Ares was watching her. Waiting, all that leashed power of his coiled and tight.

"What my mother always had, what everyone knew and agreed on, was that she was beautiful. No matter how drunk, or tired, or under the weather. Men would stop in the street to stare. Sometimes they burst into song. Does that sound ridiculous?" She shrugged. "A serenade in the street was merely an unremarkable day in my mother's life. I grew up knowing exactly what *beautiful* meant. And seeing exactly what it looked like."

"I see." Ares's voice sounded almost…strangled.

"Do you?" she demanded.

Pia didn't understand what was sloshing around inside of her then. It was too much sensation. It was too much emotion. It was *too much*.

And maybe Alexandrina had it right. Maybe it was better to make everything an opera. Because at least then you could be in control of when the curtain went up, when it went down, and everything in between. How funny that she'd never understood that until now.

She took the coverlet from around her, and tossed it aside, the way her mother would have. With flourish.

"Do you really see?" she demanded. "Look at this body, Ares. It was never much to begin with, and after this? It will be a different body altogether. Forever. It will never snap back. There will be stretch marks, everywhere. And that's the least of it. I've seen pictures of my mother when she was pregnant. She looked like at any moment, someone might happen by and write a sonnet to her beauty."

"Is this an argument you truly wish to win?" he asked.

"It's not an argument. It's reality. I'm not my mother, and I'm certainly not beautiful like she was."

"I don't know how to say this," Ares said, as if he was choosing his words carefully. "But I cannot think of much I care less about than your mother's supposed beauty."

"It wasn't 'supposed.' It wasn't an opinion, it was a fact."

"Your mother was a lovely woman," Ares agreed, shrugging one shoulder. "But what of it? The world is filled with beautiful women."

"You're making my point for me," Pia said, wishing she hadn't tossed the coverlet aside. She could hardly go scrabbling after it now she'd made such a show of casting it off. She was forced to stand there instead, tall and proud, when she wanted nothing more than to curl up in a ball and cringe away into oblivion somewhere. "The world is filled with beautiful women, and you ought to go out and find yourself one of them."

"Pia. *Cara mia.*" And Ares looked as if he was biting back a smile, which Pia couldn't understand at all.

"Perhaps you do not understand to whom you are speaking. I am Crown Prince Ares of Atilia. I have dukedoms and earldoms to spare. I am, by definition and royal decree, possessed of the finest taste. Any woman who graces my arm is beautiful by virtue of her presence there. Obviously."

Pia opened her mouth to argue, but stopped when he rolled himself up to sitting position, never shifting his gaze from her face.

"But you? The mother of my children? The only woman alive I have ever asked to be my queen? *Of course* you are beautiful." He shrugged again, so arrogant and assured that it should have hurt him. Yet clearly did not. "It never occurred to me that you could imagine otherwise."

"You can't throw compliments at me and think that it will change the fact that I am not, in any way, the kind of woman a man like you goes for."

"I suggest you look down at your very pregnant belly," Ares said, his voice slightly less patient and mild. "I have already gone for you. Repeatedly."

"Stop saying these things!" She threw the words at him, unable to control her voice—or anything else—any longer. "I know what I look like. I know what I am. Pretending that I'm something else isn't going to get me to marry you."

"Then what will?"

And Pia kept trying to suck in more air. She couldn't seem to form another word.

And that was when Ares moved again. He rolled to his feet, then came to her, wrapping his hands around her shoulders and holding her up.

"You are the only woman I have ever asked to marry me," he told her, his voice serious and his gaze darkly intense. "But if that is not enough for you, think back to the party where we met. Why do you think I was drawn to you? At first, before we spoke a word to each other? If you are so misshapen, such a hideous troll—do you imagine it was curiosity that drew me to your side?"

This was ridiculous. Tears were spilling over, tracking their way down her cheeks, and Pia wanted to die. She wanted to sink to the floor of the palace, and be swept out to sea.

"I don't know," she said, her voice cracked and much too thick. "I looked up and you were…there."

"I was there because I saw you smile," Ares said. "I heard you laugh. I was there because I followed that smile across the room, simply because I wanted to get close to it. And then, when we met, I wanted to get even closer. None of that has changed."

"Ares…"

"Marry me because every time I have asked you to follow me so far, you have," he said, words in his eyes that she was afraid to believe in. "Follow me because I have yet to lead you anywhere you didn't like. You call this palace a prison, yet here we are, together—and it feels more to me like an escape. Marry me, Pia, and we will make our marriage another kind of refuge. The sort we can take with us wherever we go."

"You only want—"

"Our sons," he finished for her. "Yes, of course I want them. Let's raise them together."

And maybe she had always been this weak. Maybe

it was the way he made her feel, and she couldn't help herself. She liked it too much.

She knew better, but Ares looked at her as if she was beautiful. And when he did, she was tempted to believe it. Here, now, she did believe it.

And that belief trickled down into her, making her feel warm. Safe.

And there were worse things, surely. There were men who didn't want their own babies and who went to great lengths to avoid their responsibilities. There were men who didn't make her heart kick at her the way it did whenever Ares was near.

A whole world full of them, in fact.

There were marriages, especially amongst the sort of people she knew, that were little more than business transactions. There were cold, brittle unions, husbands and wives who were faithless, others who exulted in causing each other pain.

There were a thousand ways to have a terrible marriage.

But maybe what that meant was that Pia could decide how to make hers a good one. Or a decent one, anyway. Better than most. And maybe there wasn't only one fairy-tale way to get there.

Maybe there were twin boys. A palace fit for Rapunzel. And months spent doing nothing but circling around and around the inevitable. Maybe there were wild, hot nights of sex and longing with the only man she'd ever wanted to touch.

Already that sounded better than half the marriages she'd ever heard of.

And Pia loved him, though she knew better than

that, too. She loved him even though she was sure that the years would pass and whatever protestations he'd made here tonight about her supposed beauty would fade. He would regret this. He might take his own father's path.

Pia knew that she would still love him then. That she would always love him. So what would be worse? Never having any part of this? Or losing what little she had?

In front of her, Ares shifted. He dropped onto his knees, his gaze locked to hers as the afternoon sun poured in and highlighted every last perfect, glorious inch of him.

Both of them were naked. Pia's belly was so big it could take over the whole of the room on its own, and maybe the world. Ares didn't put his hands there. Instead, he reached up and took hers in his.

"Pia," he said, very gravely. "Marry me. Be my queen and mother to my sons. And promise me that from time to time, you will smile at me the way you did in a stranger's party in Manhattan."

And her heart kicked at her, but she couldn't tell if it was signaling danger or excitement. Hope or anxiety. All of the above.

And she knew better. *She knew better.*

The worst thing she could possibly do was believe.

But her hands were in his much bigger ones. And his gaze was so serious that it made her flush a little.

And she had two baby boys inside her who deserved their father.

What do you deserve, dear girl? that voice inside asked her, the way Alexandrina would have. *Do you really think* you *deserve a prince?*

But Pia shoved that aside.

Right here, right now, he believed she was beautiful.

She didn't have to believe him to hold on to that for as long as she could.

For as long as he'd let her.

"Very well, then," she said, surrendering. Or, if she was honest, taking a leap into faith, despite everything. And having no idea where she might land. "I will do it, Ares. I will marry you."

Ares didn't realize until Pia finally agreed to marry him that a part of him had worried that she would not. That she would actually refuse him.

And it was one thing to make pronouncements about how he wished to live his life wifeless and childless and alone. It was another to be rendered such things because the woman he wanted would not have him.

But she had agreed at last. And he was ready—had been ready, in fact, since the day he'd met with his father and had decided on a different future.

And two days after Pia finally acquiesced, he found her on an achingly perfect morning by the sea, having her breakfast out on one of the palace's many terraces. For a moment he stood away from her, taking her in as she gazed out toward Kefalonia. This woman who had made him into a man he didn't recognize. A crown prince who wanted to claim his throne. A man who was no longer content to step aside for the father he had always hated.

Pia sat in the loose, flowing dress he had chosen for her, her dark hair back in a loose braid. The breeze from the ocean picked up strands and made them dance, this way and that, and he thought the sea itself paled beside her.

He could not believe she had ever imagined she was anything less than beautiful. Stunning, even.

He had met her mother. And he had found Alexandrina San Giacomo beautiful, yes, but brittle with it. Expectant. Her beauty was her currency, and she had been well aware of it. There was nothing wrong with that, to Ares's mind. He admired it, as he certainly knew when his own looks worked in his favor.

But Pia was beautiful in a different way altogether. Her beauty was unstudied. Artless. Her gray eyes were dreamy, her sweet mouth soft. Right now she was gloriously pregnant, ripe and lush, and it only added to her many charms.

Alexandrina had been a weapon. But Pia was a precious gem. As perfect as she was pretty.

And soon to be his princess. And one day, his queen.

He must have made a noise, because she glanced over then. And Ares had the pleasure of watching the way her eyes glowed with pleasure before she blinked it away to something far more guarded.

But the smile that curved her mouth was as bright and engaging as that first one back in New York.

It made something in him seem to turn over, then hum.

This one, a voice in him said, like some kind of gong. *This one.*

Mine, Ares thought.

He moved over to her, sliding a hand over her cheek and loving the way she leaned into his touch. The way she always did. She had no walls. She held nothing back.

She was heedless, hedonistic in bed, and he found that she made him insatiable.

There were no ways he didn't want her.

"I don't know what you have planned for today," he said.

Her gray eyes were soft and bright as she looked up at him. "I'm very busy, actually. I plan to lounge about, pretending to work, for several hours. After which I will very officiously go seat myself somewhere, open up the laptop, and type very studiously. I won't be working, of course. I'll be checking email and scrolling through things I don't care about on the internet, which is a very important part of my process. After several hours of that, I will write a single sentence, which will be so exhausting that I will instantly need to send for snacks. I plan to repeat this several times throughout the day, until I can break for an early dinner, and pretend none of it ever happened. And you?"

And that was the part Ares couldn't understand. He found her…entertaining.

He didn't understand it, but he liked it. True, he'd never seen anything like her before, anywhere in the royal family, or, for that matter, in any of the dreary noble houses of Europe. Everything was duty and history. Ancestral obligation and debts paid in to the future. Marriages were solemn contracts for the production of heirs, and everyone in those marriages worked hard to appear studiously joyless—if his own parents were any guide.

But the woman he would reign with was entertaining. She smiled, laughed. She even dared tease him. Ares chose to see it as a gift.

He went down before her, on the traditional single knee. Then he reached into his pocket, pulling out a small box with great flourish. He cracked it open, looking up to find Pia with her hands over her mouth and her gray eyes wide.

"I do not know if you recognize this ring," he said. "It has a legend attached to it. It was handed down through my family for generations, and each woman who wears it is said to be the queen the country deserves. Good, kind. It was my grandmother's. She left it for me when she died, that I might put it on the hand of my own queen one day. Will you take it?"

And he found that something in him was tense and tight until she let out a breath, nodded once, jerkily, and extended her hand that he might slide the ring into place.

Together, they stared down at the collection of three perfect sapphires, ringed with diamonds. Taken together the stones created the sense of something bigger than the sum of its parts. The ring itself was history. But on Pia, it looked like art.

"Thank you," she whispered, her voice catching. "It's so beautiful."

"I was hoping you would think so."

He helped her to her feet, aware that it was harder for her to rise these days. He swept his eye over the dress she wore, white and flowing, and making her look very nearly ethereal. He reached down to the table and picked up one of the flowers that sat there in a small vase, then tucked it into the top of her braid.

She was breathing loud enough that he could hear it. And her eyes were glassy when he was done with the flower. He wanted to lean down and kiss her, claim her—

But kissing Pia was no quick affair. It required time because Ares never stopped at one kiss. How could he?

"Come with me," he said.

And Pia held out her hand, because Pia always held out her hand. She trusted him enough to follow him into the unknown, and that was a responsibility Ares took seriously. More than seriously. He felt the weight of it move through him, and he vowed as he led her through the palace that he would honor it. Care for it.

And her.

Always her.

He hadn't planned for any of this. And he hadn't known, until that day in his father's study, how best to handle his impending fatherhood.

But now it was all so beautifully clear.

"What are we doing?" Pia asked, as he led her through the great salons and out to the wide terrace overlooking the steepest part of the rocky cliffs below. The ocean stretched itself in the sun, rambling out to the horizon. And there, beneath the makeshift canopy he'd had his staff prepare from sweet-smelling vines and bright flowers, a priest waited.

He felt her hand shake in his.

"Is this…?"

"This is our wedding, Pia," he said, looking down at her. Another tension gripping him because she could still balk. She could demand the cathedral on the Northern Island. She could refuse him. *She could still refuse him.* "Here, now."

"But…"

Ares took her hands in his. And he thought that he could lose himself forever in all that gleaming gray. He intended to. "Do you trust me?"

"I… I don't…"

"It's a simple question. You either trust me, or you do not."

"I trust you," she whispered.

"Then why wait?" he asked. "You know as well as I do what a royal wedding will be like. The pomp and circumstance, all in aid of a future throne. We can do this here. You and me, no one else. And our babies."

Her eyes glistened. Her smile seemed to tremble on her lips. Even her hands in his shook a little.

"Just you and me," she whispered.

There was a faint breeze from the sea spread out below them. The priest spoke his words, and when it was time for their vows, Pia had stopped shaking.

"I vow to honor you, keep you safe, and pledge my life to yours," Ares said, intoning the traditional vows of the kingdom.

"And I you," Pia replied.

He reached into his pocket and pulled out another box. Inside sat two rings. Two bands of gold. He slid the smaller one onto Pia's finger, so it sat flush against his grandmother's. And something dark and primitive roared through him at the sight.

He handed her the bigger ring and she took it, shifting her hand to slide it onto his finger.

And that was it, Ares thought. It was done.

"And now, Your Highness, you may kiss your bride," the priest declared.

And Pia was smiling again as he angled his face to hers, then took her mouth with his.

For a moment there was nothing but that kiss, sweet and perfect. Then another.

There was only the two of them, and the vows they'd made. Ares moved closer, pulling Pia further into his arms, because she was his. And he couldn't get enough of her.

And he doubted he ever would.

He kissed her again, deeper and wilder—

And that was when the helicopter rose up from below. It bristled with reporters, cameras in hand and pointing straight toward them.

Pia started to pull away, stiff with horror.

"Kiss me again," Ares commanded her.

"But the paparazzi—" she began.

"Kiss me, Pia," he told her, and he could hear the satisfaction in his own voice. He could feel it thrumming in his veins. He could very nearly picture the king's apoplectic rage when he saw these pictures—and understood what they meant. "I want them to see. I'm the one who called them here."

CHAPTER TWELVE

PIA DID AS Ares asked—as he commanded—because she could see no alternative.

And because she couldn't think. She kissed him, and the helicopter was right there, and everything was whipping around while she knew there were pictures being taken—

She was sure she could hear them laughing already.

Before she could object, or scream, or do any of the things that clambered inside of her and threated to come out of her, violently—Ares pulled away. He shouted something to the priest over the noise of the helicopter's rotors.

He even waved.

Then he was leading her back inside the palace, leaving the helicopter and its paparazzi cargo behind. For a moment she let him lead her on, because she was too busy reeling to do anything else. She was blind and her heart *hurt* and it was a lie.

It was all a lie.

What had happened—what had just happened—hit her, hard.

I called them, he had said.

She dug her heels in, yanking her hand from his, and moving her hands around to the small of her back as she panted a little at the exertion and the low, dull pain that bloomed there. And she didn't know whether to look at him directly, or do her best to look away, maybe up and down the gallery where they'd stopped.

"What did you do?" she demanded. "What do you mean, you called them?"

"I called them," he said again, much too calmly for her peace of mind, and even looked a bit quizzical. As if she was the one who had stopped making sense in a dizzying rush.

And he was the man she loved. The man she had married in what she'd foolishly imagined was a quiet, sweet, personal ceremony.

She'd believed his *just the two of us*, and all the while he'd had a helicopter full of reporters waiting.

Which meant none of this had been romantic.

You knew better, she reminded herself bitterly. *And you did it anyway.*

Something in her turned over, spinning around in a nauseating loop. For a moment, she thought she might be sick. A kind of cramp ran through her, centering low in her belly, and she moved a hand to curl beneath the heaviest part of it. And she held it there, wishing she could hold herself together as easily.

"Tell me why," she managed to say. "Tell me why you would do this. We ran away from my father's funeral to avoid these people and you called them here… You must know that they took pictures that will be everywhere within the hour."

He raised a brow. "That was my clear intent."

Pia looked around, wildly, because she thought her legs might cease to hold her. There was a bench to the side, beneath a huge painting that she had studied in finishing school, the better to make sparkling cocktail conversation. She waddled over to the bench and sank down on to it. Gratefully.

Though she looked at Ares—her *husband*—and that awful feeling in her belly got worse.

"I do not understand why you are looking at me as if I killed a man," Ares said.

And what struck her most was how truly, effortlessly beautiful he was. He was dressed in one of his usual royal uniforms, complete with the sash that proclaimed him the crown prince of these islands. Even here, in a controlled environment with less intrusive lighting, he looked as if the sun beamed down upon him.

Pia should have known when Marbella had laid this particular dress out this morning. It was pure white. And while the hilarity of wearing all white while this astonishingly pregnant did not escape her, she couldn't quite bring herself to laugh.

Because she had believed him, and he had been putting on a show.

And all the things she'd told herself about the heartache she'd experience had been *one day.* Far off the future. Far away from here, now, *today.*

Yet here she was anyway, with a fantasy ring on her finger and a fantasy man, and a fantasy new marriage, too. The reality was a girl the size of a whale in a white dress that seemed pointed, a staged kiss, and all the sniggering she was sure she could already hear out there—or maybe her ears were ringing. She couldn't quite tell.

"I've spent my whole life in my father's shadow," Ares was telling her, standing over her with all that *light* he made on his own, and Pia should never have let herself do this. She should never have been so weak, risking not only her own humiliation—but her sons'. "I've never been good enough for the man. He ranted at me about our bloodline until I wished I could reach my hand inside my own body, and exsanguinate myself to escape it. The only thing that worked was keeping myself away from him. Excusing myself from the damned bloodline. But then you came along and changed everything."

"And you felt the best way to celebrate this change was with the paparazzi?"

Pia felt raw inside. Torn wide-open.

And worst of all, like such a fool.

Because she'd believed him. She'd believed that not only did he care for her, not only did he want her, but that deep down—whether he knew it or not—he might even love her.

She had believed what she wanted to believe, clearly.

And Ares had been setting up a photo opportunity to get at his father.

"I realized the last time I saw my father that I have abdicated my responsibilities entirely where he is concerned," Ares told her, still standing where she'd left him in the middle of the wide hall. "And the closer we get to the birth of our own two sons, the more I realize what I owe not only them, but this kingdom. I think our subjects deserve better."

"Power infects," she said, sounding hollow to her own ears. "You told me that."

"Better to claim it, then," Ares replied, something flashing in his green eyes. He crossed to her, then crouched down to put himself at eye level. "Better that than to let it sit about, festering. I want to be the kind of king these princes—" he put his hand out to touch her belly, and for the first time she wanted to slap it away "—can look up to. No temper tantrums like winter storms, brutal and unpredictable. No shards of crystal littering the floors while they stand there, hoping not to be hit. I want to be a better man, Pia."

There was a roaring thing in her, grief and shame, and she wasn't sure she could keep it inside her skin. She wasn't sure she could survive this. Or that she wanted to.

"You're not talking about being a better man, Ares," she threw back at him. "You're talking about being a king. You begged me to marry you, and I surrendered. You didn't tell me that it would be a business arrangement. You didn't convince me by promising me a convenient union we could both use to our own ends. You made love to me. You made it *romantic*."

And she would hate herself forever for the way her voice cracked on that.

But she pushed on anyway. "How could you make it romantic?"

Ares looked floored. Astounded, as if it had never occurred to him that she could possibly have a problem with what had happened here today.

"I do not understand the issue," he said stiffly.

"You could have asked me. You could have appealed to my practical side. You didn't have to *sleep* your way into it." And there were tears then, and those were worse. They felt too salty against her cheeks. They felt like a betrayal, or one more betrayal, and her heart felt tattered. Broken beyond repair. "You could have asked, Ares, and I would have come around."

"Pia—"

"But you pretended it was something else," she said, and the cramping was getting worse with every word she spoke. She rubbed at her belly, sucking in a breath as she tried to make herself comfortable. Or just make it through this conversation. "You pretended that you cared."

"I do care."

"You even told me I was beautiful." And her voice dropped on that, into something so painful it hurt her to hear herself. "Why did you have to lie to me? Has this whole thing been a game to you from the start?"

"This is not a game." He rocked back on his heels, and even now, the moment he stopped touching her she wanted only for him to start again. "How can you think it?"

"How could I think anything else?"

"I don't know what this is, Pia. Of course I care for you. You are the mother to my—"

"You told me I was beautiful," she said again, and her eyes were too blurry to see him now, which she took as a kind of blessing. There was a strange fire low in her belly, and that cramping that wouldn't stop. "And the worst thing is, I wanted to believe you. I did believe you. Why would you do this to me?"

"What did I do to you?" he roared at her, as if even now, he didn't understand.

"You made me think that you could love me," she

told him, though she thought it might kill her. There was a sob in her voice, and something heavy, like a stone, over her heart. And yet she kept going, though her face twisted. "Because only a man who loved me could find me beautiful."

Ares's face changed then, into something like alarm, and that was even worse. "Pia."

But she'd started down this road. She'd humiliated herself. Why not throw all her cards on the table? After all, what was there left to protect?

"I love you," she told him, sealing her doom. "And I never would have told you that. I would have kept it to myself because I know better. I still know better. But you told me I was beautiful, and I hoped, and you gave me your grandmother's ring. And I wanted so badly to believe it could all be real."

He moved closer to her, a harsh look she'd never seen before on his face. "Pia, you need to—"

She lifted up her hand to keep him back, because she couldn't trust herself. And she tried to struggle to her feet, but her legs refused to help her. And she reminded herself that no one actually died of heartache, no matter how terrible they felt. No matter how awful *she* felt right now.

"It's not the first time I've been made a fool of, and I doubt it will be the last," she told him. "You have what really matters to you. Legitimacy for your heirs. But I need you to promise me something, Ares. No matter what, you must never lie to me again. I need you to promise me that whatever games you need to play, it will never be this one. Never again."

"I will promise you anything you want, woman,"

Ares all but shouted at her. “But right now, you are bleeding.”

It seemed to take Pia a lifetime or two to look down at the white dress she wore. The way it pooled around her feet.

And at the way what she’d taken for anxious cramps and heartache was instead bright red, and spreading out across her lap.

“Promise me,” she said, though she didn’t mean the same thing any longer. Or she didn’t think she did.

But then it didn’t matter what she meant, because the darkness came rushing at her, and sucked her in deep.

There was too much blood.

Ares caught Pia as she began to slump over, and he was already shouting for his staff. For someone to call back that damned helicopter. For help.

But there was blood. Everywhere.

He swung Pia up and into his arms, and he barely felt the weight she carried in that marvelous belly of hers. He strode toward the staff who yelled at him, or for him, he didn’t care which.

Her face was so pale. And the blood kept coming.

It was the longest helicopter ride of his life. And when they landed on the Northern Island, on the top of the Royal Hospital, Ares was still holding her. And found he wanted to start knocking heads together, or start tearing people apart—*something*—when the medical personnel that met them on the roof took her from him to strap her on a gurney.

“She is my wife,” he told them, aware he must sound mad with terror, with grief. Fierce with the fear that burned in him. "She will one day be your queen. She is carrying the heirs to this kingdom and you must save her. *You must.*"

And then, despite all his arrogance, all his consequence and power, he could do nothing but watch them rush her away.

Someone led him to a private room, eventually. They offered him a change of clothes, but he refused it. He sat in a chair with his head in his hands, and he waited.

While inside, his heart threatened to burst.

He could not lose Pia. He could not lose his sons.

He had spent his whole life doing everything he could to avoid having a family, and he was about to lose his before he got the chance to enjoy them.

Pia couldn't believe he had called her beautiful.

But Ares couldn't believe she loved him.

His first reaction was denial. Rage, that she would take this there, when it had worked fine as it was.

Because he knew what no one dared say to his face.

That there was nothing about him anyone could love, except his mother. And she had died a long time ago now.

But there was no one else on this earth, not even his father, who shared that sentiment. Ares was a monument to a throne, that was all. He was not a person. He existed in the first place only because his father needed an heir. Any child his mother had could have taken on that role. But no one *loved* him.

Except Pia.

And Ares could argue with himself all he liked. He could tell himself that she was mistaken. Or that she didn't know enough about men and had fallen for the first man who had ever touched her—

But he knew that wasn't true. There had been any number of men at that party, but Pia had smiled at him.

Him.

Ares knew now that she had never done anything like what she had that night in New York, but she'd done it for him. She'd given him her innocence. She had suffered his reaction to the news that she was pregnant. She'd come with him to the islands, and allowed him to lock her away for his own peace of mind, not hers.

She had done all these things, and he knew that there could only be one reason. The one reason he never would have come up with on his own, because the word wasn't in his vocabulary.

She loved him.

Once he understood that, Ares couldn't understand how he had ever managed to convince himself that it was anything else. That it could be anything else.

And now she had blood all over her. Blood, again. Blood always.

And if that blood was poisoned, the way he'd always believed, he had done that, too.

And Ares found that while he had no trouble thinking of the ways he could pay for the sins of that bloodline, he couldn't bring himself to imagine that Pia might also pay that price. Or either one of the babies she carried.

He could not lose her.

God help him, he could not lose her, not now. Not when he had only begun to grasp how very much she meant to him.

She was the only woman he had ever been this intimate with. There was the astonishingly good sex, yes, but they'd spent all this *time* together. Time enough to get to know her. Time enough to understand how much more it was he wanted to know her.

Time to understand that he wanted, badly, to meet his own sons.

Ares needed more time.

He thought he could spend a lifetime trying to imagine what Pia might say next. He thought he could spend another one learning the different shades of meaning in her smiles.

She was the only woman he had given his grandmother's ring. The only woman he had asked to marry him, not once, but time and time again.

She was the only woman, period.

She needed to live, so he could tell her so. So he could tell her a thousand things. So he could apologize for treating her like a pawn—

She just needed to *live.*

"Your Highness," came a voice from a doctor at the door, and Ares's head shot up, but he couldn't read anything on the man's face. "Your wife is stable, but the babies are in some distress. We will be performing a cesarean section immediately."

"Early," Ares managed to say, his head spinning. "It's too early."

"Twins are always early," the doctor replied. "But we must make haste."

And Ares followed, unable to do anything else.

Because he could not lose Pia. And he could not lose these babies he had yet to meet. And he had not realized until now, until he found himself in these antiseptic halls, how very thoroughly lost he had been since the first moment he'd set eyes on this woman.

His wife.

His future queen, and mother to the future king of Atilia.

Ares, by God, would make sure she lived long enough to assume each and every one of those roles.

And tell him she loved him once more.

CHAPTER THIRTEEN

Pia woke up in a panic. A desperate, confused rush—

"Pia. *Cara mia.*"

Her head snapped around, and she found him there.

Ares.

With those grave green eyes, and a stern set to his beautiful mouth. Ares, her prince, though he appeared to be wearing hospital scrubs. Of all things.

She felt herself calm, just a little. Because Ares was there, and that meant—

"My babies—" she blurted out, her heart exploding inside her. She tried to sit up, but her abdomen protested sharply, and she had the terrible notion that she'd had surgery. And that meant… "What happened to my babies—"

"We have all been waiting for you," Ares said, very solemnly, and the calm sound of his voice made her stop. Made her breathe. "Allow me to make the introductions."

And then he reached into the double bassinet she hadn't seen beside the bed, and carefully lifted up a tiny little bundle. It sported a wrinkled pink face and a shock of dark hair peeking out from beneath a little white beanie.

"I present to you our first born," Ares said, something rich and awed in his voice. "He is perfect in every way. I inspected him myself."

Pia accepted her baby, a rush of something so intense and primitive slamming into her as she took him that she was happy—fiercely so—she was already in a bed. Because she feared it would have knocked her over. She gazed down at the tiny bundle in her arms, making sounds she hadn't heard herself make before. She saw him scrunch up his nose, and his perfect little mouth, and she understood that she would never be the same again.

"And his brother," Ares said, and placed the other baby in her other arm. As if he knew that she needed to touch them both. "He is equally perfect in every way. I can verify this personally."

And that same wave took her over again. Harder, deeper.

She bent her head to one, then the other. She checked to make sure each one was breathing. And as she did, each tiny boy began to make tiny little noises, as if they understood exactly who she was and were offering their own form of greeting.

She could already tell they were that smart. That beautiful. That absolutely perfect.

"You were there?" she asked.

"They came out of you, directly into my hands," Ares said, and it sounded like another vow. Like an impossible intimacy.

And when she met his gaze, her chest ached.

"I want to feed them," she whispered.

Or, having missed their birth, maybe she needed to.

And Ares was there beside her, so she didn't have to worry over all the various things she'd read about how best to get each one of them where they needed to go. He helped her. He set a pillow over her abdomen, which stuck out significantly less than it had when she'd last seen it.

He opened up her gown, and he helped her guide one greedy mouth to her swollen, aching breast. Then the next, placing each little body beneath one of her arms, snug against her sides, so she could hold them in place like American footballs.

And she had read a thousand articles about how difficult breastfeeding was, and had read endless forums about how to manage it with hungry twins. She'd expected a battle. But there was no battle to mount, because it was happening. She felt one twin latch on, then the other. And they both began to pull at her.

Pia looked up at Ares while each of the perfect creatures they'd made together fed from her breasts, and she understood what family was on a primitive level she'd never imagined existed before.

She had known love. She had loved. She was still in love with the maddening man who stood beside her.

This was something else, this communion between the four of them. This needed a new word. This was like a new sun, bright and hot inside of her, taking her over, burning her up, terrifying and magical—and it was theirs.

They had done this. They had made this happen.

Nothing would ever be the same. But at the same time, everything was finally…beautiful.

And when the babies were fed and she and Ares had

held each of them against their bare skin a while, a nurse came in to check them again, then whisked them off for more tests. Pia tried to move in her bed, winced at the pain from her abdomen, and realized that she still didn't know what had happened to her.

"I can tell you this story using all kinds of medical terminology," Ares said. "But what really matters is that I nearly lost you. And Pia. No matter how I let you down today, trust me when I tell you that losing you is unacceptable to me. It is unthinkable."

She stared back at him, and he told her quickly and matter-of-factly about the rush to get her to the hospital. Her hemorrhage, the emergency cesarean section. How close she'd come to dying, and how terrified he had been.

"You told me you loved me," he said, as he stood there next to her bed, stiff and tense, as if that was an insult.

And Pia didn't want to remember this part. Not when she was still filled with that perfect sense of overwhelming, impossible, helpless love. She didn't want to remember their wedding ceremony. That helicopter. All the cameras.

"It doesn't matter," she said now. "We're parents, Ares, to two perfect little boys in desperate need of names. Let's just concentrate on—"

"You told me you loved me, Pia," Ares thundered at her. "And no one has told me that before, not unless they'd given birth to me themselves. That isn't the kind of thing you can just *say* to a man."

She wanted to cry again. "I'm sorry if I insulted you."

"I have spent the last five hours begging gods I've

never believed in to save you," he told her then, tall and still golden. And he had held their babies in his hands when she couldn't. He had been there. "Our wedding photos are all over every paper in the land, just as I wished, and it is like ash to me. Because there is no point in any of this, Pia, unless you are here. With me."

"Ares..."

"I have no idea how to love anyone," he told her, his green eyes blazing. "But for you, I will learn. I have no idea what a father does except crush his own son, but for the ones we made, I will learn how to do it right."

He moved closer, taking her hands in his, and then going down on one knee beside her hospital bed.

"You don't have to do this, Ares," she said.

"When I thought I would lose you, every moment we spent together went through my head in a rush," he said urgently. "And I could see it so clearly then, how much you loved me. How much you have always loved me. And how much I have failed you, time and again."

"No," she said fiercely. She winced as she sat up, but she reached out and took his beautiful, beloved face in her hands. "You are not a failure, Ares. I love you. That's not conditional on how you behave. That doesn't come with a list of duties or expectations. I just love you. It's as simple and as complicated as that, and I don't know how it works, either."

"I used you like a pawn. I will never forgive myself."

"I already have," she said, and as the words came out of her, she realized they were true. "I've spent my whole life hating how I looked because I wasn't my mother. Hating my body because it never looked like hers. But look what it did today."

"You were magnificent," Ares told her, his voice thick. "You are always magnificent, Pia."

"Let them laugh if they like," Pia said, her eyes on Ares. "They don't matter. They never did. The only thing I have to be embarrassed about is that I ever let them get to me in the first place. Even in my own head."

His mouth formed her name, but he turned his head so he could kiss her palm.

"I spent my whole life watching my parents tear themselves apart and call it love," Pia told him, a new conviction growing inside her. As if it had always been there. As if her babies' arrival had jogged it loose. "I used to think that was romantic. Now I suspect it was deeply unhealthy. What I want with you is the chance to explore the difference."

"I love you," Ares told her. "And I will spend the rest of this life proving to you that it's not only because I thought I would lose you today. But because in thinking you were lost to me forever, I understood that forever was meaningless to me without you."

"We made them," she whispered. "And Ares. They're perfect."

"They're beautiful," he whispered back. "And so are you."

And for a moment they grinned at each other, wide and bright and brimming with hope and possibility. There were two new, shiny little lives, and both of them would do their best to protect each one of them. To honor them and raise them.

Together.

"Pia," Ares said, a quiet command. "Be my wife."

"It will be my greatest honor," she said, tears streaming down her face, but this time, they were not tears of pain. This was joy, this unwieldy, unsteady thing that held her in so tight a grip. *Pure joy.* "And you must be my husband."

"It will be my privilege," he said solemnly. "You will be my queen one day. But know this, Pia. You are already, and always will be, queen of my heart."

And when he leaned over and pressed his mouth to hers, Pia tasted salt and sweetness. The great tangle that led to forever, and all the knots they'd tied in each other already that would keep them steady and connected as they headed there.

He kissed her, and it was like a fairy tale.

He kissed her, and she kissed him, and they woke each other up from that deep, dark enchantment that was the lives they'd led without each other.

Without love.

There and then, in a hospital room with the paparazzi calling their names outside, they started their new life. Together.

Full of love, light, and laughter to hold it all together, like glue.

Twenty years later, six weeks after his father's death and his formal acceptance of his new role, King Ares of Atilia was crowned in the Great Cathedral.

He took the long walk up the cathedral's august aisle that he had believed, once, he would never take.

The crowd cheered for him outside. The Atilian nobles and European aristocrats filled the pews. The famous Atilian choir sang ancient songs of power and glory.

But Ares's gaze was on his family.

His fine, strong twins, Crown Prince Pollux and Prince Castor, who stared back at him with pride and love—something Ares had done his best to earn every day for two decades. Beside them, the rest of his children stood tall. His middle children, seventeen-year-old Leto and thirteen-year-old Nyx. And his second set of twins, his mischievous ten-year-old daughters, Helen and Clytemnestra, who looked like the young women they would become someday.

Someday, Ares thought as they beamed at him, but not today. No need to rush into it.

He had never built any significant bridges with his father, who had divorced and married twice more, but had never produced another child. The old king had died in a fury, and had been found with crystal shards all around him like a halo. Ares figured that was as close as Damascus was likely to get to the good place.

The older he got, the more Ares wished he could have worked things out with the man, but he understood the ache of it had more to do with his relationship with his own children. And the man he hoped he was in their eyes, the father he was first and always, before he was a king.

And when he talked to them about bloodlines, what he talked about was love.

Ares kept walking, taking in Pia's brothers as they stood in the row behind his children. Because they were important to Pia, Ares had made them important to him, too. And as the years passed, he found Matteo Combe and Dominik James were more to him than a duty. They became more like…brothers.

And as all their families grew, with sets of twins to

go around, it was hard to remember that Matteo was the one who had punched Ares at that funeral. Or that there was ever a time that Pia didn't refer to her sisters-in-law, the impressive Dr. Sarina Fellows Combe and high-level Combe Industries executive Lauren Clarke James, as not only her sisters, but her friends.

With every step he took, Ares counted the ways he was a lucky man.

He had been born a prince, but it had taken Pia to make him a man. And it was only with Pia by his side that he could take his throne and become a king.

Ares reached the front of the cathedral and climbed the short stairs, then bent his head to accept the priests' invocations.

He thought about his kingdom. About the Southern Palace that rarely stood empty these days, and more often rang with life and laughter, as it was meant to do. He thought about his people, who had accepted it when he'd told them that he'd kept his relationship with Pia secret because the two of them had needed a time that was only theirs.

And most of all, he thought of the woman who was there at his side when the priests placed the crown on his head, then handed him the ceremonial scepter.

He watched as they fit her with a crown of her own, but her gray eyes shined brighter than any crown. Especially when she looked at him and smiled.

Ares held out his hand to her, breaking ancient custom.

And Pia took it, because she always did.

Because she trusted him. She loved him.

And the way he loved her in return would have scared him, if she didn't meet it so fiercely, so fully.

The only war he'd ever fought had been against himself, and Pia had taught him how to put down his arms.

He lifted her hand to his mouth.

"You have accepted the crown of the kingdom, and I have made you my queen," he said.

"You have."

"But there is a greater role for you to play," he told her, knowing his voice carried not only to the furthest corners of the Great Cathedral, but was being heard on television sets and radios around the world. "You are the most beautiful thing I have ever beheld. I count myself lucky every day I get to spend with you. You have made me a better man, and in so doing, will help me be the fair and just ruler my people deserve."

Her eyes gleamed with unshed tears. She whispered his name.

"I promised you a long time ago that this day would come," he said, and let himself grin, there before his children, his extended family, his subjects, and the planet. "Pia, love of my life, will you wield your crown not only as the queen of Atilia, but as the queen of My Heart?"

She stepped back, smiling, and then executed a perfect, deep curtsy.

"Your Majesty," she said, distinct and sweet, while the gleam in her gaze promised him a long, hot night ahead, "it will be my pleasure."

Ares kissed her when she rose, as if this coronation were the wedding day he and Pia had kept to themselves, and were now, finally sharing with the world. And she kissed him back as if they were alone.

The priests finished their blessings. And the roar of the crowd outside made the stained glass shake.

And then, when it was done and the bells began to toll, King Ares of Atilia took his beautiful queen by the hand, and led her into their sweet, bright, happy future. Just like those fairy tales Pia had mentioned all those years ago, when they were new.

Ares was the king. He would make it so. He would make it beautiful, like her.

For her.

And day by day, year by year, that was exactly what he did.

* * * * *